In Chaos and Destiny
The Planet of Songs
Part I

A.J. Enfictura

The Planet of Songs, Part I by A.J. Enfictura

www.enfictura.com

This book is a work of fiction. Any resemblance to real persons is purely coincidental.

ISBN: 978-1-7382405-0-0

Cover Art by Umbral Artistry

Book Design, Map and Other Visuals by A.J. Enfictura

Facebook, X, and TikTok, and their respective logos are trademarks of Meta Platforms, Inc., X Corp., and ByteDance Ltd., respectively, or their affiliates.

Content Warning

The following book contains mature subject matter which some readers may find upsetting or disturbing, including descriptions of violence, death, and sexuality. Reader discretion is advised.

Table of Contents

Preface

The following is a tale that takes place far away from our isolated corner of the Cosmos. In these worlds, there exist an abundance of things that greatly differ from the world that we know. There are cultures, species, customs, technology, and more that will be unfamiliar to us based on our life experiences on Earth and our worldviews that developed from those experiences.

One can expect from this that the contents of such a book may often come across as strange or even entirely unrecognizable to the reader. However, this is of course, a story written to be read by the denizens of the planet Earth. Therefore, it only makes sense that such a story be adapted so that it may be properly understood by such an audience.

With that understanding, the following book, along with all books that follow in this tale, should be considered more of a close adaptation of the events that occurred, as opposed to a direct transcription of all that precisely transpired.

For instance, languages both spoken and written within the story will generally be translated for the readers. As anyone with significant linguistic experience may know, this will slightly alter the meanings of the messages, changing them into imprecise approximations of what had originally been communicated in each case.

For example, "reptile" is a term with particular taxonomic implications here on Earth. Here, our reptiles are all linked by a common ancestry. And yet, the term "reptile" may be used in this story to describe creatures which have no such relationship to Earthly reptiles, save for the bearing of similar biological characteristics. There are a great many other examples, ranging from the use of familiar measurements to symbols to Earthly idioms/wordplay and beyond, all to make it easier for those of us here to understand the intended meaning in each case.

With that said, any such changes made for the sake of the reader will be kept relatively minimal. Accuracy will take priority wherever adaptations are not fully necessary. Most of the story will be told exactly as it happened in these far-off worlds, or close to it. Consequently, there will still be plenty of things that will surely seem unfamiliar and foreign to you as the reader.

Nevertheless, such unfamiliarity is, in truth, the minimum that one should expect when embarking on any adventure. And make no mistake, the following story, like most stories, is an adventure—one that will transport you to new lands where you will discover new people, civilizations, and world concepts that may challenge the reality that you know. This is an adventure that I have been on since early childhood, and one which I have chosen to now share with any who are willing to join me in it. I humbly hope that it is an enjoyable and worthwhile journey for any who choose to partake.

ANTAL

Aramont

Karris

Rikis

Rikis

Eser

Mecros

Enzod

Maram

Nolinth

Canich

Grinvell Augun
Forest

Calantia

Araf

Araf

Tarpoa

Hivich

Varith

Olan

Chal

Guun

Guun

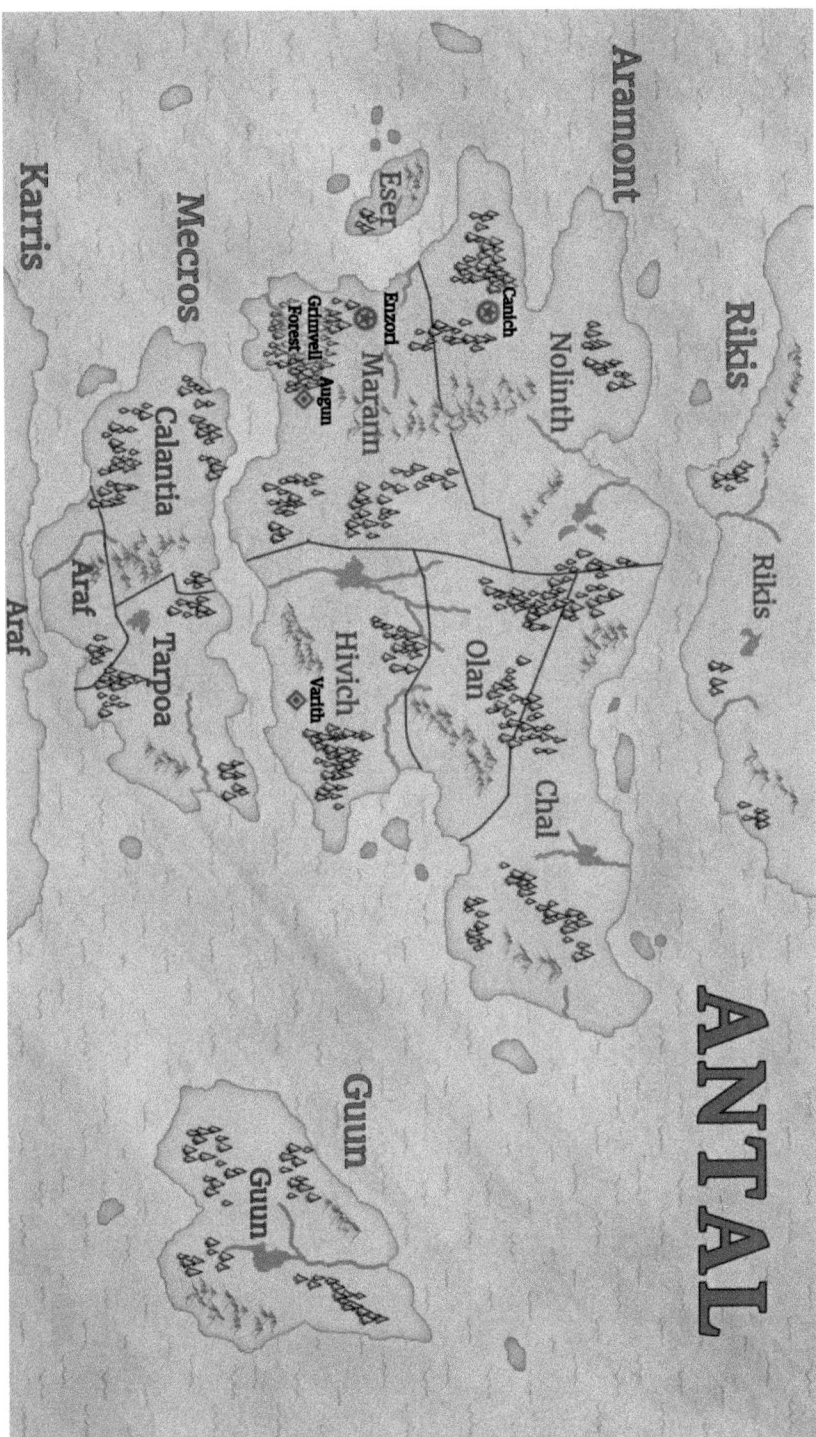

Figure 1. Antal World Map

x

Chapter 1

It was a busy night at the Silver Note Cabaret. The crowd was boisterous and cheerful, full of night-goers, all eating, drinking and talking amongst themselves at their respective tables. A quartet of the club's staff musicians stood on stage playing their early evening set. Their melodies created an upbeat and pleasing atmosphere in the cabaret, which teased the crowd of the feature performance that was yet to come.

Aren took a swig of his Antallian sweet milk as he watched the performers. This particular sweet milk was a non-alcoholic beverage unique to this planet, derived from the *Ant. glagonis interoctii* or "glago" plant. It had a flavour that was both smooth and creamy, yet also tangy and sweet. He had taken a serious liking to the drink since the first time he tried it, back when he first visited Antal.

"So, did everything go according to plan?" Anya asked him, interrupting his thoughts.

Aren flashed her an incredulous smirk. "I take it what you're really asking is 'did I get distracted along the way'?"

She didn't even feign a look of protest at the accusation. "Well... did you?"

Aren looked over at her as he fidgeted with the ebony amulet around his neck. Anya was a sturdy and beautiful woman in her early thirties. Her hair was a deep black, held up in a bun, and she had a well-defined musculature that let on to her intensive physical training. As an orren, native to Antal, she had six fingers on each hand, ridged ears, and sharp teeth. Her skin was an off-gray, with just a touch of blue. Otherwise, she was nearly human in appearance.

Aren grinned, letting go of his amulet. He pulled a data strip out of his pocket and slid it across the table to her.

"Look, I got the codes," He replied. "Mission success. Does that answer your question?"

Anya picked up the data strip with a mild look of annoyance on her face. "While I do appreciate this, you know it doesn't."

She let out a sigh. "Look, I really just want to know if you ran into any resistance."

"We-ell," Aren answered hesitantly. "Let's just say you have a few less soldiers to worry about, ok?"

"How many is a few?" Anya asked suspiciously.

"Less than Brilz, but uh… more than Glensperg," Aren admitted sheepishly.

"Seriously?!" Anya ejected frustratedly, before lowering her voice and glancing around herself cautiously. "This mission was supposed to be clandestine."

"Come on, you know how it is, Anya," Aren asserted. "Things don't always go according to plan."

Anya rolled her eyes. "You know, I have half a mind to fire you."

Aren laughed. "Come on, you could never fire me. What would you even fill your time with if you weren't cleaning up after my messes?"

A flash of a half-smile on Anya's face betrayed her amusement before she forced it back to its stern position.

"You may have a point," she conceded, relaxing a bit in her chair.

"Seriously though, Anya," Aren's tone sobered up. "Don't worry. No one had any way of knowing what I was there for, and I left no trace when I made the copy."

"Well, alright," Anya agreed tepidly. In fairness to Aren, she recognized that he had actually been doing fairly well at holding himself back lately. It would simply be unrealistic to expect him to change his nature entirely overnight.

"I am glad you succeeded in the mission," She acknowledged. "I know it couldn't have been easy, so... thank you, Aren."

Aren beamed. "You're most welcome, my friend."

"Now, before we close this matter, I have to ask—"

"No, I'm sorry," Aren cut her off, knowing what she was about to say. "The blueprints weren't there."

Anya sighed in disappointment as she put the data card in her pocket. "It's fine. That was a longshot anyway. What you got is more than enough."

Aren took another swig of sweet milk, finishing the glass, as Anya guzzled her beer. After that simple handoff, their business for the evening was already concluded. It wasn't often that either of them got a night off, so they were both looking forward to this one.

Aren, in particular, was eager to hear the feature performer that night, who was supposedly quite talented. Aren enjoyed music a lot, but rarely got the chance to see any live performances. Anya had specifically chosen this club as their meeting spot to give him that chance.

Aren's expectations were admittedly a bit high, as Anya had touted this venue as one of the best cabarets on the planet. This would be high praise on most planets, but on Antal, a world known for its music, this was an especially glowing review. Nevertheless, the pleasant atmosphere, delicious drinks, and beautiful melodies lent credence to Anya's high praises. Aren found himself really enjoying the club, even now, while the main performance still had yet to begin.

And yet, there had not been a night in existence so great that there was no room for things to go wrong. Aren was hit by this realization as he watched Anya's expression turn sour, and he turned to look at what she saw.

There, at the entrance, a group of UAPA soldiers walked in, talking loudly and acting rowdy amongst themselves.

Despite being clearly off-duty, these soldiers still wore their armored uniforms, minus the helmets, and kept their rifles on their backs, proudly ensuring everyone around them would be aware of their military status and their potential lethality. While it was a club rule for customers to check their weapons at the entrance, these soldiers simply walked right past the doorperson, without so much as a glance of acknowledgment.

"Well, isn't that just lovely?" Anya sighed before turning back to Aren. "Let's try not to let them ruin our night, ok?"

"I suppose you're right," Aren agreed.

However, he almost immediately regretted those words as the rest of the procession walked in.

Aren's gut churned as four distinct individuals, three young women and one young man, entered the club with the soldiers. Although these four people were in uniform themselves, they were clearly not soldiers. The distinct style of uniform they wore, along with the "RPW" ID number tattoos on their necks made it clear who these people were—they were slaves that the soldiers had brought into the cabaret with them.

Aren's eyes turned fiery. He gritted his teeth as he watched the group being brought over to a large table by the host. The enslaved individuals were prodded forward by the soldiers tauntingly with rifles, and then shoved into their seats.

He had checked his sword at the door, but he felt his fist fruitlessly clenching over where he normally would have kept it, nevertheless.

Anya looked him in the eye cautiously.

"I know how you feel, but I stand by what I said, Aren," Anya asserted empathetically. "It's awful, but you know as well as I do that this is happening all over most of the planet at this point. This is why our mission comes first."

Aren looked down to his glass, took a deep breath, and relaxed his demeanor. He knew she was right. He'd had to endure many such situations without making a scene lately. Restraint was not his usual style, but he was trying to learn to adapt for the sake of his employer and friend.

"You're right, Anya," He conceded. "I know that logically. I just… I don't know. There's still a part of me that wonders sometimes."

Anya looked at him sympathetically. "I know that feeling. I get it too. We just have to do our best."

Aren nodded vacantly at her. He looked around at the club surrounding them, trying to take his mind off of the injustice that had just entered the building.

It was an admittedly gorgeous venue. The club was large and open, with three semi-distinct sections—the entry area, the bar, and the cabaret itself. Of the three, the largest was by far the cabaret. Most of this section was taken up by customer tables where the audience was served food and drink. These tables were positioned across rising, semi-circular tiers expanding upward and outward majestically around a center stage, where the musicians were currently playing their tunes.

The color scheme across the venue was full of dark, cool tones that gave a relaxed but electric feel. Deep blues, particularly midnight, dominated the club's aesthetic, with accents of onyx black, shadow gray and dark purple, all illuminated with bright, neon, blue-tinted hanging lights. To top it all off, the table surfaces were a striking pattern of dark blue and black marbling with a coat of shiny wax overtop of them.

As Aren was looking around, his eye was caught by a trio getting up from their seats and pressing a button on the side of their table. This began a curious process of sinking the chairs into the floor, while rising and twisting the table in on itself. What was left was a much smaller surface at chest level. After the process was finished, the group placed their drinks on the now-shrunken table and began dancing in the new space that opened up.

Aren watched, intrigued, as the three of them moved their bodies to the rhythm. Antallian dancing had a unique, enthralling beauty to it that made it hard to pull one's eyes away.

Prior to this, he had been wondering why there was no dance floor in this club. Antallians were known for their love of dancing, and it seemed like such a missed opportunity. However, it appeared that the dance floor was there all along—under the tables themselves. Aren was impressed at the idea. He had never seen a set-up like this—not that he frequented very many clubs.

Aren's thoughts were interrupted by an orren woman approaching their table with a pitcher of sweet milk. She was an older woman, likely in her mid-to-late 60's. She was beautiful and well-dressed, with her gray hair in an expensive-appearing up-do and adorned in a number of gorgeously-crafted necklaces, bracelets, and hair accessories. She was altogether elegant in appearance—if a touch ostentatious.

"Anya, my dear," The woman greeted. "My warmest welcomes to you and your guest."

"Hey Ver," Anya responded cordially. "How's business?"

Based on the nickname, Aren realized that this must have been Verine, the owner of the club that Anya had told him about. Verine was a personal friend of Anya's, but she was also a very involved owner, so it was apparently not unusual to see her refilling drinks, interacting with customers, or helping out in numerous other ways around the club.

"Well, you know, trying to keep optimistic through all the changes these days," Verine responded vaguely, before turning to Aren and motioning with the pitcher. "Refill?"

"Yes, please," Aren requested.

"Ah, come to think of it," Anya chirped. "I'm getting low too."

Anya took a final swig of her drink, and then swiped her club card over a built-in scanner in the center of the table. Unlike with

Aren's sweet milk, beer in this club could be refilled by the customer themselves without needing a server nor having to get up.

Anya reached under her table, grabbed the beer hose, and pulled it up to her glass. As she pulled the trigger, sensors automatically detected how much was poured and added the cost to the tab associated with her card.

As their drinks were being refilled, they could hear one of the UAPA soldiers shouting from across the club.

Looking over, they saw an irate soldier with a smug look on his face and a symbol on his chestplate indicating that he was a commander in rank. He had his arm swung around one of the enslaved women's shoulders.

"I expect this first round of drinks to be on the house!" The Commander bellowed aggressively at a nervous-looking server girl. "It's basic respect for our military service. We just got back from the front lines last week. We've been out there fighting for your freedom and protection, you know?"

"Please, Jeshoa," the enslaved woman under his arm pleaded cautiously.

"Quiet, you!" The Commander pushed her head down just short of slamming into the table as he yelled at her. "I didn't say you could talk!"

The server looked over uncertainly at Verine, hoping for some cue as to how to handle this. Verine simply nodded at her, giving her the ok.

"Of course, sir," The server announced agreeably, bowing deeply to him in a show of respect. "Thank you for your service. Your free round will be with you shortly."

"See?" The Commander shouted towards the enslaved woman as he released his grip on her and pointed up at the server. "That's how you show respect. You could learn a thing or two from her."

Aren looked away. He couldn't stand to watch anymore.

"It's just awful, isn't it?" Verine muttered angrily. "They're so brazen lately. Gods, some days… Some days I wish the *Devil of Hivich* himself would pay a visit here and take these *beliks* down a peg."

"The Devil of Hivich, huh?" Anya remarked offhandedly. "Do you really believe in those tales?"

"Aye, it does sound too good to be true, doesn't it?" Verine admitted. "A UAPA boogeyman with abilities straight out of a fairy tale, hellbent on making life miserable for these soldiers... Perhaps he's real, perhaps not. Either way, it's nice to imagine him swooping in some day and scaring those pests off once and for all."

Verine sighed, looking over at the free round being delivered to the soldiers. "Until then, it's generally easier to just give them what they want."

"No one could blame you for that," Aren sympathized. "It's not like you have much choice."

"I suppose," Verine said uncertainly. "The nightly demand for free drinks isn't the end of the world. I just can't believe that they have the gall to bring *actual slaves* in here. And I don't care what they are calling them these days. 'Restitution Program Workers.' *Pft*. As far as anyone can tell, most of them are hardly criminals."

"That's just always been UAPA through and through," Anya responded in agreement. "Everything is a word game with them. Even their name, the 'United Antallian People's Army.' They're the farthest thing from being the 'People's.' And 'United'? Give me a break."

"You hit the nail on the head, love," Verine asserted.

"That said, it seems to me that they're hiding the truth less and less these days," Aren noted, watching as one of the enslaved women, looking upset, was pulled over and made to sit directly in one of the soldiers' laps in a way that did not appear to be platonic.

Verine sighed, frowning at the lurid display. "Honestly, at this point, I'd like to just ban all soldiers from the establishment, but this place would be shut down faster than a *glenth* in heat if I tried anything like that."

"Oh, Ver," Anya replied sympathetically. "Of course, none of this is on you. You're doing the best you can. Your cabaret is still the pride of Antal."

"I appreciate the kind words, dear," Verine beamed. "In any case, we'll do our best to show those poor things a good time. Maybe I'll even sneak them a few drinks. They're our guests, after all."

She shook her head and looked over at Aren. "Speaking of guests, I've forgotten my manners. Please tell me, who is this strapping young human that you brought here tonight, Anya? Is he your date, perhaps?"

Anya chuckled playfully. "Not exactly. Aren is a personal friend and a mercenary who has been working with us these past few months."

"Oh, well that's even better," Verine beamed and gave a respectful bow to him. "It's a pleasure to meet you, Aren. I'm Verine, the owner here."

"It's nice to meet you too, Verine," Aren bowed back to her. "Anya's told me good things about you and your club."

"Oh, she's too kind to me, that one," Verine chuckled. "But seriously, just know that you're welcome here anytime, love. Mercenary or not, anyone helping the cause is a guest of honour here at the Silver Note Cabaret. I do hope you enjoy what we have to offer."

"Thank you," Aren smiled. "I must say, I'm especially looking forward to your guest performer tonight. I've heard great things about him."

"Ah, yes," Verine said, looking down at the time on her wristcomm. "In fact—it's actually about time that I go out and introduce him. You two enjoy the rest of your night. And don't pay any heed to those soldiers. There's naught that can be done about those bastards. Well… for now."

Verine looked around cautiously before leaning in closer and speaking softly to Anya. "As always, thank you for everything you do, Anya… For love and freedom."

Anya smiled up at her. "For love and freedom."

Verine gave a quick bow before hastily retreating from the table and making her way backstage.

"She seems lovely," Aren remarked to Anya. "I can see why you two became friends."

"She is an absolute doll," purred Anya. "And a very talented proprietor. I wasn't exaggerating when I said this cabaret was the pride of Antal. She's done some amazing things with this place."

"I don't doubt it," Aren stated.

Anya took a sip of her beer before continuing. "Did you know this used to be an abandoned warehouse when she first bought it? She renovated it, built it up from scratch, and it's now become one of the most well-known cabarets in the astro-region."

"Wow," Aren responded. "I regret that I've been a bit too preoccupied to come here earlier, but I'm glad I finally got the chance."

"Well, joys to your first time here," Anya raised her glass up high. "And to your successful mission!"

"Joys," Aren repeated in a somewhat somber tone, lifting his glass up high with her. Together, they both slammed it down on the table at the same time, and then took a drink.

Aren was trying to enjoy the moment. He knew that things were progressing well, and they were doing all they could. But he was finding it a little hard to focus on that right now.

Verine's voice from on stage interrupted his thoughts. "My most valued guests..."

He looked up and saw that the quartet had stopped playing, and Verine was standing center-stage, smiling at the audience. She looked surprisingly dazzling and energetic for her advanced age, standing in the spotlight with her silver hair and dark makeup, adorned in her sparkling green dress and various accessories.

"It is my honour to present the one that you have all been waiting for," Verine announced proudly. "Our feature performer tonight."

The lighting dimmed, and pyrotechnics erupted across the stage as Verine spoke.

"You have all probably heard of him by now. He may be a human and an offworlder, but he is one who was trained as a musician right here, in our own galaxy-renowned Don Zai Academy. After graduating, he disappeared for a couple years, going on hiatus—you know how artists are."

The crowd chuckled lightly.

"But he has since made a grand re-appearance, making a name for himself across the galaxy and finding a beloved fanbase here on Antal. Please welcome Xander Ardentes!"

The crowd roared with applause as Xander made his way onto the stage, and Verine took her leave.

Aren felt himself taken aback as he saw the young man approaching the stage. This man was, in a word, beautiful. He was thin, just below average height with mid-length blonde hair. His face was remarkably symmetrical with a sharp nose, deep red lips, and dark, kind eyes. His pale, smooth skin shone under the stage's spotlight as he walked up to the front of the stage and gave a gentle bow.

"Gods yes!" Anya nudged Aren excitedly. "I can hardly believe I'm finally getting to see him live."

She looked down at the stage with starstruck eyes. "You know, his amazing music aside, there's something else special about him."

"Oh?" Aren uttered curiously.

"Yes," Anya replied. "He's also a talented aurimancer. Maybe we'll get to see a bit of performance magic with his set tonight."

"That would be something," Aren responded with a hint of his own excitement.

Aurimancy was the mysterious branch of magic that was cast using musical tones instead of verbal incantations. In all of his years of experience with magic, Aren rarely had the chance to witness it. It was a pretty uncommon art. However, it was hardly a surprise that Antal would be one of the few planets in the galaxy known for it, considering how deeply ingrained music was in Antallian culture. Its connection to music was so strong, in fact, that Antal was often referred to by the moniker 'The Planet of Songs' by many across the galaxy.

Xander gently walked over to the cabaret's kiardo, a large, two-handed keyboard instrument, and sat down on the bench in front of it. Of the numerous instruments utilized by Antallian musicians, the kiardo is among the most popular. It was an ancient instrument that had long been beloved across the galaxy for its deep, rich sound, and its responsive touch sensitivity, allowing a range of dynamics from daintily soft tones to thunderously loud chords.

As Xander positioned himself, Aren could see the staff musicians preparing their instruments in the background.

Xander cleared his throat. A targeted, long-distance microphone picked up the sound clearly, playing it back through top-quality speakers throughout the cabaret. These speakers were located in key points across the building, designed to optimize the acoustics so everyone in the audience could hear the performance at the same level of volume and clarity.

"Well, hello there, my good people," Xander greeted the crowd in his smooth, high-tenor voice. "It is an honour and privilege to be able to play for you all today. Inspiration can be a most fickle partner at times. Let's see how he treats us today, shall we? This is a song called *Something New.*"

And with that, he began his playing.

From the very first touch of Xander's fingers to the keyboard, his skills as a master musician were immediately apparent. His hands glided smoothly across the kiardo, hitting a flourish of keys, and creating a melancholic but powerful melody that washed over Aren like a wave crashing in from the ocean.

But as Xander continued the intro, he gradually slowed and quieted his playing. Smoothly and carefully, he came back down, releasing the tension he had built, like a steadily ebbing tide. After a period of this, he just stopped altogether. For a moment, there was complete silence.

But then, as suddenly as he stopped, he started up again. This time, he was accompanied by the staff musicians joining in with a full range of strings and woodwinds, pulling the melody back up and driving forward the theme, as if the sea had rolled back in quickly but smoothly over the shore, enveloping the entire audience in its gentle but firm embrace.

So, this is how a master musician plays? Thought Aren as he watched, enraptured.

After a few more moments of this, Xander's voice entered the mix.

"Walking through the days,
Your hollowed heart yearns.
Drudging through the weeks,
As your tattered mind spurns.
Another early wakening,
Same as before.
Locked deep in your heart,
Could you dare hope for more?"

Aren was stunned. Xander's playing was beyond spectacular, but his voice was breathtaking—angelic even. It was somehow both gentle and impassioned simultaneously, a perfect complement to the instrumentals that made the piece feel whole.

"Eyes shut closed,
Hear the unseen calling.
Do you suppose
We'll ever stop falling?
Wandering through
The endless abyss.

How did it ever
Come out to this?

An itch starts to form,
Cutting through the haze.
A desire once forgotten,
In these tumultuous days.
Love, ambition, curiosity—
These deeper profound drives
Point to something ahead,
A hope that survives.

Eyes shut closed,
Hear the unseen calling.
Do you suppose
We'll ever stop falling?
Searching for a way through
The endless abyss.
How did it ever
Come out to this?"

As Aren listened to the music, it was like rest of the world faded away, and all that was left was Xander and the notes and lyrics that came from him. The feeling was powerful and yet tranquil, all in one.

Aren was so entranced that he almost didn't notice as glowing blue doves appeared and started flying gracefully across the cabaret, leaving streams of visible aura behind them. The crowd murmured in excitement as others noticed as well.

Aren marveled, realizing that this must be the aurimancy that Anya mentioned earlier.

But as intriguing as the magic was, he was still far more caught up in the awe-inspiring music emanating from the stage. To him, that was the most incredible magic happening in that moment.

"The first step is the hardest
Into the frontier unknown.
Keep pushing and remember,
You were never truly alone.
The path ahead is new,
But the muscle memory is old,
A whole universe waiting ahead,
Worth more than its weight in gold.

Eyes starting to open,
See your loved ones calling.
Give one final embrace,
Break past the stalling.
It's time to step out
Of the endless abyss.
There are new horizons to explore
That closed eyes did miss."

The sound of the piece had been growing gradually more and more hopeful in feeling, until finally reaching the pinnacle, which culminated into a dazzling light that shone brightly into the hearts of the audience.

However, as engaged as Aren was, he couldn't help but notice some upset sounds coming from across the cabaret. He looked over and noticed the soldiers openly groping the distressed-looking slaves. Aren could feel his anger rising.

For a moment, it felt like the theater shook, but he figured it must have been in his head.

"As you open your eyes
To something new
As you open your eyes
To something new.
Wonders beheld,

Whole worlds now to view
As you open your eyes
To something new."

The crowd roared with applause as the song ended. Aren began clapping as well, but he did so while keeping a sharp eye on the soldiers. Aren loved the music, but he simply could not focus on much else as he was seeing what was happening in this very room.

He gritted his teeth and clenched his fists as he witnessed the soldiers forcibly making out with the enslaved individuals. Aren was ready to pounce over there, regardless of the consequences.

Anya must have noticed this.

"Aren," She cautioned, looking into his eyes. "I know this is hard, but we have to think of the greater mission."

Aren closed his eyes and took a deep breath. "Alright, for the greater mission."

Anya took a breath of relief. "Thank you. This will all be worth it later. We just have to be patient."

Aren tried to calm his nerves by looking back on stage. He saw that Xander had gotten up from the kiardo bench, and was talking to the staff musicians, while holding a chiambra, a somewhat smaller string instrument held over the shoulder and played with a bow. After a moment, he turned and walked back to center stage.

"My lovely audience," Xander announced. "There has been a slight change to the planned set tonight. I was considering how it can be all too easy to fall into comfort zones. When this happens, we tend to fail to do our very best. With that said, instead of doing *Whispering Winds* next, I'm actually going to play you a rather special piece on the chiambra..."

Chapter 2

There were murmurs of excitement throughout the crowd at the announcement.

Xander was well known for his inordinate skills across a variety of instruments, but one of the most sought after was his chiambra playing. Not only was he known to be particularly phenomenal with the chiambra, but it was also one of the instruments he played the least for crowds, making it one of the most special and exciting whenever he pulled it out.

Aren was intrigued, but still couldn't help but be bothered by the soldiers across the room, still continuing their abuse. He felt, after this piece, it might be better if he simply left, before things escalated any further.

On stage, Xander had closed his eyes and could be seen quietly whispering something to himself. Aren wondered if it was a pre-song ritual, perhaps for helping achieve focus.

After a moment of this, Xander stopped and opened his eyes again, looking out into the crowd.

Slowly, Xander raised the chiambra onto his left shoulder, and with his right hand, raised his bow up against the instrument's strings. He took a deep breath. And suddenly, the atmosphere of the cabaret shifted. A palpable tension filled the air as Xander's eyes turned to flame, and his body turned to steel.

In the next moment, the piece began. While the mastery of this piece was the same as the last, the feeling was entirely different. Instead of the deeper, mixed melancholic/hopeful sound from before, what followed here was a gripping torrent of notes, dark and impassioned, flowing from the chiambra and taking over the cabaret like a sudden and terrible storm as the staff musicians could only struggle to try and keep up.

It was as if Xander were engulfed in flame as he played, and that same spark traveled into the hearts and minds of the audience as they listened intently.

However, it was hard for Aren to pay full attention, as he noticed the soldiers' behaviour was only getting worse.

Cries could be heard coming from one of the slaves as they resisted a burly-looking, bearded soldier's advances. The soldier screamed at her and slapped her across the face. It took everything in Aren to remain still.

I have to remember the bigger picture, He thought to himself. *I simply can't… I shouldn't.*

The woman was in tears as the soldier raised his hand to hit her again. Aren felt he needed to leave the building right that second to stop himself from going over there. As this was happening, the chiambra music only continued building in power and speed.

Aren started to get up to leave. But he had barely stood up before, out of the corner of his eye, he saw a pillar of black flame protrude from the ground beneath the soldier, enveloping him in the flames as it knocked him back.

There was a stunned silence in the cabaret over what had just happened. As Aren looked over, he could see that the soldier was knocked out cold. However, more interestingly, the soldier somehow seemed to be the only one hit by the sudden burst of flames. Even the slave who was right next to him appeared to have somehow been unscathed.

Aren's gaping jaw quickly turned into a grin as the truth of what had happened finally dawned on him. He sat back down in his seat, looked over to Anya, who was standing up, alert, and subtly signed his realization to her. Anya acknowledged him with a nod, but stayed standing, nevertheless.

The other soldiers hurriedly got up from their seats, looking around themselves in shock and alarm.

"What the hell was that?" One of the soldiers yelled angrily. "Who did this?"

Commander Jeshoa, the one who had demanded free drinks earlier in the night, walked up to the slave and grabbed her by the arm, yelling at her. "You! Did you do this?"

But as he was shouting at her, black lightning ripped down from the ceiling and struck another soldier, knocking them clean out.

Chaos and confusion began to overtake the club at this point. Many people were running for the exits. The staff musicians had already ceased their playing and had fearfully ran for the backdoor themselves, leaving Xander as the only one left—still playing, as if nothing had happened at all.

A few of the soldiers began to give him some peculiar looks.

"Wait," the Commander said, letting go of the girl. "The aurimancer—he must be the one behind this! Take him down!"

Finally, they get it, Aren chuckled light-heartedly.

Anya looked at Aren with a look between judgment and resigned acceptance. "Of course, you'd find this amusing."

Xander smirked as the soldiers grabbed their rifles and began to take aim at him.

"Nice try, but those won't do you much good," Xander confidently asserted.

With a flurry of notes, a wave of dark flame knocked several of the soldiers back, rendering a couple more of them unconscious.

Another soldier took aim and fired with his sonic rifle. But quickly, Xander launched himself into the air, gracefully dodging it. The blast left a three-inch diameter hole that penetrated clean through the club's wall. Instead of falling after the jump, Xander then caught himself on a floating dark, multi-colored quasi-cloud, conjured through a riff that he played in mid-air.

While Aren remained seated, he did not let his guard down. He was ready to jump in, if necessary, but so far, it seemed that it wasn't. In the meanwhile, he simply watched mesmerized as Xander continued his grand performance.

Anya broke his focus a little as she addressed him.

"I'll help evacuate the civilians," She asserted. "You continue watching and only step in if absolutely necessary. We still need to try to keep a low profile."

"Got it," Aren affirmed to her, and she took off. He went back to watching Xander's fight as it unfolded.

It was as if the musician was demon-possessed. Xander did not stop playing the piece for even a moment. Even as he was shot at, he expertly dodged by jumping from conjured cloud to cloud, all the while never missing a note. Through this, he produced storms of black fire and lightning that danced across the tiers that the soldiers were positioned on, carefully avoiding the slaves with every casting.

It was not long until Commander Jeshoa was the only one left standing. With most of the soldiers gone, the enslaved people finally saw their chance and took off, bolting for the front door and getting out of there.

Despite losing his subordinates, the Commander was undeterred. In fact, his confidence only rose as he had managed to get a bio-lock on Xander with his sonic rifle. A bio-lock allows for computer-assisted aiming at a target that greatly decreases the chance of missing. The program works by locking onto a particular bio-signal picked up by sensors and uses an AI to adjust the barrel towards the target in real time.

The Commander gave a devilish grin as he squeezed his finger over the trigger. "Dodge this, belik!"

Xander wasn't sure what was about to happen, but seeing the confidence in the Commander's eyes, he did not wish to find out. He quickly engulfed himself in a sphere of dark flame. As the sonic blast came into contact with the flame, it pushed Xander back, while dissipating across the conjured shield.

As the flame shield came back down, Aren could see that Xander was a bit winded, but seemed to be ok. Xander acted quickly, conjuring more black flames with his chiambra that knocked the Commander to the ground.

After a few labored breaths, the Commander laughed from his position on the floor.

"It's too late," He shouted tauntingly. "I called for reinforcements while you were fighting my men earlier. They'll already be here by the time you get outside."

And with that, Xander cast a bolt of lightning with a final cadence that knocked out the Commander, finishing off his grand performance that had taken out all twelve of the soldiers in the cabaret.

*/

Aren looked around the club. It appeared that him and Xander were the only ones left in the building.

"That was some performance," Aren shouted up to him, walking up to the stage and clapping.

Xander jerked a little at hearing the unexpected voice. He turned and looked at Aren.

"Why, thank you," Xander grinned, hopped off the stage, and gave a deep bow, flourishing his right arm outward, while his left, still holding his chiambra, was brought up to his chest. "It's all worth it for the lovely fans, such as yourself."

Aren smiled at him. This musician certainly was charming. Up close, Aren could see that he was even younger than he had expected. He looked to be close to Aren's age or maybe a little younger—probably somewhere around eighteen years old. He saw that two of the strings were broken on Xander's chiambra, and there was some deep scuffing.

"Your instrument," noted Aren.

"Ah, yes," Xander said, looking down at it. "A little damage from that sonic shot back there. Those weapons really are quite fascinating. It seems my shield spell came up a tad short. It should be quite fixable, but my playing will be a bit impacted until then."

"Well, I'm glad it can be fixed," Aren said supportively. "But, in any case, we should probably get out of here now. If we're lucky, we can make it out of this place before reinforcements arrive."

"Sounds good to me," Xander assented.

Aren grabbed his sweet milk from the table. Then, together, the two of them made a break for the entrance.

As they neared the door, Aren turned to Xander. "Just one quick second."

Aren entered the coat and weapons check room. The door had been left open and unattended—most likely thanks to Anya on her way out. He placed his sweet milk on the counter and grabbed his sword in its scabbard. He quickly tied it back to his waist, before grabbing his drink and rejoining Xander.

"A swordfighter, eh?" Xander marveled. "That's certainly not something you see every day."

"I suppose not," Aren smirked at him. "But I will say, it certainly comes in handy whenever I forget my shaving razors."

Xander looked at him with a puzzled expression for a second before openly laughing. "You're funny. I like you."

He then motioned for Aren to follow him as he headed for the door. "Come on, let's get out of here."

As they opened the door to the outside, they were greeted by a small crowd, huddled just a little distance past the door. The outside of the club was just as nice as the inside. Beneath them, the entrance ground was comprised of eye-catching brick patterns in various blue, gray and off-brown tones. To the left was the club's private patio, which was closed off by a gated black metal fence. And ahead of them, just past the brickwork, the cabaret connected to a large paved market square with several other businesses, as well as a roadway and two underground parking lots.

The crowd near the club's entrance appeared to be mostly staff and customers, but amongst them, Aren could see Anya, the four slaves, and Verine. Looking past the crowd, there was a group of soldiers in a semi-circle around them with their rifles drawn.

Verine was shouting obstinately at the soldiers. "Let us through! We haven't done anything."

The soldiers remained silent, ignoring her as she yelled at them.

Aren scooted ahead, leaving Xander in the back of the crowd, and walked up to Anya closer to the front.

"Oh hey," Anya greeted him. "Fancy seeing you here."

"Indeed," Aren simpered, taking a sip of his sweet milk. "Ya know, I fancied a breath of fresh air with my milk."

Anya looked at Aren, seeing him casually sipping sweet milk like nothing was going on.

She rolled her eyes and sighed lightheartedly. Part of her got a little annoyed at his irreverence from time to time. Aren was often like this, no matter how serious the situation. And yet, part of her had come to appreciate this sort of levity in the midst of such tense circumstances.

Aren's expression turned a touch more serious as he began scanning over their surroundings. "So, what's the situation here, my friend?"

"Well, the good news is that Verine and I managed to get most of the staff and customers out before the soldiers arrived," Anya responded. "But as you can see, they got here pretty quickly, leaving about nineteen of us trapped, you and I included. In addition to the fourteen soldiers surrounding us in the crescent formation, two more went around back to cover the rear exit."

"What have they said?" Aren asked.

"Absolutely nothing," Anya shook her head. "Asides from telling us once not to move, they've kept their lips shut tight and ignored all questions. They've only fired warning shots whenever anyone has gotten too close to them or attempted to go back into the club. Their orders are most likely to simply hold us and keep quiet until their superior arrives."

"Sounds like pretty typical UAPA protocol," Aren noted, sighing. "Damn that we couldn't get all civilians out. This cabaret is just too close to the CNPF."

Anya gave him an 'I told you so' look. "This is exactly why I didn't want us starting anything."

"I know, I know," Aren responded. "But what's done is done."

"Well, I can't deny that," Anya remarked. "If we're really lucky, maybe we can figure out a way of getting out of here without attracting any more attention."

Farther back in the crowd, Xander was assessing the situation himself. Things seemed rather dire. His chiambra was damaged, and even if it wasn't, he questioned whether he'd be able to get a single note off before the soldiers took him out. It was one thing when he had the element of surprise, but these soldiers were actively aiming their rifles and on their guard. This was a real predicament.

As they were speaking, they heard the deep sound of an engine that was progressively getting louder. Looking over, they could see a tank rolling in, along with a procession of marching soldiers, nine of them ahead of the tank and nine behind it.

This tank was a fairly typical UAPA build, designed with thick protective metal alloys and a front-facing sonic cannon, propelled forward by sprocket wheels on tracks. On top of this tank was a pedestal with a cushioned metal seat built onto it. This seated pedestal was a common feature on UAPA tanks that was added for UAPA officials to ride on, displaying their might and military pride, either during military parades or even just during casual patrols.

In this case, a clearly decorated officer was seated at the pedestal, covered in fancy adornments and symbols across his chest and shoulders. This man had black hair and wore a smug expression on his face. Aren recognized him immediately. This was Commandant Reinault, the man in charge of Antal's famous CNPF, or Central Network Processing Facility, a UAPA military-run facility only a few blocks away.

The tank came to a halt behind the crescent-formation soldiers. Commandant Reinault rose to his feet and walked down the steps of the tank to the ground. Two soldiers quickly brought a platform in front of him and placed it on the ground before marching back into formation.

The Commandant stepped on top of the platform, and then pressed a button on his cheek, activating a cybernetic amplifier implant, which projected his voice. Such implants were relatively common on Antal, and some other parts of the galaxy among officials who regularly addressed larger crowds.

He adjusted his posture, standing as straight and rigid as a board, and held his hands tightly behind him.

"Good evening," Commandant Reinault greeted in a voice that was superficially pleasant but betrayed sinister undertones. "I understand that there was a little situation in this establishment tonight."

The crowd stood silently, paralyzed with fear as the Commandant spoke.

"But fret not," Reinault continued. "The only one we are after is the one responsible for this mess. I am told he is some sort of minor celebrity. Of course, if that one individual were to refuse to cooperate, this could get a lot more complicated."

The Commandant gave an insidious smile as he looked out into the crowd. "We'd be forced to process all of you if that were to be the case. I wouldn't be surprised if many of you were sentenced to the Restitution Program for aiding and abetting a terrorist."

Xander clenched his fists and looked to the ground. It wasn't like him to feel regret, but it also wasn't like him to allow innocent bystanders to get caught up in his impulsivity. If it were just him, he could bear it, but with this many people, the situation felt a lot more real.

He knew he had to do whatever it took to help these people. He took a deep breath and steeled his nerves.

"It was me!" Xander called out. "I'm the sole one responsible. Not any of these others."

"Ah, I should have known the perpetrator would be an offworlder," The Commandant remarked. "Well, it's certainly no surprise there. Nevertheless, good on you for doing the right thing. Now get over here and surrender peacefully, and we shall let the others go."

"And what about them?" Xander pointed to the slaves.

"Oh? The Restitution Program Workers," The Commandant responded. "They'll be returned to their work, of course. Well, after a brief punishment for their role in this situation."

"They had nothing to do with it," Xander contended. "It was all on me."

Reinault furrowed his brow, clearly not liking how much this Xander was speaking out. "It's a matter of instilling discipline. I wouldn't expect an uncivilized offworlder like yourself to understand."

The Commandant's expression shifted into a devilish smile. "Well, not yet at least. You'll be placed in the Restitution Program yourself once this is all over. You'll certainly learn then."

Xander let out an exasperated sigh. It seemed like everything he did was for nothing.

But he looked back over the crowd. There were nearly twenty people there. He couldn't just let them all suffer for his mistake. He knew what he had to do.

Somberly, he took a step forward.

But just as he began to move, he was startled by a hand shooting out in front of his chest, blocking him from taking another step. The hand was surprisingly strong, preventing him from moving another inch forward.

He looked over and saw that it was Aren holding him back, while guzzling down the last of his drink.

"Ah, the sweet milk is really something on this planet," Aren remarked. "Would you mind holding onto this for me?"

He handed the glass to Xander and took a step forward.

"I'm sorry Anya," Aren apologized. "It looks like I won't be able to keep my promise about that low profile. But this has gone too far."

"It's ok," Anya conceded, sighing. "I somehow suspected this was going to end up happening sooner or later, plans or not."

Xander looked at Aren, shocked at what he seemed to be hearing.

"You can't possibly be doing what I think you're doing," Xander stammered. "Stop it. This is on me. I attacked those soldiers. Now, I'll take responsibility."

Aren smiled at him.

"I actually want to thank you," Aren asserted gratefully. "Sometimes, we can get so wrapped up in the 'bigger picture,' that we can forget that the smaller picture is still a part of it."

"You're going to get yourself killed," Xander rebuked. "Just let me surrender myself, and everything will be fine."

Xander went to stop Aren, but Anya grabbed his shoulder with one hand and held him in place, gently but firmly.

"Relax," Anya insisted. "Trust him."

"Trust him?" Xander was baffled. "There are what—thirty soldiers out there? And a tank, for god's sake. This is suicide."

Anya relaxed her hand on his shoulder. "Have faith."

Xander, seeing her confidence, began to calm down just a little. He still thought this was insane, but it was clear that nothing that he said was going to have any impact.

Aren relaxed and closed his eyes, calming his breathing, his heart and his mind as he moved forward slowly in a meditative trance.

"You there," The Commandant yelled assertively as he saw Aren walking out past the crowd. "Stop immediately, or you shall be fired upon."

Aren stopped walking forward. He knelt down as he gently reached over and grasped his sword's hilt with both hands.

"Good, you've stopped," Reinault commended. "Now, get back in line this instant. We shall not ask again."

"*Sudis entum*," Aren muttered under his breath.

Xander watched in fascination as the air around Aren seemed to bend inward towards him.

The Commandant looked uneasy as he watched the strange scene in front of him.

"Fire at him now!" Commandant Reinault commanded.

However, before a single shot could be fired, Aren suddenly disappeared. All that could be seen in that moment was a blur of motion that washed across the line of soldiers in the crescent formation. Aren reappeared on the far end of the soldiers, his sword drawn and held outward.

The soldiers screamed and grabbed onto their bleeding wrists as their rifles fell to the ground.

Xander's jaw dropped as he started to register what had happened. In a single swoop, Aren had managed to cut across all fourteen soldiers who had surrounded them, slicing their hands clean off, and destroying most of their rifles in the process.

It took a second for the rest of the soldiers to register it too, as they looked on in shock and horror.

"No, it can't be," The Commandant uttered shakily. "It's—it's *him*."

Reinault shook his head, steeling his nerves as his fury grew.

"It's the *gods dammed* Devil of Hivich!" He roared. "He's *here*! All soldiers, shoot him, now!"

The eighteen remaining soldiers all took aim and began firing. Watching what followed next was like watching a lightning bolt dance. Xander could barely follow Aren's after-image as he zig-zagged, expertly dodging every shot as he made his way to the soldiers. In a few seconds time, he had already made it to the nine soldiers in front of the tank, where he instantly took out three with his sword.

Meanwhile, Anya quickly corralled the civilians to the west patio. She lamented that she didn't have her EK12 lightning rifle with her— a rare and powerful, electricity-based weapon that could cut through UAPA armor without issue. Nonetheless, her trusty pistol was the next best thing, and she always had that on hand.

After getting the rest of the group behind the black metal fence, Anya looked back to see Aren had already taken out several more soldiers, sprawled out on the ground with various injuries and broken rifles. However, her eyes widened as she saw movement from one of them.

"Aren, behind you!" She cried.

Aren quickly turned around. Seeing the rifle pointing his direction from the barely conscious soldier, he launched himself out of the way just as the sonic blast ripped through his robes and sliced through the edge of his calf, causing him to cry out in pain.

Anya was ready to run and help when he yelled, "Don't worry about me! Just get the others to safety."

Anya decided not to argue. She nodded and turned back to the group.

This patio wasn't exactly safe, but it was much safer than out in the open. This fence was made with thick vertical bars, with thin spaces between them, which allowed the group to see what was going on but also would provide some measure of cover if any stray shots came their way.

Looking over the crowd, she could tell some of them were starting to really panic. So far, she had kept them under control, but she was not sure how long that would last.

Just as she was considering the best way to calm the group down, her thoughts were interrupted by the sound of loud, running footsteps coming from the side of the club. Two UAPA soldiers emerged from the alleyway. Just as they rounded the corner, their gaze met Anya's.

The soldiers looked and, seeing Anya's pistol in her hand, recognized her as a threat.

However, she already knew the soldiers were there, guarding the back, and was ready for them. They swiftly began to aim their rifles at her, but Anya fired the first shot, hitting the left soldier square in the neck. The second soldier fired at her, but she dove out of the way just in time.

Anya fired back at the second soldier, also hitting her in the neck. The neck/upper collar area was one of the biggest weak points in UAPA's standard-issue armor, thin enough for bullets from her high-powered pistol to make it through with ease. Both soldiers immediately fell to the ground after being hit.

Anya heard screams behind her. She quickly turned around, fearing the worst. After taking a good look, she breathed a sigh of relief when she saw that no one had been harmed. That could have gone much worse. But her relief was short-lived as she looked at the group's faces and realized that their panic had now been setting in worse than before.

"What the hell is happening!" One of the cabaret customers cried out.

"They nearly hit us!" Another yelled. "Have they gone mad?!"

"It's ok," Anya reassured. "Both of those soldiers are down. You'll all be safe as long as we can stay together and stay calm here."

"That's bullshit!" One of the group, a rough-looking type covered in cybertattoos yelled frustratedly.

He ran over to one of the fallen UAPA soldiers Anya had shot and picked up their sonic rifle.

"I'm not gonna just stand here, twiddling my thumbs, while they kill us!" The man declared. "I can fight too."

"Wait!" Anya cried. "Just hold on!"

But he had already taken off through the patio's front gate. As he ran towards the battle, another man from the group took off in the opposite direction. Anya groaned in exasperation. She was losing control here.

The first man, running towards the battle, took aim at one of the UAPA soldiers and pulled the trigger.

But nothing happened.

That idiot, Anya thought to herself. *He must not know the first thing about UAPA weaponry.*

He pulled the trigger again and again, but it continued to not fire. He looked down at the rifle's digital display. The screen was flashing and read: *INVALID USER—LOCKED FROM USE.*

"Dammit!" He screamed out.

"Aren!" Anya cried as she saw the tank taking aim at the foolhardy civilian.

A loud whirring sound started coming from the tank.

Aren looked over, and once he saw the man, he immediately realized the situation. Focusing on his good leg, he pounced over and scooped the man up in his arms, carrying him out of the way just as the tank fired. The sonic blast from the tank left a large crater in the ground, far larger than any of the small holes left by the rifles. Aren then jumped again, wincing from the pain in his leg as he made his way behind the fence, where he dropped the man off with the rest of the group.

"Th-thanks," the man stammered ashamedly, but Aren had already taken off.

Looking out into the battle, Anya could see that nine soldiers were remaining. These soldiers had divided into two groups, one of four, coming from the west and one of five, coming from the east, each firing at Aren.

Meanwhile, Aren could feel searing pain in his leg. He knew it wasn't a full break because he was still able to run, but the limp had caused him to lose a step. He couldn't keep things up like this.

Wincing in pain, he jumped backwards again, narrowly avoiding a volley of sonic blasts. As he moved, he pointed both of his hands outwards, one towards each of the remaining groups of soldiers.

"*Scintilla dor!*" Aren shouted. Sparks flew out of each hand towards both groups, fizzling as they swiftly made their way through the air.

Once the sparks reached the center of each group, Aren again spoke, clasping his fists. "*Veit.*"

With that, the second part of the Green Dragon's Spark spell activated, and both sparks exploded into massive balls of flame that engulfed both groups of soldiers entirely.

Aren knew that these magical flames burned at a low temperature, so wouldn't do much damage from heat burns. However, the real thing that made them dangerous was how they burned directly through the life energy of those they came in contact with. This effect instantly killed a few of the soldiers and knocked the rest out cold.

With all of the foot soldiers taken out, there was only one obstacle left—the tank. It had not been firing much so far. The main reason was that Aren had deliberately been keeping close to the soldiers most of the time, so it couldn't fire at him without risking hitting its allies. However, now that the soldiers were taken out, there was nothing stopping the tank from going on a shooting spree.

A whirring sound preceded the tank firing two consecutive shots at Aren. Aren narrowly dodged each shot, but the second shook him as it hit the ground immediately behind him, causing fragments and secondary shockwaves to hit him directly.

As an astonished Xander watched all of this unfold, he wondered what Aren was possibly going to do against the tank. Even those balls of flame from earlier wouldn't be enough to take something like that out. Thankfully, the tank did not appear to have any secondary shielding. However, the thick steel alloys it was made with, in theory, should be able to handle almost everything up to specialized anti-tank guns or artillery.

The tank fired another two shots at Aren. Aren dodged both as he ran straight towards the tank at top speed. Aren gripped his sword tightly with both hands and lunged at the tank.

"*Aeras arkidt!*" Aren shouted as he struck out.

Xander watched mesmerized. It looked as if a massive amount of wind had suddenly engulfed Aren's blade and was moving with it as he sliced the tank upwards, ripping through steel and caving in the front of the tank as the entire 100-tonne contraption was flipped onto its back.

Xander was stunned. He had never seen or even imagined that anyone could fight like this before. He himself had some tricks up his sleeves. But the way Aren disposed of these soldiers was on a whole other level.

Xander's thoughts were interrupted by a sinister voice sounding out suddenly.

"Stop right there!" Commandant Reinault cried out, walking towards Aren.

Aren stopped his movement and looked at him. It appeared Reinault had caught the man who had run away earlier. The Commandant held the man tightly with one hand while another held a pistol to his head. As he looked more closely, Aren could see that it was one of the four enslaved individuals—the young man, specifically.

"Stop immediately and give yourself up, or I will kill this man," The Commandant commanded. "I know you, *Devil of Hivich*. I know how much you value what you consider to be 'innocent' life. Now drop the sword, or I fire immediately."

Aren complied, instantly dropping his sword to the ground by his side.

"*Scintilla esher,*" Aren whispered under his breath.

"Good," Reinault commended, sounding a little less panicked. "Now, get down on your knees. And don't get any funny ideas. This isn't my only hostage, you know. Try anything, and I'll start firing straight into that crowd after killing this one. That pitiful fence won't be enough to stop this sonic pistol."

Aren complied, slowly getting down on his knees, but as he did, a tiny spark appeared right next to the Commandant's hand.

"*Veit,*" Aren called out.

Suddenly the spark ignited into a small ball of flame, engulfing the Commandant's hand, causing him to drop the pistol, and cry out in pain.

"*Sudis entum,*" Aren intoned.

Like at the beginning of the battle, the air began to pull in around Aren. In the next instant, Aren disappeared, along with his sword from the ground, into a sudden blur. When Aren re-appeared, he was standing several feet past Commandant Reinault, holding his sword in hand.

The Commandant, looking confused, reached up to touch his neck. Looking down, he saw that his fingers were covered with blood. He coughed deeply, spurting up crimson as his neck began to leak out. He fell to the ground.

Chapter 3

It was over three years ago, on Aren's 16th birthday that he officially completed his apprenticeship with the Dehnovai. He had only been with them for a year and two months, making this one of the shortest apprenticeships in Dehnovai history. The average length was four years, and the clan record was only a week shorter, held by the current Grandmaster Hallamaine.

That night, they were holding a Consecration Feast at the dojo to celebrate Aren's ascension into the rank of warrior.

Aren was feeling strangely conflicted as he left his quarters and made his way to the hall where the celebration was being held. He knew he had no reason to feel anything but good. He had just reached a major milestone. His entire goal in joining this clan was to become stronger, and to achieve the things he never could with the Magi Academy. Today's achievement showed that he was making progress towards that goal. And yet, for some reason, he found his thoughts currently stuck in the past.

Over his years, he had been through a lot. The destruction of his home world as a young child was not the only tragedy he had had to go through, and these experiences had all cast a dark shadow over his heart.

He had vowed to get stronger, so that he could retake control of his life and protect those he cared about. But lately, it just didn't feel like enough. Every sparring session, every workout, every magicks exercise, every assignment—it had all begun to feel like he was just going through the motions. He felt aimless and without direction.

Nevertheless, he did his best to shake off the feeling as he approached the hall. There was a celebration waiting for him, and he didn't want to bring down the mood of his fellow clan members. He took a deep breath and put on the best smile that he could before entering.

Aren looked around as he crossed the threshold into the hall. It was a gorgeous room, around 2000 square feet, with burgundy wooden floorboards, and walls made out of special paper contained between wood pillars and patterned frames. Large, glassless windows opened up to the serene, moonlit training grounds outside, while wall sconces illuminated the hall with enchanted flames that would turn on or off with a word from any member.

A wonderful aroma hit Aren's nostrils as he entered the room. He couldn't wait to try the meal tonight.

As Aren looked around, he could see over ninety people in the hall. The clan had a current total of 106 members, including 1 grandmaster, 5 masters, 58 warriors, 6 apprentices, 7 utility members, 12 retirees, and finally 17 kin-members, who were accepted into the clan as spouses or family of other members. With the number of people Aren could see in the hall, that meant that only around a dozen or so were out on assignment that day.

It was unusual for so many clan members to be present at the dojo at the same time. There were even a couple members here that Aren didn't recognize— who had likely been out on assignment so often that he had never had the chance to see them before now. It was clear that some of the people who came here for the feast were hoping to scope out the new warrior joining their ranks. Aren expected that the training grounds tomorrow would be full of challengers looking to test his skills.

As Aren walked further in, he was met with a handful of cheers from some and calculating stares from others. He waved cheerfully to the former and ignored the latter, as he continued over to where the apprentices were sitting.

As he began to approach the table, Gueri, an androgynous apprentice and one of his closest friends in the clan, ran up to Aren's side and threw their right arm over his shoulders, sloshing their beer so that a few drops splashed into Aren's shirt.

"Happy birthday Aren!" Gueri declared. "And congratulations at beating us to warrior, you lucky bastard."

They took a swig of their beer and patted Aren on the back, before pulling their arm back.

As the two of them took their seats, Julien, the oldest apprentice of the group, smirked and nudged Aren with his elbow.

"I can't believe the disrespect here," Julien teased. "Didn't you know that I was here first? It was totally my turn, you know."

"Yeah, yeah, Julien," Aren rolled his eyes as he took his seat. "Maybe you'll get there… in the next decade… If you speed up your training a little."

"Ohhhh," the other apprentices responded, laughing playfully at the jest.

"You know I kid, Julien," Aren chuckled, patting him on the back.

"Sure, sure," Julien rolled his eyes.

"Personally, I say it's about damn time Aren," Tersha, another apprentice, quipped playfully. "You've been beating up most of the warriors in this place for months now in training. And that assignment success record of yours is stunning."

"Thank you, Tersha," Aren responded graciously.

The light, playful atmosphere was suddenly interrupted by Julien yelping in fright. "What the hell is that?!"

Aren looked down, seeing what appeared to be a large arachnid of some kind on Julien's plate, looking up curiously at him.

Julien raised his hand and brought it swiftly downward to crush the creature. However, just before his hand could touch it, Aren's own hand lashed out and grabbed Julien's wrist, holding it tightly in place.

"What are you doing?" Julien asked flusteredly. "That thing is on my plate!"

"Come on. It's just a bug," Aren reasoned assertively. "Let's bring it outside."

The arthropod made a terrified squeaking sound and ran off the plate.

"Taloy!" Gueri cried out, scooping up the little creature in their arms. "I've been wondering where you crawled off to."

Gueri looked down worriedly at it, cradling it softly. "Don't be scared little guy." They glared at Julien. "The bad man can't get you anymore."

"I swear to the gods, Gueri," Julien furrowed his brow in frustration. "Is that another of your damned robots?"

"His name is Taloy!" Gueri corrected. "And I would appreciate if you didn't try to crush him in the future."

Gueri looked over to Aren and nodded gratefully towards him. "Thank you for saving him."

"It was nothing," Aren replied, nodding back.

"Whatever," Julien rolled his eyes. "Just keep that thing away from my dinner plate."

"*Hmph,*" was Gueri's only response as Taloy climbed into the chest pocket of Gueri's robes, where the little robot made himself cozy.

As the excitement died down, Aren could feel his stomach grumbling. He looked over the banquet before him. As much as he had been masking it, the inner turmoil he was feeling was still eating away at him. And yet, it was no match for his hunger, which offered a welcome distraction.

While stress might curb some people's appetites, Aren generally preferred to eat through his feelings—that is, when he wasn't training or fighting through them. As the food finally started to be passed around, Aren eagerly helped himself to an assortment of meats, breads, starchy root vegetables, and an extra big bowl of fresh salad with a *boliart* cheese dressing.

Gueri looked judgmentally at Aren's large helping of salad and laughed. "I'll never understand why you're so into that stuff. That's *pelit* food."

"Laugh all you want," Aren chuckled. "I don't know how you aren't constipated eating nothing but meat and bread all the time."

Gueri rolled their eyes and gave a light chortle. "I promise you my bowel movements are just fine, thank you. I'd much rather take that dressing on bread or pasta."

Aren shook his head. "To each their own, I suppose."

Aren took his first bite of salad and felt his mouth fill with ecstasy. This was the best dressing he had ever tasted. He tried the meat next, and then the fresh baked bread. The reaction was the same with each. With every bite into the meal, it was like his tastebuds were teleported to the gates of Elysium.

"My god," Gueri commented, as if reading Aren's mind. "This is amazing. Venler outdid himself."

Aren couldn't help but agree. Venler was the Dehnovai's chef who had formerly been a warrior in the clan. He changed his vocation over to chef two years ago when he lost his legs during an assignment. He could have continued working as a warrior with cybernetic prosthetics or retired with the compensation he received from the Dehnovai, but he unexpectedly chose to try his hand at cooking instead, filling the vacancy from the recently retired chef. Since trying it, he discovered that he had a love for the work.

Admittedly, it was a bit rough when Venler started. It took some time and more than a few burned dishes for him to develop his culinary skills. However, as Aren again bit into the succulent and well-seasoned red meat from his plate, every bit of the progress Venler made was apparent. This meal was incredible.

"Yes, it's fantastic," praised Tersha next. "Venler really outdid himself this time. I've gotta give him my compliments later."

"Why, thank you," Venler replied proudly, as if on queue, wheeling himself in next to the group.

"Venler!" Tersha greeted. "It's wonderful to see you! I assumed you'd be eating separately, like usual."

Aren and Tersha both scooted over to make room for him to join them.

Venler laughed as he pulled into the table. "Come now, you didn't really think I'd miss this celebration, did you? I prepped everything ahead so I could join you folks tonight."

Venler looked over and winked at Aren while scratching his salt-and-pepper hair. "Happy birthday and congratulations, both, ya godsdamned prodigy."

"Thank you, Venler," Aren voiced his appreciation.

"I can't believe you're still using that artifact," Julien commented, looking at Venler's wheelchair. "I know you don't like the idea of cybernetics, but you know that the clan could still get you a hoverchair, no problem, right?"

"Naahhh," Venler rebuffed. "That kind of thing is just not for me. I'm happy with my wheeled chair."

"What is it you like about that thing?" Aren questioned curiously.

"Well, part of it is just that I understand this much better," Venler replied. "I would have no idea what to do with a hoverchair if it ever broke down and I had no engineer nearby. On the other hand, I could easily rebuild this whole damned thing from the ground up given the right materials."

"Interesting," Aren acknowledged. "I think I can understand that."

"Well, not only that though," Venler continued, looking thoughtful for a moment. "The truth is, I also just like the feel of it. I like the control. Every movement, every turn, every brake—all of it is powered by me and my arms. I'm completely in tune with every part of this old thing. It's like an extension of my body. I like that. It makes me feel like *I'm* the one driving it, and not that it's driving me, ya know? A hoverchair just isn't the same."

Aren nodded sympathetically.

"That makes complete sense," Aren affirmed. "I never really thought of it that way."

"Well, luckily, you've never had to," Venler guffawed light-heartedly. "But don't worry about it, I'm happy with how things are for me. Now, come, let's enjoy this night and eat."

"You don't have to tell me twice," Aren chuckled as he looked hungrily down at his food.

Venler looked Aren in the eyes with a warm skepticism. "Seriously though, Aren. I hope you're able to enjoy tonight."

Aren hesitated for a moment as he looked Venler back in the eyes. The words were vague, but it was clear that Venler was speaking with concern.

While part of Aren felt awkward and vulnerable to have his inner struggling acknowledged like that, there was another part that felt grateful—relieved even, to hear such support from a friend.

"Thank you," Aren stammered awkwardly but appreciatively in response.

Venler nodded to him, before turning his attention to his plate.

Together, they ate and drank. As alcohol, dionyl and herbal vices were passed around, Aren opted not to have any of the above. Instead of beer, he chose to wash down his delicious meal with a fresh mug of crystal-clear, glacier water. Tonight, he wanted to keep a clear head.

*/

After the feast was over, Aren went straight to his quarters.

As he closed the door behind him, he headed straight over to the bed. The Dehnovai had quite nice bedrooms for their members—nicer than Aren had expected for a clan of warriors specializing in bounty hunting and assassination. The room was fairly spacious, around 15 x 20 feet. The construction was the same as the dining hall, with paper walls, wooden floors/supports, and high ceilings. Filling the room were elegant wooden furnishings, including an armoire, desk and chair, and an ornate king-sized bed.

"*Kassekari*," Aren spoke, activating the enchanted sconces in the room

Aren sat on the bed and put his head in his hands. It really wasn't a bad night. There was great food, good friends, and an achievement worth celebrating. Yet somehow, he still felt lost.

Slowly, he reached over, opened his bedside drawer, and pulled out a deep scarlet, jeweled brooch. This piece of jewelry, given to him by his mother, was the only thing he had left from his home world of Dracosia.

It was nearly nine years ago now that his home world was devastated by a series of four hyperstate explosives known as "world destroyers". These demolitions extinguished nearly 2/3 of life on the planet within minutes. The environmental and climactic devastation that followed killed most of what was left.

Experts projected that, of the 5 billion original population of Dracosia, there should have at least been survivors numbering between 100,000-1,000,000. However, inexplicably, despite rescue efforts, not a single surviving person had been found. It was a mystery that baffled the galaxy, and which only made this horrible tragedy even worse.

Aren looked down at the jeweled piece in his hands. It had been some time since he looked at this thing.

The brooch was quite well-crafted with an exquisite mix of rose-gold and silver surrounding a large, beautiful gemstone in the center. The gem itself was particularly beguiling. It was a deep, translucent crimson with unique, ribbon-shaped inclusions beneath the surface that, when exposed to light, glinted in a way that looked like there was a crackling fire in the center of the ruby.

Aren admired the beauty of the piece, and yet, he couldn't help but feel the urge to put it back away.

Why is this so hard to look at? Aren pondered. *Is it because it simply feels pointless? I barely even remember Dracosia.*

But looking deep into his heart, Aren realized that this wasn't the truth. The memories may have been a bit distant and foggy from his younger childhood, but they were still there. The problem was the ache that he felt thinking about it. The fact wasn't that he ignored Dracosia because he couldn't remember—it's that he didn't want to.

But there was something about tonight that made him feel extra nostalgic. On this night, for whatever reason, he didn't want to forget. Tonight, he wanted to remember, even if it was hard to think about.

Aren laid down on his back with the brooch in hand and closed his eyes, rolling the jeweled piece between his fingers, trying to remember.

As he thought back to his childhood, flashes of his thoughtful teacher, his stoic father, and lastly, his loving mother all cycled through his head. They were good memories, but painful, knowing they were based in people and an entire world that were now lost to him.

Out of everything from back then, the memories of his mother were the strongest. He felt a deep panging as he thought about her kindness and warmth. She used to make him feel so protected and cared for.

He recalled an old lullaby she used to sing to him at night to help him sleep. The memory of the lullaby was a bit foggy, but he could remember that its name was *The Emerald Caves*.

"Hmm, how did that go again?" Aren asked thoughtfully, opening his eyes again and sitting up in his bed.

"Was it, 'over the'?" Aren wondered aloud. "Wait, no. Not quite."

He closed his eyes and took a moment to think. It had been years since he had attempted to recall the piece. And yet, as he emptied his mind of everything else, he could slowly feel the memories returning to him. He took a deep breath, and when he started up again, the words and melody flowed from his mouth, as if he had just heard it yesterday.

"O'er summit peak and through mountain pass,

Across windswept valley and fields of grass,

The Emerald Caves lie, hidden from sight,

Where the old ones lie slumbering for the thousand-year night.

Sleep soundly sweet angels, keep your wings held close,

Dream of feasts in the heavens, of joys in high dose,

Rest peacefully beloved guardians, so old and so wise,

Until the time comes again to waken and take to the skies."

He felt a warmth in his heart as he finished singing the lullaby. It was such a peaceful melody. His mother had told him that the lyrics were about the ancient dragons of Dracosia that supposedly watched over the lands. He could hear his mother's voice from his childhood, explaining it to him.

"Wow, dragons were really here?" A younger Aren chimed with a gleeful curiosity, cuddling up to his mother as she told him the story.

Aren's mom gave out a pleasant laugh.

"Why yes, my dear," She replied sincerely. *"And it wasn't just dragons either. There were many other magical creatures and nature spirits as well. You see, long ago, our kind used to live together peacefully alongside all of them on Dracosia."*

"That's amazing!" Aren marvelled. *"But then, where did they all go?"*

"Well, Aren," His mother replied sweetly. *"One day, the spirits and their magical creature kin were called away and had to leave to a faraway place. And that's when the dragons decided to take their deep and long slumber. But one day, just like the poem says, the dragons will awaken, and we shall see them again."*

"I can't wait!" Young Aren replied eagerly.

His mother gave a warm chuckle as she smiled down at him.

"Oh, my dear Aren," she spoke tenderly. *"Neither can I."*

Aren smiled at the memory. The feeling was bittersweet. It had been so long since he had allowed himself to reminisce about his mother. There was pain, but also warmth in it.

It had been even longer still since he had thought about the Dracosian myths. He chuckled as he remembered one of his childhood peers making fun of him for believing in the old legends.

But, despite the teasing, his mother had told him that it was true, so he continued believing it with all of his heart.

Aren jerked suddenly as he realized that something was off with the brooch in his hands. He had been so focused on the memories, he hardly noticed as the jewel had started emanating a warm, tingling sensation in his fingers.

Slowly, he opened his eyes. To his shock, the brooch was glowing brightly with a mix of brilliant white and red light.

This immediately put him on his guard. All of these years, and he had never seen his heirloom do anything like this. He was just about to cast a defensive spell when he suddenly stopped. He was unsure why, but there was something inside of him staying his hand, that told him to relax and have faith.

He stared deeply into the brooch. As he did, the jewel slowly got brighter and brighter, until the light had enveloped his vision entirely, and all he could see was white.

Aren closed his eyes to protect them from the blinding light. When he opened them again, the light had died down and he was no longer in his room in the Dehnovai dojo.

He looked around himself. It appeared he was in some kind of library. There were tables and chairs, and the walls were covered in shelves full of old books, and modern data tablets.

"Hello?" He called out. "Is there anyone here?"

But he could hear only silence.

He began to walk around carefully.

Based on the lighter gravity he was feeling, he could tell that he wasn't on Halos anymore. Aren had finely tuned senses, but hardly needed them in this case. Halos was a very large planet with a strong gravity, and the gravity here was maybe just over half of that. But that brought up the question of just where he could possibly be.

Have I been brought to another world? He pondered to himself.

But there was something else that felt off in the atmosphere. Something that he recognized from his time at the Magi Academy. He suspected there was something more going on here.

"Aspetus vweir," Aren commanded.

In an instant, his vision had shifted. Flowing purples, blues, greens and reds flooded his sight as the spell took effect, allowing him to see the underlying dimensional fabric of the area surrounding him. What the makeup of this fabric revealed to him caused him to gasp.

The colors and composition of the vweir in this place pointed to one truth and one truth only. He was standing inside a pocket dimension.

Aren had known many incredibly powerful and talented sorcerers in his time, but there was only one he knew of, maybe two, who were capable of forming a pocket dimension of this size and stability. Creating even an unstable pocket dimension was no small feat, let alone one as steady and well-developed as this one.

This was undoubtedly a rare and unexpected sight.

Aren blinked, ending the spell and changing his vision back to normal.

He looked down at the brooch, still in his hand. It had, again, returned to looking normal.

"I can hardly believe it," Aren said aloud, still focused on the glimmering jewel. "All this time, this little thing was hiding this big secret."

Aren placed the brooch back in his pocket, and again continued exploring. The room he was in was very large and elegantly designed. Both the architecture and furniture in it were strangely familiar to him, from a time long past.

As he continued, he came across a large, dark brown door. Embedded into the wood of this door was a magnificent relief carved with ornate depictions of dragons, gods, woodland spirits, and magical creatures. It was a wondrous work with incredible detail. Aren was curious what sort of room such a door would lead to.

After taking a few moments to study the relief, Aren gently turned the knob and pulled the door open. His wonder turned to awe as he entered the next room. Filling this room was a number of glass display cases, containing all manner of artifacts, and some strange-looking devices.

There were swords and weapons, ancient tools, cultural artifacts, enchanted items, and modern, unique Dracosian inventions, all side-by-side.

In the center-back of the room, three pedestals stood out against the rest of the displays. He could see large piles of parchment on the outer two pedestals. He walked over to one of them, starting on the left. The front page read:

DRAGON SCROLLS, SERIES I

THE SCROLLS OF PROGRESS, V. 144

Dracosian Practical Arts and Applications in Agriculture, Medicine, Conservation and the Betterment of Life

Aren could hardly believe what he was seeing. This was a truly special find. While bits of Dracosian culture had been preserved in parts of the galaxy, there were no known copies of the famous and secretive Dragon Scrolls, containing hidden Dracosian techniques and specifications, that had been saved.

As special as this find was, most would have assumed it to be one of cultural significance only. For instance, many of the technological components in this document would certainly be outdated, as the latest version was written well over a hundred years ago. However, Aren knew that the much greater significance of these scrolls was the timeless and purportedly highly effective magical art contained within, known as Dracanis, the magic of the Dracosians.

If the Scrolls of Progress are on this pedestal, Aren thought to himself, *then that must mean…*

Eagerly, Aren ran over to the right-side pedestal, and looked down at the pile of parchments, where the front page read:

DRAGON SCROLLS, SERIES II

SCROLLS OF COMBAT, V. 128

The Dracosian Art of Guardianship and Defense through Combat and Magic

"I knew it!" Aren cried enthusiastically.

He had heard stories of the powerful and effective Dracosian combat magic, once infamous across the galaxy, but the only times he had ever gotten to see it firsthand was as a young child. He thought that the art was forever lost.

Finding the Dragon Scrolls here was a seriously incredible discovery. While thousands of Dracosians were safely off-world during the time of the planet's destruction, every known master of Dracanis was on-world and lost during its demise, essentially eradicating most knowledge of this magic.

Although both series of scrolls were important, Aren was most excited for this second half—the Scrolls of Combat. He could hardly wait to see the combat techniques and magicks utilized by the masters of the world that he came from.

However, he was too curious what was on the last remaining pedestal, so he left these scrolls for the moment, and walked over to the center pedestal, standing between the other two.

On this pedestal, stood a lonely note with a data card attached to it.

Shaking, Aren picked up the note. Tears began to form in his eyes, and he placed his hand over his mouth as he read the only two words written on the parchment, in his mother's handwriting, which read:

TO AREN

Chapter 4

Aren flicked off what little blood had clung to his sword and sheathed it as Commandant Reinault fell to the ground behind him, clutching at his throat.

Aren stood up straight and turned to the young, enslaved man who had been held at gunpoint by Reinault moments ago.

"Are you ok?" Aren asked, looking him in the eyes with concern. "Were you harmed at all?"

The young man averted his gaze nervously.

"I-I'm ok, I think," The man responded. "I wasn't hurt at all."

"Good," Aren replied, sounding relieved. "What's your name?"

"My name?" The young man asked with some hesitancy, almost as if he didn't trust the question. "It's Jem."

"It's nice to meet you Jem," Aren greeted him. "Do you think you could walk back with me to the others?"

Jem nodded.

Together, the two of them walked back towards the group hiding behind the patio fence.

The bystanders here had seen the entire thing. Many were too stunned to even speak. However, the owner Verine, beaming, walked straight over to Aren with open arms, her dress sparkling in the light of the streetlamps.

"*Mesana, mesana!*" Verine cooed affectionately, using the Antallian term for a person you consider to be admirable. "Look at the amazing thing you have done here today. I can hardly believe it."

She gave him a big bear hug, squeezing him tight. He winced as he hugged her back.

Anya rushed over to him, looking down at his leg. "Are you ok?"

"I'm fine," Aren smiled through gritted teeth. "It's just a flesh wound. I may be shit at healing magic, but paired with a little regenerative gel, even I should be able to get this fixed by morning."

"Fine, but at least let me bandage it," Anya insisted.

"Yes, yes, you bandage him," Verine said in agreement. "I will go check on the others here—make sure they are all ok."

Anya nodded to her.

Verine turned and started to walk away, chuckling as she made her way back to the crowd. "'Do I really believe those tales,' she asked me. *Ha!* And all the while, he was right there, in front of me—in my own club."

Anya pulled out first aid supplies from her satchel and sat down next to Aren. A little of the tension in the air seemed to dissipate and people began chatting nervously amongst each other as Anya got to work.

Aren winced as she poured disinfectant on the wound.

He scratched his head bashfully. "Sorry I couldn't keep my promise to stay out of it."

She chuckled. "As if you weren't over the moon about it… But really, don't worry, I know it's not your fault."

"You are correct," A voice behind them asserted. Aren turned around, to Anya's annoyance, messing up her bandaging progress, to see Xander behind them, bowing deeply in their direction. "The true fault lies with me. Please accept my deepest apologies, and my greatest appreciation for cleaning up after this awful mess that I made."

Aren placed his hand on Xander's shoulder and looked sincerely into the young man's deep blue eyes.

"You have nothing to be sorry for," Aren assured him. "Maybe it was a bit poorly thought through, but your heart was in the right place… If we had a bit more of that, of people like you, standing up to evil, rather than sitting silently and worrying about the consequences, I think perhaps, that this galaxy would be a better place."

Anya rolled her eyes as she finished on Aren's leg and stood back up. "It's talk like that why you so often find yourself in these kinds of situations, you know?"

Aren laughed. "Maybe so."

"So much worrying, mesana," Verine said as she rejoined them, getting between Aren and Anya and patting both on the back. "Come now, we're all safe. That's what's important. You all did a wonderful job."

"Thank you," Anya replied gratefully.

"I just—I have to say, that was extraordinary, Aren," Xander exclaimed. "I'm not entirely a stranger to combat, myself, but I've never seen anything like that before."

Aren smiled. "I felt the same way listening to your music earlier. You were really something on that stage."

Xander blushed.

"I hate to break this up," Anya asserted teasingly. "As much as I'd like Xander's autograph myself, we need to get moving here. We have maybe ten minutes tops before this place is swarming with soldiers."

"Agreed," Aren affirmed.

"So, it's safe for us to leave?" One of the club's customers from the crowd inquired. "We can go home now?"

"Well, yes, but you need to be prepared first," Anya asserted. "Verine can delete the security footage, but there are still witnesses, including their own surviving soldiers. There's going to be an investigation, and most of you will likely be taken for interrogation."

"But we're innocent!" One of the customers exclaimed.

"I know that, and they know that, but it doesn't matter," Anya explained. "I guarantee they're going to try to frame this all as a terrorist attack. All the soldiers dead and injured here are going to be propped up as heroes. If you don't want to end up enslaved in the Restitution Program yourselves, you need to agree to go along with whatever narrative they try to force on you."

"Can't we just tell the truth?" one of the customers asked incredulously. "Surely, they can't actually convict us just for being caught in the crossfire. We didn't do anything."

There were murmurs of agreement from the crowd.

"That doesn't matter," One of the enslaved girls spoke up. "Listen to me, everyone! My name is Reo Fastia. I know the truth of UAPA firsthand."

The crowd quieted down, looking at her and listening curiously as she continued. "They claimed I was convicted for treason, but in truth, the only crime I committed was allowing my father to live with me in my apartment.

"I never knew at this point that he was illegally giving shelter to Tarpoan refugees. He lied to me and said his apartment was being renovated. When we were both arrested, I thought I'd be fine if I just told the truth, but that wasn't enough for UAPA, even with saved messages as proof.

"They demanded that I publicly condemn my father as a Tarpoan spy who was giving aid to their military—even though the refugees were only civilians. I refused to spread this lie and was shortly after convicted of treason. They sentenced me to indefinite labour under the Restitution Program, where I have since faced abuses you can hardly even imagine."

"You poor child," Verine patted her on the back. "I have seen similar things happen far too many times. People go missing who even just speak out against UAPA."

"It sounds like we don't have any choice," One of the customers lamented.

Another one perked up. "Maybe so, but it won't change the truth of what happened. I'll know what UAPA did—how they threatened us and nearly shot us while you defended us."

"Aye," Another customer agreed. "We might have to lie to officials, but I promise you, I'll be talking about what really happened here to all of my friends. The truth might not make it to the media, but it will get around, one way or another."

"Thank you," Anya smiled and nodded to them. "That is greatly appreciated."

Anya turned to the four former prisoners. "I do need to mention, however, that not everyone will be able to go to their homes. There's no chance they'd let you four go, sadly."

Anya then pointed to the customer covered in cybertattoos who had, earlier, jumped into the fight and who tried unsuccessfully to take and use a UAPA rifle. "And you as well. It's too risky that a soldier might remember your face as someone who tried to fight them."

"Dammit," the man groaned. "I guess that only makes sense."

"Hmm, what are you thinking Anya?" Aren scratched his head thoughtfully. "Do you think they'd be ok in the Varith safehouse? Or do we need to find other accommodations?"

Before Anya could say a word, Verine stepped up.

"There is no need for that," she announced. "I will take them in. I'm overdue for a vacation anyway."

Anya looked at her. "Are you sure, Verine?"

"Yes, yes, of course," Verine asserted. "I have a secret vacation house in the mountains that UAPA doesn't know about. There's plenty of space, and months of food stockpiled. It's probably better that I don't stick around for interrogations anyway; I'd only give them a piece of my mind and probably end up convicted to multiple life sentences for the things I'd say."

"Probably," Anya laughed. She took a few moments to work on her wristcomm, before looking back up. "I've just messaged my contact and forwarded the conversation to you—he'll meet you in town asap to get those RPW trackers disabled. You should be fine to go to your vacation house then."

Anya was referring to the geolocation trackers that every Restitution Program Worker had surgically implanted in their necks.

"Thank you, mesana," Verine smiled.

"Of course," Anya agreed. "Alright, everyone, we should all get moving. I'm sorry for everything, but I promise, you'll all be fine if you stick to what we talked about."

There were murmurs of thanks and nods from the customers to Anya, Aren and Xander as the majority of the group began to disperse.

Verine motioned to the group who was coming with her. "You five, come with me now. We'll get to my van in the east parking garage."

Verine began leading them to the garage, but just as she started walking, Reo spoke up. "Please, just give me one moment."

Reo turned, ran to Xander, and pulled him into a deep hug.

"Thank you," she said, as her eyes filled with tears. "Thank you so much."

A bit shocked, Xander hugged the woman back. He had felt so guilty about the situation he created that he had momentarily forgotten that he did anything at all to help.

"You're welcome," Xander replied. "I just... I couldn't stand by. But truth be told, I'm really not the one to thank here."

"But you are," Reo refuted, burying her head into his chest. "We never would have escaped if not for you. You have done a greater thing than you know."

She let go of him, turned to Aren, and bowed. "And thank you too, great warrior. I did not forget your kindness either. I did not think we could get out of that. That strength of yours is really something… Please use it to help others as well."

Aren bowed back to her. "I will. I promise."

"Truly, thanks to all three of you for helping us together," Reo again bowed, this time to all three of them.

"Yes, thank all of you," Jem agreed, bowing as well.

"Thank you," the other two formerly enslaved women also stated in unison and bowed.

"You're welcome," Anya replied.

"You're all most welcome," Xander agreed.

"It was my pleasure," Aren responded lastly with a grin.

With that, the four former slaves turned and went back to Verine, who nodded to Anya one last time before walking away, leading the group to the parking garage.

Anya turned to Xander. "You should be heading out with them. Things won't be safe for you either. Verine can help you arrange a way offworld after things cool down a little."

"Actually, I had been thinking," Xander stated. "You're Oppori Qala, aren't you?"

Anya was a bit shocked at the question. It wasn't often that strangers were simply guessing her organization like that. It was especially surprising from an offworlder. "What makes you say that?"

"Come on, the way you both just instantly stood up against UAPA like that, and then all the talk about failing to lie low," Xander pointed out. "I may have been away for these past couple years, but even I could piece that together. It's my understanding that well over

90% of resistance fighters have banded under the Oppori Qala banner. It wasn't likely to be anything else."

"Fair enough," Anya replied sturdily. "I suppose you have proven your trustworthiness. Yes, I am indeed from Oppori Qala. I am the Second-in-Command of Operations, Vice-Chair Anya Allister. This is Aren. He is not a formal member of Oppori Qala but is a good friend and a mercenary that I have hired to help us with the cause."

Aren was slightly shocked at the admission. While Xander did seem trustworthy, Anya was normally much more tight-lipped than this. He suspected that her admiration for Xander as a musician may have loosened her lips some.

Anya continued. "Now, why is it that you ask?"

"I want to join you," Xander implored, bowing to show respect. "Please, let me travel with the two of you."

"Wait, what? Anya responded quizzically. "But why?"

"I want to fight," Xander answered. "I can't stand what I've seen since returning to this planet. Disturbed doesn't even begin to cover it. Tonight was the first night I finally felt some peace since arriving here."

Anya looked at him thoughtfully, considering the request. "Is that really the only reason?"

"Well," Xander looked to the ground, his expression turning serious as a tear trickled down his cheek. "Maybe not the only thing. I'll admit, I have reason to believe that UAPA is behind the disappearance of someone I care about."

Aren put a sympathetic hand on Xander's shoulder. "I'm sorry, Xander. I understand completely."

Anya seemed a touch less convinced. "You understand this will be incredibly dangerous, right? Don't get me wrong, I can't deny you'd be useful with the combination of your celebrity influence and aurimancy skills."

She looked at him sternly before continuing. "But with what we're up against there's still a very good chance that you could get seriously injured, or even die."

Xander looked up at her. There was a sudden fire in his eyes that hit her like a wave. It reminded her of when he was on-stage with his chiambra earlier that night, before taking on those soldiers.

"I promise you… I'm prepared for whatever may come," He responded somberly, with a quiet but powerful determination.

"Well, I'm convinced," Aren chimed in. "But then, it's not my decision. What are you thinking, Anya?"

Anya took a moment, looking pensively at Xander, as she considered his request. She couldn't deny that he certainly seemed resolved.

"I'm getting there," Anya asserted. "But one last thing. If you work for me, there can be no more reckless stunts like this, ok? Whether or not your heart was in the right place, it was not ok to risk so many civilians like that."

"I know you're right," Xander hung his head in shame. "I'm deeply sorry. I promise though, from here on out, I will be much more prudent."

"Ok, well, if I have your word then," Anya responded tepidly. "And you're absolutely positive you don't want to leave? This may be your last chance to go offworld."

Xander nodded.

"Very well," Anya assented. "Then I happily welcome you to join us, Xander Ardentes."

"Thank you," Xander beamed. "I really appreciate it. I can promise you, I'll work hard to do my part."

As they were speaking, Anya's automated car pulled up next to them. The door opened.

"Hello, Anya," The car's automated voice greeted.

"Alright, before we go, do you have everything you need?" Anya asked Xander.

"Oh, that's right. My belongings are in a suitcase back in the club," Xander announced. "Just give me a moment, please."

"Ok, just be quick," Anya responded.

He looked down at his wristcomm and pressed a few buttons.

A few moments of silence went by.

"What are you waiting for?" Anya asked Xander who hadn't moved an inch.

"Just one second," Xander assured.

As he said that, a faint whirring sound became audible coming from the cabaret. A second later, a dark leather designer suitcase could be seen wheeling itself towards Xander.

As it got to him, it beeped and flashed its lights. Xander picked it up.

"Fancy," Aren commented with a smile.

"Alright, I'm ready to go," Xander piped.

Anya rolled her eyes and chuckled. "Alright, shall we?"

The three of them entered the vehicle.

"Where shall we go today?" The car's bright, automated voice asked her.

"Back to 137 Grenfri Road, please," Anya commanded.

"Sure, Anya," The car responded. "Taking you to 137 Grenfri Road."

"Thank you," Anya stated, then looked to Xander and Aren. "We'll get some rest at the safehouse first. Tomorrow is going to be a big day."

"Sounds good to me," Aren agreed.

"Yes," Xander concurred. "I think I could also do with some rest."

Several minutes later, the car arrived in front of a small house on the outskirts of town. The trio left the vehicle, entered the house, and shortly after, found themselves in separate bedrooms.

Xander spent a brief amount of time repairing his chiambra, using the tools and materials he had brought with him. As soon as he was done, he collapsed onto the room's bed.

Despite all of the stress and excitement of the day, Xander felt that for whatever reason, tonight he would sleep quite soundly.

*/

The next morning, Xander awoke to the feeling of being shaken.

Groggily, he opened his eyes and saw Aren standing over him, rocking him awake by the shoulders.

"Come on, sleepyhead," Aren teased. "We tried calling for you, but you wouldn't wake up. I hope you can get ready quick. We've got a train to catch."

Xander yawned and stretched. "I'm getting up, I'm getting up."

"Good," Aren smiled at him. "I'll see you out there in a bit."

"Sure, sure," Xander yawned again.

Once Aren had left the room Xander slowly pulled himself into a sitting position. He looked at his wristcomm. It was still early.

He groaned. He was not a morning person.

Nevertheless, he knew they were on a deadline, so he summoned all of his willpower to get up and head over to the shower in the adjoining bathroom.

He was debating whether or not he had time to do any body shaving. But, realizing that he might not get this opportunity again for a while, he decided he would try to do it quickly.

After starting up the shower, he worked on his hair first, cleaning and conditioning it. Then he washed his body, before finally moving on to shaving. He was proud of how fast he had been moving.

Several minutes into the shower, as Xander was nearing completion, he heard a knocking at the door.

"Hurry up," He heard Anya's voice calling. "We're going to be late."

Yaesh, he thought to himself. *Good thing I've been moving at record pace or I might have had to stop halfway through.*

Xander hurried to finish up. After getting out of the shower, he briskly dried himself, moisturized, deodorized and sprayed some light cologne before emerging from the bathroom in fresh clothes. His suitcase followed behind as he left the bedroom.

"Hey there," Aren greeted him as he came out. "You ready to leave?"

Xander looked over at him. Aren was already fully dressed and packed, holding a conspicuously long suitcase, presumably hiding his sword. Aren wore interesting robes and an ebony amulet, both offworld in style, but they suited him well. He had medium-long brown hair, light skin, and a face that could be described as both handsome and pretty at once.

"Well, hello there. If it isn't the dashing swordsman," Xander greeted back coquettishly. "Indeed, I am ready."

Aren winked playfully at him. "Glad to hear it."

Xander looked down at Aren's leg, noticing that he was no longer walking with a limp. "Have you healed already?"

"Yup!" Aren chirped. "Well, for the most part. The regenerative gel did most of the work, but the little healing magic I could muster helped. Thankfully, the wound wasn't too deep."

"Well, I'm glad you're ok," Xander stated.

"Thanks," Aren smiled.

While they were speaking, Anya handed Xander a fresh, hot breakfast wrap and a juice container.

"Alright, let's get moving," Anya ordered. "These are for you. You can eat and drink on the way. We've already had our breakfast."

"Why, thank you," Xander said graciously, accepting both items from her.

Hungrily, Xander took a bite of the wrap. He could taste egg, meat, vegetable *tomakes*, and a delicious sweet and savory sauce.

"Mmmm," Xander moaned, looking over to Anya. "Where did you get this?"

"I made it," She smiled at him proudly. "Do you like it?"

"I love it! You'll have to share the recipe sometime."

"Sure thing," Anya chuckled. "It's actually quite simple."

Xander continued scarfing the wrap down and chasing it with juice as they all exited the house together and entered Anya's car, which had been waiting for them.

"Where shall we go today, Anya?" her car asked.

"To the train station please," Anya commanded.

"Sure, Anya," the car predictably responded. "Taking you to the Varith Arrow Train Station."

And with that, the car took off.

As they drove through the city, Xander looked out the window of the car. He watched the buildings, streetlamps and people passing by. Varith was one of only a handful of large cities on Antal, with its population just over 400,000. The city stood out in a planet that was mostly rural, with massive tracts of land that were entirely unpopulated. With Antal's total population of 82,000,000 people, there weren't enough denizens to come close to filling out the roughly 90 million square kilometers of landmass across this planet.

Behind music and sonic technology, the next thing Antal was most known for was its beautiful, sprawling forests that have largely been untouched by industrialization. Such pristine nature wasn't entirely uncommon in the galaxy, but Antal had its own unique variety that many found particularly attractive. It was also the planet that glenths originally came from—one of the domestic animals bred for its meat in many worlds across Auros, which had first been discovered in Antal's forests.

Nevertheless, here in the bustling city, there were only fragmented signs of that nature that could be seen—some odd trees and shrubs, as well as the random park here and there between all of the many manmade structures.

The city stood in stark contrast to the copious nature covering most of the rest of the planet. Still, Xander enjoyed the metropolitan visual for what it was. There was a certain beauty that could be seen in the streets and buildings surrounding them—an art form in the architecture, and a majesty to the achievement of their creation.

Admittedly, the largest skyscrapers on Antal hardly compared in size or architectural marvel to many of the superskyscrapers found on certain other worlds, and yet the ones here still stood, majestic and visually impressive, even so many millennia after such buildings had first been designed.

After a few minutes, Xander turned his head and looked at Anya.

"So, I'm a little curious," Xander began as he continued eating. "If we have this car already, why would we take the train?"

"Well, unless you want to spend almost an entire day of nonstop driving, the arrow train is the way to go," Anya responded. "That thing has top speeds of over 1500 kph. That's around five times faster than the best we'll get from this thing on the highway."

"Oh wow," Xander replied. "I had no idea it was that fast."

Aren looked at him curiously. "Didn't you live here on Antal for a few years a while back? Did you not use the train back then at all?"

"Well, truth be told, I spent almost all of my time here on Antal in the Academy," Xander replied. "I was very absorbed in my studies."

"The Don Zai Academy, right?" Anya inquired.

Xander took the last bite of his breakfast wrap, satisfyingly swallowing before answering.

"Yes," Xander answered. "I rarely left, and when I did, I usually just took an autocab to somewhere in town. I never really had the need to take the train."

"Well, I guess this will be your first time then," Aren stated.

"I guess so," Xander responded. "But anyway, trains aside, I have some questions about what's been going on here since I've been gone."

"Right, that only makes sense," Anya sympathized. "A lot has happened in these past few years. What exactly do you want to know?"

Xander took a moment to mull the question over.

"Well, the truth is, I want to know more about UAPA and everything that's been going on these past few years," Xander clarified. "I do know some, of course. I mean, I was here on-world when UAPA was founded by Hamish Drulth around three years ago. I remember when UAPA successfully led their coup, taking over the country of Nolinth, and starting all of this."

"I don't think any of us could forget that," Anya commented.

"Indeed," Xander agreed. "Anyway, by the time I had left Antal about a year later, they had already conquered three more nations. However, I don't know much past that. I have tried to do my own research, but Antallian media seems to be *flooded* with UAPA propaganda, so I've had difficulties finding trustworthy information. I'd like to hear more from someone who really knows what's going on."

He hesitated for a second before adding. "Well, that is, if you don't mind."

Anya looked at him with a thoughtful appreciation. She always found it refreshing to work with people who were willing to listen and learn. In Oppori Qala, she led many passionate people, but admittedly, not a lot of them had much interest in learning history or any politics significantly more deep than "UAPA bad, Oppori Qala good." She found that this was especially the case with the younger soldiers who were around Xander's age, which made his curiosity especially refreshing.

"I don't mind at all," She responded readily. "You're honestly right not to trust the media right now. It's especially been a major problem since UAPA now controls nearly all of the internet radio networks."

"I'm not surprised, from what I've heard on the radio," Xander remarked.

Anya nodded to him in acknowledgment. "In any case though, everything you said about UAPA is true. They've claimed from the start that their goals have been to unite the planet and remove offworld influences, but they have shown through their actions that what they really want is to dominate the planet and oppress offworlders. Hundreds of thousands have already been killed in their invasions, and they're not going to stop until they control all of Antal.

"Of course, they *claim* that all of this bloodshed is worth it for the greater good of the planet—that they'll make things better when they're in full control, but everything they've shown us proves that to be a lie. I mean, they have now conquered seven of Antal's eleven nations, and what have they done with their newfound power? They've censored free speech, instituted oppressive and xenophobic policies, and enslaved thousands, all while spreading lies and misinformation. This is why Oppori Qala fights. UAPA must be stopped. This is not the Antal I know."

"Wow," Xander replied. "I had no idea it was quite that bad. I am curious though. How have they had so much success? It's not every day you see some organization come out of nowhere and take over most of a planet in three years time."

"That is a good question," Anya replied. "Well, to be honest, they've had a few big advantages. For example, they have unique sonic weapons that Hamish supplied for them, developed by the infamous engineer and close friend of Hamish's, Lester Kanan."

"Interesting," Xander responded. "I had been curious about those weapons since I first heard of them, and even more so after I saw them in action back at the cabaret. They seem to be very powerful."

"Indeed," Anya replied. "Here on Antal, we've been well-known for our unique sonic technology, used in mining, medicine, entertainment, and industry across the galaxy. However, no one had ever weaponized this tech nearly as effectively as Lester has. Thanks to her, UAPA's military is loaded with those powerful sonic rifles, pistols and cannons. They even have them digitally networked and bio-locked so only UAPA soldiers can use them. In other words, even if we stole them, they'd be of no use to us."

Anya's explanation had Xander thinking back to the battle at the Silver Note Cabaret. He recalled the cabaret customer who had attempted to use one of those sonic rifles without success and nearly died for it.

"That makes sense," Xander acknowledged, rubbing his deeply bruised chest from the shot he partially took. "Those weapons really are something. You know, I tried blocking one with my magic and it still managed to break through and do some damage."

"I know that feeling," Anya stated. "Even with my ballistic armor on, an indirect shot was enough to break my arm a few months ago. Even my lightning rifle, as great as it is, can't quite match the damage those things do.

"In any case, those weapons aren't UAPA's only advantage. They also have been very effective at PR, using misinformation and propaganda to manipulate the public to their favour.

"It all started on Hamish's personal Internet Radio show ironically named 'Real Talk,' but it's become much worse ever since UAPA took over the CNPF—that's the Central Network Processing Facility. That takeover is what gave them control over nearly all global internet radio networks. Censorship, misinformation and propaganda are now the hard and fast rules in the media across the board on Antal."

"Does that really work on people though?" Xander asked incredulously.

"You'd be surprised," Anya replied. "I wouldn't have expected so before UAPA, but it's become clear to me that there are certain people who will believe anything when it suits them. Not everyone falls for it, but you'd be surprised how many do. Without a doubt, it has helped UAPA plenty with military recruitment and in making the public more amenable to their takeover."

The car interrupted them. "Now arriving at Varith Train Station."

"Ah, I see we are here," Anya said. "Any more talk on this will have to wait. I hope that helped for now."

"It did," Xander replied sincerely. "Thank you. You are most gracious, mesana."

"Oh, you," Anya blushed. "You're most welcome. Now, before we go in, hold still, please."

Xander held perfectly still as Anya pulled a small, strange-looking device out of her pocket. Slowly, she scanned over Xander's face with it.

"Facial calibration complete," A voice from the device stated.

She then placed the device behind Xander's ear, which made a buzzing sound for a moment before turning quiet.

"What was that?" Xander inquired.

"See for yourself," Anya replied, handing him a small mirror.

Looking curiously into the mirror, Xander could see that his facial features had been slightly altered. It wasn't that far different than normal, but enough that he was unlikely to be recognized, even by someone who knew him.

"Remarkable," Xander commented. "What is it?"

"Cosmetic Alteration Holoprojector, or as it's more commonly known, a holo-mask," Aren answered. "They were originally designed for modelling but found popularity in the criminal underworld. They were often used in my old line of work as a bounty hunter. Oppori Qala has recently taken to using them to protect the identities of some of their top agents as well. They can't make you look like someone else entirely, but they can change your features enough to fool most people and can even trick some surveillance systems."

"Why weren't you using these before?" Xander inquired.

"Well, they're highly illegal in UAPA territory, and most places in Antal to be honest, so it's less risky to avoid using them when we can," Anya explained. "However, now that our faces have been seen, it's much safer for all of us to start wearing them every time that we're in public, just to be safe. Luckily, I had a few stashed in the safehouse, in case our cover was blown. We should be fine as long as we don't advertise that we're using them."

"Well, I can't exactly say that it's an improvement," said Xander cheekily as he looked at his new features. "But I certainly don't mind it either."

"You look good," Aren assured him with a smile.

"Well, thank you," Xander said, smiling back.

"If you two are done," Anya teased them playfully as she exited the car. "We have a train to catch."

Chapter 5

The arrow trains were a transportation technology uniquely developed on Antal. When Aren first used one, he had been struck by the fact that they had no wheels, no magnets, and no hover technology. Instead, the way these trains worked was by creating a virtually frictionless connection between themselves and the railway tracks using sonic vibrations that also helped to propel them forward at high speeds.

However, what perhaps stood out more to Aren than the technology was the experience of riding them. He found that he really enjoyed taking them since he first arrived on the planet. Their interiors were always perfectly clean and comfortable, there was usually good food and drink, and the rides gave him the opportunity for some relaxed, peaceful reflection. This was his first time on the train with company, but he felt that only made the trip more enjoyable.

After sitting down for lunch together in one of the dining cars, the group decided to go to a café car next to enjoy some tea while waiting to reach their destination.

Upon entering the café car, they were greeted with a notably pleasant atmosphere. It was reasonably lively, with several patrons across the car all talking cheerfully amongst themselves. However, it also was not crowded, with a number of empty seats and no line to the barista.

The aesthetic in this car was modern but inviting. Freshly waxed, dark grayish-brown hardwood floors lay beneath a series of café furnishings, including tables and a bar which all had polished, marbled-gray surfaces. Wainscoting followed the walls with gentle blue paint covering the top half and dark gray paneling along the bottom.

The car was split lengthwise into two sections. One section was for seating customers, while the other, smaller side was the bar with the barista. On the customer side, windows lined the walls, giving a view to the outside. Behind the bar on the opposite side was a narrow countertop covered with appliances, and above that, an assortment of shelves, displaying various coffees, teas, syrups, biscuits, and other snacks and ingredients.

The trio walked up to the bar, where a handsome barista stood, waiting to take their order.

"Hey, Anya, Xander, would you two like some *baleroot* tea lattes?" Aren asked. "My treat."

"Yeah, sure," Anya replied. "Thank you."

"Yes, please, Aren," Xander perked up. He knew he could use a little caffeine.

"Three baleroot tea lattes, please!" Aren made his order to the barista. "And could that be with steamed sweet milk, please?"

"Absolutely," the café worker responded. "That'll be 105 marks please."

Aren handed his money to the barista, who then promptly got to work preparing the drinks.

The three of them sat on stools at the bar, next to an older orren man who was drinking his coffee quietly, with a mild scowl on his face as he looked at them.

"So, where are you folks headed?" the barista asked them in a friendly tone.

"You know, come to think of it," Xander looked over at Anya and Aren. "I don't think I ever actually asked where we're going, myself."

"Our destination is the Augun Station," Aren answered honestly, careful to withhold further details.

"Oh, Augun, huh?" The barista responded. "You know, my sister lives there. It's a gorgeous city. Not big like Enzori or the other metropolises, but very quaint."

"I've never actually been there before myself," Xander commented.

"Ah, well, if you have time you have got to check out the holo-plays while you're there," the barista noted as he began steaming the milk for the drinks. "They have a beautiful, new theater worth checking out."

The old man sitting next to them at the bar grunted irately.

What's his problem? Aren thought to himself.

The barista then looked at them more seriously. "If you want my advice though, it would just be to stay far away from Grimveil on the outskirts of town, if you can. It's unfortunate that Augun had to be so close to that cursed place."

"Grimveil?" Xander questioned. "What's that?"

"It's a forest," Anya answered. "One with quite a reputation to it."

The barista nodded. "Since taking over Marann, UAPA has banned entry completely, and with good reason. The damned place is cursed. Legends say demons roam there… or was it one demon? Either way, it doesn't matter. Even if you don't believe the legends, it's unquestionably dangerous."

"Oh?" Xander voiced inquisitively. "What makes you say that?"

"Well, just take what happened a few months ago," The barista responded. "According to news reports, there was a group of ecologists that snuck past security into the forest. Apparently, there were some unique species they wanted to research, and they were willing to risk charges for it."

"What happened to them?" Aren inquired.

"No one knows," the barista shared forebodingly. "*Poof!* Vanished into thin air. Search and rescue parties tried to track them down, but not a trace could be found."

The barista lowered his voice. "There are many who believe that it was the demon who got to them."

"That's horrible," Xander shuddered.

"Indeed," The barista nodded. "Just thought I'd give a word of warning. It's important for people to look out for one another, ya know?"

He handed them their drinks and began to speak louder again. "On a lighter note, I really hope you folks get a chance to check out that new theater. It really is worth the trip."

"Sounds great," Xander enthused.

The old man sitting next to them at the bar scoffed. "Just make sure you mind your manners while you're there, ya hear?"

"Oh, well that goes without saying, doesn't it?" Xander assured, uncertain why this elderly stranger would demand such a thing out of the blue.

"You'd think," The old man snorted. "With offworlders, you never really know."

"Excuse me," Anya interjected angrily. "Offworlders are not any more likely to be rude than any Antallian. You're proof of that."

"Whatever," the old man grumbled.

"Ugh," Anya rolled her eyes. "Come on, guys, let's go."

She looked at the barista as she grabbed her drink. "Thank you very much."

Aren and Xander also grabbed their drinks and thanked the barista before the three of them headed over to a corner table, a bit of a distance from everyone else.

"Sorry about that," Anya apologized. "Some orrens are a lot less progressive than others. It's been especially bad since UAPA came into power."

"Oh, it's no worries," Aren smiled at her to show her he wasn't upset. "No sense letting a man like him ruin our day."

"I agree," Xander said, taking a sip of his drink.

Xander looked up above their table, noting a screen up there for customers, currently playing a live broadcast from a channel within one of the Internet Radio networks.

"You know," Xander stated. "When I first came to Antal, I always assumed 'radio' would be audio-only, like it is on most planets. It shocked me to find out that some of the channels include video as well."

"Actually, video wasn't always a part of it," Anya clarified. "It was before my time, but it was only added a few decades ago."

"Really?" Aren asked. "Honestly, I find that surprising. Video tech is basically ancient at this point. Did you guys really just go that long without it?"

"Well, keep in mind that we orrens tend to value sound above all," Anya explained. "That's really reflected in our culture. It's not that we don't like visuals, but admittedly, they're more of an afterthought."

"Interesting," Aren responded. "I suppose it makes sense with how incredibly good orren hearing is."

"Maybe so," Anya conceded. "But we're not the only ones. You have weirdly good hearing for a human yourself Aren. And Xander, I'm assuming it must be the same for you, considering what I've heard from your music."

"To be honest, my hearing is still well below the average orren," Xander explained. "Back at the academy, I had to work twice as hard to be able to pick up what most of the other students could hear naturally."

Anya looked taken aback. "Wow. Well, honestly, that's maybe even more impressive."

"Thank you," Xander smiled warmly at her.

"So, Antallians just really never felt the need for video media?" Aren asked, bringing the conversation back to the topic at hand."

"Well, it's not like we didn't have cameras, we just didn't use them for any mainstream media," Anya explained. "However, our networks have always been focused on the highest quality and depth of audio—unmatched in most of the galaxy. Video only came much later.

"To be honest, some traditionalists actually want to get rid of it. They believe video muddies the auditory experience. I think that's silly, personally."

"I think I somewhat understand," Aren empathized. "When media is designed to be seen, it's not the same as audio-only media, right?"

"That's true," Anya agreed. "But it's not like the choice has been taken away from people. Anyone can always switch to an audio-only channel if they choose."

"Perhaps they just don't like change," Aren replied.

"I think you struck the *miyar's* tail there, Aren," Anya agreed.

As they sipped their teas, they heard intro music playing from the screen as the commercial break ended. They looked up in time to see a new program starting up on the network.

On the screen was a handsome, dark-haired orren man in a suit sitting in a chair and smiling. After a brief musical intro, the camera zoomed in on the man, and he began to address the audience.

"Hello, and welcome once again to our show 'Real Talk,' recorded live in the Capitol Palace Studio, where we tell you the truth about Antal. I am your host and Head UAPA Media Correspondent, Jun Karlsen," Jun announced from the screen. "Today, we have a real special treat for you. Our guest is someone you all know and love. He's arguably the greatest musician and aurimancer in Antal and, dare I say, the galaxy. He is the newly appointed Ear of Media and Arts, the brand-new department in our glorious UAPA, here to talk about some of the changes he'll be making. Please give a warm welcome to Lant Morr!"

Bombastic music played as a tall, strong-looking, blonde, orren man walked across the stage, smiling and waving to the audience. He took a seat near Jun, as the musicians finished their piece.

"Hey, I know him," Xander expressed to the group with a hint of unease in his voice. "I went to the Don Zai Academy with him."

"Really?" Anya asked. "Lant was your classmate?"

"Yes," Xander confirmed. "Is that so shocking?"

"Well, I knew that he went to the academy," Anya explained. "But I didn't know it was at the same time as you. Isn't he a lot older than you?"

"Yes, he's probably in his thirties now, I think, but what lots of people don't realize is that all ages attend the Don Zai Academy," Xander explained. "There weren't many who were younger than me in my classes, but there were some who were even older than him."

Hearing the interlude music dying down, the three of them looked back up at the television, just as the host began to speak.

"Welcome Lant, and thank you for being here," Jun greeted him.

"Thank you for having me here, Jun," Lant greeted back.

"So, first of all, congratulations at becoming UAPA's first ever Ear of Music and Arts," Jun commended. "That must feel pretty amazing."

The audience clapped and cheered.

"Thank you," Lant replied with a tone that was brimming with confidence. "It does feel pretty good—I can definitely say that."

"So, talk to us about this new department, Lant," Jun said. "Tell us what we can expect from it."

"Well, I can tell you I'm very excited Jun," Lant exclaimed. "A department of Music and Arts has been something Antal has needed for a very long time now."

"Really?" Jun inquired. "Can you tell us why that is?"

"Absolutely," Lant replied. "You see, our music industry has unfortunately lacked some major quality control over the years."

"Quality control?" Jun questioned.

"Yes," Lant answered. "You see, and our Supreme Executive personally agrees with me on this, but we've sadly allowed our musical culture to be corrupted. This inclusivity movement nonsense has especially been damaging."

"You certainly don't have to tell me," Jun responded. "We've talked plenty about that movement before here on the show. However, I'm curious how this applies to the world of music and arts. Would you care to tell us a little more?"

"Absolutely Jun," Lant assented. "You see, for a long time now, among other things, this movement has tried to force offworld music down our throats. I'm sure they have good intentions, but let's be frank here. We all know offworld music is generally inferior. I mean, if you need an example, most offworld musicians don't even utilize del-tones in their music."

Anya scoffed as she continued to watch.

"Nevertheless, to appease the masses, our radio networks are still regularly playing offworld music," Lant expressed. "And the problem is not only on the radio either. Nearly a quarter of music played in our live venues is by offworld musicians. They come from everywhere, trying to force their way into our culture."

"Nearly a quarter, huh?" Jun responded. "That's no small amount."

"Yes, and that's only the tip of the iceberg, Jun," Lant asserted. "Hell, our academies are still teaching offworld music in their curriculums for no rational reason. It doesn't do anything to improve Antallian music."

"Oh, I'm sure it doesn't," Jun agreed.

"Really, this inclusivity movement wants to give 'everyone' a chance, regardless of merit," Lant continued. "Of course, what they don't tell you is that for every offworld musician being given an 'opportunity', a much more skilled Antallian musician is being left behind."

"You don't have to tell me," Jun asserted. "We've talked many times about Antallian jobs being stolen by offworlders on this show."

"It is a real problem, Jun," Lant explained. "But it's not all about the musicians either. Did you know that 31% of audience members for live music on Antal are also offworlders?"

"Wow," Jun responded. "They're taking up a lot of space in our venues, huh?"

"Of course, don't get me wrong here," Lant continued. "I understand their love of our music. But the problem is that they can often ruin the musical experience for the rest of us. Many of them come from uncultured worlds, and do not have the same respect for music as us. It only takes one bad offworlder at a concert to ruin the experience for everyone else."

"Interesting points, Lant," Jun commented. "But on that note, it's now time for a quick break. We'll be right back after a word from our sponsors."

"Ugh, what ridiculousness," Anya burst out as soon as the ads came onto the screen. "I can hardly believe that people really buy into this. As if the inclusivity movement is the only reason offworlders deserve the same basic rights and opportunities.

"Hell, the only reason we have high rates of offworlder musicians is because so many musicians tend to travel and tour offworld. There are countless Antallian musicians on other worlds too. As for audience members, of course we'll have a lot of offworlders in our venues. We have a thriving tourism industry."

Anya shook her head in frustration. "Lant and Jun both know these things, but they don't care. The prejudice—it's just so... transparent."

"It's about time!" They were interrupted by the old orren man from the bar shouting happily to the barista, taking a swig of his tea. "Nice to finally see a politician with some sense."

"Not so transparent to everyone, apparently," Aren lamented, looking over at the old man.

"Apparently," Anya agreed with a disappointed sigh.

She sipped her tea quietly for a minute until she heard the music indicating that the commercial break had ended.

As annoyed as Anya was, she also had a morbid curiosity, so she continued watching, as the show started back up.

"Welcome back," Jun greeted. "Now, before we left, Lant, you had some words you shared about offworlder audiences. Now, I wanted to respond and say I agree completely that they can be a real problem. I don't mean to be offensive to anyone here, but I think many of us know exactly what you're talking about."

Anya rolled her eyes.

"It's not offensive to tell the truth," Lant responded.

"Oh, I think the inclusivity movement would disagree with you there," Jun jested with a chuckle.

"I'm sure they would," Lant laughed heartily. "Now, I want to be clear here—I do sympathize with offworlders. They just don't have the same hearing that we do, so how could they appreciate music the same way?"

"That is absolutely true," Jun agreed. "So, what is the solution your department is looking to bring here. Are you going to start barring offworlders from music venues? That might be a bit extreme, wouldn't it? Our economy relies on tourism, right?"

"Oh, nothing like that, don't worry," Lant refuted. "I mean, don't get me wrong, we will be banning offworld musicians. Antallian talent must be prioritized above all. But for audience, we understand that all kinds of people want to listen to our music. I mean, how could they not, right?"

Loud applause came from the audience.

"You got that right," Jun agreed. "Our music is the greatest, hands down."

"Absolutely," Lant agreed. "Now, instead of banning offworlders, our solution will be to make sure there are separate sections for them in music venues, generally at the far back. This will keep them from ruining the experience for others, while allowing them to enjoy our galaxy-class music. This will also ensure that the front rows are saved for Antallians, who can much better appreciate the music anyway."

"What an ingenious solution," Jun heartily endorsed. "Can we give a round of applause for that, everyone? Finally, some much-needed changes."

The audience clapped and cheered.

After the audience quieted down, Jun continued. "Really wonderful stuff. I do have to ask, though. With all of these new regulations relating to offworlders, how will your department deal with offworlders who were born on Antal? I know there's been some debate over whether to even call these people offworlders or not."

"Look, Jun," Lant responded. "And I know you have the same feelings as me on this, so I'll say it outright. It doesn't matter whether you're born here, or whether you're second, third, or even eighth generation. An offworlder is an offworlder, and that's how they will all be regulated."

Anya shook her head angrily. "I can barely believe they're saying it outright. 'Offworlders born on Antal.' In other words, all non-orrens."

Anya looked over at Xander and saw how upset he looked.

"Don't worry about them," Anya reassured. "This whole interview is *ogni-dung,* and most of the planet knows it… For what it's worth, your music is as good or better than any top orren musician."

"Oh, it's not that," Xander said. "I just can't believe I went to school with someone that ignorant. But truth be told, he was the same way in the academy too. He made it clear he hated me from day one and treated other offworlders with similar contempt."

"Oh, Xander," Anya sympathized. "I'm sorry you had to deal with someone like him."

"It's not like he was alone or anything," Xander sighed. "But he was the worst. He even butted heads with our professors over offworld issues. He claimed any offworld music he was assigned was a 'waste of his time.' It's just sad to see that he never grew out of that. Seeing him up there now trying to influence others with that hatred is… disappointing."

Aren patted him on the shoulder sympathetically. "I understand, Xander."

"Same here, Xander," Anya added. "I know I don't have your same experience as an offworlder, but I have seen many of my friends fall for UAPA propaganda, and it's always upsetting when it happens."

"I feel that," Xander related. He took a deep swig, finishing the last of his tea.

"Attention: We are now arriving at the Augun Train Station," a robotic voice over the intercom announced.

"Ah, well, at least we're here," Aren said. "Come on, let's get moving."

Chapter 6

"So, now that we're finally alone, I have to ask," Xander mentioned as they were leaving the station, his suitcase following close behind. "Where exactly are we going? What's the plan here?"

Aren began leading them down a park trail away from the station.

"Well, ultimately, we're going to be headed to Enzori, the capital city of Marann, where we have an important meeting," Aren explained. "This is just a stop we're making along the way."

"Ok, well, then what are we stopping here for?" Xander asked. "What's here for us in Augun?"

"Oh, nothing," Aren answered. "We aren't going into Augun."

"Ok, I'm confused, we're at the Augun Station, right?" Xander responded. "If we aren't going to Augun, then that can only mean… We aren't going to Grimveil, are we?!"

"You nailed it," Aren said sprightly, disregarding the clear alarm in Xander's voice. "Yes, Augun is east of the station, and Grimveil is to the west, just through this park. We have no need to go into Augun at all."

"The barista just warned us about that damned place," Xander exclaimed with alarm. "Don't you think this might be a bad idea?"

"It'll be fine," Aren assured him with a smile. "Don't worry, you've got me to protect you."

While that did help Xander to feel a bit better, he was still nervous. The barista's warning had made a serious impact. He especially didn't like not knowing exactly what kind of dangers lurked within the forest. While he did not believe in demons, it seemed clear there were things of some kind to be afraid of in that place.

"I actually didn't know we'd be going into Grimveil myself," Anya admitted. "So, that's where she wants to meet us then, Aren?"

"Yes," Aren confirmed. "Sorry, I didn't mention it earlier. She insisted that it had to be there. She'll update you on her progress when we get there."

"Wait a second, who is this 'she'?" Xander asked inquisitively.

"Sorry, I guess we really haven't kept you up to speed," Aren apologized. "'She' is a good friend of mine we're going to meet. I'm sure you'll like her."

"I actually hired her and Aren at the same time to work for me as mercenaries," Anya explained further to Xander. "Although admittedly, she went dark on her last mission. I haven't been kept up to date on what she's been doing, except that she's been following up on an important lead."

As they continued, a sign came into view. Within moments, it became close enough to read:

Restricted Area Ahead. Turn Back Now. Violators will be Prosecuted.

–UAPA Health and Safety Commission

"Are we sure this is the best meeting place?" Anya asked uncertainly. "UAPA has had this forest locked down for nearly three years now, citing safety concerns. Don't get me wrong, I certainly don't trust UAPA, but it is a little worrying, nevertheless."

"I agree wholeheartedly," Xander stated. "I can't help but think about those missing ecologists. It's my understanding that ecologists are professionals who usually know what they're doing in a forest like this. It can't be normal for an entire group of them to disappear like that."

As they were walking, a 16' security fence came into view in the far distance along with a line of large, ashen trees behind it.

"Ah yes, the story of the ecologists was very sad," Aren replied somberly. "I think it takes a special sort of person to take on that kind of risk for something that they're passionate about."

"Agreed," Xander said. "But you're missing the point. We're going into that same forest?! The one they went missing in. The woods that, true or not, locals claim is home to demons."

"Yes, exactly," Aren responded candidly. "That forest."

Aren looked over and saw them both looking a bit concerned. "Come on, we'll be fine."

"Alright," Anya asserted. "I do trust you."

Xander was less convinced, but held his tongue, nevertheless.

Anya looked over at the security fence, which was still some distance away, but getting closer each second.

"I do wonder though—how exactly do you plan to avoid the sensors and get us past the fence?" Anya inquired. "I didn't know we'd be coming here, so I didn't bring my impulse disruptor. Also, keep in mind, that fence is electrified."

"What's an impulse disruptor?" Xander asked curiously.

"It's a device that disables any standard security sensor within range," Anya explained. " Usually around 100 meters or so, depending on the model. You have to adjust it depending on what sensor you're disabling, and it only works for a short time, but it's pretty reliable if you use it correctly."

"Yes, and there's another advantage to those things too," Aren pointed out, remembering something Gueri had taught him when he was with the Dehnovai. "The effect of these things looks like a malfunction or a glitch on their end, so security isn't likely to be tipped off of your presence."

"Interesting," Xander responded.

"But in any case, we'll be fine without it here," Aren asserted. "Those types of security sensors need at least 0.3 seconds of uninterrupted scanning to detect an intruder. Also, their range is 100 feet at most. All of that is easily workable."

Aren stopped moving. "Actually, I'd say we are about close enough at this point. Both of you come here and hold on to your luggage tight."

"Close enough for what?" Xander asked.

"Ugh, this again?" Anya voiced as she walked closer to Aren. "Get yourself ready Xander."

Xander cautiously followed suit, picking up his suitcase, and walking in close next to Aren. Aren had begun stretching his arms and legs. "You may want to brace yourself."

"*Acari paraskina,*" Aren commanded.

Large, flat protrusions that appeared to be made of dark energy instantly folded outward from Aren's back as he cast the spell Wyvern's Wing.

"How beautiful," Xander observed as he looked at them in awe.

Completely focused, Aren gently reached an arm around both of their waists from behind.

"*Sudis entum tero!*" Aren commanded.

Xander remembered the first two words of this incantation from the battle yesterday. He had a guess for what was coming and quickly tried to brace himself as best he could. The air began pulling in around them. In the next second, the three of them were launched forward, moving at what Xander would estimate to be somewhere around the speed of the arrow train they had just been on.

At the speed the air was hitting Xander's face, it felt nearly solid. It was mildly painful, but an exhilarating ride, nevertheless. With the conjured wings, the trio were launched forward in an upward arc, moving safely over the security fence to the other side.

And in practically the same moment it had begun, it was already over.

Xander immediately fell to his knees, panting. He looked around himself. They had started about 200 feet behind the fence, and they were now nearly the same distance past it. There was no doubt about it, they had now officially entered Grimveil Forest.

"You know, maybe you could try counting down next time to give us a bit more warning," Anya reproached Aren, trying to catch her breath. "Some of us aren't used to moving like that, you know."

"Oh?" Aren voiced. "Sorry, I'll try that next time."

Xander laughed, brushing himself off and standing up straight. "That was kind of fun, actually. Thanks for that."

Anya rolled her eyes. "Don't encourage him."

"You're most welcome," Aren beamed at Xander. "Glad you enjoyed the ride."

"Well, in any case, we are well past the security fence and sensors, so I appreciate that, Aren," Anya conceded. "Do you know how deep into the forest we need to go?"

"I'd estimate it'll be a few hours, by foot," Aren answered. "We should find a place to hide our luggage here. We will be returning for it."

Xander took a moment to look around them. The forest was surprisingly dark for the late afternoon. As he looked up, he could see why. Not only was it a cloudy day, but the giant trees that seemed to fill this forest grew with a thicket of dense, overgrown branches and leaves overhead, which filtered out a lot of the sunlight that had made it through the clouds.

As he looked back down, he could see Aren and Anya taking their weapons out of their luggage, before stashing the rest under a particularly large bush.

Xander decided to follow suit, taking his own chiambra out of its case and strapping it to his back. He then walked over to the bush. He pushed through the bramble, scratching up his arm a little as he did, and hid his luggage next to Anya and Aren's.

Xander hurried to catch up with the two of them, as they walked deeper into the forest.

He shuddered as he looked around himself. It turned out that the forest seemed to be every bit as spooky as he had worried it would be. The darkness in the forest was the worst part, lending credence to imagined terrors, which were only heightened by strange forest sounds, coming from all directions around them.

Xander closed his eyes and inhaled deeply, trying to relax himself.

It's just a forest, he reminded himself. *Nothing more than a bunch of trees, plants and animals. You'll be fine.*

He opened his eyes, releasing his breath as he continued forward.

As he started to calm down, he began to realize that there was actually a strange sort of serenity to the wood. Spooky or not, this forest was still just as full of lush, beautiful life as any other. Natural environments had their own brand of peacefulness, and even a forest as dangerous as this one was no exception. He could feel musical inspiration bubbling from beneath the surface. He hummed to himself as he began to come up with an original melody based on this wood—something eerie on the surface, but soft and beautiful in the layers beneath.

However, this period of relaxation did not last long. Over the next few hours as night fell, the woods got darker and the sounds got louder, the foreboding feelings became more dominant again, and his creative inspiration took a backseat.

He thought back to the story of the missing ecologists. The more he thought about it, the more questions flooded into his mind. What could they have run into that could have killed them? How were their bodies never found? Were him, Anya and Aren now headed towards the same fate?

He could hear the sound of a branch snapping next to him, causing him to jump. His eyes shot downwards towards the noise, where he saw a fluffy rodent with large, beady eyes, and even larger, round ears staring up at him curiously.

"Well, hey there, little guy," Xander knelt down next to it, and it scurried off.

"Careful that the rodents don't get you," Aren teased him playfully.

"Yeah, yeah," Xander laughed. "This place has got me a little jumpy. How much further would you say we have to go, anyway?"

Aren looked down at his wristcomm which he had been using to track their geopositioning.

"Not much further," he stated. "We should be getting quite close now, based on the coordinates I've been given."

As they walked, Xander could hear a deep, guttural sound from off to the distance.

"Please tell me that was one of your stomachs," Xander hoped aloud.

"Unfortunately, not," Anya responded.

Aren sniffed the air pensively.

"Nope, not this time at least," Aren laughed, before turning more serious. "Don't look back, but we're being followed right now. There are about four or five of them currently, but the number seems to be steadily growing as we move."

"Really?" said Xander in shock. "You could tell that from the smell?"

"Well, that, and the sound of their footsteps and growling," Aren added.

"Every time I think I've noticed something before you do," Anya complained to Aren playfully.

Xander listened carefully. Now that they mentioned it, he too could just barely hear gentle rustling some distance behind them as they walked. He shuddered as his mind wandered, thinking about who or what could possibly be following them.

"Are you sure that looking back would be a bad idea?" Xander asked. "I don't know about you guys, but I'd kind of like to see whatever is stalking us."

"You probably wouldn't see anything anyway," Aren responded. "They're too far away and staying hidden. But they can probably see us, and if they notice us looking around for them, it'd likely only agitate them."

"I suppose that makes sense," Xander begrudgingly agreed.

"I've never smelled anything like them before," Aren remarked. "There's something…"

He stopped and sniffed in the air again before continuing "…off about them."

As they continued, they emerged into a large clearing. The light of both of Antal's twin moons shone down, reflecting off a large pond in the center of the glade. Littered across the ground were bundles of strange, bioluminescent plants that glowed a gentle blue.

It was a beautiful and tranquil scene that made Xander forget, for a moment, the horrors that lay behind them. But he was suddenly made to remember as loud, guttural screeches came from all directions around them. Anya pulled out her pistol, and Xander pulled out his chiambra. It seemed that whatever was stalking them had finally caught up.

"Back-to-back!" Aren shouted.

Xander immediately understood the order. The three of them backed up into each other, all facing different directions, so nothing could sneak up behind any of them.

Out of the woods emerged a large beast, growling and walking on six legs, covered in thick black fur. It had wide onyx eyes and a gaping, elongated maw filled with several rows of razor-sharp teeth. Squirming feeler tendrils protruded from its upper lip, while pools of corrosive drool dribbled down its chin, hitting the ground in large drips that slowly melted through the plants beneath. However, more alarming than any of that was the beast's shape. It was noticeably twisted, like parts of its skeleton had been contorted. Patches of fur were also missing, revealing dark scales underneath.

Slowly, more and more beasts emerged, until there were ten surrounding them, all circling them slowly, stalking their prey.

"If you were waiting for the right time to bring out those combat skills, Aren, I'd say now might be good," Xander pointed out anxiously.

"I agree," Anya concurred. "We need to fight together, but I need you to make the first move and draw their attention, Aren."

"Wait," Aren requested. "I'd really like to try something."

He slowly and gently walked up to one of the beasts, keeping eye contact with it. He cooed softly at the animal as he approached very carefully. The creature growled deeply at him, as if warning him, and Aren stopped in his tracks.

"*Bhiast kalarost,*" Aren voiced in a soothing tone.

As he spoke the words, the beast visibly calmed down. The anger in its eyes and lashing of its teeth stopped, as it began happily panting and looking at him. Aren calmly walked closer, brought his hand to the side of the beast's jaw, and stroked it gently. The other beasts watched cautiously, growling uncertainly as they saw this happening.

"Incredible," Anya marveled.

Xander, too, was impressed. He was thinking about how he could help with Aren's efforts here if he had only brought his flute. His chiambra was not well-suited for calming magicks.

However, shortly after Aren had cast the enchantment, a pain could be seen forming in the beast's eyes. This pain seemed to grow worse and worse until the creature began screeching again, breaking free from Aren's spell.

"Damn," Aren said jumping back. "There's something seriously wrong here. Get yourselves ready."

The beasts were growling and screeching more ferociously at the trio now than before. It seemed Aren's move only served to further tick them off.

Aren held his right hand tightly over the hilt of his blade, while Xander gripped his chiambra and bow, and Anya aimed steadily with her pistol. Suddenly, three of the beasts broke out from their circling formation and began to lunge at the group.

They were about to strike at the coming beasts when suddenly a thundering sound blasted out of nowhere.

Xander was startled when he heard it, and further confused when he saw the three beasts going limp mid-lunge, collapsing to the ground as blood pooled under them.

Then, a faint-but-consistent, high-pitched whine sounded out. Anya and Aren both seemed to wince at the sound and covered their ears. The remaining beasts screeched again, this time sounding like they were in great pain, and all of them ran off.

As Xander was looking around, wondering what was going on, he heard a rustling sound. He turned around just in time to see as a shadowy figure drop down from the trees behind them.

Chapter 7

Aren looked over at Gueri apprehensively. He couldn't help but feel uneasy about this assignment.

It had been over a year since his promotion to warrior and his discovery of the secret Dracosian Archive hidden in a pocket dimension. This was the first time, since that promotion, that he failed to do the proper legwork for an assignment like this. Generally, he would case the target's location and gather proper intel on their security situation before making a move.

However, this time they were very rushed and decided to suffice with only a quick assessment of the facility. There were two reasons for this decision. First, this target was a slippery one, constantly disappearing mysteriously the second anyone took notice of him. So, once Aren and Gueri discovered his location, they knew they needed to move fast before he could disappear again. The second reason was that this contract had a rather strict time clause, and they were on their last day left to capture him.

The terms of the bounty contract presented to the Dehnovai were a pretty standard "dead or alive," and the pay was twenty million marks, which was double the Dehnovai's usual rate for a job like this, but with the stipulation that they only had one week to complete the contract.

The target of this contract was a former CEO of a pharmaceutical company and a lowlife who was wanted for defrauding millions of people out of nearly a trillion collective marks for a so-called "life-saving treatment," named Isifur, that was later found to be nothing more than an elaborate placebo.

Worse than the loss of money, tens of thousands of people died, and millions of others faced deleterious effects as a result of relying on Isifur. These people would have potentially all been able to receive alternative treatment with better results if they knew they were wasting their time and money on this product.

In the first couple of months after Isifur had been launched, there was confusion over why the patients using it were still getting worse and dying. Not only was Isifur marketed as extremely effective and fast-acting, but the clinical trials also had some incredible results to back up the claims. However, an investigation by the GDR (Galactic Democratic Republic) brought to light that the results of the clinical trials had been faked, and the product itself was virtually worthless. Over a dozen people were arrested as a result of this investigation, but the man most responsible at the head of this conspiracy, Marqus Leuran, managed to get away, along with the majority of his fortune.

It had been four months since Marqus had been outed as a fraud and no one seemed to be close to capturing him. The few times anyone happened to discover his location, he would escape before they could move in.

One of the victims of Marqus' scheme, Haenes Clorusen, got sick of waiting for the GDR to do their jobs and arrest him. Haenes wanted to see "justice served," and as a billionaire, he had the resources to make it happen. So, he decided to put up his own money to hire the Dehnovai to either capture Marqus and hand him over to the GDR authorities, or to kill him and deliver proof to Haenes in the form of a paired holo-recording/bio-scan of the body—the standard for the industry. Aren and Gueri were here to complete that contract.

They had seen Marqus through the window of the penthouse in the building not long ago, confirming he was in there, and they were about to move in.

"Alright Aren, you ready?" Gueri used sign language to communicate to him, as they stood next to the door of the security outpost.

"Yes, let's move," Aren signed back.

Aren counted down from three with his fingers. On zero, Gueri opened the door and Aren burst in. In the building, Aren could see two guards sitting next to each other in front of a security station full of computers and monitoring equipment. Before either of them could move a muscle, Aren was instantly behind them and had placed his bare hands on the back of both of their heads.

"*Mahi ret,*" Aren whispered.

Both of the guards instantly fell in a heap to the floor. The *Paralyzing Touch* spell from the *Fuinshai* magical art would last for a few hours. That would be far more than long enough for them to complete their objective.

Gueri was about to lunge in with their *guando* pole weapon but relaxed once they saw that Aren had already taken out both guards.

"You know, you could try to leave me one once in a while," Gueri teased.

Aren looked down.

"Actually, I think that I saw that one twitch just now," Aren said, pointing at one of the paralyzed guards. "Maybe you could still fight him."

"Pfft," Gueri responded, chuckling. "Quiet you."

Gueri sat down in front of one of the security terminals. Immediately they went to work, typing away rapidly as they worked their way into the system.

"So, how's digital security looking?" Aren inquired.

"It's looking good for us," Gueri responded confidently. "Thank god for Tel-el security systems. They're a cinch to break into once you get to know them as well as I have, and all the rich people in this astro-region are using them these days."

"I'm glad to hear," Aren responded. "Can you access everything you need from here?

"Absolutely," Gueri asserted. "It's all networked from this station. I should be able to control it all from here—turrets, doors, and cameras. I should be good to go."

"Good," Aren stated. "I'll see you again when I have Marqus in binds."

"Ooo, sounds romantic," Gueri jested playfully. "I'll make sure to have a horse and carriage ride ready for you two."

"Don't forget the mood music," Aren joked back.

"I would never," Gueri chortled lightheartedly.

With that, Aren took off, stealthily making his way towards the fortress.

In the past, Aren had preferred to work alone, but he had started to change his outlook recently as he had been taking on more jobs with Gueri after they were promoted to warrior.

Gueri may not have been the Dehnovai's greatest fighter. Even after training hard for their recent promotion, the fighting side of the job was still not their forte. However, their skills with both computers and security hardware were world-class. Whether it was security systems, traps, sensors, locks, etc., Gueri was among the most reliable in the clan.

This made the two a strong pair. Aren was decent enough when it came to noticing security hardware, but actually dealing with them was not his specialty. When dealing with them on his own, he often found himself having to either side step them or fry them with a spell, but when he worked with Gueri, he generally didn't have to worry about them at all.

As he got closer to the facility, the forest coverage was greatly reduced. All bushes, trees and foliage were cleared in an approximately 150-foot radius around the facility, leaving nothing but barren, empty ground in the surrounding area, illuminated by bright security lights. This open perimeter was plainly established to give a clear line of sight to any incoming threats.

Aren knew that he wouldn't have to worry about any cameras or silent alarms, thanks to Gueri, but he still had to consider the guards themselves, and their line of sight.

"*Yingin kleok*," Aren whispered.

A slight cold washed over him as he could feel the *Shadow Cloak* spell taking hold. When he looked down at his hand, it had become translucent and dark, allowing him to blend in better with the environment, especially while he was still under the cover of night.

Aren struggled with illusion magic in his studies at the Magi Academy. At the Dehnovai, he had had to work hard to improve, as it was a staple of the *Fuinshai* magical art used by the clan. It still wasn't his best class of magic, but he gotten fairly competent at it at this point.

Circling the building from in the bushes, Aren managed to see the backdoor into the facility. He looked up and saw snipers perched on the building, facing outward and looking alert.

If there had been better cover, Aren would simply sneak over, but with this long open stretch and security lights, the chance of detection were too high for his comfort. Even with the shadow cloak spell, he was not invisible, and there was every possibility of being seen by one of those snipers, or even some guard looking out one of the windows. Therefore, he knew he would be best served doing something a little extra to make it across this stretch unseen.

"*Sudis entum*," Aren whispered.

He could feel space and time bending as he cast Hurricane Sprint, the speed-enhancing spell that he learned back at the Magi Academy. With this spell, he was able to move several times faster than usual for up to two seconds. The spell also somewhat sped up his perception of his surroundings—however, at a significantly lesser rate than it enhanced his movement.

The biggest difficulty to Hurricane Sprint, however, was that it was easy to build momentum under the spell, but much more difficult to fight against that momentum until the spell ended. This made stopping or changing directions mid-spell difficult and meant that this spell was best suited for one-way, fluid motions—either in a straight line, or in a curve. Aren, however, had gotten used to this over the years he had known it, and learned to work with the mid-spell momentum, rather than against it.

Approximately a second after casting, Aren could feel the spell turning active. He bolted forward at a meteoric speed. When Hurricane Sprint combined with his other agility-enhancing abilities, he was able to move at over 800 feet per second on the average planet's gravity.

In order to keep quiet and to avoid conspicuously disturbing the area, he kept his movement down to about half of that. Still, this was more than enough to bring him instantly over the stretch of open ground, and next to the fortress' back door where he came to a sudden halt at the end of the spell.

"I'm at the back door," Aren whispered in his earpiece connected to Gueri.

"Excellent," Gueri stated. "Let me get that for you."

As soon as Gueri finished speaking, the door popped open for Aren.

Aren peered in carefully. The door led to a wide, empty hallway. He sniffed deeply while listening carefully. Smell and sound both confirmed that no one was nearby. He walked in cautiously.

Aren smiled when he thought back to how differently he would have done this when he first joined the Dehnovai. Back then, he was all about running in guns blazing.

Truth be told, he still much preferred that method whenever it was possible. However, working with the Dehnovai, he quickly learned how crucial stealth was to many of his assignments. On this mission, for instance, stealth was critical so that Marqus wouldn't try to escape before Aren could get to him.

"You know," Gueri's apprehensive-sounding voice came through Aren's earpiece, interrupting his thoughts. "I'm starting to think that I spoke too soon earlier. I thought this security would be easy to deal with, but I'm picking up some red flags."

"What do you mean?" Aren whispered.

"Well, for one, even for a Tel-el system, this has been admittedly a bit too easy to hack and to keep under my control,"

Gueri explained. "Normally, I would have had more hoops to jump through, but it just seems like this system wasn't set up right. With Marqus' security budget, you'd think he'd have hired professionals who would have done a better job of this."

"Is that all?" Aren asked. "You and I both know a big wallet doesn't exactly mean a smart spender."

Gueri was silent for a moment.

"Gueri?" Aren called quietly.

"Sorry, I was just thinking," Gueri responded. "But no, that's not it. It's more than that. It's also this networking. It's too clean and well laid out for me—as if they're just showing me what they want me to see. I don't know. I know it's nothing concrete, but I can't help but get the feeling that we're being manipulated here."

"Hmmm," Aren responded thoughtfully. "Well, I trust your intuition, but keep in mind, this is the last day we have for this assignment. If we abort now, we won't get another chance at this."

"Mm, I get you," Gueri acknowledged. "I don't think we should abort either. It might be nothing anyway. Just be careful, please. And keep your eyes open. I just would rather you be safe than sorry."

"Will do," Aren affirmed. "I appreciate the heads up."

"No problem," Gueri responded. "Alright, the false feeds have now been successfully rendered and uploaded across all levels now, so you should be able to move freely throughout the facility without raising any alarms."

"Thanks, Gueri," Aren said appreciatively.

Aren looked up to the penthouse of the six-story building, where Marqus was currently located. Under other circumstances, Aren might have scaled the wall, or used a spell to help him jump up straight to the roof, but the problem was that there was no easy access point. Gueri's scans revealed the walls and roof of the building were heavily fortified, and the only access point from the roof was a three-foot steel alloy hatch that only opened from the inside.

While Aren knew he could get through it with enough time, it would be loud and chaotic, and Marqus would likely find some other means of escape in the meantime. Therefore, Aren knew his best shot at accessing the penthouse was starting at ground level and working his way up stealthily.

Moving through the first hallway, Aren pulled his electric body cuff out and checked again to make sure it was in working order. While the contract was an indiscriminate "dead or alive," with no higher reward one way or the other, Aren always went for "alive" regardless.

While he understood that killing on the job was sometimes inevitable, taking an assassination contract felt different to him. It was no longer a case of killing in response to a "kill or be killed" circumstance that happened to come up on the job. It was the entire job. His discomfort with this went doubly when the target was a civilian, as these contracts often were.

He didn't always feel this way, however. Even after he was promoted to the rank of warrior, where he was granted the right to choose the jobs he took, he still continued to take almost any contract that came his way, so long as the target appeared to "deserve it," which they usually did with Dehnovai contracts.

However, his outlook changed several months ago, when he decided to never take another assassination contract again. He now specializes in either "alive" or "dead or alive" contracts with the focus always being on alive.

As Aren made his way from one floor to the next, he noticed a conspicuous lack of guards. With Gueri's earlier warning in mind, he was more and more suspicious that a trap may be lying ahead.

However, as he continued moving, he thought more of it and realized that made no sense. Having no guards at all was simply too conspicuous to be part of some trap. There was likely something else going on here.

He sniffed the air curiously. After a few whiffs, he realized he could smell the scent of people coming from down the hallway. Cautiously, he followed the scent over until he came to a doorway, where the scent was the strongest.

After drawing his blade, he opened the door, fully prepared for whatever was on the other side. He was met only with silence and what was clearly a simple storage room, full of barrels and shelves packed with supplies, with no people in sight.

He sniffed again, and realized the scent was coming from a stack of barrels in the corner of the room. He walked over to the barrels and moved them to the side, revealing the bodies of three dead guards hidden behind them.

"Aren," Gueri suddenly spoke up, sounding alarmed. "There's something you need to know."

"Let me guess," Aren stated. "You've found evidence that a different, third party is in the system."

"How did you know?" Gueri exclaimed. "But yes, it appears we have competition here."

"I figured as much," Aren responded. "I just found a pile of dead guards hidden on the third floor. I'm guessing there are more on each level. Whoever it was likely arrived only minutes before us."

"I suppose it's a race to finish the contract then," Gueri mused. "Think you can finish first?"

Aren hesitated before responding. "In all honesty, I'm not sure. There are a lot of unknowns at the moment. This is turning out to be a bit of a strange job."

"Well, shit must be serious if *you're* saying that you're not sure," Gueri responded teasingly. "I was expecting you to respond with something all smug like 'do you even have to ask?'"

"Well, hey, I didn't say I'd lose," Aren smirked. "Just be ready to pull the ship around when I make the capture. We don't have any time to waste here."

"There's the confident bastard I know and love," Gueri chuckled. "I'll be ready and waiting, Aren."

Aren swiftly made his way up two more levels. Here, he finally saw an active, upright guard, standing some distance down the hallway. Aren was about to make a move when he saw a dark figure emerge and break the guard's neck from behind.

Aren was shocked. With his superb hearing, he could hear a pin drop across a field, and yet, he failed to hear this person's footsteps or breathing until the second they moved to strike. In fact, even as they were moving, he could still hardly detect a trace of this person with any of his senses. It was almost like seeing a ghost. There were very few even out of the Dehnovai who could hide their presence this well.

Aren decided to hang back and watch. The figure hadn't noticed him yet, so he was keeping his breathing and movements as silent as possible.

The figure immediately took and moved the body into a side closet, before emerging again.

As the figure walked closer into the light, Aren could see that they were a girl, likely around his age, in military garb. Peering more closely, he could see the emblem of the Arlodt Empire over the left breast of her uniform.

Could this be who I think it is? Aren pondered curiously.

There had been rumours that the Arlodt Empire had one of their Weapons of War working in this astro-region in recent years. Supposedly, this weapon was a young girl who was said to deal death like it was an art form. While her real name was not public, she was most widely known by the moniker *Greivilder*, which translated to "Grief's Child" in the common tongue.

Aren could hear someone opening the door into the hallway from an adjoining room. His competitor clearly heard it too, as she silently rushed into another room to hide.

The door opened and three people walked out. Aren tensed up as he saw his target, Marqus Leuran walking so casually in front of them. Alongside him were two women in armored suits, likely bodyguards. Before Aren could act, they started talking. He decided to wait and listen before making a move.

"So, is everything set for me to finally get off this gods forsaken planet?" Marqus asked, as they walked across the hall, stopping in front of a door.

"Yes, sir," one of the bodyguards responded, as they opened the door. "Everything is ready to go."

Aren's anxiety immediately shot up. Questions flooded his mind. This was not according to plan. Why was Marqus leaving? Had they been detected?

However, he also realized there was no time left to think as Marqus and the bodyguards swiftly entered the room, followed by his competitor who slipped in silently behind them.

Oh no, you don't, Aren thought to himself determinedly. *That bounty is mine.*

He pushed his worries aside and dashed in after her, making it in just before the door closed behind both of them. In that instant, the door sealed and locked itself on its own.

Aren breathed a sigh of relief as he made it into the room. He had cut it really close to avoid detection, but it had almost been too close.

However, Aren's relief quickly turned to alarm as the lights in the room were turned on, and all of his senses instantly informed him of his mistake.

Dammit, Aren lamented frustratedly. *How could I be such an idiot?!*

Before him were thirty or forty armed guards and two ceiling-mounted artillery turrets all focused on him and the other bounty hunter or assassin. They were trapped.

His competitor was frantically looking around herself, presumably assessing the situation and looking for an escape route, but for an ambush this well-orchestrated, Aren doubted there would be any.

Aren anxiously wondered how he didn't see this coming. But taking a look around himself, he quickly saw the answer. This was a sealed room surrounded by heavily reinforced walls and blast doors, likely originally designed for weapons testing. Not a sound or smell could have escaped this room except during the brief moment that the door had been opened. However, Aren was too focused on getting to the target in that second to pay attention to his environment.

Gods, Gueri is never going to let me hear the end of this one, he thought to himself.

*/

Kyara looked frantically around her. There were a total of thirty-six soldiers armed with energy rifles positioned in front of her, and two heavy duty artillery turrets pointing in her direction from the ceiling. She recognized several of the rooftop snipers among them. They must have been called down to help with the ambush.

The only two ways she could see out were the blast door behind them, which had been locked and sealed, and a more basic metal door on the opposite end of the room, past all of the soldiers and turrets, next to where Marqus, her target was standing.

She could hardly believe she allowed herself to get caught in a trap like this. In all of her years working for the Arlodt Empire, she had never made such a careless mistake.

That comment Marqus had made about leaving the planet had startled her into giving chase rashly. In hindsight, it was obviously a part of the trap, but at the time, an ambush like this didn't seem like a possibility from someone like Marqus. It was clear that she had seriously underestimated this white-collar grifter.

However, despite the impossible situation before her, she was almost more curious about the man standing beside her. He was another part of the reason she had been thrown off of her game. She had noticed him watching her back in the hallway, despite his amateur attempts to conceal himself. She had tried to goad him out of hiding by revealing herself, but Marqus interrupted her cat and mouse game when he showed up out of nowhere.

The man was likely an assassin or a bounty hunter, clearly after the same target as her. He was shrouded in some sort of camouflage effect, that made him partially see-through and a bit dark, almost like a shadow. However, she could still make out that he was young, like her, with facial features that were soft and almost feminine, besides a decently strong jawline. He wore strange robes, and had an amulet around his neck, as well as a sheathed sword attached at his waist.

His appearance, although a bit unusual, did not indicate anything particularly special, and his stealth abilities were nothing to envy. Yet, despite this and despite that she couldn't put her finger on exactly why, her instincts were screaming at her that this was no ordinary bounty hunter.

"Well, well, well, look at what we have here," Marqus asked smugly, standing safely behind three lines of his hired mercenaries. "My security chief called me paranoid, but it looks like my so-called paranoia has paid off. Having a second, hidden security system worked like a charm for detecting the two of you after you both hacked the first one. All I had to do was wait until you were both together, and then luring you in here was a piece of cake."

He laughed maniacally.

"You should have turned yourself in," The swordsman next to her responded to Marqus calmly as his camouflage effect dissipated. "You must know what you did was wrong. If you just accepted responsibility, all of this could have been avoided."

"Wrong?" Marqus stated. "All I did was sell hope to people. I don't see the wrong in that."

He grinned confidently. "Besides, you don't seem to be grasping the situation. You're dead already. You might both be skilled, but as you can see, I was more than prepared for just two of you. Your deaths will serve as warnings to anyone who even thinks about coming after me."

"What you did was lie and manipulate vulnerable people into relying on your medicine that you knew wouldn't help them," The swordsman asserted angrily, letting out a half growl as he spoke.

"Thousands of deaths are on your head. What's coming next is on you."

"Whatever," Marqus brushed his words off. "The words of a dead man are meaningless. Kill them!"

Kyara took a deep breath as she drew her rifle.

In this moment, she was prepared for death. She could see the ambush before her and could see Marqus wasn't bluffing. For most assassins, this sort of trap would have been well over-the-top, but for her, she calculated that it was probably just enough to ensure her death. She would fight with every ounce of strength she had, but she knew that it was a near-certainty that it was over for her.

Rather than fear, she felt a strange sense of peace at the revelation.

But then, she heard the man next to her speak.

"*Kurami envelo,*" He voiced softly.

In that instant, Kyara's vision went completely dark. Instinctively, she leapt backwards. Having memorized the complete layout of the room, she aimed her jump so that she landed behind a nearby desk for cover.

"What the hell?" she heard one of the soldiers yell. "Why were the lights turned out?"

"My flashlight won't turn on!" Another shouted.

She realized then, it wasn't her vision that went dark, but the room itself, and everyone else was experiencing the same thing.

"It doesn't matter, just shoot them!" she heard Marqus shouting.

She could hear the sound of explosions, of energy rifles going off, and slicing sounds, followed by screams and the thumping of falling bodies, but not the faintest glint of light could be seen through any of it.

Suddenly, the lights came back on. She could see that ten of the soldiers were on the ground with deep slice wounds across their torsos.

She didn't see the swordsman at first, until she looked up and saw that he had jumped at one of the artillery turrets with his sword drawn. She was sure he must be insane to go near those giant, metal beasts with only his sword in hand. That turret was huge and fortified.

But then she saw what appeared to be powerful gusts of wind enveloping his sword. The swordsman then lashed out, ripping through the turret, and cutting it clean in two.

The other turret shot at him with powerful energy blasts, but he dodged mid-air. The blasts ripped a hole straight through the steel-reinforced floor. As soon as the swordsman hit the ground, he launched himself up at the second one and repeated what he did to the first, tearing it apart with the thunderous sound of hundreds of pounds of metal being ripped through at once.

Who is this man? Kyara thought in wonder.

Realizing she couldn't just keep watching him, she looked back down at the soldiers. They were all re-orienting themselves after the sudden return of the light, and a few were already preparing to take aim at her again. Without a thought, she pounced into the air, dodging a few shots, and took out four of them with her rifle before she hit the ground again.

"Dammit!" Marqus screamed furiously as he saw his ambush failing.

Kyara watched as Marqus ran through the backdoor, shutting and locking it behind him. She wanted to take off after him, but there were still twenty-two mercenaries left in her way.

She looked at the swordsman, and their eyes met. Not a word was spoken, and yet, both knew exactly what they had to do.

She went left as he went right. The two moved swiftly, fighting those who were left while dodging all shots fired their way. It was like a synchronized dance as the two of them took out mercenary after mercenary with sword and rifle working together side-by-side.

"Gods dammit," one of the mercenaries cried out. "How are they doing this?"

"These aren't people," another shouted. "They're demons!"

And true to his words, they were fighting as if they were demons, refusing to give an inch as they wiped the floor with the mercenaries together. It was only a matter of seconds from that point until the last soldier finally fell, defeated.

"That was... impressive," Kyara said to the swordsman. "Who are you?"

"I am Aren, Clan Warrior of the Dehnovai, at your service," Aren bowed. "You have some pretty incredible moves yourself, I must say."

"I appreciate that, but we should get going," Kyara responded as she shot off the lock to the backdoor of the room and opened it, revealing a staircase. "We need to move quickly if we're going to catch him."

"Oh, I'm sure he's already gone," Aren lamented while following her up the stairs. "At least one of his ships is just on the roof above here. We'll have to track him through space."

"You mean that you already knew about his ship, and you didn't disable it beforehand?" Kyara probed. "I would have thought better of Dehnovai operational procedures."

"Well, uhm, to be honest, I didn't think I had to," Aren sheepishly stammered. "I thought I'd get him before he could escape. I generally always do. But I suppose you already took care of it, then?"

"Affirmative," Kyara confirmed. "It was an operational necessity. He won't be going anywhere."

"But you were going from the ground level up, weren't you?" Aren queried. "Did you really go to the roof just to disable the ship and then go all the way back down to ground level?"

"Yes," Kyara stated. "That's exactly right."

As the two of them emerged from the open hatch at the top of the staircase, they could see Marqus frantically trying to get his small one-person ship started in vain. Once he saw them, he panicked, and began trying to undo his seatbelts.

"Here, you can have him," Kyara told Aren.

"Wow, are you sure?" Aren asked. "I mean, we both worked hard to get him. Maybe I could at least split the bounty with you?"

"You can keep it," Kyara responded nonchalantly. "This mission was never for the money. My superiors only wanted him punished after a member of the royal family fell victim to Isifur. It doesn't matter who deals that punishment."

"Right, that would be the Arlodt royal family, I suppose," Aren surmised. "Well, I plan to take him alive. He'll be headed for prison. Is that an issue?"

"Hmm, they'll complain a little about that, sure," Kyara replied thoughtfully. "But it's fine. They'll be satisfied enough once they learn he's no longer walking free."

Kyara was almost startled at herself as she spoke. This was the first time she was deliberately choosing not to complete a mission she had been tasked with. But something inside her told her that this was the right thing to do.

"Well, thank you a lot," Aren smiled at her. "I really appreciate it."

He looked at her inquisitively. "I must ask though. I'm really curious here. You wouldn't happen to be the Arlodt Weapon of War—the one known as Greivilder, would you?"

"Technically, that isn't my official designation," Kyara answered. "Although yes, I am commonly known by that name."

Aren grabbed Marqus as he was exiting the ship and placed him in binds.

"Huh," Aren replied thoughtfully. "Do you mind if I ask what your real name is?"

"My real name?" Kyara responded to the question with a hint of mild shock, like it was something she wasn't used to being asked. "It's Kyara."

Chapter 8

Xander looked on carefully, keeping his guard up as the figure began to move towards them, still hidden under the shadows of the trees. Whoever or whatever this was had likely been responsible for taking out those three creatures and scaring off the rest. No matter who they were, it was clear they were highly dangerous.

As the figure emerged into the moonlit clearing, Xander could start to make out their features. They were cloaked, but he could see that they were wearing what appeared to be some kind of dark fabric armor and carrying a strange hunting bow made out of a charcoal-colored wood. The bow had an unusual shape that twisted in on itself in curved spirals along its upper and lower limbs, straightening out only in the center, which was covered in a textured, deep black coating, likely for grip.

Aren began moving towards the figure.

"W-wait," Xander warned cautiously to Aren.

Could this be the demon of the forest? Xander thought nervously.

Aren continued forward, disregarding Xander's warning. Xander braced himself for whatever might be coming.

"My gods, it's good to see you!" Aren rejoiced, holding his arms out.

"It's good to see you too, Aren," the figure responded, meeting him in a warm and lasting embrace.

Xander's fear turned to confusion, and then finally to relief as it suddenly dawned on him who this was before them.

"Right, of course," Xander said with a sigh of relief, regaining his composure. "This must be the woman that you two came here to meet."

"Indeed, she is," Anya confirmed. "Xander, meet Kyara Lex'hawa, another excellent mercenary working with us towards the cause. Kyara, this is Xander Ardentes, who's newly joined our cause."

After the hug with Aren had ended, the figure pulled back the hood of their cloak, revealing a gorgeous young human woman with light brown skin, a strong jawline, and long dark hair, shimmering in the moonlight. She turned to Xander and bowed to him. Still a bit shaken from before, he tentatively bowed back.

"I wasn't expecting Aren and Anya to bring anyone else," Kyara expressed. "But if you're with them, I trust you must be a good person. It's nice to meet you, Xander."

"Likewise," Xander responded warmly.

"I have to admit, I wasn't expecting to meet you here in the infamous Grimveil of all places," Anya expressed. "But I'm very interested in what you've been up to."

"Sorry I didn't contact you sooner," Kyara apologized. "I get limited reception out here due to UAPA jammers, and Aren had managed to contact me one of the only times I had been in range. I trusted he'd bring you here though."

"No worries," Anya assured. "Aren told me you were having reception issues. Although I will admit, I'm quite curious what you've been doing out here. To be honest, we've had some suspicions about this forest for a while now, but we've never had anything concrete on it."

"The answers to your questions are just a short distance away from here," Kyara asserted. "I'd be happy to lead you there now if you'd like."

"Please do," Anya agreed.

With Kyara at the lead, they exited the clearing, making their way back through the trees.

Xander was still a bit unnerved after everything that happened. The darkness didn't help. The light from the group's wristcomms illuminated their immediate surroundings, but beyond that was still pitch black, and there were random sounds coming from all around them. This seemed to be a rather active forest in the early evening.

Xander looked at Kyara who was leading the group through the woods. "So, to be clear, it was you that took out those creatures, right? What did you use? I have to say, I'm not really sure what happened back there."

"Yes, that was me," Kyara confirmed. "I used arrows to take out the first three, and then a sonic deterrent to drive off the rest."

"But wait… that can't be right," Xander replied hesitantly. "What were those loud sounds then? It was like thunder or maybe gunfire."

"You know, I've said it before, Kyara," Anya lectured. "That bow is not going to add any stealth value over a rifle if you keep doing that."

"I know, I'm working on it," Kyara agreed sheepishly. "This new bow is difficult to get used to. None of my old ones could go sonic. Luckily, we're still some distance away from where anyone could hear us though."

"Wait one second, you're not saying—" Xander exclaimed in disbelief. "Are you implying you created a sonic boom with your arrows—as in, they were moving past the speed of sound?!"

"Unfortunately, yes," Kyara admitted. "I wasn't trying to, but honestly, I probably pulled back just millimeters too far."

Xander was dumbfounded. "I have—just—so many questions. But for now, I'll just ask, what was that about a sonic deterrent?"

"Oh, that was this," Kyara pulled a small, metal, cubic device with dim, flashing lights from her waistband. "It's a miniature one. They're used to scare off certain types of animals like those shreen back there."

"Wait a second, those were shreen?" Anya exclaimed. "I didn't think that shreen were usually that aggressive around people. Also, I don't remember them looking like that."

Kyara looked sad for a moment. "I think that will be better explained once we reach our destination."

"What are shreen?" Xander asked.

"Aren't you a curious one?" Kyara smiled. "Shreen are the apex predators of this forest. They're the only species on this planet with more sensitive hearing than orrens, which is convenient for driving them off with a sonic deterrent like this."

Kyara pointed again to the sonic deterrent. "Normally, for shreen, this thing would be set at a frequency too high for humans and orrens to hear. However, when shreen are in the middle of the hunt like that, the standard frequency doesn't always work.

"When that happens, I set it to a wider frequency range. That's why you could hear it earlier. It would probably have been much more excruciating to Anya and Aren with their hearing though. Anya as an orren, and Aren, as well, Aren."

"It definitely wasn't pleasant," Anya asserted, gently nursing her ear with her hand as she remembered the shrill sound and the pain associated with it.

"In any case, it's still on but it's back at a normal range now," Kyara explained. "This is probably the only reason we haven't seen another of those predators in the time we've been walking. They're very active in this part of the woods."

"Well, I'm glad for that," Xander said nervously. "That thing seems to be handy in a forest like this."

"You know, you probably actually saw some of these earlier without realizing," Kyara commented. "UAPA uses similar ones on the security fence you would have passed on your way here."

"Actually, we didn't really get close enough to see anything like that," Xander explained. "We kinda just flew right past the fences."

"Oh?" Kyara voiced questioningly. "I suppose Aren used magic to get you over, then? I'm surprised you didn't just use an impulse disruptor to get past the sensors."

"Well, we would have," Anya stated, glowering at Aren. "If a certain individual had warned me that we needed it, so I could have brought one."

"Come on, the glide wasn't that bad, was it?" Aren nudged her lightheartedly with his elbow.

"That's easy for you to say," Anya chastised. "Some of us aren't used to suddenly being pulled forward at ludicrous speeds."

"I actually thought it was fun," Xander piped up.

Anya rolled her eyes. "I suppose if you consider a near-heart attack to be fun."

Xander chuckled lightly.

"Alright, we're almost there," Kyara informed them. "Just a few minutes of a mostly uphill hike to go."

"Thank the gods," Xander remarked. "My legs could really use some rest. We've been going for hours now."

"You do know, we still have the return trip, Xander," Anya reminded him. "And I don't think we'll be stopping for very long."

"Gods, don't remind me," Xander complained dramatically. "But I'll take whatever break I can get at this point."

As they walked, Xander began to notice that they were coming across more and more dead trees. Looking around himself, he realized it wasn't just the trees either. Most of the other plants, bushes, ferns, and vines either looked dead or barely clinging to life.

What on Antal could possibly be causing this? Xander thought to himself.

He could hear running water nearby. As they continued forward, a large, snaking river appeared off to the side. The water was rushing in the opposite direction they were heading. Curious, Xander walked over, knelt down next to it, and slowly began to reach his hand towards it.

The voice of Kyara interrupted him. "Hey, your name is Xander, right?"

"Yes," Xander affirmed.

"Well, Xander," Kyara addressed him. "I wouldn't go near that water if I were you. It's not safe."

Xander hurriedly pulled away, imagining what terrors could be lying beneath the surface. He rejoined the group, continuing to walk forward.

"Also, I'm sorry, but I have to ask," Kyara spoke to him. "I know it's unlikely, but you look kind of familiar, and, well... you wouldn't happen to be Xander, as in Xander, the musician, would you?"

"Indeed, that would be me," Xander smiled and gave a deep, flourishing bow in her direction. "The one and only."

"Seriously?!" Kyara said in shock. "I didn't really expect it to be true. You know, Anya had told me about you actually. She really likes your music."

"You were talking about me?" Xander cheekily asked Anya. "I'm flattered."

"Well, I mean," Anya stammered, blushing. "I had been trying to get her to listen to a bunch of artists to be honest. You know, your first public release was really big here on Antal, so it would have been weird not to include you, really."

"Well, I'm still flattered nevertheless," Xander's playful grin turned into a warm smile as he spoke.

Anya smiled back, before blushing and looking away in embarrassment.

"That actually brings me to my next question," Kyara said curiously "I didn't want to say anything before... It makes a bit more sense now that I know who you are, but... is that really a musical instrument you brought here?"

"Oh, my chiambra?" Xander quipped. "Well, of course, you never know when a bit of music could come in handy."

"Is that so?" Kyara lilted, sounding a bit confused.

"He's teasing," Anya explained. "He's actually a talented aurimancer. He took out a dozen UAPA soldiers with that thing last night. I'd definitely say it's a good idea for him to bring that around."

"Impressive," Kyara praised. "I've heard about aurimancy, but I've never actually seen it for myself."

"It's really something," Aren stated. "I got to see his casting first hand. Anya's right—he's quite talented."

"Ah, Aren, you're too kind," Xander replied, blushing and scratching his head with his bow hand bashfully.

"Huh, well, I hope I get the chance to see it," Kyara remarked.

"I'd be more than happy to give a demonstration at some point, Kyara," Xander offered.

"I appreciate that," Kyara smiled at him.

Kyara turned back forward and continued leading them towards their mysterious destination. Xander could see the edge of a cliff coming up ahead of them past some trees.

Kyara turned the light off on her wristcomm, walked up to the cliff's edge and then came to a sudden stop.

"Ok everyone, we're here now," She announced in a grim tone.

*/

Anya was stunned as she looked through the night-vision binoculars. "I can't believe it. You've found the last one!"

"The last and the largest," Kyara added. "From my surveillance, I'd estimate there are over 25,000 in this camp alone."

"25,000!?" Anya repeated in alarm. "That would make this more than double the next largest one that we've found."

"Over 25,000 what?" Xander inquired. "What are we looking at?"

From their vantage point on the cliff, he could see in the distance that there was a group of buildings and lights nested in the forest and surrounded by walls. He could also make out some movement—possibly vehicles. It looked like a small town—but no town should have been here in this condemned forest.

He squinted to see better, but at a few hundred meters away and with this dark, he couldn't make out any significant details.

Anya passed him the binoculars, shaking her head in disgust. "No matter how many times I see this kind of stuff, it always still gets to me."

When Xander first peered through the binoculars, he wasn't exactly sure what they were talking about. It really appeared to just be a small town, but with no houses, and large industrial buildings. He could see that the forest's river cut through the town, entering and exiting from underneath two different points in the walls.

However, as he looked more closely, he started to notice more key details. The biggest thing to jump out at him was that there were lots of UAPA soldiers prowling about who appeared to be guarding the facilities. He wondered if this was some kind of military base. This assumption, however, was cut short when he saw the other type of uniform there.

It took him a little longer to notice the people wearing this uniform as there didn't seem to be many wearing it outside. However, when he looked through the windows of the larger buildings was when he particularly began to see many who were wearing it, hard at work in what appeared to be factories.

Xander had known this uniform well since he arrived on Antal, looking for Matlex. It was unmistakably the official UAPA Restitution Program uniform, and when he zoomed in on the people wearing them, he could see the distinctive Restitution Program Worker ID markings on their necks. This was a slave camp.

"My gods," Xander expressed in shock.

Xander could feel his heart drop as he gripped tightly onto the binoculars. The more he looked, the more disgusted he felt. Many of the slaves here looked little more than skin and bone—deeply malnourished. A fair number had injuries as well. These people were clearly being treated horrendously.

"I'm sure you can see that things are pretty bad, even at a glance," Kyara stated dismally. "I've been doing some surveillance for a while now, assessing the security and general situation in this camp, and I can say assuredly, this is worse than most forced labour camps I've seen across the galaxy, and I've seen a few in my former line of work."

Xander was about to look away when his eye caught an annoyed-looking soldier approaching one of the prisoners. The soldier and this prisoner began exchanging words. The prisoner appeared to be pleading, while the soldier continued looking angrier and angrier. In the next moment, the soldier pulled out what appeared to be an electrified nightstick and began beating the prisoner relentlessly. Xander turned his head away from the binoculars. He couldn't stand to watch anymore.

"This is just awful," Xander announced.

"It really is," Kyara agreed somberly. "And truth be told, it's not only the slaves being harmed here. They're also polluting this forest with some pretty intense toxic waste from the weapons they're making, dumping it straight into the river—that's what's been killing this forest."

"Seriously?" Anya exclaimed. "It feels like these *beliks* won't be satisfied until they've ruined everything on Antal."

Kyara nodded. "Actually, this brings us back to your question earlier about the shreen. I believe that the pollution has caused them to mutate. The effect has been twisting their bone structure, causing patches of fur to fall off, giving them more teeth and sometimes more eyes. Also, it's made them far more aggressive and irritable, likely from the pain the mutations have caused them."

"That makes sense. Those things did seem to be acting bizarre when we encountered them," Xander said empathetically. "It's awful to think that UAPA is doing this to them."

"They have no respect for nature," Kyara replied with a sadness in her voice.

"So, is that why they came after us earlier then?" Xander asked.

"It definitely is part of it," Kyara answered. "It's worth mentioning that the pollution has also killed off most of the shreen's usual prey, leaving them hungrier and more aggressive than usual."

She looked at Xander and pointed over at the edge of the slave camp. "Look down there, along the tree line."

Xander looked curiously back through the binoculars at the tree line some distance away from the camp. He could see packs of shreen pacing along to the trees parallel to the wall, staring at the camp hungrily as they moved.

Aren's voice interrupted Xander as he was watching.

"Mind if I borrow those?" Aren asked him quietly.

Xander looked over at Aren, realizing he had been conspicuously silent this entire time. He handed over the binoculars, allowing Aren to look at the camp.

"I saw the shreen," Xander said to Kyara. "They all seem to be pacing some distance from the camp's wall. It's a bit unnerving to be honest."

Kyara nodded in acknowledgment. "That's about as close as they can get to the wall before the camp's sonic deterrents start to cause them pain. But they're always there waiting. Especially at night."

"I'd understand a few," Xander stated. "But why so many?"

"Most likely, it's because there are so many people there," Kyara responded. "That camp is, by far, the biggest, most densely packed collection of potential prey in the forest. Shreen can smell and hear their prey from hundreds of meters away, so they can easily tell that there's a feast behind that wall. Those sonic deterrents are the only things keeping them at bay."

As they were talking, Xander suddenly noticed Aren was no longer standing next to him. Xander looked around himself in confusion, wondering where he went.

"Wait, where did Aren go?" Xander asked in alarm. "He was just here a second ago."

Kyara looked around for a moment, and then sighed. "Gods dammit."

Without any hesitation, Kyara began running for the side of the cliff.

"Wait, don't!" Xander cried out as she reached the edge.

However, Kyara ignored him, and to his shock, jumped right off the cliff. Xander ran forward and looked down over the edge, where he watched in fear as she landed on the ground below.

He was about to call down and ask if she was ok, but before he had a chance, she bolted forward into the woods, in the direction of the camp. It seemed that she was fine.

Xander turned to Anya, who was sighing frustratedly.

"What's happening?" Xander asked worriedly. "Is Aren alright? What's Kyara doing?"

"Oh, I suspect Aren is just fine," Anya answered with a hint of exasperation in her voice. "Let's just let Kyara handle this."

The next few moments felt like an eternity as Xander's anxious mind wandered, wondering what was going on.

Breaking the stillness was a giant projectile launching up from the forest below. Fearing he would be hit, Xander jumped out of the way.

A moment later, the projectile crashed next to them. Xander, looking over apprehensively, felt his eyes widen as he realized that the "projectile" was Aren, who was currently grimacing, laid out on his back after crash landing.

Immediately after, Kyara hopped back up next to them, having rapidly scaled up the side of the cliff.

"Ugh, you didn't have to throw me," Aren groaned, as he got back onto his feet. "I was only going in for a closer look."

"Really?" Kyara asked skeptically. "Is that why you have your sword drawn?"

Aren blushed as he looked down, almost as if he was only just realizing that it was out. He quickly sheathed the blade.

"Look, I just don't see why we should be standing around like this," he protested. "The camp is right there!"

"Really, Aren?" Anya rebuked. "I thought you had gotten over these reckless stunts."

"I just—" Aren stammered. "I mean, I get how it looks, but there are thousands of people there. If we could even just—I don't know—sneak in and save one or two of them, maybe they could help us in saving the rest, or something?"

"If you saved one or two, all it's going to do is lead to them greatly beefing up their security," Kyara explained. "And considering there are already 2000 guards posted here, it'd be a really bad idea to attract more. And that's only the beginning to the holes in your plan."

"Yes, absolutely," Anya said assertively. "I'm glad we have someone else reasonable here. I don't know what you were thinking, Aren, but there's nothing you could do there that would end well."

Aren sighed and grumbled. "I see your points."

"The real solution is that we need to take down all of the camps at once, when we're actually prepared," Anya asserted. "Don't worry though, Aren. Morgas and I have had a plan in the works for a while now. All we were waiting for was the location of the final camp, which we now have. Just a little more patience is all we need."

"I'm sorry," Aren looked downcast. "I just—I just wasn't thinking. There are just so many people right there in front of us suffering right now."

"I understand," Kyara assured him, placing her hand on his back and rubbing it comfortingly. "I don't like this either, but we're not going to be doing nothing. We just need to be cautious if we actually plan on helping. We need to plan and prepare first."

"I-I know," Aren replied. "You're right. I'm sorry."

Kyara pulled Aren in for a hug. Aren embraced her warmly.

"We will find a way to help them," Kyara reassured.

"Yes, absolutely," Anya affirmed. "So, no more reckless stunts, ok?"

"Ok," Aren conceded.

He let go of his embrace with Kyara.

Breaking the tension of the moment was the sound of laughter, coming from Xander.

"What's so funny?" Anya asked.

Xander looked at Aren. "I can't believe you seriously were going to storm that massive camp all by yourself."

Aren blushed and rubbed the back of his head sheepishly. "Well, I mean, that wasn't what I was going for… but well, I guess I don't really know what I was going for, to be honest."

Xander patted Aren on the back as he continued laughing. "Gods, have I found some interesting travel companions, it seems."

Anya sighed. "Interesting is one word for it."

After a moment of quiet, Xander looked back over at the camp. Without the binoculars, the view from the cliff was strangely serene. The twin moons were out in full, the river was flowing peacefully, and the stretch of trees between them and the camp was swaying gently in the night breeze. It was hard to imagine the horror and suffering that lay in the midst of all of this beauty.

"By the way," Xander looked over to Anya, his expression turning more grim. "I've been curious if I heard you right earlier. Are there really fourteen of these camps across the planet?"

"Yes," Anya confirmed sadly. "None of the others are quite this size. But even those camps all have between 4,000-12,000 enslaved people each. With this one at around 25,000, that puts the total estimate at around 130,000 across all of the secret camps."

"Wow," Xander expressed in shock. "That's unbelievable. I didn't think they had nearly that many people in the Restitution Program."

"Very few do," Anya explained. "Publicly, they've only claimed about 18,000 total 'Restitution Program Workers'. But in truth, those numbers only account for the ones who are working out in the open—not any of those in the camps. The real number is over eight times that."

"Why the lies?" Xander questioned, confused. "They're open about part of the program—why bother covering up the rest?"

"It's all about optics," Anya explained. "UAPA is big on that. They really want to make themselves appear to be the good guys to everyone. The nicer public face of the Restitution Program makes it easier for them to hide the darker underbelly of these camps."

"I think I get that," Xander acknowledged. "But why are people ok with the program at all? Even that public face seems pretty messed up from what I've seen, even if it is a few steps better than the camps."

"True enough—people's values do seem to be twisted" Anya agreed. "But there is a history here. The Restitution Program they have now used to be called the Penal Servitude program, which had existed only in the country of Nolinth. The Penal Servitude program had actually been quite unpopular, so UAPA worked hard on rebranding it. They marketed their 'new' version as being a more merciful program designed solely to help society's worst criminals to rehabilitate and pay back their debt to society.

"I know that isn't likely aligned with what you've seen, but it is what they have been effectively leading most people to believe. That's why they have to cover up these camps. If people saw the horrid things going on in these places and also realized the massive number of people sentenced to them, it would shatter the illusion they've been so carefully cultivating."

"I had no idea that Nolinth had its own version first," Xander remarked. "I thought the Restitution Program was purely a UAPA invention."

"Sadly, that isn't the case," Anya shook her head. "UAPA may have put a fresh coat of paint over it to make it appear nicer, but it is essentially the same program that has existed in Nolinth for decades.

"In the past, the rest of Antal turned a blind eye to the Penal Servitude program. They didn't like it, but no one was willing to go to war with Nolinth over it. It didn't help that their government adamantly claimed it was a tool to help serve justice and nothing more. In truth, I don't know how the program was really like in Nolinth. It might have been true back then, but as you've seen yourself, the Restitution program is nothing more than a façade today."

"How do they keep it up though?" Xander asked. "Isn't there some trail of evidence? Aren't there trials?"

"For the most part, they do a good job of covering their tracks, sadly," Anya explained. "It is true that there are public Restitution Program trials, which are focused on the worst offenders. But the majority of those in the Restitution Program are quietly sentenced, outside of the public eye, and for all manner of 'offenses'. To our knowledge, the majority of them are sentenced simply for dissidence—in other words just for public disapproval of UAPA. Not only that, but offworlders are clearly targeted at much higher rates than everyone else."

"That's despicable," Xander stated. "But it is in line with the rumours I had heard."

Xander took a deep breath. "To be honest, I think that's what happened to my friend."

"Right, you had mentioned that they took someone you cared about," Aren stated sympathetically. "Who is it, if you don't mind me asking?"

"To be honest, he's an ex-boyfriend of mine," Xander responded. "We used to date back when we were at the academy together. He's actually made a bit of a name for himself since then, so you may have heard of him. His name is Matlex Winslow."

"You don't mean Matlex Winslow, as in, *the* Matlex Winslow?!" Anya exclaimed in astonishment. "You're friends with him? And you even dated him?"

Xander blushed. "Yes, that is correct."

"I'm sorry, who is Matlex?" Kyara inquired curiously.

"See, this is why I've been trying to introduce you to new musicians, Kyara," Anya expressed. "Matlex is one of the most famous Antallian musicians across the galaxy—even more famous than Xander. I mean, Xander, as a new musician, you do have the spotlight now, but Matlex is an established name in the music scene across Auros."

"He sounds impressive," Kyara remarked.

"He is very talented," Xander affirmed. "He has a very unique, smooth sound, reminiscent of the jazz masters of the fifth century, but with a modern twist."

"On top of all of that, he's also well known to be a good guy," Anya added. "In fact, he's one of the few celebrity musicians on Antal brave enough to outwardly criticize UAPA. It probably wouldn't shock you to hear that he's one of my personal favorite musicians."

Anya's eyes lit up as she looked at Xander. "Which is why it's so unbelievable that I never knew that you two dated. You know, all of the gossip radio shows would have a field day with that information if they ever caught wind of it."

Anya's expression quickly turned from swooning to worried as the reality of what Xander said hit her. "I'm sorry. You say that he's missing? I thought he went on hiatus, taking time to explore the galaxy or whatever, similar to how you did before."

"That was the official story," Xander confirmed. "I mean, to be honest, my own hiatus was a bit more complicated than that. But well, as for Matlex, the story just never added up from the get-go."

"What do you mean?" Anya asked.

"Well, for starters," Xander continued. "I went to the planet he was supposed to have traveled to, but according to customs, he never actually arrived."

"How strange," Aren expressed. "Is it possible he went elsewhere instead?"

"There's no record of him traveling anywhere else," Xander answered. "But more importantly, he had left me a holo-message before he left. Here, you can listen for yourselves."

Xander proceeded to press a few buttons on his wristcomm, and then held his arm out for the group to see. Suddenly, a 3D holo-image of a heavyset, dark-skinned orren in stylish clothing appeared above the wristcomm's screen. Anya's eyes lit up as she instantly recognized her idol, Matlex.

"Hey Xander," Matlex stated with a hint of worry in his voice. "Look, things are getting pretty hot here on Antal. I know we rarely talk these days, but I may need to come hang with ya offworld, if you don't mind. If I don't make it, don't believe a word of what they tell you. It was UAPA, got it? Sorry, I gotta go. Call me back."

The message ended with a click, and the image of Matlex disappeared.

"When I finally listened to the message a couple days later, I immediately called him back, but he was already gone," Xander lamented, looking down to the ground sorrowfully. "I was very troubled, considering what he had said in the message. I began looking into it right away. When I found out he never made it to his destination, I booked a long series of gigs on Antal, knowing that my musician work would give me the perfect cover to come here and check things out in person. Frustratingly, I was quite some lightyears away at the time, so it took some traveling, but I got here as quickly as I could."

Xander gave a deep sigh. "However, I can't shake the feeling like maybe I could have prevented all of this if I just checked my messages sooner and then gotten right back to him. The truth is, I had seen he had left a message, but I was busy at the time and I just, well, didn't want to answer it right away. I had figured it could wait a couple days. Turns out I couldn't have been more wrong."

"That doesn't sound fair to yourself," Anya commented. "What could you have even done from so far away?"

"I could have called him and talked some sense into him," Xander stated. "If he just took local private freighter offworld rather than holding out for a public transport, he might have been fine. He was never practical when it came to self-preservation, but he would have listened to me if I told him to smarten up."

Aren patted Xander on the back supportively.

"I know how it feels to regret—to want to change the past," Aren related to him. "But it's all just hindsight. There's really no way you could have known."

"I agree," Anya chimed in. "You can't blame yourself here. You know, sometimes I leave messages from friends unchecked for a lot longer than a couple days if I'm really busy."

"Thanks, you two," Xander stated gratefully. "I will try to keep that in mind, but it's hard sometimes."

He took a deep sigh before continuing. "Really, I had no idea how bad things had gotten on Antal until I actually got back here and saw things firsthand. Those first couple weeks looking for him were rough. That about brings me to when I met you guys at the performance—when I finally lost it on those soldiers. I'm just glad you guys were there to clean up after my mess."

"Think nothing of it," Aren stated cheerfully. "I'm glad we were able to help those people out."

"Well, it was reckless," Anya added. "But I am glad that it all turned out mostly ok… I will admit, it was nice to see someone standing up to UAPA. It was impulsive, but also brave. Besides, I'm sure Aren is grateful you gave him an excuse to get out there and scratch his own itch against those soldiers."

Aren laughed at being called out. "Ok, I can't deny that."

Xander chuckled, lightening up his dark expression a little. He turned to Aren and gave him a charming smile. "Well, I'm glad to have been of service in that case."

"We'll find him, don't worry," Anya consoled. "If he's going to be anywhere, it's almost certain to be in one of the camps. We'll have our reconnaissance teams looking out for his face in all of the camps before we make our move.

"I will say—him being your friend would make him a priority no matter who he was, but to be frank, knowing there's a VIP like that who may be in the Restitution Program makes it doubly critical. We will find him, Xander."

"Thank you," Xander responded gratefully. "I appreciate it."

The group sat together silently for a moment, taking in all they had just seen and learned.

"Well, we should probably be headed back to the station," Xander broke the silence. "I don't think we have anything left to do here, right? And you said we still have to get to Enzori, capital of Marann, right, Anya?"

"Yes, we do," Anya agreed. "If you've had enough of a rest Xander, then absolutely, we should get moving."

"I can assure you I have not," Xander stated only half jokingly. "Nevertheless, I would like to make it to the station by midnight if possible. I'm used to late nights, but I still would like to get my beauty sleep at some point."

"As if you need it," Aren winked at him. "But I won't argue. Let's get going."

With that, the group turned around and headed back, making the trek first towards the luggage they had stashed before heading to the train station.

Chapter 9

Gran Deigas hurried through the winding hallways of UAPA's Capitol Palace.

Although he had been working long hours in this building since he was first hired two weeks ago, he still often had a hard time finding his way through these labyrinthine halls.

Today, trying to find his way through this building felt extra frustrating as he was on his way to see his hero, the great leader of UAPA, Supreme Executive Hamish Drulth, or at least attempting to. Gran was supposed to escort the Supreme Executive to the Capitol Palace Studio where he worked as an assistant.

He worried that, at the current rate he was going, he might actually end up being late.

"Right, so, here are conference rooms F–H," He mumbled to himself as he read the room labels next to the doors. "Ugh, no, I passed by here earlier. This can't be the right way."

He immediately turned around, going back in the opposite direction, and then took the first right turn that came up. He knew he should have spent a bit more time familiarizing himself with the building, but at over 100,000 square feet across 5 levels, that was not an easy task to accomplish.

In fact, beyond the size, the bigger difficulty that Gran was finding was with the layout. The hallways were all winding and seemed to start and stop at random intervals, with seemingly little planning behind them. As a result, it often took an inordinate number of twists and turns to get from point A to point B in the palace, and dead ends were often hit along the way. This often made even short trips through the palace more confusing than most would expect.

Gran sighed as he saw yet another dead end approaching.

"Dammit!" He cursed. "Who designed this building?!"

"That would be the nephew to the Supreme Executive, Olaf Drulth," a voice came from behind him. "Hamish himself hand-picked him as Grand Architect."

Gran quickly turned around, revealing Jenika, another assistant working in the building, emerging from one of the rooms into the hallway.

"Oh, uhh," Gran blushed and tensed up. "Right, I didn't mean to insult anyone. It's a lovely palace."

Jenika laughed.

"Relax, Gran," She reassured him. "I think we both know this building isn't going to receive any architectural awards."

She looked both ways, as if she was checking if anyone was there. "But maybe we should keep that to ourselves in this building."

Gran let out a sigh of relief. "Do you happen to know how I can get to the Supreme Executive's quarters? I need to get to him pretty quickly here so I can bring him over to the studio."

"Oh wow, so you're really getting the chance to work with the Supreme Executive?" Jenika asked excitedly. "And after already getting that cushy gig working as Jun Karlsen's personal assistant too. I'm jealous... Even though I'm in the same building, I rarely get to interact with any of the big shots here. Hell, I still am stuck in the comms room half the time these days."

"Yes, I am lucky," Gran asserted proudly. "I'm sure you've heard by now that Supreme Executive Drulth is getting interviewed by Karlsen today? I'm supposed to be escorting him to get ready for the interview."

"Ah, yes," Jenika replied. "Everyone's been buzzing about that lately. It's so exciting to hear that Hamish will be back on Real Talk. It's been what—months since his last interview? I can hardly even remember what it was like when he was on regularly."

"Yeah, something like that," Gran affirmed.

"You know, I've heard rumors," Jenika mentioned. "Give me the inside scoop—is it true that Hamish plans to come back for regular interviews on the show?"

"To be honest, I don't really know," Gran lamented, scratching his head. "Even as Jun's assistant, I often am kept out of the loop, to be honest. But anyway, I really gotta get going. Did you know the way?"

"Oh, of course," Jenika responded. "Sorry, I just got a bit excited. You're actually pretty close. If you turn around, you need to take the third left, and then it's just the second door on the right."

"Thank you, Jenika!" Gran said appreciatively. "It was nice talking to you. I'll see you later."

"Yes, nice talking to you too," Jenika beamed. "Good luck with the Supreme Executive."

"Thanks," Gran responded as he began heading back down the hall.

On his way to the Supreme Executive's suite, he glanced at some of the artwork adorning the walls. He was often floored by the incredible, expensive pieces Hamish filled this palace with. The pieces didn't exactly follow any theme or even match each other, but they were impressive, nevertheless. As much as the layout was frustrating, there were still many impressive things in this building worth taking a second look at.

Following Jenika's instructions, Gran took the third left down the hall, and then stopped at the second door to the right. Big, bold, golden letters on the dark, wooden door read:

SUPREME EXECUTIVE'S QUARTERS

"Finally!" Gran declared enthusiastically.

He stopped and took a second to mentally prepare himself for his big meeting with his hero.

He looked down at his wristcomm. He had made it here with better time than he had expected.

Alright, Gran, he thought to himself. *It's now or never.*

He knocked on the door.

"You can come in," A voice called out from inside the room.

Gran's heart nearly jumped out of his chest. He would know that voice anywhere. That was Hamish Drulth, the Supreme Executive, actually speaking to him—a nobody, fresh out of college, who got this executive assistant job to Jun Karlsen by the skin of his teeth.

Gran's hand was shaking as he reached for the doorknob, turned it, and slowly pulled the door open.

"Thank you, sir, it's a real hono—" Gran stopped talking dead in his tracks as the door finished opening.

The bedroom before him was quite large, and very opulent, even beyond the rest of the palace. This room was filled with what looked like the most expensive of everything, from pure gold dressers to designer wardrobes to the massive bed, with imported *moxi silk* sheets and drapery. There was even a desk made entirely out of what appeared to be ultra-expensive and illegal, poached *prapana bone* ivory. There was little doubt in Gran's mind that the value of everything in this room must have totaled into the tens of millions of marks.

However, it was not the expensive furnishings or lavish adornments that had caught Gran's eye in this moment and caused him to stop mid-sentence. It was what was happening on top of the bed that caused his jaw to drop.

On top of the silk sheets, with the covers cast aside, there were two individuals facing Gran. One was Hamish Drulth himself, looking over at Gran from a higher angle, positioned on his knees. The other individual, Gran recognized as the master engineer Lester Kanan, a notably beautiful woman who, at this moment, was naked, on all fours, her large breasts heaving as she was being plowed into by the also nude Hamish behind her.

"I'm so sorry," Gran hastily apologized, quickly grabbing the doorknob to close the door. "I'll come back later."

"No, no," Hamish said, continuing his periodic thrusts into Lester. "It's fine. You can stay. Come on in. Tell me, what are you here for?"

Gran hesitated for a moment, then obediently walked into the room, shutting the door behind him. He had heard the rumours about Hamish and Lester. Although they weren't in any official relationship, the gossip around the palace was that Lester had apparently been receiving massive amounts of money from Hamish to sleep with him. Supposedly, they were even said to be pretty open around some of the workers at times.

Previously, Gran had dismissed the notion as mere rumor. Lester was already making massive amounts of money as UAPA's top engineer—as she should, considering it was her who designed UAPA's sonic weaponry that helped them so much in this war.

Such weaponry had been considered theoretically possible in the past, but only she was able to make it a reality. In truth, she may have been the most talented engineer on Antal, and her connection with Hamish was definitely one of the big reasons for his success. There was good reason she should be making good money from her career.

However, once Gran saw pictures of Lester's incredible 30,000 square foot mansion, and later, saw her in the palace wearing designer clothing and jewelry valued in the millions of marks, he did begin to question the possibility of whether the rumors might be true. Her lifestyle admittedly seemed out of even a celebrity engineer's budget.

Regardless, whether it was true or not, he did not expect to see anything happening first-hand, and certainly not when meeting the Supreme Executive for the first time.

Gran averted his eyes, trying to focus on the floor, rather than the lurid display on the bed. However, he could not help but occasionally sneak peeks. Some things were too hard to look away from. He could hardly believe that they were actually doing this so openly in front of him.

"Oh, uhm," Gran spoke up, realizing he had just been asked a question. "I'm here to tell you that you're needed at the Capitol Palace Studio, sir. Your interview on Real Talk is in 45 minutes. I've been instructed to escort you."

"Ah, of course," Hamish responded. "I suppose you must be Jun's new assistant."

"Dang, he's cute," Lester chimed in flirtatiously, biting her lip as she looked Gran up and down.

Gran was a bit nervous at hearing the compliment. Previously, he would have loved to hear such praise from such a beautiful and talented woman as Lester. But that was before now—before seeing undeniable proof that she was Hamish's lover, with every risk that his hero might get jealous over such a remark—especially one made right in front of his face.

However, as Gran looked up at the Supreme Executive, the man seemed completely unfazed by her words, putting Gran back at ease.

"Yes, sir," Gran replied to Hamish with just a hint of discomfort in his voice. "My name is Gran Deigas. Like you inferred, I am Jun's new personal assistant. I just started two weeks ago."

"Well, congratulations on getting hired in the greatest place in the world," Hamish asserted. "So, tell me. How are you liking working in my Capitol Palace?"

This entire time they had been talking, Hamish had never slowed down for a second, and neither Hamish nor Lester made any attempt to cover up.

"It's a wonderful opportunity, sir," Gran responded truthfully. "I've really been enjoying my time here."

"Good, good," Hamish replied. "Did you know this is the most expensive building ever made on the planet?"

"Oh yes, I actually had learned that before I started working here," Gran asserted. "It's a very impressive architectural feat."

Hamish smiled. "You have good tastes. I think you may just do well here."

Gran saw Hamish's face go red as he began grunting heavily, while his strokes started moving slower and harder. Gran blushed as he realized the Supreme Executive was in the midst of climax. Lester on the other hand, seemed neutral, still holding the same expression she had had this entire time, which seemed to border between mild amusement and boredom.

After panting for a few moments, Hamish pulled back and got up and off the bed. Gran quickly looked away, trying to avoid looking directly at the Supreme Executive's genitalia.

Hamish walked into his private washroom, leaving the door open and turned on the shower.

Lester got up and did some quick clean-up with a towel before throwing her own clothes back on. As soon as she finished getting dressed, she headed straight for the door.

"Bye, Gran," Lester simpered, waving coquettishly to him as she walked past.

"B-bye," Gran responded nervously as his face went red. Even forgetting the power dynamics at play here, Lester was incredibly gorgeous. He had a hard time talking to her without stuttering, even despite—or perhaps especially because of—what he had just seen her doing here.

"So, tell me Gran," Hamish ordered from the other room, interrupting his thoughts. "What am I talking about on my show today? I never really got to ask Jun what he had planned."

Gran watched, entranced, as Lester left the room, closing the door behind her.

"Well, sir," Gran responded, clearing his throat and snapping back to Hamish and the topic at hand. "Today we're going to be talking about the Restitution Program. Jun is going to be asking you about how it's going, about whether it's successfully rehabilitating the workers, and just about how it's helping your plan to make Antal a better world."

"Ah, the Restitution Program," Hamish stated as he washed himself. "Did you know I came up with that myself? I mean, Jun may have said something first or whatever, but it was really my idea. Just like I was the one who started Real Talk. It's a great program and a great show."

"I did know that," Gran replied positively. "It's really amazing everything you've accomplished, sir. I had actually meant to say it earlier, but it's a real honour to meet you."

"Sure, sure," Hamish replied. "You seem like a decent guy. So, tell me, what do you think about my glorious Restitution Program?"

"Well, sir, I think it's a brilliant program," expressed Gran. "Undoubtedly, it's a huge improvement from Nolinth's Penal Servitude program, which was just outdated and a tad barbaric. This new program is a wonderful way for the most heinous criminals and terrorists to pay back society. It really shows how merciful you are to give them this chance."

"Of course," Hamish replied confidently. "You know, nobody gives me credit for it, but I really am a very merciful guy. I love this planet. I just want to see it become great, you know?"

Hamish stepped out of the shower, quickly toweled off, and then began getting dressed in an expensive Antallian suit.

"The only thing is…" began Gran before hesitating.

"The only thing is what?" Hamish asked. "Tell me."

Gran looked over at Hamish nervously. There were certain rumours he had been curious about, but he felt reluctant to share a negative question with such a powerful man.

However, when reflecting on it, he considered that this was not just some ordinary man. This was his hero standing before him. Hamish might have been a bit eccentric and overly open with his sex life, but he was still the same amazing Supreme Executive who started UAPA. Of course, it would be fine to ask such a great man as this.

"Well, admittedly, I was wondering about some of the rumors," Gran stated. "There are claims that the Restitution Program is a lot bigger than has been stated. There have been rumours of people going missing, of secret trials—"

Gran stopped mid-sentence as he saw Hamish had stopped getting dressed and was staring furiously at him, shooting daggers with his eyes.

"Nonsense!" Hamish yelled. "Utter nonsense and lies from those trying to make me and UAPA look bad."

Gran quieted up immediately. He didn't expect the question to piss Hamish off so much.

"I'm sorry," Gran apologized. "Of course, that makes sense."

Hamish was quiet for a moment before again responding. "Look, you seem like a good kid. I'm guessing fresh out of college? But what you gotta realize is, there are a lot of people who are jealous and spiteful because of my success. Lots of people want to hurt UAPA and me along with it. They'll say absolutely anything. Anything. The truth doesn't matter to them. Do you understand?"

"Yes, sir," Gran replied. "I'm sorry, sir."

"Good, glad you get it," Hamish said coolly as he quickly finished getting dressed. "Now, let's head over to Real Talk, and share the truth with the people, shall we?"

Chapter 10

To Aren, the train ride to Enzori had an almost completely different feel to it than the one to Augun. For starters, the night service was livelier and while many of the passengers chose to rest at that hour, those who were up often seemed more happy and friendly, if occasionally inebriated or high.

Furthermore, there was also something special about the view out the train windows at night, especially as they trailed through the mountain pass and across the ridge. Looking down into the moonlit valley below revealed a captivating landscape of forests alongside cities and towns that were covered in beautiful architecture and infrastructure that were glimmering brightly in the distance.

The group reversed their order of activities on the train this trip. The four of them started off going to the café car this time, as Xander wanted a little caffeine to help him stay awake for the rest of the trip. After getting sufficiently caffeinated, they then moved to one of the dining cars for a late dinner.

The aesthetic in the dining car was completely different than that of the café car. As opposed to the cool tones and modern look of the café car interior, this dining car had a focus on warmer tones and a more traditional look. For instance, instead of the sleek blue paint covering half of the walls in the café car, the walls here were comprised of rich mahogany paneling. The tables and chairs were also a high-grade orange-brown wood. The lighting was strong but warm, coming from faux sconces adorning the walls between the windows.

The dining car was mostly empty at this point, save for one server, and a handful of drunken customers, dining on an extra-large platter of chips and chatting amongst themselves.

"Hello there," greeted the smiling server approaching the group's table. "Are you all ready to order?"

"Yes, I think so," Aren asserted, looking around at the group. "Are you all ready?"

Everyone in the group nodded. The server looked to Anya first.

"I'll have the Ongorian wine pasta," Anya requested. "And a large beer with it, please."

The server wrote it down.

"Beer with wine pasta?" Xander asked in a slightly critical tone. "A bit of an unusual pairing. You wouldn't prefer a nice dark wine with that?"

"Whatever," Anya responded. "I like what I like. Beer is great and wine pasta is great. Why shouldn't I have the two together?"

"Huh, to each their own, I suppose," Xander conceded.

He turned to the server. "I'll have the *demiure* leaf salad please, with boliart cheese dressing and a serving of seared poultry on the side. Oh, and a glass of your finest wine please."

The server nodded, indicating she wrote it down.

"Ok, then," Aren began. "I'll admit, that demiure leaf salad sounds delicious. Could I please have a serving of that, the same way that my friend here asked for it? And along with that, I'd also like to have: a fried cheese appetizer, one serving of Armiian cream pasta, three glenth steaks, and the roasted vegetable platter, please?"

The server looked stunned for a moment. "Are you sure, sir? I would like to remind you, besides the fried-cheese appetizer, the rest are all full-sized entrées you just ordered, with their own sides and everything."

"Yes, I am," Aren confirmed. "If it isn't too much trouble."

"Alright," the server took down the order.

Xander's jaw dropped.

"Are you really going to eat that much?" He asked in astonishment. "You didn't have that much for lunch."

"I like to keep things light during the day," Aren clarified. "But I'm hungrier now."

The server finished writing down his meal and turned to Kyara. "And for you?"

"Oh, what he ordered sounds pretty good," Kyara stated. "But I'll have four glenth steaks instead of three, please."

"Oh, uhm, ok," The server said in shocked acceptance as she took down the order.

Aren gave Kyara a petty side eye as she placed her slightly bigger order. "You know what, I'd like to change my order. I actually still haven't recovered my energy from last night and am feeling quite hungry. I'll take five glenth steaks instead of three, please."

"Ok, five steaks for you, I got it," the server acknowledged, getting more wide-eyed with every order. "Will that be everything for all of you?"

Her question almost sounded more like a request than an inquiry.

Kyara glared back at Aren. "Actually, I've changed my mind as well. I've been focused so hard on my work that I've been barely eating for days now and could use some replenishment. Please make that six glenth steaks for my order instead, and I'll also add a second serving of the roasted vegetable platter as well. I need my plant nutrients too, of course."

"I'll match her order!" Aren announced competitively without missing a beat.

"Ok, I'll go tell the cooks right away," the server responded nervously, not giving them time to order anything more as she took off to the kitchen car.

Xander could hardly believe how much these two were ordering. He was certain their mouths must have been bigger than their stomachs here. Competition has a way of building up confidence on stilts of glass, and that was a lot of food for anyone.

However, once the food had finally started arriving, Xander watched stupefied as they devoured each course like it was nothing. One after the other, they cleared each plate as it arrived, even as the cooks had clearly been working at top speed.

Xander had hardly gotten through half of his salad by the time they had already devoured an appetizer and four entrées each.

"Don't worry," Anya chuckled, looking at Xander's dumbfounded expression. "They're always like this. Both of them are very big eaters, not to mention how competitive they can be with each other. In fairness, I know both of them burn a ton of calories in their day to day, but it still blows my mind how fast their metabolism seems to burn through it."

"No kidding," Xander said looking at both of them.

Despite their diet, Aren and Kyara both appeared to be in excellent shape. The pair had fairly similar body types too. In terms of size, they were probably around average—not exactly skinny, but they certainly weren't ample either. However, their musculature within their frames was anything but average, with some impressive muscle tone and definition among both of them. They were too skinny to be mistaken for bodybuilders, but there was no questioning from looks alone that they were both strong and athletic.

The only two clear differences between the pair's bodies was, first, that Aren was a bit taller, and second, that Kyara had a slightly more feminine figure than Aren, with hips and waist that were a little curvier, and breasts that were more pronounced than Aren's pecs.

However, both of them were a little androgynous overall. Aren had softer facial features than the typical man, with long eyelashes, a waist that was a bit narrow, hips that were a bit wide, and luscious, flowing, mid-length hair. Kyara on the other hand had broader shoulders, more muscle bulk, and a stronger jawline than most women.

Looking over the two of them, Xander was curious about the features he hadn't seen between them. He found his eyes trailing down Aren's torso, as he pondered what Aren's abs looked like under those robes. Realizing his thoughts, he quickly blushed and looked away.

"You eat almost as well as you fight," Xander commented to Aren. "It's impressive."

Aren laughed.

"Thank you," he responded between bites. "Train food is always so good on Antal."

Xander looked as a second stack of three large steaks was placed in front of Aren besides his other food. "Wow, that really is a lot of meat."

Aren looked over at him coyly. "What? Not a fan of meat?"

Xander blushed again. "Oh no, I enjoy it just fine, I can assure you."

"Oh, I bet," Aren flashed him a playful, toothy grin, surprising Xander with his unusually sharp teeth, before going back to his food.

The four of them ate silently for a while. By the time Anya and Xander had finished their meals, Aren and Kyara had somehow made it to their last plates as well. It was only moments later that they completed their final entrée, finishing at roughly the same time each.

"I suppose it's a tie," Aren said, panting.

"Oh, were we competing?" Kyara teased with a light-hearted chuckle.

As he rolled his eyes in response, she leaned over and gave him a sporting hug. "Gods, I missed you, Aren."

Looking around, Xander noted that the last of the drunken customers from the dining car had finished their chips and left, leaving their group alone. He realized it must have been pretty late.

"I have to admit, when you both first made the orders, I didn't really think you were going to finish," Xander confessed. "But damn, did you both prove me wrong."

"My personal rule is to never doubt these two when it comes to fighting or eating," Anya expressed lightheartedly, patting him on the back.

"Well, I certainly can see why," Xander said with a chuckle.

Aren laughed heartily. "You two have seen nothing. There was an angossin in my old clan, Master Ofrike, who could eat me under the table. Now, don't get me wrong, I know angossins are typically twice the size of humans, and boy can they eat, but I'm telling you, he was different. He could eat everything Kyara and I just had combined and still be hungry for dessert."

"Wow, that's unbelievable," Xander expressed.

"You can say that again," Kyara responded. "I was actually a bit dubious about everything I'd heard until Aren introduced me to the man, and I saw it for myself. He's quite something, that Ofrike."

"Wait a second here," Xander said hesitantly. "You wouldn't happen to be talking about Ofrike as in the assassin, Ofrike the Twice-Cursed, are you?"

"Oh, you've heard of him?" Aren replied casually.

"Heard of him?" Xander voiced, dumbstruck. "He's one of the most infamous assassins in this astro-region, especially after he took out the warlord, Izak. It's said that Ofrike is indestructible, and that his hammer is capable of crushing buildings and cracking earth."

"Ah, yes, it makes sense that his name would be out there," Aren laughed. "Out of the entire clan, he probably was the worst at keeping a low profile—even worse than me. Although, I can tell you those stories aren't all totally accurate. He may be hard to hurt, but he's certainly far from indestructible. His hammer does hit pretty damned hard though. I'll admit that much."

Aren rubbed the back of his head tenderly, as if he was remembering some past pain back there.

"Ok, but that would have to mean," Xander was slowly putting two and two together. "You were a warrior of the Dehnovai Clan, then?"

"Yes, I was," Aren admitted. "I just quit a few months ago, actually."

"He was more than just warrior," Kyara pointed out nonchalantly. "He had actually just become a master before he left."

Xander looked at Aren in awe and admiration. While he did not know much about the clan, he knew enough to understand that was no ordinary feat.

Overall, the Dehnovai was a clan that was mired in mystery. But there were some facts that Xander knew about—things that were public knowledge in this region of space. For starters, he knew that they were a warrior clan specializing in bounty hunting and assassination contracts in the astro-region. They had an infamous reputation for being able to complete the jobs that others couldn't.

Few of the Dehnovai's members were publicly known, but among them included Ofrike the Twice-Cursed who was one of the Dehnovai's masters who did not seem to care for stealth nor hiding his identity on the job, which often led to him being identified and reported to the media.

However, perhaps even more infamous, yet also more mysterious, was the Grandmaster of the clan, Takeda Hallamaine, also known as Hallamaine the Unbroken, who was likened to the devil themselves by any who were unfortunate enough to witness her on the job.

Hallamaine was easily recognizable by her unique fox mask, which she supposedly always had on. That mask was associated with death in this region of space. Outside of Ofrike and Hallamaine, there were supposedly many other incredible warriors in the clan, but most of their identities were unknown to the public.

"Well, I will say, that certainly does explain a lot," Xander expressed thoughtfully. "Would you mind if I asked why you left?"

Aren's expression suddenly turned serious, and a little sad. "It just… It wasn't what I thought it was."

Aren looked down uncomfortably as he took a sip of water. "But anyway, enough about me. Xander, how are you feeling about everything? Are you still resolved to continue this fight after what you've seen?"

Xander looked back at him with a fierce determination. "Everything I've seen has only strengthened my resolve. I'm determined to see this through to the end."

"That's what I like to hear," Aren beamed.

"I'm honestly impressed," Anya praised. "It's not even your home planet, and you're willing to go into the line of fire for it. I know you didn't ask for it, but I want to let you know, I will make sure you get compensated."

"Antal has been like a second home to me for a long time now," Xander expressed. "As for compensation, please no. I'll be fine. You guys spend it wherever else it could help. Between my digital releases and concerts, I've actually been doing really well for myself since my debut. Money is not currently a worry of mine."

"Well, we must do something for you," Anya protested. "Aren and Kyara actually aren't getting paid in cash themselves, you know. They have other arrangements with us. Perhaps there's something besides money we could do for you?"

Xander paused and thought for a moment.

"It'd be more than enough if you guys could just help me find Matlex," Xander asserted. "I'd consider that to be ample payment."

"Of course," Anya agreed to the terms in a sympathetic tone. "I can promise you that we'll do everything in our power to help you find him."

"Good," Xander smiled. "Then we'll be square."

"Excellent," Anya beamed back at him.

Anya sipped her beer and looked at the time on her wristcomm. It was well past midnight at this point. Thankfully, her apartment wasn't far from the Enzori station, so it would be a short trip after they arrived.

"So, changing the subject here for a moment," Xander began. "I wanted to say that I appreciate how you guys have been filling me in on what's been going on, particularly you, Anya. However, there is still one question that I've had at the back of my mind, that's been bugging me."

"What is it?" Anya inquired.

"Well, Antal is still a member of the Galactic Democratic Republic, that is, the GDR, right?" Xander questioned. "Which of course, is the largest inter-governmental organization in the galaxy, correct?"

"Yes, that is correct," Anya responded. "Even though UAPA is trying to get us to secede, we still currently retain our status as a part of the GDR. Anyway, I think I see what you're going with this, but go ahead and ask your question."

"Well, frankly, I am curious why they aren't intervening here," Xander expressed. "To my knowledge, for the past three years, UAPA has been steadily invading country after country, causing deaths and injuries well into the hundreds of thousands, and then enforcing a global slavery program on top of it all. I'll admit, I don't have much of a mind for politics or legal what-not, but doesn't that violate some kind of law?"

Anya sighed deeply.

"You're really not wrong," She acknowledged. "At least, in theory. However, it's a complicated situation."

"How so?" Xander quizzed.

"Well, for starters, Hamish may be many things, including a bit of an overall idiot most of the time," She began. "However, to his credit, he can definitely be very resourceful at times too. For instance, he has long since been a member of the Antallian GDR delegation, well before UAPA was even a thing, and that has allowed him to negotiate with the GDR directly."

"Oh?" Xander voiced. "Interesting. I'm surprised a man like him got a position like that. He doesn't seem the type for high-brow diplomacy from what I've seen."

"Yes, well, family connections and money go a long way getting you into high places like that," Anya explained. "His father had many friends in the GDR."

"Oh really?" Xander responded. "How was his father so well-connected?"

"Well, his dad was actually president of Nolinth some years ago," Anya explained. "And before that, he made a fortune in the financial industry, all of which was inherited by Hamish when he passed away around 20 years ago."

"Well, that doesn't surprise me," Xander remarked. "Men like him rarely attain that kind of money and power from nothing."

"Indeed," Anya agreed. "In any case, I will also credit Hamish with the fact that he surrounds himself with many capable and savvy people."

Anya quickly finished off her glass of beer as she spoke. Kyara and Aren were both quietly listening, alongside Xander. Aren knew about the situation already but was happy to listen as Anya explained. On the other hand, Kyara actually didn't know anything about this and was intrigued. She wasn't used to receiving more information than necessary for her jobs, so this was an unusual experience for her.

"In truth, there actually had been a big attempt to petition the GDR for aid," Anya continued. "Several of our nations' leaders and top politicians were behind the petition. UAPA had clearly been violating established GDR peace accords. However, Hamish's lawyers and consultants helped him to make a counter-petition to designate the war as a 'multi-sided internal conflict,' which would bar the GDR from any interference. Sadly enough, a GDR tribunal awarded UAPA their petition, and that is why they won't interfere. Well, the official reason, at least."

"What?" Xander asked in bewilderment. "Forgive my ignorance here, again, I don't know much about politics or legislation, but a 'multi-sided internal conflict'? How can attempting to conquer an entire planet be considered multi-sided? That cannot be right, can it?"

"That is absolutely correct," Anya exclaimed. "The decision pissed off countless Antallians, myself included. Hamish and his team really focused their arguments on a number of legal loopholes in the legislation, and then topped it off with their typical ogni-dung spins, making themselves appear to be simultaneously victims and heroes in this situation, without accepting any culpability whatsoever."

Aren sighed angrily as he listened. Even knowing the situation already, it still was upsetting to hear.

"That tribunal was a bunch of idiots," Aren exclaimed frustratedly. "There's no justifying a decision like that."

"Sadly, it's not unlike what I've seen many times before," Kyara chimed in. "In the Arlodt Empire, the truth was always whatever the royal family decreed. The real facts always came second."

"It's hard to wrap my head around, to be honest," Xander said with a disappointed sadness in his voice. "I'm shocked that such a powerful organization would allow such a farce."

"It is very disheartening," Anya agreed. "However, UAPA's nonsense arguments aside, I honestly think the GDR was happy to accept any excuse at all to not send help."

"Why is that?" Xander inquired.

"Well, they try not to advertise this, but they've been spread very thin lately," Anya explained. "They're not nearly as powerful these days as they used to be. And their military resources are currently all being utilized protecting their established systems from pirates and bandits, who are more active than ever. Rumor is, the Uomak have been giving them serious trouble lately too."

"The Uomak?" Xander asked. "Oh right, that's that species from Outlying Region-Beta, right? I've heard they're at war with GDR, or something along those lines."

"Well, that's kind of true," Anya asserted. "It's more a bunch of disjointed raids, skirmishes and pillaging than actual warfare, but I suppose it's still war of a type—probably similar to our own Raider Wars from not long ago actually."

"Makes sense," Xander acknowledged.

Anya nodded to him. "In any case, the Uomak are not just a single government, but a species with a number of clan-houses, both great and minor, each with unique politics and beliefs. Many of these clan-houses have taken to warfare, and because they're close to many GDR sectors, this has made the GDR a big target. I'm sure this is part of why the GDR was so quick to accept UAPA's petition."

"I see," Xander responded thoughtfully. "It still doesn't excuse such egregious apathy though. I understand that they're struggling, but that's no excuse to leave an entire planet behind to suffer like this."

Aren smiled at him. "I couldn't agree with you more, Xander."

Anya and Kyara both nodded in agreement.

"It really is inexcusable," Anya added. "Other Antallian politicians have since put in for an appeal of the GDR's decision, but there's a good chance that will fall apart too. There are many reasons for this, but the biggest is that, as I mentioned earlier, UAPA is also working towards Antal's official removal from the GDR. They claim it's for their global pride and independence, but it's clear that Hamish just doesn't want GDR interference. With the number of countries UAPA now controls, they finally have a majority, and may just get their wish soon."

"Well then, I suppose we'll just have to do something before that happens," Aren exclaimed confidently. "GDR or not, we'll take those beliks down."

"You're damn right we will, my friend," Anya beamed and slapped Aren on the back supportively.

"I think we can say joys to that," Xander said, lifting his wine glass up with the last sip still in it.

Aren and Kyara lifted their waters. Anya, noting that her beer was finished, grabbed her water as well.

"Joys!" They shouted, bringing their glasses down onto the table in unison, and then taking a drink.

A voice suddenly rang out from the PA system. "Attention passengers. We are now arriving at the Enzori Central Station. For those getting off here, please prepare to disembark now. Thank you for riding with Antal Railway."

"Perfect timing," Xander said with a yawn as he started to get up from his seat. "I think my caffeine is starting to wear off."

The rest got up from their seats too.

"Well, you'll be resting quickly enough," Anya stated. "We'll be at my apartment in ten minutes after catching an autocab. Make sure you all get a good sleep tonight. That meeting tomorrow is no small matter."

"Now that is an order that I am happy to oblige," Xander smiled sleepily.

The group went to the dining car's service machine to pay for their meal, and then headed to the nearest transition car to prepare for their arrival.

Chapter 11

Xander yawned and took a sip of his grain coffee as he sat at the conference room table. Despite his usual affinity for lattes, he took his coffee black this morning, and extra strong, as he felt he could use all of the caffeine that he could get.

The bed at Anya's apartment had been comfortable enough, but the problem came with how early he had been woken up. Anya wanted to make sure they were all prepared for the meeting well before it started, so she made sure everyone was up bright and early in the morning. However, Xander ended up being the sole target of these efforts, as Aren and Kyara, as usual, had gotten up quite early on their own.

Xander was a night owl and accustomed to sleeping in, so he found himself having a difficult time adjusting to these early mornings. Nevertheless, he complied, getting up and going along with Anya's explanations and preparations for the meeting that was coming that day.

The first thing Anya informed them of was the fact that, because none of the three of them were technically even members of Oppori Qala, let alone the council, they did not yet have the right to actually sit through the council meeting.

However, as Vice-Chair, Anya had the authority to bring them into the building, where she planned to petition for them to join the council under the rank and title of Specialists before the meeting officially started. If her petition went through, they would be allowed to stay, which she was really hoping for, as she believed that they would bring valuable insight and support to the meeting.

After a long morning of getting prepped and then traveling to the secret headquarters, Xander found himself in the conference room where the meeting was scheduled. Here he was sitting at the table, alongside several top officials of Oppori Qala, all waiting patiently for the meeting to get started. Looking around, he could see that, of the ten people currently in the room, only he, Aren and Kyara were not orren.

The rest of the council were all talking amongst themselves. He noticed two of the officials here murmuring excitedly and pointing in his direction. He couldn't hear most of what they were saying, but he did manage to overhear his name being spoken. He realized that it was likely that those two and possibly others in the room had recognized him. It wasn't unusual for this to happen since he started gaining some renown as a musician. And, to his pride, Antal had been one of the planets his music was most popular on.

In his first weeks after arriving here, he found himself being recognized and approached by fans often. He didn't mind it before, but now that he was wanted by UAPA, he was grateful for the holo-mask given to him by Anya, which changed his features and prevented him from being recognized in public. However, since he was not wearing one now, it seemed that at least a few people in the room had realized who he was.

Xander scanned over the people in the room, noting a few interesting characters. There was one in particular who really caught his eye. She was a beautiful orren woman, likely in her early twenties, in tight, black clothing and dark makeup. She looked rather bored as she was fiddling around on a palmcomm—a reasonably popular alternative to a wristcomm that was held in the hand. Even despite this woman's apathetic demeanor, Xander could feel an intensity to her bubbling beneath the surface, like there was a sleeping tiger hidden under that cool exterior.

Xander felt himself being nudged by an elbow from Anya beside him.

"Alright, I know we've already gone through everything," Anya murmured to him. "But I just want to double-check. Are you positive that you're ready? Do you feel comfortable making your case if need be?"

"Yes, I think I'll be fine," Xander grinned cheekily. "This won't have been my first time having to plead my case in front of officials before. Granted, it may be the first time while not in cuffs."

"Come on," Anya rolled her eyes, trying to hold back a chuckle. "Are you taking this seriously?"

"Yes, of course," Xander assured in a more serious tone. "Jokes aside, don't worry, I am ready."

"Ok, good," Anya smiled. "I'm glad to hear it."

The door opened, and everyone suddenly got silent as two figures walked into the room. Xander was surprised to see that the first to enter the room was a human. She was a tall, dark-skinned woman with gorgeous, woolly hair, likely around her early forties, and she was the only non-orren besides Xander, Kyara and Aren in the room. She carried herself with a strong posture, and a fast-but-steady step that exuded the confidence of a powerful, self-determined woman.

Trailing behind this human woman, was a short orren woman in a blouse, pencil skirt, and glasses, carrying a clipboard.

Anya got up from her chair, and walked over to the human woman, with her arms outstretched, greeting her with a hug.

"Greetings Morgas!" Anya welcomed her warmly. "It's great to see you."

"You as well Anya!" Morgas spoke with a strong but calming voice as she returned the hug.

"Wait, that's Morgas?" Xander whispered to Aren, who was sitting on his left side. "She's a human?"

"Yes," Aren whispered back in confirmation. "That's her—the infamous and beloved leader of Oppori Qala."

Anya and Morgas both let go of the embrace and Anya returned to her chair.

"I'm glad to see you all here," Morgas announced. Looking over the people in the room, Morgas' eyes fell on Kyara, Aren and Xander. "I see we have some new faces here today."

"Yes, I've been wondering about that myself," said an orren man sitting across the table from the group. "Who are these people you have brought here, Anya? I was under the impression that this was supposed to be a council meeting. I had been told of two guests who would be joining us on holocomm, but I didn't expect anyone else to show up here in person."

Xander looked over at the man speaking. He was a middle-aged, orren man, with sharp cheek bones, a long, pointed nose, and beady, dark eyes.

"Yes, well, General Ollit, I was just waiting for our Chair to arrive," Anya explained. "But now that Morgas is here, I would like to officially petition for these three to be allowed to join the Oppori Qala council as Specialists, so that they could share their experience and expertise with us, here at the top level of the organization."

"On what grounds could you possibly expect us to grant that?" Ollit asked her. "That is not a privilege we give to just anyone. The Specialists we allow into our top council include only the very few in our organization who have displayed the top level of skills, reliability and trustworthiness in their respective fields. Forgive me, but I have skepticism that these people meet such stringent criteria."

He looked directly at Xander with a disapproving expression. "Even if one of them happens to be a celebrity."

Anya narrowed her eyes at the overtly critical statement, but her demeanor remained calm and composed.

"Skepticism is fine," She asserted. "However, I am prepared to make the case that each of these individuals meets all of the requirements for the title and more. None of them are currently official members of Oppori Qala, but all of them have shown the dedication, fortitude, competency, and character worthy of being included in our council. I vouch that all of them are trustworthy and will be great assets as council officers if given the chance."

"Are you serious?" General Ollit scoffed. "Forgive me, Anya, I know you outrank me as Vice-Chair. But isn't this a tad ridiculous? You're telling me they're not even official members at all, and yet you took the huge security risk of bringing them here to our headquarters, and you then dare ask if they can join the council, right before we're supposed to have our meeting?"

"I'll admit, I don't see eye to eye with Ollit on much," A silver-haired orren woman with a strong posture and steel eyes spoke up from the far end of the table. "But I'm afraid I must agree with him here. Even as our Vice-Chair, it was rather presumptuous of you to bring non-members to a council meeting, Anya."

"I apologize about that, General Clodwyn," Anya responded genuinely. "However, I give my personal assurance that they are not a security risk, and it was necessary to bring them here in order to make this petition in a timely manner. I also wanted it to be done before our meeting, as I believe their inclusion in the meeting would be an asset."

"Well, regardless, I still have serious doubts," Ollit asserted, looked over at the group disapprovingly. "Not only are they not members, but I'm guessing, based on their appearance and clothing, that they're offworlders too."

"That's enough Ollit," Morgas commanded. "That last comment was uncalled for. Don't forget that I'm still technically an offworlder by most definitions myself. Not only am I human, but I wasn't born on Antal either."

"But you moved here in your childhood," Ollit protested. "You were raised here. None of us here would call you an offworlder where it counts—we're not UAPA here. Besides, I have nothing against actual offworlders, as you know, of course. I just think it's worth noting that most of our organization are fighting for their homes. If they're not from here, I simply question what their motives are in helping us."

"Well, the only way we can find out is to hear their case, isn't it?" Morgas pointed out. "You can go ahead Anya. Tell me about these three you have brought here today."

"Thank you Morgas," Anya smiled at her. "The full names of the three of them are Xander Ardentes, Kyara Lex'hawa, and Aren Sperosun. The first I will discuss is Xander, since he is already known to most of you."

She motioned towards Xander who nodded in acknowledgement towards the group.

"As you all are likely aware, this man is a bit of a star on Antal at the moment, to put it mildly," Anya began her pitch. "Among his successes include his release 'Something New' hitting number one on the Antal charts last week and being recently named as musician of the month by *The Antallian*. He also has great charm, as well as intellect and passion for social justice, as noted in his public appearances, and I believe his celebrity influence could be a valuable asset in recruitment."

Looking around, Anya could see the officers were listening intently. It was a good idea to start with Xander. He was the least likely to be a controversial choice here due to his popularity.

"Furthermore, you may have heard him mentioned in the news as a wanted felon recently," Anya continued. "However, what they failed to mention was that Xander put himself in danger to free four Restitution Program slaves and took out twelve, fully-armed UAPA soldiers by himself in the process. I will also add that all four of the enslaved individuals are now free and safe with a personal friend of mine."

"A dozen UAPA soldiers?!" Ollit balked doubtfully. "Armed with sonic rifles? How did a musician possibly manage that? I don't know if I have any trained operatives in my regiment capable of such a feat."

"Xander is a very talented aurimancer," Anya explained. "Dare I say better than what I've seen from the academy aurimancers here."

"Ah, aurimancy, of course," An old man, stroking his beard spoke up. "I've heard it said that it could be very useful in combat by a skilled practitioner, but I've never actually seen it used in that way before. Even here on Antal, there aren't many who have mastered the art. That's very impressive at such a young age."

"I agree, Elmenz," Anya concurred. "Xander has demonstrated both his virtuous motives and his skill through his actions. I will admit he can be a tad reckless at times, but he has also shown he can be reined in. Altogether, with his skills and celebrity influence, I believe he would be an excellent Specialist, in charge of public relations and aurimancic applications."

Xander smiled silently. He had been prepared to help make his case if need be, but it seemed that Anya had done more than a good enough job without him having to say a word.

"Fine, I can understand your argument for him well enough," Ollit accepted. "But what about these other two."

Ollit pointed at Aren and Kyara.

"Both Aren and Kyara here are mercenaries I hired for ongoing contracts about three months ago," Anya explained. "Both of them have done extremely well, completing many high-level missions in that time."

"Mercenaries, huh?" Ollit said in a critical tone. "Well, I can't say that speaks well to their motives. Mercenaries work for whoever pays best. I don't think they're the type who can be trusted for a council officer title."

"Well, first of all, they are not your typical mercenaries and are uninterested in cash here," Anya retorted, before turning to Morgas. "These are the two mercenaries I talked to you about, Morgas, who have been working with me in exchange for your old Arc-I spaceship you so graciously donated to the cause and a special concession once we are victorious in this war."

Morgas nodded at her. "Understood. I had been curious to meet these two for a while now."

Anya nodded back to Morgas before continuing.

"Furthermore, while I may have only hired the two of them a few months ago, I have known Aren for significantly longer," Anya pointed out. "Him and I have been good friends for nearly a year now. In that time, he has demonstrated superb moral fiber, as well as total loyalty to the cause. As for Kyara, not only does Aren vouch for her on his life, but she has also shown the same qualities and dedication in the entire time she has been working for us."

"Fine, fine," Ollit conceded. "But what about the skills of these two mercenaries? Do you really feel they deserve to hold the same title held by such people as the infamous, master thief Henrika that we have under the rank of Specialist?"

He motioned over to the woman in dark makeup that Xander had noticed earlier. At this point she was chewing gum and sitting upside-down, with her head dangling off the base of her chair, still on her palmcomm, looking bored and not paying attention to the meeting.

"Hmph, ignoring the issues with her etiquette, anyway," Ollit stated judgmentally. "The point is that the Specialist title is not one that would be fit for any ordinary mercenaries."

"Ollit, for starters, I do recall you protesting Henrika's appointment when she started too," Anya retorted. "You came around on her though, I will remind you."

"Well, that was only because I questioned her motives," Ollit stammered, his face reddening in embarrassment from being called out. "Although, almost everyone on Antal knows her reputation as a master thief. Her skills were never in question. Here, I question not only these newcomers' motives, but also their credentials—making their appointments doubly dubious."

"Well, if you're looking for credentials, I'm assuming you've heard of the infamous Devil of Hivich by now?" Anya asked. "The one who single-handedly took down a quarter of the 14th regiment and who has been wreaking havoc for UAPA in the nation of Hivich. That's your territory, so I assume you must know about it."

"You're not telling me that's him?!" Ollit scoffed. "If so, why am I only just hearing about this now? Like you said, yourself, that's my jurisdiction!"

"That's true Ollit," Anya replied with a hint of exasperation. "However, you explicitly told me that my operations in Varith city and the marchlands were both my prerogative, and that you were too busy with your own operations, so you didn't want to hear any details from my side of things."

"Fine," Ollit relented in a slightly annoyed tone. "I guess I'll allow for that, but I will state that I have been skeptical about the rumors, in any case. I've suspected that this 'Devil of Hivich' was a hyperbolized UAPA boogeyman more than anything else. I'd like to know this man's background for starters, and maybe see a demonstration of his skill to show that he's not full of it."

In that moment, Aren disappeared from his seat, just as a gust of wind rushed along the conference room table where they were seated.

"What in the blazes?" Ollit called out, looking around frantically.

Ollit heard the sound of a blade being sheathed behind him and turned his head around to see Aren, just as the bottom half of Ollit's shirt fell down into a heap along his waist.

Ollit looked down in shock and saw that Aren had somehow cut his shirt horizontally on all sides around his waist in under a second, leaving him with essentially a crop top. The cut was clean and even all the way across, and more startlingly, Ollit did not feel a thing. The blade never so much as grazed his skin.

"H-how?" Ollit attempted to articulate.

Xander noticed, for the first time all meeting, the bored-looking woman in dark makeup, who Ollit had called Henrika, had put away her palmcomm and was sitting upright, watching intrigued at the events that were unfolding.

After putting away his sword, Aren bowed to Ollit. "Aren Sperosun, freelance mercenary, at your service."

"It may be helpful to mention that Aren here used to be a master of the Dehnovai clan before joining us," Anya pointed out. "He quit only right before coming to work for us, in fact. As you can see, he has some incredible skills when it comes to combat, utilizing a combination of battle magic and his own physical prowess. He also has a wealth of experience in stealth and tracking."

It took Ollit a few moments before he managed to pick up his jaw and compose himself.

"Right," Ollit acknowledged. "I'll admit that was… impressive. I suppose, then, that you'll tell us that this Kyara was also a former Dehnovai master? What skills does she have?"

In that instant, Ollit felt himself get knocked back. His heart jumped out of his chest as a volley of ten arrows pierced the sides of his crop top, pinning him to the chair he was sitting in.

Ollit was breathing frantically as adrenaline rushed through him, but like with Aren, he again realized that he was completely unharmed. The arrows were fine-tipped and had somehow pierced the edges of his clothing without so much as breaking any of his skin.

He looked over and saw Kyara standing across from him with her bow in hand, which she had already begun to put back away.

The woman with dark makeup, Henrika, giggled while looking at Ollit in his newly tailored crop top, pinned to his chair by the arrows.

"Well, no, admittedly, Kyara never had any affiliation with the Dehnovai," Anya responded to Ollit's comments. "However, you may know her by her other name, well known across this Ereva astro-region: Greivilder."

"She's one of the Arlodt Empire's infamous Weapons of War?" Ollit exclaimed in a combination of disbelief and alarm.

"Former, actually," Kyara responded a bit defensively, looking over to Aren. "I don't work for the Arlodt Empire anymore. I'm a mercenary now."

"Whatever her past, Kyara has a diverse set of skills, including a mastery of martial arts, marksmanship, reconnaissance, military tactics, stealth, tracking, and more," Anya endorsed. "I believe her and Aren would be excellent Specialists, both in charge of special operations and military strategy."

"Whatever, but I still don't know what these people have against my clothing," Ollit murmured angrily as the shock began to dissipate and he started attempting to pull arrows out of his shirt and chair.

Morgas began laughing and clapping her hands, applauding all she had seen and heard.

"Well, it seems you brought some rather interesting people to our organization, Anya," Morgas commended. "Well done. I think what we have seen here can attest to their skill, and if you can vouch for their character, that's enough for me. I've always trusted your judgment, Anya. Are there any objections?"

The entire room, including Ollit, was conspicuously silent.

"Very well then," Morgas announced. "I hereby appoint Xander Ardentes, Kyara Lex'hawa, and Aren Sperosun into the council of Oppori Qala under the title of Specialists, along with all associated privileges and responsibilities."

Aren, Kyara and Xander all stood and bowed to Morgas, as they had been told by Anya was customary in this situation to show appreciation and respect for the appointment.

"Thank you Morgas," Anya smiled. "I appreciate it."

"Just doing what I believe is best for Antal, as always," Morgas replied sincerely. "In any case, I think we've wasted more than enough time on preliminaries. Let's get this meeting started, shall we?"

Chapter 12

Aren was, in general, not a huge fan of meetings. While he hadn't experienced that many in his life, he found the ones he had attended were typically no better than his lectures at the Magi Academy, which often seemed to drag on forever, and left his mind wandering.

Although, there were some times that weren't as bad as others. For example, he found that he enjoyed meetings more when they were more engaging, paced well and full of intriguing content. But quite often, it felt like most meetings were frustratingly full of unnecessary fluff and could have been reasonably substituted with a few electronic messages.

Nevertheless, today he found himself actually excited to be a part of this particular meeting he was currently sitting in. That is because he knew that, in this meeting, Anya was planning to bring up a topic that had been on his mind since arriving on Antal—the matter of the "Restitution Program".

With the excitement from earlier over, everyone was now sitting quietly in their seats, with their eyes on Morgas, awaiting the start of the meeting.

"To start, we should introduce everyone to the new members," Morgas announced. "I'll begin with myself. I am Morgas

Yen, Chair of Oppori Qala. It is my job to oversee operations across all of Antal, with the help of my wonderful officers."

She then motioned to Anya. "You of course all know Anya Allister, our extraordinary Vice-Chair and Second-in-Command. It is her job to assist me in overseeing Oppori Qala operations, but she also often goes out of her way to personally lead her own operations across the planet wherever needed."

Morgas then motioned to the woman with the clipboard who had entered the room with her earlier. "Following Anya is our Head Administrator Taran Let, Third-in-Command, who is the true backbone of this organization."

Taran gave a friendly wave to the group.

"Next are our three generals," Morgas continued. "They are in charge of coordinating the resistance cells all across UAPA territory."

She pointed to a large, hulking, bearded man around 7' tall who was holding his hands gently in his lap. "First is General Argim Brunick. He commands our western resistance cells, which includes Marann, the nation we currently are residing in; Eser, the island nation further to the west; and finally, the southern half of Nolinth, which is the nation north of here, the seat of UAPA."

Morgas smiled at Argim. "Don't let this man's size fool you, he may actually be the sweetest member of Oppori Qala—although, that has never stopped him from getting the job done either."

"Hey y'all!" Argim greeted sweetly, as he smiled and waved to the group. "It's nice to meet you."

Despite Argim's friendly greeting, Xander could see why he was a general in the military. With his incredible size, giant muscles and rough appearance, including beard and tattoos, this did not appear to be a man to be trifled with.

Meanwhile, Aren, looking Argim over, felt surprised that this man was in the military at all, let alone a general. From the way that he moved and spoke, Aren got the impression that this man wouldn't hurt a fly. He would have sooner pegged him as a baker or a caretaker at an animal shelter than a general.

Morgas then motioned to Ollit, sitting next to Argim. Ollit was just pulling the final arrow out from his chair and shirt. "Next is General Ollit Krafts, who you've had the lovely opportunity to interact with plenty already. Ollit is in charge of the Eastern resistance cells, including the nation of Hivich—which I believe was where you had been working, Aren. He also is in charge of operations in Olan, the nation just north of it."

"Welcome," Ollit greeted them sternly as he pulled the last arrow out of his shirt and chair, adding it to the pile of arrows on the table in front of him. "Skepticism aside, I sincerely hope that you all do well in our organization."

His words sounded as much of a warning to them as they were well-wishes.

Next, Morgas pointed to the stern-looking woman with steel eyes, silver hair, and a rigid posture sitting at the end. This was the same woman who had spoken earlier in criticism of Anya bringing them to the meeting.

"And this is General Clodwyn Begue," Morgas introduced. "She coordinates the northern resistance cells in the nations of Chal, Rikis, and the northern half of Nolinth. She also has been behind some of the most decisive victories against UAPA out of anyone on this council."

"It's a pleasure to meet you all," Clodwyn greeted them in an austere tone. "I acknowledge that the group of you may be significant assets to our organization, but I would like to remind you that you will be closely observed over the next while. Please do not make any of us regret your appointment into this council."

"Finally, we have our three other Specialists who are currently here in attendance," Morgas explained.

She started by pointing to the older, bearded man who had commented on Xander's aurimancy earlier. "First is Specialist Elmenz Makiree, Oppori Qala's Master of Sorcery, and one of the greatest mages on Antal."

Elmenz gave a brief courtesy bow.

Morgas then motioned to a woman sitting next to Elmenz, in a baggy t-shirt and glasses, with messy, vibrant, purple and blue hair, looking like she just got out of bed. "Next is Specialist Orita Merne, our Master of Digital Infiltrations and Cyber Security."

"Sup?" Orita greeted, displaying three fingers to them in a friendly, youthful gesture.

Morgas then motioned to Henrika, who had gone back to focusing on her palmcomm. "And finally, this is Specialist Henrika Juliette. Henrika was formerly the most infamous thief on Antal, but some months ago she decided to join our cause and became our Master of Special Acquisitions and Sabotage."

Aren did a double take as Henrika disappeared from her chair after the introduction. Suddenly, he sensed something coming towards him from behind. He shot his hand out instantly, grabbing what he quickly realized was a slender wrist.

He turned around and saw Henrika smiling down at him. She appeared to have been reaching for a handshake. Although, her hand was currently stuck in place as Aren had a tight grip on her wrist.

"Well, hello there," Henrika gave him a sly smile. "It's nice to meet you, Aren. You have some pretty impressive reflexes."

"Thank you," Aren sat still, transfixed.

"Mind letting go of my wrist?" Henrika asked politely. "You have a rather strong grip."

"Oh, sorry about that" Aren quickly let go and withdrew his hand. "I'm not used to people being able to sneak up on me."

"Oh, I bet," Henrika giggled, pulling her hand back. "I'd only been here less than a second, truth be told."

Henrika lifted a small, dark object to her face, which she opened up and began studying intently.

"Oh, so that is your real name," Henrika mentioned curiously. "How interesting."

It suddenly dawned on Aren that she was holding his wallet in her hands, and she was reading off of his GDR photo ID.

He laughed out loud, impressed by both her skills and her audacity. "Took that with your left hand, while I was focused on the right, huh?"

"Ooo, he's a smart one," Henrika patted him on the head playfully. "I'd give you a cookie if I had one."

"Henrika!" Anya scolded. "These antics of yours are not appropriate."

"Oh, come on, Anya," Henrika laughed playfully, while placing her free hand on Aren's shoulder gently. "We're just playing around here. He doesn't mind—do you?"

She turned to him as she asked the question.

"Not at all," Aren responded cheerfully. "But if you don't mind, I'll be taking that back."

In that moment, the wallet flew from Henrika's hands and back into Aren's.

"Oh, you are full of surprises, aren't you?" Henrika grinned. "Well, I should be headed back to my seat. Hope you don't mind that I kept a little souvenir."

She flashed a few bills at him that she had slipped from his wallet. Before he could say a word, he watched as a shadow appeared in front of her, which she walked into, re-emerging from another shadow on the other side of the table, where she sat back in her seat.

"Thank you all for kindly welcoming us into your ranks," Aren expressed graciously. "Kyara and I may be mercenaries, but I can assure you, we plan to stay until UAPA has been defeated, and Hamish is brought to justice."

Kyara nodded. "I'm with Aren on that."

"Yes, I feel the same way," Xander agreed. "I mean, I'm not a mercenary, but Antal has long been a second home to me. If possible, I'd like to see UAPA taken down as well."

"Very well," Morgas announced. "Now that the introductions are over, let us get down to business."

At this point, the Head Administrator Taran got up and rolled over two holoprojectors from the corner of the room next to the table where they were sitting. She began pressing some buttons on both of them, getting them warmed up. Finally, she hit the call button on one of them.

"Now, as some of you already know, we have two very special guests joining us today," Morgas announced. "The first one, joining us now, is President Lodin Pleat, from the continental nation of Guun, currently the only neutral nation on Antal at the moment. Guun has been in talks about signing a non-aggression pact with

UAPA, but Lodin here is considering delaying the signing and possibly even joining the war effort on our side.

"The second guest, coming later, will be Chancellor Hans Frolick, the leader of the nation of Tarpoa, one of the three remaining nations embroiled in war against UAPA at the moment. He is quite busy, so he will only be joining us for part of our meeting later on. Frolick is not a stranger to any of us, as we often have worked with him and the other leaders of nations fighting UAPA, but his presence in this meeting tonight was a special request from Anya."

Just as she was finishing speaking, the holo-image of a broad-shouldered orren man in a suit sprang up from the projector.

"Hello, Morgas," Lodin responded appreciatively. "Did I hear correctly that Chancellor Frolick will be joining us later? That'll be nice. I don't think I've seen him since the last National Leaders Summit, back before UAPA put a stop to those."

"Hello President Lodin," Anya confirmed. "Yes, Frolick will be joining us later. He'll only be on the holocomm for a short while, but I'm sure he'll be glad to see you too."

"Thank you, Anya," Lodin nodded to her. "Anyway, I'll get straight to the point here. As Morgas already stated, I'm expected to sign a non-aggression pact tomorrow. UAPA has been pressuring us to formalize our neutrality for some time now. I've been holding them off for as long as I can, but the pressure is continuing to mount. My people are scared and a sizeable portion of them have fallen for UAPA propaganda."

"Your efforts at holding off are appreciated," Morgas said diplomatically. "Of course, we understand the political pressure you've been under."

Lodin nodded to her. "Thank you Morgas. I'll admit that part of me is not entirely against this signing though. My people's safety is a big priority of mine and war is not something I consider lightly. However, if what you people have told me about the slave camps is true, then I certainly won't be signing any such treaty with them. If you can provide enough compelling proof, I believe I could even convince the senate to commit to war. Although, I will admit, I am skeptical that a handful of recordings taken from a distance will be enough for them."

He cleared his throat before continuing. "And I have to be honest, if I can't get them to commit to war, I don't know how long I can avoid signing this pact. It is getting to the point where it has to be one or the other."

Anya couldn't help but feel a little annoyed at his speech. It was easy enough for him to talk about wanting to avoid war, living on an isolated and far-removed continental nation with strong defenses that UAPA has avoided completely so far. Most of the other nations of Antal have not had that luxury.

But she bit her tongue, knowing that calling him out here would not do her any good.

"Well then, I'm glad to inform you that, in four days from now, you will have all the proof you need and more to convince your senate," Anya announced. "I believe that should be long enough to delay the signing without your senate interfering."

"What do you mean?" President Lodin questioned. "I thought you only had the photos and recordings we spoke of earlier. And I thought those were going to be shared with me tonight—not in four days from now."

The rest of the officers all looked quizzically over to Anya as well, also unaware of what she was referring to.

"Of course, you'll get those tonight," Anya assured. "However, that will only be to start. We always knew you'd need more than that if you really wanted to prove to your senate of UAPA's horrific misdeeds, but we now have the means to guarantee that proof, if you can just delay signing the pact a little while longer."

Anya stood up as the others watched her. "I know that it's a bit sudden, and originally, this meeting was strictly to bring Lodin into the fold and deliver him some preliminary proof, but I have some news to share with you all."

"What is it?" Clodwyn inquired curiously. "Don't leave us all in suspense here."

President Lodin and the Oppori Qala officers were all listening intently, curious about what Anya had to share.

"Thanks to the efforts of Kyara here, we have discovered the location of the fourteenth and final slave camp," Anya announced. "The one we found mentioned in those hidden UAPA records that Henrika recovered for us, and the only one we had been unable to find up until now."

"This is amazing news!" Argim shouted cheerfully. "Fantastic work."

"Indeed," Ollit conceded. "Well done, I suppose."

Anya pulled out a data strip from her pocket. Aren recognized it as the one he had given to her back at the Silver Note Cabaret.

"Not only that," Anya continued. "But Aren has recovered officer credentials for one of the commanders working at the CNPF — that is, the Central Network Processing Facility. In other words, we now have means to access the facility that processes more than 80% of Antal's internet radio networks, currently owned and managed by UAPA."

"That is commendable," Clodwyn praised.

"Ok, yes, that is great and all," President Lodin acknowledged. "I'm glad you folks are making progress. But I am curious, what's the significance of that to what we're talking about now?"

"The significance is that we're going to raid the camps," Morgas announced excitedly, picking up from Anya after only just hearing the news for herself. "And furthermore, we're going to broadcast it to every network on the CNPF, so the world can know what UAPA has really been up to."

"Oh wow," Lodin interjected. "And you're already prepared to move so quickly after discovering this information? Four days seems like a very short period."

"Well, in truth, this is a plan we've had in the works for some months now," Anya explained. "We always planned to simultaneously take down all the camps and to broadcast it to the world. But we were only missing two things: the location of the last camp, and the means for infiltrating the extremely secure CNPF. Thanks to Aren and Kyara we now have both."

"This really is excellent news Anya," Morgas commended. "We'll certainly be getting to work on this right away. The four-day timeline should be very doable."

"I agree," Anya stated.

"Ok, but do we even have blueprints of the CNPF?" Ollit probed. "That's a very large and complex facility. Blueprints will be critical for a timely and effective operation. And even though that building is technically ancient, it's changed countless times with renovations, so any information we've had on it is completely outdated at this point—unless you managed to get recent blueprints that I am unaware of."

"I had tried to get blueprints," Aren responded. "Unfortunately, though, the records facility I infiltrated didn't have any. I had heard rumours that UAPA deleted all of their copies of the blueprints out of paranoia, and it seemed those rumours were true."

"Not to worry Aren," Anya reassured him. "That is actually related to the second guest we have coming tonight."

Taran, recognizing her cue, quickly went over to the second projector and turned it on. Suddenly, a tall, bald orren man appeared. He was wearing traditional, Antallian, ceremonial garb associated with the leaders of the Antallian nations.

"Please, everyone welcome Chancellor Hans Frolick, the leader of the proud nation of Tarpoa," Anya announced.

"Welcome Chancellor Frolick," President Lodin spoke up. "It's good to see you."

"You as well Lodin," Chancellor Frolick responded with a strained voice, looking around at the faces of everyone at the meeting. "And thank you for the introduction, Anya. Although, I hope you can make this quick. Like I told you before, I am quite busy these days, and I've already been waiting for a few minutes."

"I'm sorry that we're a little bit behind," Anya apologized. "I know you're very busy with the war lately. We'll try not to take too much more of your time."

"I appreciate that," Frolick stated anxiously. "Things have been brutal, you know. UAPA has been breaking more ground every day. I agreed to this call as a favour to you. I owe you a lot for everything you've done for my nation, but I simply cannot afford much time."

"That's very understandable, Chancellor," Anya acknowledged. "I'll cut right to the chase then. I brought you here to formally request the CNPF blueprints."

The Chancellor paused for a moment as he contemplated the request.

"I'm surprised you know about that," Chancellor Frolick commented. "I suppose you must have talked to one of the engineers or contractors, then?"

"Wait, really?" President Lodin questioned. "I'm curious why you would have them? The CNPF has never been a Tarpoan facility."

"I have no problem answering that," Chancellor Frolick responded. "As you are surely aware, us Tarpoans are highly renowned for our skills in architecture and engineering.

"While it was not made public, our Public Works department was responsible for the re-design of the CNPF for those massive renovations 15 years ago. Few people knew about this though, so I'm assuming Anya must have a source."

"Yes, you got me," Anya admitted. "I talked to one of the renovation contractors, who shared this information with me. I was hoping your government kept records of the updated blueprints."

"I must ask, why do you want them?" Frolick inquired. "What use does Oppori Qala have with such documents? Are you planning on launching an operation there?"

"I'll spare you the details, but to be frank, yes," Anya stated. "This will be a huge help in our fight against UAPA."

Frolick paused for a few moments, considering what she had to say. "Ok, well, I suppose I can get them for you. I'll be sending them through the usual encrypted channels. I need to be going now though."

"I understand," Anya stated. "Good luck fighting the good fight, Frolick. For love and freedom."

Frolick nodded at her and responded somberly. "For love and freedom."

Frolick's hologram promptly disappeared as he cut off the call.

"Well, it seems like you have all of your bases covered now," Lodin stated. "I'll be expecting the first recordings tonight. It won't be hard to hold the signing off for a few days until your big operation, but I warn you that I will not be able to wait much longer than that."

"Thank you, President Lodin," Morgas replied graciously. "We really appreciate your patience and willingness to work with us on this."

"And I appreciate your efforts as well," Lodin responded. "UAPA is an organization of tyrants and oppressors. It's well past time for the facts about them to come to light. Godspeed and good luck to you all."

With that, Lodin's holoprojection disappeared as he signed off.

"Well then," Morgas exclaimed. "It appears that we all have a lot of work to do over the next few days."

Chapter 13

Kyara was on the ground of the Dehnovai's Yahata Ring, gasping for breath, trying to collect herself after a particularly brutal sparring session.

"So, that's what? Four for you and four for me, now?" Aren remarked, also trying to catch his breath.

Kyara didn't process what he had said, as she was lost in thought.

"Kyara?" Aren called to her.

"Oh, sorry," Kyara responded, realizing what had just been said to her. "I think that's right."

Aren reached his hand out to her. She took it and allowed him to help her stand back up.

"You seem to be distracted today," Aren observed. "Is everything alright?"

"It's fine," Kyara asserted. "Nothing to worry about."

"Well, in that case, shall we go again?" He offered. "One last match to determine who's the winner for today?"

Although she had barely had a chance to catch her breath, she smiled up at him and nodded, signalling silently that she was raring to go again.

She took a few deep breaths to collect herself as she walked along the Yahata Ring towards her starting position.

Despite the fact that her and Aren had been friends for over a year and a half now, she had only first been allowed access into the Dehnovai dojo two months ago. Outsiders were only given conditional access to the dojo when they were named clan-friend with unanimous consent from all of the Dehnovai masters, and the grandmaster.

The title of clan-friend was not commonly given in the Dehnovai. Typically, the clan was distrusting of outsiders. Even spouses and family members were expected to vow into the clan as full kin-members in order to gain access to the dojo. On top of this, Kyara's particular case was even worse than usual, as her military connections made her more of a security risk to the Dehnovai than the typical outsider.

Nevertheless, at this point, every single Dehnovai master had owed Aren a personal favour. Calling in those favours, along with support from Gueri's testimony, who had worked alongside Aren and Kyara a few times, the masters agreed to allow it. As for Grandmaster Hallamaine, she took a bit more convincing. However, she always had a soft spot for Aren and eventually caved as well.

It had taken a couple months of pleading their case all-in-all, but afterwards, Kyara was finally named clan-friend, giving her access to the dojo as long as she remained under Aren's supervision.

Aren and Kyara took their opposite positions across the ring. Kyara gripped her bow tightly. Attached to her waist was a quiver filled with blunt, soft-tipped arrows she used for training.

Aren stood on the other side, holding a wooden training sword in both hands.

There was a tension in the air as they both gripped tightly onto their weapons, mentally preparing themselves for the coming bout. Kyara's breathing had slowed back down, and she could feel her heart rate steadying.

Then, suddenly, Kyara drew five arrows from her quiver and fired each in rapid succession at Aren.

Aren quickly brought the wooden blade up and deflected all five of them. He then lunged at Kyara at top speed.

Just as he came into range, Kyara kicked some dirt into his eyes and then pulled out twin, wooden training daggers, striking at Aren with both at once. Even blinded, Aren somehow managed to sweep his sword to deflect both daggers.

Kyara pulled back and then attacked again, and then again. The two of them quickly became trapped in a flurry of feints, attempted strikes and blocks as they each tried to gain the upper hand.

This was a non-magic training day for them. Under these conditions, the two of them often found each other as a near even match in sparring, with a slight advantage to Kyara. However, with magic, Aren was always hands down the winner.

It wasn't that Kyara had no magical skills. She herself was a practitioner of Ineyem, one of the most effective forms of enhancement magic that increases the strength, speed, and durability of those who cast it. Ineyem is categorized as a *simple magical art*, not because it is easy to use, but because it does not require complex energy interactions in order to cast and control.

One of the biggest defining features of simple magical arts, like Ineyem, is that they do not require any incantations to cast like the better known *complex magical arts* do. Simple magical arts manipulate life energy using only the mind, which allows them to, in turn, impact their environment in various ways.

However, this was often not easy. Ineyem, in particular, required intense and continuous focus to cast, and had a high life energy drain. This made Ineyem magic very taxing and especially difficult to maintain in battle. Most who attempted learning the art for combat tended to quickly abandon it when they would come to realize how difficult it was. However, those who did master the art found themselves with a significant combat advantage as a result. At her current abilities, Kyara could more than triple her already impressive natural strength, double her natural agility, and give herself a significant protective boost using the art.

Nevertheless, despite being a master of Ineyem, Kyara's magic was no match for Aren's. Aren had not only mastered Ineyem himself, but also several other strange and powerful magical arts that Kyara had little-to-no familiarity with. Overall, he was clearly a far more experienced and powerful magic user than her, which gave him a huge upper hand whenever they allowed magic use in their sparring sessions.

As they were fighting, it was clear that both of them were starting to lose a bit of steam. Both of them had a full workout before sparring that day, and they had each been giving it their all in every match against each other. The fatigue from it all was finally starting to get to them.

However, Kyara was determined. She kept going for strike after strike, moving in for the kill. She slashed with both daggers horizontally. Aren blocked vertically with his blade, and she saw the opportunity that she had been waiting for. While their wooden blades were locked, she kicked directly upwards, connecting her foot with Aren's jaw.

From the successful upward kick, she transitioned into a backwards flip, drawing her bow again as she did so. When she landed back on her feet, she immediately loosed an arrow that hit Aren directly in the stomach. The arrow's soft and flat tip could not penetrate his skin or clothing, but the powerful force of the arrow being launched from the 280-pound compound bow knocked him flat on his back.

"Oh my gods," Aren sputtered, clutching his stomach. "You got me, damn."

After he had a moment to recover, Kyara reached out her hand to him to help him up. He took her hand, and she quickly pulled him up onto his feet.

At this point, even in Halos' immense gravity, both of them had the astounding physical strength to the point where getting up from being knocked on their back, even while fatigued, was remarkably easy without any help. Doing so was an act comparable in difficulty to just lifting up one's own arm by a person with the average physique. However, the helping hand they gave each other was a courtesy that both of them simply felt good about offering and being offered.

"I guess that makes you the winner for today," Aren announced cheerfully. "Come, let's head to my quarters. There's this new drink I recently discovered—it's a special kind of sweet milk. I have a few bottles waiting for us in my mini-fridge. You have got to try it."

Kyara followed silently behind him as they headed to his room. After they entered, Aren turned to her and saw her with a sad expression.

"Why do you look upset?" Aren questioned. "You won today. You should feel proud. You know, those moves of yours are really impressive. You've got to teach me some of your martial arts at some point."

"I only won because we didn't allow magic today," Kyara spoke candidly with just a hint of frustration. "I know I don't stand a chance against you when magic is involved."

"Perhaps," Aren conceded, opening up his mini-fridge and grabbing two glass bottles filled with white liquid. "But we all have our strengths. I mean, you are a far better sharp shooter than me; I can't come close to your speed or accuracy with a bow or rifle."

He paused in thought before continuing. "You also are better when it comes to stealth; and on top of all of that, you're the better strategist."

"I don't know about that last one," Kyara contended. "You're not a bad strategist yourself."

"Maybe so, but I think we both know that you're better," Aren responded. "That ambush you planned back at the Chiev job we worked together? Absolutely brilliant. The way you used the enemy's scanning systems against them was really impressive. I wouldn't have thought of something like that."

Kyara thought back to the job. It was one of several that Aren and Kyara had worked on together since they had met. Under ordinary circumstances, working jobs together might not have been possible, considering they had such different employers. However, the two of them had caught quite a liking for each other after meeting, and actively sought out ways to spend more time together, despite their busy work schedules. After some thinking, Aren had suggested to Kyara that she request jobs hunting down the Arlodt Empire's enemies with posted bounties. This would allow her the option of coordinating with bounty hunters like Aren.

When Kyara had first started working for the Empire, she did not have the right to make any such requests for the type of jobs she wanted to work—especially considering she was a prisoner working off her sentence in the Imperial Military. However, over the years, she had earned leeway in her position through her many successful missions—especially after becoming recognized as one of the empire's eight Weapons of War. She therefore made the request to her handler, the 27th Prince Haros vul Arlodt, who, to Kyara's delight, granted it.

As for Aren, as a consecrated warrior of the Dehnovai, he had the right to choose his own jobs, so long as these jobs met certain criteria, and they were run by Grandmaster Hallamaine first. Bounties posted by the Arlodt Empire almost always met these criteria and paid very well, so Hallamaine was happy to give her blessing to Aren for each of these contracts. Aren was also personally happy that the Arlodt Empire kept their assassination jobs in-house. This meant that they exclusively posted "Alive" or "Dead or Alive" jobs for bounty hunters, allowing him to continue avoiding assassination contracts as he worked with Kyara.

"Chiev was an interesting job," Kyara noted. "I suppose when you put it that way, perhaps I may have a teensy edge in strategy."

"So modest, as always," Aren laughed.

"I don't know about modesty," Kyara dismissed. "I just like to focus on where I could improve. I could always be doing better, you know."

Aren handed her the sweet milk with one hand and placed his hand on her shoulder gently for a moment with the other as he looked into her eyes empathetically.

Before meeting Aren, Kyara had not been used to physical affection. In fact, she found she did not enjoy it from the few who had attempted it with her. However, with Aren, it somehow felt different. Even something as simple as putting his hand on her shoulder often made her feel warm and safe, as it did now.

"I get that Kyara" Aren empathized. "I often feel the same way. Just try to remember, you are not only your weaknesses, but your strengths too."

"I mean—" Kyara stammered, trying to find the words to respond. "But don't you think we should be focused on improving ourselves?"

"Of course, I do, Kyara," Aren affirmed. "I agree completely, working towards improvement is important. But you can't forget, there's plenty of value to who you are now. I mean, you are an incredible individual and one of the most talented warriors I've ever met. You have so much to be proud of."

"You really think so?" Kyara queried hesitantly. "I mean, you're surrounded by Dehnovai masters here."

"Absolutely, and you'd hold your own against any of them," Aren assured. "But honestly, even without your talent, it wouldn't make a difference. I truly believe that everyone across the galaxy and beyond has innate value."

"What do you mean?" Kyara questioned.

"Well, I just don't think we always have to be the best at everything we do to feel good about ourselves, who we are, and what we've accomplished, no matter how small," Aren expounded. "You are valuable Kyara, not only because of your skills or accomplishments, but also simply your personhood."

Kyara stood silent for a moment. She was at a loss for words. She wasn't used to anyone saying such things in her life. Prince Haros had been nice enough to her whenever she successfully completed a mission. However, whenever he spoke of her performance, it was almost exclusively about what she could have done better. And god forbid, the few times she ever did fail any mission—things were far worse then.

"T-thank you," Kyara blushed. "I appreciate that."

"Any time, Kyara," Aren smiled at her. "I really mean it."

The two of them removed the caps from their bottles. Kyara curiously sloshed the milk around in the glass container as she looked down at it. When she looked back up, she saw as Aren chugged half of his bottle like it was nothing.

Kyara brought her own bottle slowly to her mouth. She took a small sip at first. Her initial impression was how creamy and rich the drink was. It was a pleasant taste. She tipped the bottle more, drinking a few gulps. As she continued drinking, she began to notice more depth to the flavour, including an intriguing tanginess that gave the drink an extra kick.

"Wow, this is good," Kyara exclaimed excitedly.

"I told you, didn't I?" Aren smiled enthusiastically.

As Aren looked at Kyara, he noticed her looking down again, like she was deep in thought about something.

"What's on your mind, Kyara?" Aren asked. "Are you still worried about the magic thing?"

"No, no," Kyara assured. "It's not that."

"Well, what is it, then?" Aren questioned. "You've been distracted a lot lately, like you've been lost in thought. You know you can always share anything with me, if you want."

"Is it that obvious?" Kyara asked. "I suppose I have been doing a little thinking—about life and such."

"Would you like to talk about it?" Aren asked with a compassionate tone.

"I just—honestly, I sometimes just don't know," Kyara expressed. "For years now, the Imperial Military has been my entire life. I had always felt that the best I could hope from the future is to continue to work hard, bringing honor to the Arlodt Empire, and making my superiors proud."

She took a deep breath before continuing. "But since I've been with you, I've begun to question if maybe there's more for me. You've shown me music, games, holo-plays, sweets—all kinds of things I never felt I had time for or even the right to indulge in. And then, you follow it up by praising me, and telling me I'm allowed to feel pride and self-worth, along with other things that no one has said to me before."

She looked up into Aren's eyes. "Honestly, this past year and a bit with you, it has been like experiencing an all-new galaxy, one that I never realized existed. I want to experience more of it, but I've started to realize that I can't—not while I'm still a part of the Imperial Military."

"I understand Kyara," Aren acknowledged sympathetically. "I'm glad that I've been able to help show you a different side of Auros. It saddens me that you've gone through your life having seen so little of it."

He looked down at the bottle in his hands contemplatively. "In any case, I can relate to no longer feeling like you fit in anymore. In all honesty, I'm not sure I feel at home with the Dehnovai any longer."

"Really?" Kyara responded. "I had no idea you were feeling that way."

"It seems we both have had some things we've been keeping to ourselves," Aren commented. "But we can talk more about that another time. I have to ask, Kyara… Have you considered leaving the empire?"

"It was never a thought that used to cross my mind," Kyara replied. "Prince Haros has always told me about how I'd be receiving a promotion and things would get better for me as soon as my sentence was over. He always just assumed I'd voluntarily sign up for another 5 years. To be honest, until recently, I had been assuming the same."

"I can understand that," Aren sympathized. "As you said yourself, that military has been your entire life for some time now."

"That is true," Kyara agreed. "However, I'm now thinking I might actually leave when my sentence ends next year."

"Wow," Aren voiced excitedly. "That's big news, Kyara, but also really awesome. I say, if that's how you feel, you should definitely go for it."

"Thank you, Aren," Kyara smiled at him before looking down again in thought. "The problem is that I just don't know what I want to do instead. I had never considered life outside of the military before."

She was silent for a moment before looking up at Aren quizzically. "You know, we've never really talked about it, but I'm very curious. What do you have planned for your future, Aren? Do you have any ambitions or goals you're working towards outside of the Dehnovai?"

Aren paused for a moment as if he was caught off guard by the question.

"I will say, as much as I don't really talk about it, this is something I've put a lot of thought into in recent years," Aren began. "To be honest, there's part of me that doesn't like fighting and would like to do something else. However, the truth is, I've seen too much to stop. My experience has shown me that there are a great many evils in the galaxy, some lurking in the shadows and some out in the open, but all looking to cause harm."

Kyara listened intently as he spoke.

"I just don't feel it is within me to turn a blind eye to these evils," Aren continued. "There are too many out there who are suffering. Conversely, there are those with strength and power, abusing what they have to the anguish of others. I want to stand up against these people who abuse their strength and to protect those who are vulnerable. That is my biggest ambition in life."

"I can't say that I'm surprised, to be honest," Kyara noted. "You've always prioritized protecting people first and foremost."

"I've certainly tried," Aren replied.

"I appreciate you sharing, Aren," Kyara said gratefully. "That gives me something to think about. But I do wonder—standing up for the vulnerable—that's just so broad. Do you have any more specific plans?"

"Hmmm, well, if I'm going to get into that, there's something I think I should show you first," Aren stated, reaching into his desk drawer and pulling out a red-jeweled brooch. "Something I would say has been long overdue to be shared…"

Chapter 14

Kyara looked around herself, amazed at her surroundings.

One moment, she had been in Aren's quarters, and the next she been teleported to some strange library. Looking around, she could see shelves filled with books and data tablets covering the walls, while beautiful antique furniture and decor adorned the great room.

"Where are we?" She asked in wonder.

"This is a pocket dimension," Aren answered. "One that I've never actually shown anyone else before."

"A pocket dimension?" Kyara responded, mystified. "I've heard of them before, but I didn't know they really existed."

"That's understandable, considering how rare they are," Aren explained. "Dimensional magic is among the most advanced and mysterious of magical arts in the galaxy. Creating a pocket dimension is a fairly incredible feat only accomplishable by few. Even just accessing one requires pretty advanced capabilities. Well, unless you have a portal key."

"Huh, so this is a pocket dimension," Kyara commented aloud. "I suppose that explains the lighter gravity. On Halos, I weigh nearly 400 pounds. Here, I'm feeling like maybe 250. Although, in

Galactic Standard, I'm only 150, so this still must be the gravity of a relatively large planet."

"Indeed, it is," Aren corroborated. "Interestingly, I don't think this level of gravity is an accident either. Masters of Aspat Recti, that is, Dimensional Magic, can be capable of altering gravity and other laws of physics within pocket dimensions. I was curious, so I checked, and it turns out that the gravity here matches perfectly with a particular planet…"

"Oh?" Kyara questioned. "And which planet is that?"

"Dracosia," Aren responded candidly.

Kyara was taken aback.

"Dracosia?" She exclaimed. "As in your former home world? The one that was destroyed?"

"Yes, that's exactly right," Aren confirmed.

Kyara again, looked around the room in wonder. "What is this place, really?"

"Well, I don't know what its actual name is or if it even has one," Aren explained. "But I've come to refer to it as 'the Dracosian Archive.' This place is the last remaining vestige of the knowledge and culture of the world I came from."

"That's incredible!" Kyara declared. "I had no idea such a place existed… Not that I know much about Dracosia, but I was under the impression that most of everything had been eradicated."

"Most of it had been," Aren nodded. "However, this place managed to save a fair amount."

Kyara could see that the statement was not unfounded. This room was huge, likely around 2000 square feet, and two stories tall.

And the shelves here ran across all of the walls, spanning from floor to ceiling, all packed with books and data tablets.

"Since we're here, I think it'd be a good time to share a bit about one of the magical arts that I use," Aren announced. "Of course, I've told you about a few in the past, like Mivana, which was one of the primary arts I learned from the Magi Academy, and Fuinshai, which was one of the main arts taught to me by the Dehnovai."

"Yes, I remember," Kyara confirmed. "Although, I've been most curious about the ones you haven't mentioned. There are some powerful spells you use regularly that don't seem to be from any of the arts you've told me about."

"Yes, sorry for all the mystery," Aren replied, scratching the back of his head sheepishly. "It's not exactly a secret, but I find it can sometimes be difficult to explain. The truth is, that last magical art I haven't told you about is called Dracanis, which is the legendary magical art form developed by the Dracosians."

"Dracosian magic?!" Kyara exclaimed in surprise. "Now that is something I know I've been told had been lost in that terrible tragedy."

She looked around in wonder at the library surrounding her. "So, I guess you're telling me this place managed to preserve that magical art somehow?"

"Exactly," Aren confirmed. "It was here that I found copies of the legendary Dragon Scrolls—likely the only ones remaining in the entire galaxy. It was thanks to those scrolls that I was able to learn that magic."

"That makes so much sense," Kyara remarked. "I had always heard that Dracosian combat magic was really something. So, I suppose that would include that powerful fire magic you use, huh?"

"Yes, that is correct," Aren nodded. "Most of the combat magic in Dracanis involves the manipulation of various natural forms of energy. The fire-magic I use is just one of several types that it teaches. The wind pressure I use to fortify my sword sometimes is another. That latter spell is known as 'Black Dragon's Claw.'"

"Ah yes, I've seen you cut through some pretty tough metals with that technique," Kyara recalled, thinking back to the large, steel turrets he took out when they first met. "It's certainly very impressive."

"Thank you," Aren said appreciatively. "It can really come in handy sometimes."

"No kidding," Kyara replied. "So, does Dracanis include any non-combat spells?"

"Yes, actually, Dracanis has many other spells, including some healing, and some involved in the protection and restoration of nature," Aren explained. "Dracosians may be known in the galaxy for their strength, but their military and combat techniques were mainly just for self defense. In truth, Dracosian culture had a greater focus on nature and the arts."

"It sounds like it was a really interesting world," Kyara remarked. "I'm very sorry that it got destroyed."

"I am as well," Aren lamented. "But I am happy that this place was saved, at the very minimum."

Kyara nodded. She walked along the shelves, scanning over the books curiously. The collection here was awe-inspiring. She had had just one childhood novel that she loved to read before joining the Arlodt Empire, but since then, her only real reading material had been military manuals, supplemental training packets, and a handful of encyclopedias.

"So, besides the Dragon Scrolls, what other kind of books are kept here?" Kyara asked.

"Basically, every kind," Aren responded. "There are books on astronomy, on medicinal plants, on ancient farming techniques, on the mechanics of hyperstate drives, and far, far more. There's even a fairly vast fiction section. Of course, the data tablets here hold far more information than the books, but I always found something satisfying about reading through a physical book with real parchment. I'm glad this library includes both."

Kyara pulled a book off of a shelf that caught her eye. It was titled *Empires, Republics and Alliances Across the Stars: A Political History of the Auros Galaxy*. There was a beautiful, artistic depiction of Auros on the front cover.

Kyara always found it mesmerizing to look at depictions of the galaxy. The idea that she was such a tiny speck within such an unbelievably enormous collection of stars, planets, nebulae, and more was both awe-inspiring and humbling.

"Come, follow me," Aren instructed. "It's time I showed you the reason why I brought you here."

"Ok," Kyara assented.

She was very curious what it was that he could possibly want to show her.

Aren led her over to an oaken doorway. As they walked through the door, Kyara was surprised to see a very long stretch of hallway before her, with a full series of doors on both sides.

"How big is this place?" Kyara asked, intrigued.

"Well, including the main library, I've counted a total of 32 rooms," Aren explained. "These include four hallways, a lounge, a training room, a utilities room, a study, six bathrooms, a kitchen, a dining room, a storage room, a display room, ten bedrooms, and two conference rooms. Altogether, I'd estimate the building at somewhere around 14,000 square feet."

"Wow, that's bigger than I would have expected." Kyara replied. "It's almost like a palace. I bet this place would make an excellent base of operations."

"Absolutely," Aren agreed. "The facilities here are quite handy, and it's a good size for any building, let alone one contained in a pocket dimension."

Kyara continued looking around her. It was strange to think that the entire building they were standing in was contained in another dimension—a plane of reality separate from the universe that she knew.

"Also, in case you were wondering," Aren added. "I've checked, and the pocket dimension doesn't go any further than the boundaries of the building. In other words, these rooms include everything contained within this dimension."

"Really?" Kyara responded. "How does fresh air get in here?"

"I actually had been curious about that too," Aren noted. "I checked it out, and the whole building is equipped with a life support system similar to space ships. To keep a fresh supply of oxygen, there's an air recycler hooked up to the ventilation systems. Those systems, along with the rest of the building, run on special hybrid-nuclear batteries. There's enough energy to keep this place running for thousands of years."

"Interesting," Kyara remarked. "I suppose the creators really thought of everything. Speaking of, I am very curious—who was it that actually built this place?"

Aren stopped walking and turned to a door on his right. "That's part of what I was hoping to show you."

Aren opened the door and led Kyara into what appeared to be a conference room. In the center of the room stood a large table that was surrounded by chairs. On top of the table was a holo-projector.

"Sorry to lead you all this way," Aren apologized. "This was one of the few rooms in the building with a working holo-projector."

"It's no problem," Kyara assured him. "So, you wanted to show me a holo-projection then?"

"Yes," Aren smiled, before adding somewhat sarcastically. "I suppose you figured it out."

"Indeed," Kyara responded in a teasing tone. "I have some excellent observational skills, I'll have you know."

"Oh, I know," Aren laughed.

It was a rare thing to hear sarcasm from Kyara, and he always appreciated the few times he got to hear it.

Kyara watched curiously as Aren walked over to the holo-projector and pulled out a data card from his pocket.

"So, I discovered this place for the first time about two and a half years ago now," Aren explained. "It was the same day I was promoted to Warrior with the Dehnovai—which also happened to be my sixteenth birthday. It was a complete and total accident the first time I came here."

"How did you come into a pocket dimension by accident?" Kyara inquired.

Aren pulled out his brooch and handed it to her. She took some time to study it closely. It was a remarkably beautiful and ornate design. The scarlet gemstone was especially enchanting, but the patterned gold and silver framework surrounding it was also full of gorgeous, intricate detail. Together, the precious metal surroundings and ruby centrepiece made for sublime complements to one another.

Kyara moved the brooch into the light. This caused the jewel to glimmer as if a fire was crackling deep inside of the gemstone.

"This brooch was the last thing that had been given to me by my mother before I was sent away from Dracosia as a young child," Aren recounted. "I had no idea at first, but it turned out that it was a portal key this entire time. On my sixteenth birthday, I had spontaneously decided to sing an old Dracosian lullaby called *The Emerald Caves*. My mother used to sing me that lullaby and I had fond memories attached to it. To my surprise, the lullaby turned out to be the activation phrase for the portal key, which sent me straight here."

"That's really interesting," Kyara responded. "I didn't hear you sing the lullaby to activate it when we came here, though."

"Yes, well, after activating once, the brooch has since recognized my energy, and allowed me to activate it by simply making direct contact with the jewel against my skin for about fifteen or so seconds," Aren expounded. "It's a little more convenient than having to recite a full lullaby every time, I'll say that much."

"That makes sense," Kyara acknowledged, handing the brooch back to Aren who placed it back in his pocket. "So, if your mother gave you that brooch, I'm assuming she must have been involved in making this place then?"

"That is correct," Aren asserted. "I'm sure creating this archive took a lot of people. I don't know who most of the people involved were, but my mother was definitely amongst them."

Aren fiddled around with a few buttons on the holo-projector. It quickly turned on, revealing a menu, which Aren navigated through. After pressing a couple more buttons, a tall woman in an elegant gold and white dress with a warm smile appeared above the projector. There were remarkable similarities in some of her facial features to Aren.

"Is that—" Kyara began to ask.

"Yes," Aren confirmed. "That is, or rather was, my mother. The former High Sorceress of Dracosia, Aurielis Sperosun."

Kyara looked quietly up at the figure as Aurielis started to speak.

"My dear Aren," Aurielis spoke in gentle tones. "Before anything else, I need to say that I am sorry to you. I am sorry I sent you away. I am sorry that I could not come with you, and if things turned out the way I suspect, I am sorry for the most terrible loss you have had to endure. I cannot imagine what you must have gone through."

Kyara turned to Aren and could see the sadness in his eyes. She walked closer to him and put her arm around his back, resting her hand on the side of his shoulder as they watched together.

"I'm sure you have many questions," Aurielis continued. "Unfortunately, I will not be able to answer all of them. However, I left this message in the hopes that perhaps I could help illuminate things just a little."

Aurielis spoke with a voice that was soft and warm, yet held a subtle power behind it, like someone who was used to speaking as a figure of authority.

"First of all, I am sure you are wondering where you are right now," Aurielis asserted. "This is a place that I created with the help of others in order to preserve parts of our knowledge and culture. Not only is it a complete archive, full of an abundance of valuable data, books and artifacts, but it is also a fully equipped facility for living, studying and training. The intention was always to leave this place to you, my child. I am trusting you to take good care of it, and I hope that it will serve you well.

"Now, undoubtedly, you will have many questions about Dracosia, and what happened to it. I'm sure that the media is likely saying that anti-GDR terrorists were behind what happened. I know this because we have already seen the false seeds planted by our enemies to make it look as if that's what occurred.

"I'm going to tell you right now, that isn't who is behind it. Although we are still investigating, we have reason to believe the group conspiring to end our world is the Kingdom of the Red Sun, Galvara."

Kyara's eyes widened at hearing Galvara brought up. That was not a name she expected to hear.

There was very little known about the Galvarans, but the rumours were that they went from planet to planet, wreaking havoc, destroying entire governments and wiping out full militaries with them. Most believed the Red Sun Kingdom to be completely made up—nothing more than an excuse used to explain away the destruction that planets caused to themselves during their own internal wars.

However, her handler, Prince Haros had once claimed to her that they were real and warned her to stay far away. In fact, she had never heard the prince speak in such a grim manner before. It had left a lasting impression on her that led her to decide to follow the advice to the best of her ability.

"I'm sure you've heard that Galvara is a myth," Aurielis acknowledged. "However, some of our operatives discovered some years ago now that that is not the case. We have been investigating and have learned that they have been around for decades, working in the shadows across the galaxy, conspiring with governments and criminal syndicates alike."

Aurielis took a deep breath and looked down somberly for a moment before looking back up.

"These people… I truly think that they believe that what they're doing is right," Aurielis explained. "But it's so far from it. Countless people have been hurt, and recently, we've gained intel that Dracosia is expected to be next, in a way that may be worse than anything they have done before.

"We hope to stop them, but honestly, I'm not sure that we can, which is why we've also been considering another alternative. I won't get into too many details as doing so may lead you into a fruitless search, but I will mention that we are working on something that might save all of Dracosia. It's risky, but even if it does work, I am saddened to say that you will still never see any of us again. Either way, I ask that you move on, and please do not come looking for us. One way or another, unless we can somehow stop the attack, our time in Auros will be over—that much is assured."

Kyara rubbed her hand on Aren's shoulder. She wasn't always in tune with the emotions of others, but even she knew that hearing this must have been hard for Aren, no matter how many times he may have heard it before.

"However, because our plan is risky, we decided that it would be best to leave you behind," Aurielis explained. "Thus, we decided to leave you in the care of your teacher, Jadyn. If you are seeing this, I trust that it is because he felt that it was finally time and instructed you on how to unlock the portal key.

"Aren, I humbly request that you do not be cross with Jadyn for not having shared this information with you earlier. In truth, he was not aware of most of it. For his safety and yours, we had to keep him in the dark on a great many things. However, he is one of the most wise and knowledgeable Dracosians that I know. There is no one I trust more to care for you."

Kyara recognized the name Jadyn, and quickly understood why Aren had to find out about this portal key on his own.

Aren had told Kyara all about Jadyn, his old teacher who had brought him from Dracosia to Ohira as a child. Unfortunately, Aren also mentioned that Jadyn had died shortly after their arrival to Ohira. This would explain why Jadyn never would have been able to tell Aren about the portal key, probably along with a lot of other things he would have been expected to teach and share with Aren over the years he was supposed to have raised him.

"Again, I cannot say enough how sorry I am that I left you like this Aren," Aurielis apologized. "I couldn't bear to have you go through the risks of staying here. I'm still holding out hope that we can either stop the attack or that our alternative solution works out, but I know that there is every chance things can go wrong."

Aurielis sighed somberly before continuing. "I know it isn't much but attached to this data card are photos of our family and a few letters, some written by me and some by your father. I hope you can forgive me, and that you lead a wonderful life. Goodbye Aren."

With that, the holo-recording suddenly ended, and the image of Aurielis disappeared. Kyara looked at Aren and could see a single tear rolling down his cheek.

"I'm so sorry Aren," Kyara empathized. "That must have been hard to watch."

"Well, it's easier than it was the first time," Aren expressed, wiping the tear. "I mean, I have come to terms with it at this point, at least."

He walked to the holo-projector and removed the data card before turning over to her.

"Anyway, you're probably wondering why I decided to show you this now," Aren stated. "The reason is because you asked me about my goals—my plans and ambitions for the future outside of the Dehnovai, and in truth, it all relates to what you just heard."

"Oh?" Kyara voiced. "Please, tell me more."

"Ok, well first, I should tell you that I already spent some time investigating the destruction of Dracosia," Aren explained. "You may have noticed that my mother mentioned in her message that she was working on a way to save the people of the planet. No bodies had ever been found after Dracosia's destruction, so I was very curious if they somehow escaped, but unfortunately, my investigation only led to a dead end."

"I'm sorry Aren," Kyara consoled. "I did notice she seemed to imply they might have some unusual solution, so maybe they're still out there somewhere?"

"Maybe," Aren agreed solemnly. "But in any case, with that investigation at a standstill, I have instead turned my focus towards justice. I've therefore been looking into Galvara, the secret nation my mother cited behind the destruction of my home world."

Kyara felt a pit in her stomach as Aren brought Galvara up. Part of her had been hoping it wouldn't come back up after the recording.

"What did you find out about them?" Kyara asked hesitantly.

"Well, through some investigating, I've confirmed they are real," Aren responded. "And despite the mystery surrounding them, they are undoubtedly behind an immense amount of death and destruction across the galaxy."

"Yes," Kyara responded in a cautious tone. "To be honest, I've heard some disturbing things about them in the Imperial Military myself. But even knowing that they're real, you must understand that they're not a group to be trifled with. Supposedly, they're an entire nation of warlocks and killers, led by a man rejected by death itself. These people have led entire planets to ruin and managed to stay hidden from the public eye throughout it all."

"So, I've heard," Aren responded assuredly.

"I know it's hard, but I think it'd be best to leave them alone," Kyara stated with a mild anxiety behind her voice. "However, knowing you... Well, I'll just ask; what exactly are your plans here?"

Aren looked into Kyara's eyes with an intense resolve.

"My plan is to put an end to the Red Sun Kingdom... I'm going to take down Galvara."

Chapter 15

There was a heavy tension in the air as Xander made his way through Grimveil Forest alongside Anya, Kyara, Morgas, and more than 500 Oppori Qala operatives and officers.

Xander felt that it was something of a miracle that they managed to get so many across the forest's security border undetected. To accomplish this, they had to create a power surge across a full section of UAPA's security fencing, designed to look like a naturally-occurring incident.

However, as the engineers of Oppori Qala had calculated, this barely gave them the time to get even this many across, which unfortunately, was a relatively small number against the looming threat ahead of them. The forces at the Grimveil Slave Camp outnumbered them nearly four-to-one.

Nevertheless, the plus side of Oppori Qala's low numbers was that fewer operatives here could mean more in other parts of the operation. There was a total of fourteen camps that Oppori Qala would be raiding tonight on top of the concurrent operation at the CNPF, so every agent counted.

Furthermore, they weren't without a plan here. Kyara had come up with something to help even out the odds. She had pointed out there was the possibility of things going wrong, but Morgas loved it, and Xander felt it was pretty solid as well.

Logically speaking, it sounded like everything should work perfectly. But then, why did he feel so uneasy?

Xander took a big gulp as he continued the trek through the wood.

Perhaps it was that he still didn't like knowing how outnumbered they were, or maybe it was the foreboding atmosphere of the dark forest. But whatever it was, something was causing a growing pit in Xander's stomach as they got closer to their destination.

Nevertheless, he was still wholly determined. Shortly before this operation began, he had gotten some hopeful news. He looked down at the photo Anya had given him yesterday and felt a surge of motivation as he clutched to it in his hand.

"Don't worry," Anya reassured him, patting him on the back as he gripped the photo. "If he is there, we're definitely going to save him, alright?"

"Thank you," Xander replied appreciatively.

He looked down at the photo. It was hard to say whether or not the person in this photograph was truly Matlex. It was a rough side profile taken from a distance with mediocre night-vision tech. It didn't help that, if it was Matlex, he clearly was looking different than usual, having lost some weight, and looking very dishevelled, in contrast to his usual clean and well-groomed appearance. Xander couldn't be certain, but he felt confident there was a good chance it was him.

"You know, I honestly can't decide whether I want it to be him or not," Xander admitted. "On the one hand, if he truly has been captured, of course I hope that he is there, so that we can save him tonight.

"But on the other hand, part of me wishes that I'm just wrong altogether. It would just be so much nicer to think that he took his trip early on some unregistered freight, and that he lost his wristcomm along the way and couldn't get in touch with me. I just hate to think that he's been living in that hell for months now."

"I understand," Anya sympathized. "I have friends in these camps myself. We're going to do everything we can to save everyone tonight. I'm sure that things will turn out ok in the end. Just have a little faith."

"I'll try my best," Xander replied sincerely. He hesitated for a moment before adding. "By the way, I'm grateful that you got the word out so quickly. It's amazing that your operatives managed to get this photograph this fast, even if it isn't a positive ID."

"It was nothing," Anya replied. "They had to scope out the camp anyway. And to be honest, they were just as shocked. To think there's even a chance that Matlex might be in the Grimveil camp… It's not something any of us expected."

Xander pushed through some thicket to continue forward. "It really is crazy to think we may have been less than a kilometer away from him when we were here before."

"It really would be," Anya agreed. "But fate can be a strange thing at times."

"I'm not sure I believe in fate, but I see your meaning," Xander replied. "I will say, though, it would make sense for him to be in Grimveil of all places. This camp is not only the closest one to his home, but also to where he was reportedly last seen, at the Enzori train station."

Xander looked over at Anya. There was something different about seeing her in full tactical gear, complete with body armor, her EK12 lightning rifle on her back, and pistol on her side. She had always had an air of authority about her, but she somehow had an even more powerful presence in her full gear.

"If you don't mind me asking, why were you looking for him in Hivich, before?" Anya inquired. "I mean, if he lives in Marann and was also last seen here, what were you doing over in Varith city, where we met you?"

"Well, I started looking here in Marann, but I eventually moved to Hivich when I had no luck," Xander explained. "Hivich was where he was booked to leave Antal from. His tickets were for a ride from the Varith Interglobal Spaceport. Honestly, as silly as it might sound, it was probably to save money. He had a sponsorship deal with one of the interstellar carriers there, so he got huge discounts if he traveled offworld from that port. He was very proud of that."

"Seriously?" Anya exclaimed incredulously. "Isn't he one of the richest people in Antal? And you think he was trying to save money while running for his life?"

Xander laughed.

"Honestly, he does it without thinking," he explained. "Even before Matlex made it big, he was always well-off, thanks to his family, but that never stopped him from being surprisingly cheap."

"Really?" Anya asked.

"Yes," Xander affirmed. "I mean, don't get me wrong, there are things he'd spend lavishly on—especially when it came to looks or style. I've seen him buy a shirt worth 100,000 marks without batting an eye.

"But then he'd be very stingy when it came to the most random of things. You know, he once vented to me about a mistake made by a comms provider on his account. Apparently, he had spent half the day on the phone trying to correct it."

"Wow," Anya responded. "A man like him spending half a day dealing with a comms error? It must have been some mistake."

"That's what I thought too," Xander responded. "So, imagine how floored I was when I found out that it was only a 300-mark charge accidentally put on his account... I mean, he made well over that for every second that he sang at the Auros Sports Festival, Antrogonis, last year."

"Wow, that's unbelievable," Anya remarked. "Some people are truly full of some strange contradictions."

"I would say most are in one sense or another," Xander stated. "That can be part of what makes them so interesting though."

Xander found himself huffing a little bit as they hiked up a stretch of hill through dense thicket.

He noticed some rays of moonlight ahead of them and looked up. The trees here were more sparse, and as he looked to the sky, he could see Antal's twin moons peaking through. That light illuminated the plant life along their path, from the giant, majestic trees, to the gorgeous, flowering bushes. This forest may have been terrifying, but it was equally beautiful.

Xander looked back down to Anya.

"I did want to say that I appreciate you all allowing me to come along," Xander expressed. "I know that the council was really on the fence about it, but I simply couldn't stay behind, knowing that there was even a chance that Matlex was here."

"It's no problem," Anya replied. "And to be clear, it's not that anyone doubted that you'd be an asset in this raid. It's only because you're a VIP, valued for your celebrity status and influence. We only questioned the wisdom in allowing you to come on such a dangerous mission. The Generals protested Morgas coming for similar reasons. But at this point, we all generally know better than to think that she can be dissuaded."

"I understand," Xander nodded. "But in any case, I appreciate that you all came around. This was important to me."

"Of course," Anya smiled at him. "I'm glad you were able to as well. I have faith in you, Xander."

As they reached the crest of the hill, their destination finally came into sight. Staring back at Xander ominously from a few hundred meters away was Grimveil Slave Camp, with over 25,000 slaves, 2,000 soldiers, and an unforgettable battle awaiting them.

*/

With Aren at the head, the CNPF infiltration team had been walking for nearly an hour now through the maintenance tunnels beneath Varith.

In most cities on Antal, there were not large underground tunnels like this dedicated only to cable infrastructure. However, Varith was special in that it housed the CNPF, which was the hub of most internet radio networks across the entire planet. This meant that there was a very high concentration of cables within the city borders before they branched out and distributed information across Antal. The tunnels built here allowed for all of these cables to be easily accessed by workers for maintenance and repairs.

Originally, the plan had been to storm the CNPF right in the open, going straight for their front door. However, this plan had drawbacks. It would have meant facing a large number of sonic turrets outside, for starters. This would have required far more operatives to deal with, while they were already stretched thin from the simultaneous raids on the slave camps. It also would have taken out some of the element of surprise, as they would have been forced to face the security forces outside the CNPF before entering the building, giving the security in the building a better chance to prepare.

These maintenance tunnels were not originally considered an option. Although they were not guarded, it had been believed that there were no direct access points into the facility through them.

However, the blueprints that they had received from the Chancellor, Hans Frolick, showed that there was another access point inside the facility itself that did not exist on any official records. This access point was a single, solitary emergency hatch between the CNPF and the maintenance tunnels. This hatch existed as a failsafe in case things went seriously wrong, such as fire or flooding, giving repair workers instant access between the tunnels and facility for faster and more efficient repairs.

However, for security reasons, this hatch was kept off of public records, and designed to be nearly impossible to find unless you already knew where to look. Furthermore, even if you found the hatch, it was blocked by a high-end sonic repulsor shield that prevented entry to anyone without digital officer credentials. Thanks to the blueprints, they were able to find and include this hatch in their plans, and thanks to an earlier mission from Aren, they also had the officer credentials that they needed.

The team included eighteen people in total—a fraction of the number they would have needed for storming the front gates. However, these were all highly skilled and experienced operatives and officers, including such people as the infamous former burglar, Specialist Henrika Juliette; Oppori Qala's top sorcerer and battlemage, Specialist Elmenz Makiree; and the head of the infamous resistance cell E7, Commander Irven Wo, alongside his top lieutenant and twelve of his operatives. Wo's resistance cell, E7, was the top resistance cell in Hivich, with countless successful operations under their belt.

Leading this entire team was General Ollit Krafts, who despite his friction with Aren, had jurisdiction over this region along with all of the eastern resistance cells.

Although Ollit was in charge of this team, Aren was the one physically leading the group at the head, as he was the one with best knowledge of these maintenance tunnels out of anyone here, since he used them regularly in his missions in the city of Varith.

Aren looked back at the group. Not far behind him were General Ollit and Commander Irven, smiling and talking up a storm. It was clear that the two of them had a strong relationship. Perhaps they were old friends, or maybe even something more.

Whatever the relationship, the two made an interesting looking pair. Ollit was a somewhat shorter orren man, around 5'7" with beady eyes, sharp features and a short, military haircut. Irven, on the other hand was a handsome, proud-looking human man, one of only three humans and four total non-orrens on this team, including Aren. Irven was tall, around 6'2" and broad-shouldered. He had smooth, amber skin, dark, narrow eyes, and a gorgeous head of dark brown hair, a few inches long and styled nicely.

Besides the notable size difference between the two, Ollit looked more rigid next to Irven, who had a more relaxed posture, style and general demeanor. Although, surprisingly, Ollit was smiling and laughing quite a bit as the two of them spoke.

Aren looked away with a smile of his own. It was nice to see that Ollit could get along with some people, at least.

As he continued walking, his sensitive ears picked up Ollit's footsteps speeding up and approaching him.

"How close are we getting?" Ollit asked Aren as he caught up to him at the front.

This was the first time that Ollit spoke directly to Aren this entire trip. Part of this was certainly related to how wrapped up Ollit was in his conversation with Irven, but it had also felt like Ollit had been avoiding Aren somewhat until this point.

"It shouldn't be too long now," Aren answered. "We're most of the way there."

"Good," Ollit responded. "I'm glad to hear it."

As they continued walking, Ollit cleared his throat. "So, Aren, I had been wanting to bring up the council meeting from the other day."

"Oh, there's no need to apologize or anything," Aren reassured him. "I understand why you were skeptical."

"Oh, I wasn't going to apologize," Ollit asserted pointedly. "I stand by everything that I said. All I wanted to say was that I still don't trust you."

"Oh?" Aren responded. "Is that so?"

"Yes," Ollit reaffirmed haughtily. "Look, I recognize that you've done some good work for us. However, I still don't trust your motives here. You're a mercenary—a soldier for hire—and I don't hold any delusions that UAPA pays better than we ever could."

"I understand," Aren sympathized. "However, I'm not in this for the money."

"That's what Anya said, but I don't buy it," Ollit accused. "Maybe I could believe it for Xander. He has a history here on this planet, and I know he's rich enough that UAPA could never buy him, but you? You're just a merc who recently left their clan for some unknown reasons and are claiming to not be in this for the money, despite that being your *entire job*. And you've been here what, two or three months, and I'm supposed to trust that that proves loyalty? Honestly, I don't think that proves much at all."

"You're welcome to believe what you want," Aren asserted. "However, everything I have said has been the truth. My only interests are both taking down UAPA, and the two rewards Anya has offered to me and Kyara upon our success."

"Right," Ollit noted. "I remember Anya mentioned that we'd be giving you our Arc-I spaceship. It's a fine craft—the one Morgas used in the Raider Wars. It's small, but fast and stealthy.

"However, I'm assuming Anya let you know its condition, right? It's pretty worn out now, and the weapon system is no longer functional. With a market value probably between two to three-million marks that'd be very low payment for all of the work you and Kyara have been doing, especially on a contingent contract like this where you get paid nothing unless we are completely victorious."

"I see you've really done your homework," Aren remarked. "But the fact is, we do need a ship, and that one should do the job just fine. Besides, it's not the main thing I'm here for."

"I figured as much," Ollit declared. "So, tell me, what is this other reward that you're after then? Anya said it was some kind of special concession, right? I want to know what that is."

"Well, it's not a secret," Aren responded. "So, of course, I don't mind sharing. My goal is to interrogate a certain member of the UAPA administration after we take them down."

"Really?" Ollit expressed. "What could any of them have to say that's so important to you?"

"Now, *that* is personal," Aren asserted.

"Ok, fine," Ollit responded. "But if you won't talk, it's certainly not making it any easier to trust you."

Aren sighed.

"Look, Ollit," Aren started to sound frustrated. "I would like if you could start to trust me—I really would—but to be frank, I was hired to help bring down UAPA—not to prostrate myself to you."

Ollit was silent, as he appeared completely taken aback.

"I'm happy to continue doing my job, but I have no interest in entertaining every doubt you have," Aren continued sternly. "If you have a problem with that, then I suggest that you bring it up with Morgas or Anya, because I'm done justifying my presence to you."

Henrika, who was trailing a bit behind them, began laughing out loud as Aren finished his speech. Ollit appeared stunned.

"Hmph, well then," Ollit stammered. "If that's how it is, I will be expecting much from you during this mission."

"Sounds good to me," Aren asserted.

Ollit let himself fall back in the group, next to Irven, who he immediately began talking to again.

Henrika clapped her hands as she continued laughing and walked up next to Aren.

"Well, that was fun to listen to," Henrika grinned. "Hardly anyone ever stands up to Ollit. I thought he might crap himself for a second there."

"I don't have any qualms with him," Aren stated. "Maybe I was a little harsh, I don't know. But I do think boundaries are important."

"Of course, they are," Henrika giggled. "Either way, it was entertaining to watch though. Most people's boundaries tend to crumble in the face of stern, overbearing authority like him. Personally, I prefer to just ignore or tease him, but your method ain't so bad either."

Aren looked over at her. She was strikingly beautiful. She had pale skin for an orren, and dark black hair. She had a very beautiful face, with high cheekbones, a large nose, playful eyes, and thick lips curled into a grin that betrayed just a hint of her mischievous nature.

For clothing, she wore a long black coat over top of a dark maroon halter top, tightened with an overwear corset around the waist, and black leather pants underneath. Despite her dark clothing and makeup, she had a noticeable glow about her, emanating especially from her hair and skin, but also from her personality.

From his experience with her so far, Aren could tell she was trouble. And yet, he still felt drawn to her. Perhaps it was her beauty, perhaps it was her carefree vibe, or perhaps it was that, despite her seemingly chaotic tendencies, he had yet to detect an ounce of malice from her.

"Everyone has their own way of doing things, I suppose," Aren remarked.

"Thank gods for that," Henrika chuckled. "How boring would life be if everyone did everything the same way?"

Aren laughed. "I think you have a point."

There was a faint sound that Aren heard coming from beside them. It was hard to qualify exactly what it was, but it almost sounded like a muffled cough. Aren jerked his head forward, turning away from Henrika.

Using his hands, Aren signalled to the group to stop, and to be quiet. Everyone immediately recognized the signs and abided.

It was most likely nothing, but he needed to be certain, so he scanned his surroundings carefully. From what he could see, nothing seemed to be out of place. The maintenance tunnels were normally dark, depending on flashlights or wristcomms from maintenance workers for light. Their surroundings were currently lit by a combination of the team's helmet lights, and Aren's light magic. Aren silently cancelled his magic and signalled for the others to tone down their helmet lights. They all obliged. It was now much darker, but Aren's excellent night vision allowed him to still see fairly competently.

He looked around them. They were currently in the largest section of the tunnels under Varith. Here, the tunnel spanned 26-feet in width, and stretched for nearly a mile in length. Their team was currently walking on a steel-grate, raised platform situated in the center of the tunnel that took up about a third of its width.

Positioned underneath them on both sides were large masses of cables running in tandem with the direction of the tunnel and spanning across the full width of it. It was impossible to tell exactly how deep the masses of cables were, but, based on the shape of the tunnel and look of the cables, Aren figured that it was probably quite deep.

There were railings on both sides of the platform, but with many intermittent spaces for maintenance or repair worker to walk out into the cables to work on them. Although, Aren imagined it must be hard to access the cables closer to the bottom of the mesh, considering how many layers they likely would have to go through.

The more Aren looked, the more it appeared like everything was normal. He was sure that he heard something, but it was only for the briefest moment, and he wasn't positive that it wasn't some sort of surge from the cables. The mesh was emitting a consistent electrical humming sound that sometimes had rare hiccups. However, it didn't escape his notice that this humming could possibly mask low-level sounds from potential threats as well.

To be safe, Aren took a sniff of the air, trying to see if his powerful olfactory senses might pick anything else up. The first couple of sniffs eased his mind, as he couldn't smell a thing.

Just to be sure, he sniffed one last time. Immediately, alarm bells went off in his head and his full body tensed up as he finally smelled it. It was faint, but there was no doubt in his mind that was the scent of gaucifin, a specialty chemical used specifically to mask scents, usually from wild animals.

"Everyone, get down, now!" Aren screamed.

But it was already too late.

Chapter 16

After Grimveil Slave Camp had come into view, Kyara stopped moving and made the signal for everyone behind to do the same.

"Alright, this is the closest we can get as a group for the moment," Kyara spoke softly into her radio piece, which was currently set to broadcast to the earpieces of the top officers in the raid.

"Understood," Morgas affirmed, also speaking via radio. "All agents, excluding K-1 and X-1, hold position and standby for now. We'll begin moving again once the operation reaches phase two."

Xander's ears perked up at hearing the code names for him and Kyara.

"Roger that," Anya replied.

"Roger," affirmed each of the seven commanders present in the raid, one-by-one.

These orders and responses were a standard part of the chain of command in Oppori Qala. The structure of this chain of command was fairly simple. The Oppori Qala council stood at the top of the organization's hierarchy, presiding over the more than 9000 Oppori Qala members. Within the council, the ranks went, from top to bottom, the Chair, the Vice-Chair, the Head Administrator, the Generals, and lastly, the Specialists. Then, answering to the council, the rest of the members were divided into resistance cells. There were 108 of these cells in total, and all of them were overseen directly by the Generals.

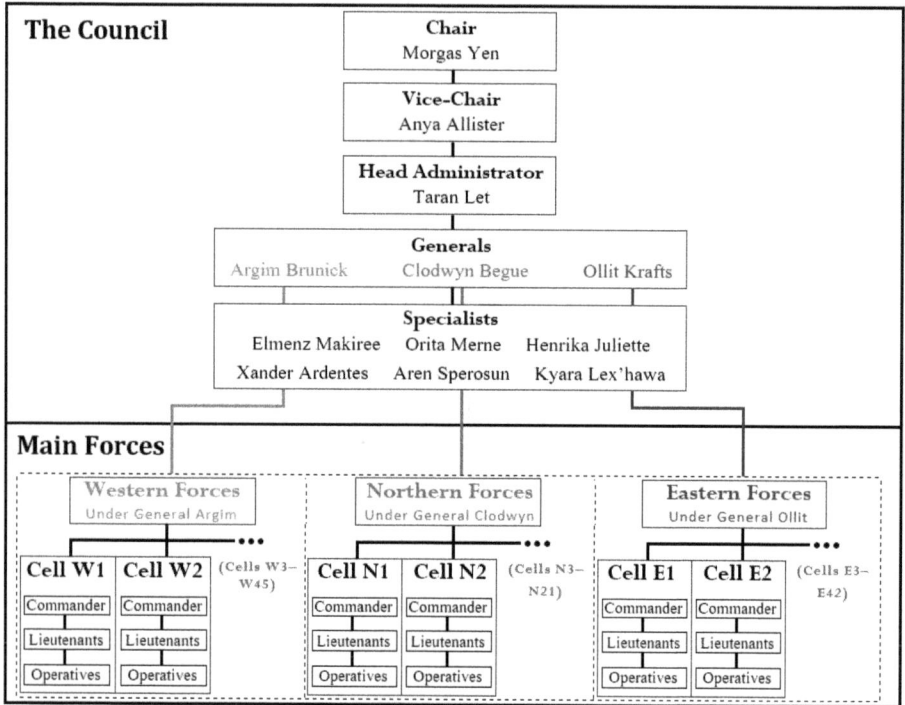

Figure 2, Oppori Qala Organizational Chart

Within the resistance cells, there were three ranks: the commander in charge of each cell, the lieutenants answering to them, and then the operatives at the bottom, who made up the vast majority of Oppori Qala agents.

The reason for structuring the organization into cells like this was so that they could be kept separate and insulated for information security purposes. Towards this end, those within each resistance cell were kept in the dark about the operations and identities of those in other cells.

Moreover, with the exception of Morgas Yen and Anya Allister, who were known to all in Oppori Qala for leadership purposes, the identities of the rest of the Oppori Qala Council were only known to the top commanders of the resistance cells. Even for Anya, only her name was known throughout the organization—only the council and a select few other agents had seen her real face without holo-mask modification (while UAPA did have a likeness up along with Anya's bounty, it had the wrong face, based on a falsified license photo that Anya herself had planted in Marann government records in anticipation that it would be used against her).

This insulated system helped prevent UAPA from gaining much intel whenever they were able to capture and interrogate Oppori Qala operatives. That way, even if they could break or turn an operative, there was limited damage that could be done to the organization as a whole.

The only times Oppori Qala risked breaking this insulation were in crucial joint operations, such as this one, which required that multiple cells work together towards a common goal. However, even in these cases, they still took some precautions, such as using code names, and trying to keep each cell functioning separately under their respective commanders as much as possible.

This was also why they used secure, selective radio channels limited to set groups, rather than just allowing open communication between all operatives. In many cases, these channels would be limited to two to four people at a time. However, in cases like this, where Morgas and Kyara both had to relay information to the entire army, they had to use a broader channel. This officers' channel included all council officers and the cells' commanders, but not lieutenants or operatives. The expectation was that the commanders would then pass on the information to their lieutenants and troops themselves.

This still kept most front-line communication isolated within each cell. If a commander died or was compromised during an operation, only then did lieutenants have permission to take over command of their cells and join the officers' radio channel in their commander's place.

Kyara looked over to Xander and promptly walked up to him.

"Are you ready?" She asked him.

"As ready as I'll ever be," He confirmed, with just a hint of nervousness behind his voice.

"Good luck you two," Anya wished to them. "If you run into any trouble, notify me on the radio immediately."

Xander nodded. "Will do, boss."

With that, him and Kyara began their approach, moving stealthily through the trees, heading towards the western wall of the camp.

Originally, Kyara was supposed to complete phase one of the operation alone. However, while they were planning this raid, Xander realized that he was actually better equipped to deal with one of the biggest obstacles than Kyara was. The council had been hesitant to allow him to go at all, but once he pointed out his capabilities to them, they tepidly relented and agreed to include him right from phase one.

Xander was quite happy about this, as he wanted to get into the camp as early as possible. If Matlex was there, Xander wanted to find him as fast as he could, preferably before things got too chaotic in the camp.

As they approached the wall, Xander could see that Kyara's information had been good. There were no visible guards in the vicinity. This area was probably considered a low security risk since it was so far from any gates. However, despite the lack of guards, there still was the 20' tall, fortified wall to contend with, along with security sensors that would detect them if they got too close.

Kyara switched on her impulse disruptor. This initialized the device on standby mode, preparing it to activate at a moment's notice when she was ready.

"Well, I'm glad to see that you have a plan for the sensors," Xander noted quietly. "But how are we scaling that wall? Rope and hook?"

"Nope," Kyara responded. "It's not a terrible idea, but it's also not the ideal method. With how slow it is, there's some risk to us getting caught."

"Ok, then what?" Xander asked, confused. "I mean, I could easily get up there with an aurimancic spell, except the guards would almost certainly hear my playing."

Kyara didn't respond. Instead, she silently grabbed her bow, which was attached to her back from a sling around her torso and flipped it around, so the bow was now being held at her front. She then turned away from Xander, got down on one knee, put her arms by her sides, and motioned to him.

"Come, hop on," she instructed.

"What?" Xander asked in shock. "Do you mean like, piggyback?"

"Yes, the optimal method is for me to jump us both over," Kyara responded. "Don't worry though, it won't lead to us getting caught. The dirt around this area is soft, and I've been trained to land quietly from large falls. Also, there's a tall building on the other side of this wall, so our visibility will be minimized from any guards in the area. Overall, we have a very low chance of being detected this way."

"I mean, that isn't really the issue," Xander asserted, his face going red. "For starters, can you really jump us both up that high? That's gotta be around 20 feet."

"Yes, it's no problem," Kyara replied. "Maybe not with my natural strength alone, but it's a sure thing using Ineyem. It'll be a bit tight, but it should be fine in Antal's lower gravity. I've done more difficult jumps under heavier gravity before."

"Oh, you use Ineyem?" Xander's eyes widened. "That would explain a few things. Still though… I've met Ineyem users before, and I don't think they could jump this high—especially not while carrying someone on their back."

"I understand, but trust me, I've got this," Kyara assured. "Now please, get on. We're wasting time here."

"Sorry, it's just," Xander hesitated, rubbing the back of his head bashfully as the redness in his face deepened further. "I haven't had a piggyback ride in some years now."

"I don't really understand the issue, but I can assure you, it will be fine," Kyara asserted, starting to sound a bit impatient. "Now come on, let's go. We're wasting time here."

"Ok," Xander reluctantly agreed.

Slowly, he walked over to her and carefully hopped onto her back, wrapping his arms around her, while she cradled his legs with her arms. He was surprised at how sturdy she was. Her body didn't bend so much as a millimeter in response to his weight. It was as if a feather had jumped onto her back rather than a person.

Xander's blushing intensified as he felt her strong muscles pressed against him. Kyara's tactical armor was made of a surprisingly thin, special fabric with no hard plating, meaning he could really feel her hard body against his own. Part of him felt like a kid again, being held like this.

Kyara didn't waste any time. She hit a button on her disruptor, activating it. She then quickly ran forward at full speed. Once they got relatively close to the wall, Xander braced himself. He did this just in time before Kyara launched them both from the ground, making a small rumbling sound as she took off, amazingly making it just over the top of the wall.

It was at this point that Xander realized the bigger problem in this situation. This was not just a long way to go up, but it was an equal distance to fall. Kyara might have been ok with her Ineyem protecting her, but Xander did not have that benefit.

Nevertheless, he knew how important it was to avoid being heard here, so he bit his tongue and stopped himself from screaming, holding his terror inside as they plunged towards the ground at full speed. His heart was racing, and he closed his eyes as the ground got closer and closer. Finally, they hit the soil with a gentle thump. Breathing heavily, Xander realized that the landing somehow didn't hurt.

"How am I ok?" Xander whispered, mystified. "I was sure that was going to be painful. That's a high drop."

"Oh, I'm surprised you didn't ask earlier if you were worried about that," Kyara commented. "I could have told you before I jumped."

"I may or may not have been a bit distracted," Xander admitted bashfully. "I didn't exactly think about it, in any case."

"Ok, well, you can partially thank what you call the 'piggyback ride'," Kyara explained. "It distributed the impact of the landing across most of your body, instead of at any one point. That's why this was the optimal way to carry you."

"Wow, I guess I never really thought of that," Xander responded. "You said partially though, what else is to thank?"

"Well, I also bent my knees when I landed to absorb part of the impact," Kyara explained. "And the soil here is soft, which helps too. However, likely more important was that I extended my Ineyem around you on the moment of impact, to give you a little extra protection. Extending Ineyem past my own body is not an easy thing to do, but I can manage it in short spurts for people or things in close proximity to me. It's weaker when extended outside of me, but I'm sure it helped."

"Ah, now that makes sense," Xander expressed. "Well, I appreciate it. I really could barely feel a thing."

"I'm glad to hear it," Kyara responded sincerely. "We really should get moving though. Someone is likely going to come check up on the 'malfunctioning' sensors soon."

"Understood," Xander acknowledged. "Let's go then."

His face went red again as he realized he was still latched onto her back. He quickly let go and jumped off. She didn't give him any chance to worry about it though, as she immediately began moving forward through the camp and he had to get moving quickly to keep up.

Kyara led him through alleys and across streets, careful to avoid any patrols and stay out of the sightlines of any guards. There were no cameras anywhere in the camp. This was likely to avoid a potential scandal if the footage of this place somehow got out to the public, but this worked to Kyara and Xander's advantage as they slipped through the camp entirely undetected.

Xander took a moment to look around at the structures surrounding them as they were moving. Most of the buildings in this camp were earth structures in a style that Xander recognized from an Antallian history documentary he had watched back at the academy. These buildings were made from mudbrick baked around prefab metal frames. Mudbrick buildings like these ones tended to be valued for being cheap, as well as quick and easy to build, which made sense for a work camp that likely had to be built on a very short deadline.

The origins of this type of building was speculated to come from the culture of the orri who were among the first to colonize Antal thousands of years ago, alongside a group of humans. Although this type of construction had not been actively used through most of Antal's history and it was rarely seen in the modern day, it had made a temporary comeback in the previous millennium when a severe economic depression over 1600 years ago gave necessity for cheaper construction methods.

Xander was so lost in thought about architectural history that he didn't notice that Kyara had stopped, causing him to bump into her.

"Oops, sorry," Xander apologized again, turning red in the face.

"Ok, the security station is just up ahead," Kyara pointed out, hardly seeming to notice the accidental collision as she looked down at the time on her wristcomm. "We should have a decent window before the next patrol comes through here. Are you ready? Once we get started, we're going to need to be moving quickly from beginning to end."

Xander looked around the corner. As she had said, the security station was right there. It was a relatively small building, but well-fortified, and surrounded by visible vibrations in the air, denoting an active sonic repulsor shield protecting it. Furthermore, there were two guards stationed in front of the door. Xander knew there would be several more inside.

He took a deep breath and closed his eyes. This was the moment of truth. The rest of the operation hinged on their complete and total success here. Not only did they have to infiltrate the station and gain access to the security grid, but they also had to make sure that not a single guard raised the alarm when doing so. This was going to be an uphill battle.

Nevertheless, Xander had been prepared for this from the start, and he knew that it would be now or never. He exhaled gently and then opened his eyes.

"I'm ready," he said.

"Ok, let's go," Kyara instructed.

She took out her bow, along with two arrows from her quiver. Xander noticed that this was not the same strange, twisted wooden bow that she had before, but a large and heavy-looking metal compound bow instead. He surmised that she must have wanted to avoid accidentally creating a sonic boom during this mission. It still blew his mind that such a thing was even possible, but he appreciated Kyara's mindfulness in avoiding the risk with what was likely a much weaker bow.

Kyara took a deep breath. In the next second, she turned the corner, drew her bow, and simultaneously shot both arrows at once, hitting the guards in their necks.

Both guards fell to the ground, and Xander and Kyara dashed towards the station. In only a few fluid motions, Kyara swooped over the bodies of the guards, scooped them up beneath each arm, and brought them over to the alley next to the security station where she hid them behind a stack of barrels.

"That won't hide them for long, but it should be long enough," Kyara asserted. "Are you ready?"

Xander looked at the vibrating sonic repulsor shield surrounding the building. This repulsor shield was particularly powerful and made the building nearly impenetrable to anything short of major artillery.

The only time this shield was lowered was during the guards' shift change. It had originally been Kyara's plan to attack during this shift change. However, she would have had twice the guards to contend with—the ones from the previous shift, and the ones for the next shift. While she was confident that she could technically beat them, the risk that one of them would raise the alarm first would have been high. This would have taken away some of the element of surprise they were hoping to keep, which was why it was so helpful to learn that Xander believed he would be capable of taking down the shield with his aurimancy.

"I'll do my best," Xander asserted.

While aurimancy had a great variety of applications, if there was one thing it was particularly well-suited for, it was the manipulation of sound waves. The fact that Antallian repulsor shields relied primarily on a special, manipulated form of sound energy meant that Xander's aurimancy was particularly well-suited for disabling them. Unfortunately, the problem here was that volume was a component of aurimancy and playing quiet enough to remain undetected meant that his spell would not be as strong.

Thankfully, Oppori Qala had a similar repulsor shield that Xander could practice this spell on a number of times to try and get it just right. It took him a long time, but he eventually got it to the point where, even at a low volume, he could accomplish a weaker version of the spell that was just strong enough to penetrate the shield for a very short time.

The problem was that this modified version of the spell took both very intense focus and a precise crescendo. He had not fully mastered the quiet version of it yet, and he sometimes found himself slipping and playing too loudly at the last note of the spell, which could risk alerting nearby guards of their presence.

Nevertheless, Xander was prepared to give it his best shot. He pulled a special tuning device out of his pocket, pointed it towards the shield, and pressed a button in the center of the device. The display on the device showed a reading of 174.319 Hz. This would do just fine.

Xander pulled out his chiambra and bow. He did not have time to worry about possible mistakes. All he could do was try and hope for the best.

"We'll have about seven seconds to get through after I hit the final note of the spell," Xander explained. "I'll start now."

With that, he began with very soft and gentle playing. The tune was layered with subtle harmonies that helped to bring out a pronounced melody. With each note, the volume continued to rise ever so slightly. This was the way it had to be played, but the key here was precision. Not only did Xander have to be careful not to get too loud, but he also could not remain too quiet or else the spell might be too weak to penetrate the shield, or worse, it might not even activate at all. The goal was to go from a precise pianissimo volume and end with the final note at the lower end of mezzo-forte. Any louder or quieter at all could pose a problem.

Furthermore, he also had to be simultaneously manipulating his life forces with his mind in order to cast the spell, as was the case with all aurimancy magic, but which made it hard to focus on the demanding volume precision that was needed here.

The spell took him around 20 seconds altogether, but to his delight, he managed to keep the precision all the way through to the final note. This final note was designed to precisely match the shield's frequency at 174.3 Hz, and due to the effects of the spell, would continue playing without him for seven seconds after he stopped. As long as this note was sustained, the spell's effects should hold strong.

Xander put his bow down and looked at the building. Despite having played the song perfectly, to his dismay, he could still see the air vibrating quite visibly around the security station. It looked like it had become significantly weaker, but not by nearly enough to get through.

Kyara could see it too. She touched the tip of her bow in range of the vibrations only to have it violently pushed back at her.

A couple seconds later, the sustained note stopped, and the vibrations were visibly back at full strength again.

"What happened?" Kyara whispered to him. "Why didn't it work?"

"Dammit," Xander cursed. "I don't think this was the same model as the one Oppori Qala let me practice on. This shielding seems to be stronger."

"Ok, so we move to plan B, and ambush them during the shift change then," Kyara asserted. "It'll be harder since we took out those guards at the front. They'll be on alert when they see those two are missing, but I think we can still manage it."

Xander clenched his teeth. He knew that option was much riskier. He couldn't stand by and let this plan possibly fall into shambles.

Kyara began walking back to the alley in preparation for the ambush.

"Wait, no," Xander protested. "I can do this. Just let me try one more time, please."

"Ok," Kyara relented. "But this is the last attempt. We don't have much time before the next patrol."

"Understood," Xander responded.

He took a deep breath. There was a lot of pressure on this, but he couldn't let that get to him.

He knew, if he was going to accomplish this, he had to draw up more power. However, he also knew he could not play at a higher volume, or else he would risk guards hearing him. Therefore, that meant that he needed to draw more life energy through a more intensive focus, which would make the volume precision even more difficult to pull off.

If there weren't so much riding on this, he would have insisted on months more practice for such a feat. But he knew he had no choice but to try anyway.

He exhaled. To say that the odds were against him here was an understatement. While he could feel the pressure mounting, however, his determination was rising faster.

He thought about the countless victims who were imprisoned at this camp, where they were brutally mistreated and forced into slave labour. He thought about Matlex who could be with them right now. Pangs of compassion and righteous anger consumed him, steeling his mind to the task at hand. This injustice could not last for a second longer.

With all of the strength and resolve of one who was carrying 25,000 lives on their shoulders, Xander pulled the chiambra up to his chin once again, and gently lay his bow upon it. There was a deafening moment of silence, and then the playing began.

In that moment, his world dissolved, leaving only the notes to fill his entire universe. His body and mind were transformed into mere vessels for the melody that would end the suffering surrounding him.

Kyara gasped as she listened to his playing. She had thought the piece sounded masterful enough the first time he played it, and yet, it somehow felt like it was on a completely different level this time.

The notes were the same, and yet it inexplicably had transformed into a new piece. There was an intense energy behind every tone that Xander played—a passion and power within them that was not nearly as present the first time.

Kyara could hardly believe her eyes as what appeared to be the glowing silhouette of a giant swan manifested itself around Xander. This had not happened the first time he cast the spell.

After it finished forming, the swan began flying at the building, quickly and gracefully.

The moment that the swan hit the building and dissipated into it was the same that Xander hit the final note once more. In that moment, it was like a wave had washed over both Kyara and the building, visibly neutralizing the shield in its entirety while sending shivers down her spine.

However, Kyara realized what this meant and that there was no time to waste. She looked over at Xander. As their eyes met, she nodded to him. He nodded back in response. Without hesitation, Kyara opened the door and threw a flashbang grenade into the room. There were ten soldiers in here altogether. Every one of them appeared shocked at the sudden intrusion, and none were prepared to respond.

Xander put his chiambra away, rushed in and closed the door behind them. Him and Kyara both quickly closed their eyes tightly and covered their ears, just as the flashbang went off.

While everyone was in a daze, Kyara put special earplugs into her ears, while Xander pulled out his flute. The melody he began playing was haunting—a piece that reached deep into your soul and caressed it gently, while relaxing both mind and body, like a tender but evocative lullaby.

Kyara had her bow drawn and was watching the guards carefully, having been warned by Xander ahead of time that this spell did not always work on everyone. However, without fail, every single individual in that room collapsed where they sat or stood, falling into a deep slumber instigated by Xander's spell.

"Wow," Kyara marvelled, taking out her ear plugs. "I'm starting to think I wasn't needed in this phase of the operation at all."

Xander blushed and rubbed the back of his head sheepishly. "Well, thank you Kyara. That means a lot coming from you."

Kyara and Xander both got to work binding and gagging all of the sleeping soldiers in the room. Although they were fast asleep now, the spell's magic wouldn't hold them for long, and once it wore off, it was relatively random when a person might wake up. It might take hours after the magic wore off under the right conditions, such as if they were a heavy sleeper and if they were exhausted at the time the spell was cast. However, they also might wake very quickly after the magic wore off under the wrong conditions, like if a sudden loud noise disturbed their sleep. Either way, it was safer to have them tied up, which would help keep them immobilized for as long as possible, even after they awoke.

It went against Kyara's instincts to tie up guards like this. Kyara had always been taught to kill guards over incapacitating them. A living guard, even unconscious, and even tied up, posed a significant risk in missions. Not only did tying them up take up crucial time. There was also always the chance of the guard waking up and either finding some way out of their bonds or figuring out a way to alert others.

However, as Kyara spent time with Aren, she realized that killing maybe wasn't always as necessary as she had been taught to believe. Despite the mountain of bodies that she had left in her wake, there was a part of her that always hated the killing, and she welcomed the idea that she didn't always have to. She still knew there were many times that she could not avoid it, but she felt good about the times that she could, like now.

In any case, even if these soldiers did wake up and somehow escape, it would be too late for them to do anything by that point.

After they finished, Kyara sat down at the security console. The computer was on, and the interface was open, but it was not logged in. She clicked a button to gain access to the security grid.

Facial scan required, read a prompt on the screen.

Orita warned her that this would most likely happen, based on her analysis of the camp's security. Kyara looked over and saw the highest-ranking officer, as evidenced by the symbols on his chest and shoulder. She gently reached down to the sleeping person and picked them up. She then grabbed the back of his head and gently held it in front of the scanner for a few moments.

Facial scan accepted. Access granted. A new prompt on the screen read.

She felt grateful that UAPA used outdated bioscanning software that was not programmed to detect consciousness.

She put the officer back on the ground, and then went to work quickly, first disabling the security sensors, then opening all gates, and finally, disabling all sonic deterrents throughout the camp.

She then plugged a device into the console, given to her by Oppori Qala's top computer expert, Orita, that began installing a virus, preventing any changes from being made to the security settings that she had just set in place.

After the installation was complete, Kyara got up, drew her bow, and fired into the computers and consoles, destroying them as an extra precaution.

There was quiet for a few moments afterwards, until suddenly, a shrill, guttural screech broke that silence. The sound started out fairly quiet, clearly originating from some distance away, but built up quickly in volume as many more distant screeches began to join in to the dreadful chorus. A shiver ran down Xander's spine as he listened to this bloodcurdling cacophony resonating throughout the camp.

The shreen were coming.

Chapter 17

The second that Aren had warned the team, black ops agents in tactical gear revealed themselves, emerging from beneath the cables on both sides of them, and aiming sonic rifles in their direction.

Aren was shocked to see these soldiers here. These tunnels had been entirely unguarded every time he had been through here in the past. But then, normal guards also wouldn't have been hiding under the mesh of cables. The only conclusion here was that this had to be an orchestrated ambush. But there was no time to think about that now.

Aren quickly launched into a backflip, dodging a volley of sonic shots aimed at him. He was tempted to draw his sword and counterattack, but with all of his teammates behind him, he knew that defense had to take priority.

"*Ashaid cubri*!" Aren cried out.

Pouring his focus into the incantation, Aren drew energy from within himself to produce a barrier around him, using a shielding spell known as Spirit Guard. He did not have any spells that could protect the entire group, but with this one protecting him, he could safely draw fire to himself, and hopefully prevent the others from getting hit in the process.

Aren looked back. The emerging UAPA agents extended far in front of them, but only a little behind them, meaning that the safest place for their team to go was backwards.

"Everyone, fall back!" Aren yelled.

"Do as he says!" Ollit somewhat surprisingly confirmed Aren's order.

Thankfully, it seemed that Aren had detected the enemy somewhat early, before their team had been caught in the dead center of the ambush. However, it was not early enough, as they were still surrounded on three sides.

Dammit, Aren thought to himself in frustration. *Why couldn't I have noticed them sooner?!*

But he knew there was no time to waste on regret. His teammates were already ducking low and exchanging fire with the enemies on all sides. It had only been seconds since all of this began, but three of the team were already dead and a few others were injured.

Aren considered the possibility of using the Fuinshai Shroud of Darkness spell to remove all light from the tunnel, but he changed his mind when he noticed that UAPA agents were wearing tactical goggles. This meant they would very likely have visual access to infrared and/or other frequencies in the EM spectrum, meaning that they would likely be able to see just fine even in the total absence of light.

Aren turned and saw Elmenz casting spells against the enemy. Elmenz took out one of the soldiers with a small, magical dodecahedron that pierced straight through the soldier, armor and all. However, the problem was that he was standing upright and unmoving, right in the line of fire.

What could he be thinking? Aren worriedly wondered.

Aren swiftly dove at Elmenz, tackling him to the ground, just as a sonic blast flew past where he had been standing, hitting the railing beside him. Elmenz had a terrified look in his eyes as the railing was blasted away.

"Thank you!" Elmenz said gratefully to Aren. "That was a close one."

"No problem," Aren responded. "Just make sure to stay low and keep moving."

"Noted," Elmenz acknowledged.

Aren turned his wristcomm light on in an attempt to draw attention to himself and away from his team, while trying to swiftly think of the best way to defend the group.

The biggest issue were the enemies flanking them on both sides. They simply had no means to defend against three fronts—left, right and forward—all at the same time. Within the next minute, chances were high that most or all of the team would end up dead.

Aren wanted to rip all of his hair out in desperate frustration as he realized there was nothing he could do. He couldn't cast destructive combat spells with his teammates around and taking out the enemy with his sword would be too slow.

Nevertheless, he knew he had no other option, so he drew his blade, and he gave one last quick look back at his team in dismay, knowing he was helpless to save them.

However, to his shock, half of the team seemed to be missing. He frantically worried that they were dead but he realized there were no bodies that he could see besides the three who had died early on—the rest had simply vanished.

Adding to his confusion, Henrika suddenly appeared out of nowhere, seeming to jump out of the ground itself. He was about to ask her what was happening, when he saw her grab two of the team's operatives and then suddenly disappear again, along with both of them.

In that moment, his confusion turned to a surge of ecstasy and relief as he realized what was going on.

He turned his head and saw the team, who had been brought about 80 feet back.

Even though Henrika was only teleporting two at a time, she was moving so swiftly that in another moment, Aren and Elmenz were the only ones left there. Aren grabbed Elmenz and with his full strength enhanced by Ineyem, pounced eighty feet back, landing where Henrika had brought the rest of the team.

They were not safe yet, as they were still in the range of the enemy's rifles, but thanks to Henrika, the group was far enough back that they were no longer surrounded, and the enemy would have more trouble aiming. They were still outnumbered, but no longer as disadvantaged as before.

"Thank you, Henrika," Aren stated. "You may have just saved the team."

"Aw, don't mention it, love," Henrika, panting from the exertion, leaned over and kissed him on the cheek gently.

Aren blushed as he turned his focus back on the enemy.

"It's time we ended this," Aren said heatedly.

"*Scintilla ekrix,*" Aren cried, pointing his palm at the enemy.

A spark appeared in front of his palm and began making its way to the center of the enemy soldiers.

"Wait, stop!" Elmenz cried.

Aren cancelled the spell, snuffing the spark. "What is it? We don't have much time here."

"I may not be familiar with that spell, but I recognize fire magic when I see it, and well," Elmenz began to explain. "My daughter's an electrician, and she's complained to me about the cheap materials used in these tunnels…"

"Please get to the point," Aren ordered, as he continued trying to draw fire to himself and fend off the blasts from several feet in front of the team. "We don't have much time."

"Fire magic could melt straight through those wires, electrifying that section of tunnel," Elmenz declared. "It could make it impassable, ruining the mission."

"The flames from this spell are a lower temperature," Aren stated. "Are you sure that'll still be a problem?"

While they spoke, Aren attempted to dodge as many shots from the enemy as he could. However, he was not moving at full speed since he did not want to discourage the enemy from aiming at him entirely. He was hit a few times as a result.

While they didn't do much damage with his Spirit Guard spell up, he knew he had to be careful. These sonic blasts were clearly more powerful than typical projectile rifles. Each hit took more of an energy drain than he had expected. His shield could still handle the occasional blast, but he needed to make sure that he didn't take too many.

"I can't be positive, but I don't think it's worth the risk unless you want to abandon the mission," Elmenz responded.

"Understood," Aren acknowledged. "Thank you for the warning."

Aren looked over at the enemies with a fierce determination. He was not about to let any more of his team die, but he also wasn't about to abandon this mission. Countless lives were at stake.

Aren extended his right arm towards the enemy.

So, I can't use fire, Aren thought to himself. *But if those cables are properly insulated, however cheaply, then this should work just fine instead.*

"*Fulgur tempes!*" Aren cried out, wincing in preparation.

Intense pain seared through Aren's arm, as a massive amount of energy surged from every pore of the outstretched limb, from shoulder to fingertips. At the same time, all of the lights in the area dimmed and he felt his own strength being sapped, as the spell drained energy both from him and from all active electronics around him.

It was little surprise that this was considered among the most brutal spells in Dracanis. It was a very difficult and unpleasant spell to cast, not only because it came with a very high energy demand that few casters could keep up with, but it also expected the caster to endure an incredible amount of pain while keeping perfect focus during the process of casting.

But in the following few seconds that the spell lasted, it became easily apparent why these costs were worth it.

The bolts that sprung from Aren's arm grew rapidly in size as they snaked outwards. In a flash, these bolts had filled the entire width and height of the tunnel and made their way over two hundred feet forward, capturing every single UAPA agent in an intense electrical surge. This was the power and fury of the spell known as Wyrm's Tempest.

After the spell was over, Aren quickly looked down at the cables and gave a sigh of relief. Just as he hoped, their insulated coverings were perfectly fine, with only slight singeing at a few parts, having mostly resisted the electrical blast.

Elmenz could hardly believe what he had just seen. In his decades as a sorcerer specializing in the magical art of Mivana, he had never seen anyone cast a spell this powerful so quickly, and without a single support caster to assist them.

Ollit's jaw had dropped, and he was similarly stunned as he looked over the scene. From his count, there were nearly fifty soldiers that had been taken out in an instant from that devastating blast of lightning magic that Aren had cast. Prior to that, their entire elite team put together had maybe taken down six or seven UAPA soldiers altogether.

"Aren—" Ollit began.

"Wait a second," Aren interrupted him.

Aren could hear a faint whirring sound, off in the distance, that put him back on guard. It sounded strangely familiar to him, but he couldn't quite put his finger on where he knew it from.

Then, it clicked. This was the same sound he had heard from the UAPA tank before it fired its sonic cannon back at the Silver Note Cabaret. However, with how long this one was charging, and how loudly that he could hear it, despite being out of visual range, he surmised that this one was likely larger and more powerful.

"Everyone, off the platform!" Aren ordered. "Get to the sides of the tunnel, now! They have a sonic cannon."

People immediately began sprinting to the sides. Aren looked back, where he saw Commander Irven struggling in the dead center of the tunnel. Aren was wondering what was going on, but quickly saw that not only did Irven seem to have broken a leg, but some of his torn armor had somehow gotten fully caught in part of the platform's broken grate. Aren could see that there was no way that he was going to make it in time.

"Irven, no!" Ollit screamed desperately.

Knowing there was no time to waste, Aren dove towards Irven, putting himself between the Commander and the cannon.

"*Ashaid cubri maxun!*" Aren yelled.

Bracing himself in a low stance, Aren threw his hands forward and put everything he had into this spell, conjuring the most potent shield he could muster. This was the most powerful variation of Spirit Guard, but it came with an intense energy drain, and would only last for a moment.

He hoped with everything he had that it would last long enough as the sonic blast made contact with him

Every tenth of a second that Aren was defending against the blast felt much longer, as it pushed and pushed against his shield. The blast quickly blew through the steel platform in front of them, blowing chunks of metal grating into Aren's shield along with the massive wave of sonic energy.

The sonic blasts from UAPA rifles were powerful, but this cannon was in a whole other league. Aren was only blocking maybe half of the blast's radius, and yet it took everything he had and more.

This artillery cannon was likely designed for destroying tanks and aircraft. Here, it had likely been prepared as a back-up plan in case the original ambush failed, to wipe out any surviving enemies.

Aren was doing everything he could to keep the shield up, putting every ounce of his power into it, but he could still feel it starting to crack. He pushed back harder, but he could not stop it, and his shield quickly shattered, ending the spell.

Aren used all of his strength to hold himself steady as he was forced back a step, and his arms were flung back to his sides. He was expecting the worst as his main defense was broken against the continuing blast. He still had his Ineyem, but the increased durability that gave him would not be enough against such a destructive force. Undeterred, however, he planted his feet firmly into the ground, refusing to allow himself to move another inch from his position in front of Irven. If he were to die here, he would at least save this one person behind him.

And yet, nothing more came. Aren slowly opened his eyes back up. It seemed that the blast ended just as Aren's shield had been destroyed. He fell to his knees, gasping for air.

He looked down. The front of his robes was torn, and his chest, which was at the focal point of the blast, was bloodied and deeply bruised. He suspected he may have fractured something, but besides that and some soreness in his hands, he otherwise didn't seem to be too injured. He looked behind him and saw that Irven appeared to be fine too. It looked like none of the blast had made it to him.

"Are you ok?" Aren asked him in a raspy voice, wanting to be sure.

"Yes," Irven responded, sounding shaken.

"Good," Aren asserted weakly, immediately collapsing to the ground and blacking out.

*/

Aren awoke to the feeling of being shaken. He groggily opened his eyes, seeing Elmenz above him.

"Aren, there you are!" Elmenz stated. "Are you alright?"

"I—wait, the cannon!" Aren suddenly sat up.

He jumped at the sudden sound of metal hitting metal. He turned his head to see a large mechanical implement had been dropped right next to him.

"Hey there, love," Henrika patted him on the shoulder as a shadow disappeared behind her. "Have a good nap?"

"Wait," Aren exclaimed, still waking back up. "Is that—"

"Yes, it's the cannon's energy converter," Henrika expressed. "I also knocked the operator unconscious, just to be safe."

"Wow," Aren laughed. "Thanks, Henrika."

"Thank you both," Commander Irven spoke up. "That was some amazing work. You two really saved us."

Aren shakily stood up and looked over to see Ollit helping Irven to his feet. He could see the pain in Irven's eyes behind his smile. Aren wasn't surprised at this though. From the appearance of his leg, Irven's tibia seemed to have been shattered, probably from the blast of a sonic rifle. However, he was still lucky that he had his body armor on, or else the leg might have been blown clear off by the shot.

He also noticed that Ollit was helping Irven with only his left arm. Aren looked at Ollit's right arm and was surprised to see that the armor had been shattered and it was in similar condition to Irven's leg.

"Your arm!" Aren exclaimed to Ollit, concerned.

"Don't worry about it," Ollit instructed as he finished setting the splint on Irven.

Ollit stood up, turned to Aren and began walking towards him. Aren stood guarded, unsure of Ollit's intentions as the General got closer and closer to him. What Aren was not expecting, however, was to be embraced in a tight, one-armed hug.

"Thank you," Ollit sputtered, tears flowing down his cheeks. "Godsdammit, thank you!"

After getting over his initial shock, Aren brought his arms up and hugged him back. After releasing, Ollit looked at him.

"*Devil of Hivich*, indeed... They should really call you the *Angel of Hivich*," Ollit expressed gratefully. "I thought Irven was dead for sure. What you did back there was incredible."

"Oh, it really wasn't so much," Aren dismissed somberly. "We still lost three people, and a few more are injured, yourself and Irven included."

"True, we did lose people," Ollit acknowledged, pulling out of the hug. "However, while I may have been skeptical, I'm not stubborn enough that I can't admit the truth in front of my face. And the truth is that we would have lost a lot more, maybe everyone, if you and Henrika weren't there. That ambush was the worst I'd ever seen."

"Thank you, Ollit," Aren stated, turning to Henrika. "I really want to thank you myself, Henrika. Not only for taking out the cannon, but also for getting everyone out of the way when this all started. I couldn't have done a thing if it weren't for you."

"Thanks, love," Henrika smiled coyly. "I believe that's what they call teamwork."

"Yes, Henrika's performance was excellent," Ollit acknowledged. "However, I need to address you Aren, because Henrika was not the one I had been doubting."

Ollit looked straight into Aren's eyes.

"Look Aren, I still may not understand your motives," Ollit expressed. "But you've proven you're one hell of an asset. I owe you for saving us."

He looked back at Irven with a longing look in his eyes. After a moment, he looked back over at Aren.

"Anyway, with my good arm broken, I'm in no condition to continue with this mission," Ollit admitted. "I'll take those who are injured, and we'll head back to base for treatment. With me gone, this operation needs a new leader. I doubt Henrika would be interested, and Elmenz doesn't have the right experience. That said, if you're not too injured, I'd like to leave you in charge, Aren. Think you're up to it?"

Aren was taken aback. He did not expect to hear such a concession from Ollit, and he definitely didn't expect Ollit to put him in charge. That ambush must have had a serious impact on him.

"You can count on me, General," Aren assured him.

"You know what," Ollit responded in a sincere tone. "I think I might actually believe that."

Chapter 18

After the shreen's howls died down, there was a moment of silence in the Grimveil Slave Camp's security station. Xander looked at Kyara with a worried expression. Although Xander had always known that letting the shreen into the compound was part of the plan, there was a growing part of him that felt uneasy about it. His experience with shreen was limited, but he couldn't shake the memory of his one encounter with them—those hungry, drooling jaws, those desperate, pained eyes.

However, he brushed it off as jitters.

Kyara's plan is a good one, he reasoned. *There's no reason to let doubts start to creep in now.*

"Great work, X-1 and K-1," Morgas' voice came in on Xander and Kyara's earpieces, breaking the silence. "I can see by the open gates that your mission was successful. Has the enemy been alerted of our presence?"

"That's a negative, Morgas," Kyara responded with Morgas' real name, as her and Anya were the only ones to never use a codename on open comms. "To our knowledge, our presence has not been reported. They will be on high alert and know that something is wrong with all of the gates opening, but they shouldn't know that Oppori Qala is involved yet. For all they know to this point, it could be a malfunction or user error. I'm sure they'll be scrambling to investigate though."

"Of course, no worries on that front—it's to be expected," Morgas asserted. "As you planned, K-1, we'll wait until they've diverted more of their forces to the gates. When they're all focused on the shreen we'll use explosives to blow holes in the eastern wall and move to flank their forces from there. Will you two be ok without us for a while?"

"Yes," Kyara asserted. "We will be fine on our own. Take however long you need."

"Yes, we'll be fine, Morgas," Xander agreed. "If it's alright, I'd like to move to my other objective at this point though."

"Ah, X-1," Morgas acknowledged. "Yes, you have the greenlight to go ahead with your own objective now. We'll take over the primary raid from here. You two have done a superb job, so thank you."

"I'm glad I could help," Xander replied.

"That you certainly have," Morgas affirmed. "Now, good luck. And X-1... I hope you find him."

"Thank you Morgas," Xander responded gratefully.

A click sound from their earpieces indicated that Morgas had disconnected from the line.

"We need to get out of here," Kyara asserted. "They'll be here any second."

"Agreed," Xander nodded.

Kyara walked up to the door control panel. Thankfully, getting out of the security station was much easier than getting in.

For security reasons, the only means to deactivate sonic repulsor shield from the outside was from bio-locked security remotes held only by the camp's top officers. However, from the inside, the repulsor shield could be easily temporarily disabled from a panel. Kyara pressed a few buttons on this panel, which opened the door and temporarily disabled the shield.

Together, Kyara and Xander exited the security station. As they emerged from the building, they saw a group of four UAPA soldiers running down the street in their direction.

Xander panicked, wondering if they could hide, but quickly realized it was not possible as the soldiers were already looking straight towards them.

"What the hell?" one of the UAPA soldiers exclaimed. "We've got intruders!"

However, Kyara didn't give them a chance to react. In a flash, she got her bow out and fired four arrows in rapid succession. Three of the four soldiers were hit straight in the neck, collapsing to the ground, but the last one had tilted his head down at just the wrong time, causing the arrow to be deflected by the chin of his helmet, saving him, but knocking him backwards.

Jarred by the hit, he began randomly firing his sonic rifle very roughly in their direction. However, within a split second, Kyara had drawn another arrow and shot at him again, hitting her mark this time.

Without wasting a second, Kyara quickly grabbed all four bodies, throwing two of them over each of her shoulders, almost like they weighed nothing. Xander marveled at her strength and speed as she brought them into the alley and hid them alongside the two bodies from before.

"Sorry about that," Kyara apologized. "Now let's get out of here."

"What do you mean by sorry?" Xander asked, but she was already darting through the alley and across the adjacent street.

He followed at the fastest sprint he could muster, trailing a bit behind, until they found their way safely behind a stack of crates a bit of a distance from the security station. Despite the short distance, he was already out of breath. Kyara was very difficult to keep up with when she moved seriously. Although, he suspected that even at this speed she had been slowing down for his sake.

As they hid behind the crates, they could hear shouting from UAPA soldiers along the street behind them. It seems they crossed at just the right time to avoid more enemies.

"Did you really just apologize for needing one extra shot to take down four soldiers?" Xander inquired quietly, huffing as he tried to catch his breath.

"Mistakes like that can cost lives and ruin missions," Kyara asserted. "People likely heard those sonic rifle blasts and will be coming to investigate. That's probably what those guards back there are looking for."

"Come on," Xander reasoned. "They already clearly know something is wrong from the opened gates and incoming shreen at this point. I doubt a couple sonic blasts are going to do much of anything. Besides, perfection is a ridiculous standard to hold yourself to."

"Perhaps," Kyara half-heartedly conceded. "Either way, we don't have time to discuss this. We need to keep moving. Even this hiding spot won't be safe for long."

"Alright, that's fine, but before you go, can you just let me know if you have any idea where I can find prisoner records?"

Xander inquired. "This camp is huge, but if they have Matlex, they have to have some information on him somewhere here."

"Yes, actually, there's a processing building ahead that should have access to prisoner records," Kyara answered. "Unfortunately, it's pretty close to the main southern gate, where a lot of the guards will be gathering at the moment, but we should make it through ok if we're on our guard. I'll lead you there."

"Wait, aren't you needed elsewhere?" Xander asked. "I can do this on my own."

"It's ok, I actually already told Morgas I'd be going with you," Kyara informed him. "Besides, we'll be assisting the raid by taking out guards and causing some extra chaos along the way."

"Wow, really? You planned this all along?" Xander asked with gratitude in his voice. "Well... thank you. I really appreciate the help."

Still sweating and feeling a burning in his chest from that last sprint, he looked at Kyara pleadingly. "However, is there any chance that you could move just a little slower this time?"

"Sorry, it's been a while since I've worked with anyone besides Aren on an operation," Kyara explained. "I can try to slow down a bit more for you."

"Thank you," Xander replied appreciatively, then adding with a hint of sarcasm. "So sorry to burden you with my regular human speed."

"Oh, it's fine," Kyara responded nonchalantly. "No need for you to worry. We should get going though."

Kyara continued leading him down streets, alleys, and pathways. As they made their way closer to their destination, they could hear the sounds of shouting, sonic blasts, and the shrieking of the shreen.

"I wasn't expecting it to be so loud out here," Xander said to Kyara. "Is this all part of the plan?"

"I'm not sure," Kyara responded hesitantly. "But we need to keep our guard up as we go along, nevertheless."

It was not long after Kyara said this that they were startled by a screaming UAPA guard, running past the alleyway where they were hidden. Before the guard could even make it past them, a shreen pounced onto him, tearing through his armor with its teeth and biting deep into the soldier's flesh.

"Holy shit!" Xander shouted.

Kyara grabbed his shoulder to get his attention. He looked over and saw her motioning that they needed to get away. He nodded, and the two of them quickly went in the opposite direction, making their way into another alley a bit of distance away.

"What the hell?" Xander blurted. "What are the shreen doing all the way over here? We're still some distance from the main gate here, aren't we?"

"Yes, we are," Kyara answered. "I'll admit, this is a bit unexpected. They weren't supposed to make it this far—especially not this quickly. They were really only supposed to be a diversion so our main forces could sneak in behind... Hold on a second, I'm going to contact Anya."

Kyara pressed a few buttons on her wristcomm, connecting her to a secure radio line with Anya. Kyara then pressed a few more buttons to add Xander into the call.

"Anya, what's going on?" Kyara queried. "I'm seeing shreen deep into the compound here. Have you guys started moving in to flank yet?"

"No, not quite yet," Anya answered. "The plan has changed somewhat. There are far more shreen than we anticipated. Those ones always pacing outside the camp didn't attack alone, like we expected. It seems they called a bunch of their friends from across half of the damned forest to join them."

"Well, that's a bit terrifying," Xander stated with a feeling of unease.

"Honestly, I was worried something like this might happen," Kyara added candidly. "They are social creatures after all, and their behaviour has been unpredictable lately."

"Yes, you did warn us, Kyara. However, in all honesty, this may actually end up working to our advantage," Anya responded optimistically. "They're taking out a lot of UAPA soldiers."

"I agree that's a benefit," Kyara replied. "However, I still don't think we should take this lightly."

"Don't worry, we're aware," Anya reassured. "All of our teams have activated their sonic deterrents, and we're going to be moving very carefully from here on."

"I'm glad to hear it," Kyara replied. "How many shreen are there anyway?"

"Well, at the beginning, I'd say it was around two hundred," Anya answered. "It's hard for me to be sure exactly how many there are now, but definitely over a thousand at this point. They've completely breeched into the camp. It's a good thing we waited until after curfew, so prisoners won't get caught up in this mess... From what you've seen, do you really think they'll be safe in their bunks?"

"Yes, the residency buildings are well-fortified to keep the prisoners contained," Kyara explained. "They should be safe in there until we can get them to the transport vehicles."

"That's a relief," Anya responded. "Just be careful you two. I know you gave up your sonic deterrent to another team that didn't have one, Kyara. I hope you'll be ok without it."

"Oh, I'll be fine," Kyara assured her. "They need it more than I do."

Kyara could hear someone talking to Anya on the other end of the line.

"Sorry Kyara, I've gotta go," Anya stated. "Morgas has made the call and we're going to be moving in now. Good luck you two!"

"Thanks," Kyara responded. "Good luck to you too!"

"Good luck Anya!" Xander added.

A click sound indicated that Anya ended the call.

"I don't suppose there's somewhere else we could go for prisoner records?" Xander asked nervously. "Preferably somewhere with a bit more distance from the main gate, considering what Anya just told us."

"None that I know of," Kyara responded. "I think this building is our safest bet for finding him."

Xander sighed. "I worried as much."

He looked over at the path ahead of them, listening to the screams and howls in the distance. "I suppose we should get moving then."

Kyara nodded. "Yes, we should."

As much as the sounds ahead of them sent chills down his spine, Xander felt some comfort as he looked over at Kyara by his side. Even if he had been alone, he knew he was not going to let whatever lay ahead stop him from searching for Matlex. Nevertheless, having someone like her around definitely did not hurt.

Again, Kyara and Xander began moving down the streets and alleyways together. As they moved, they came across an increasing number of shreen and UAPA soldiers, both living and dead. Moving cautiously, they managed to make their way through the area without being detected.

It did not take long for them to reach the epicenter of this chaos. After entering an alleyway closer to their destination, they looked out into the wide, main street on the way to the primary gate. This street seemed to be where most of the sounds were coming from.

Xander put his hand over his mouth. It was worse than he had imagined. Ahead of them was a bloody and brutal battlefield. Hundreds of dead bodies, both of shreen and UAPA soldiers were strewn across the large stretch of street with thin pools of blood covering most of the ground between them.

Standing atop this bloodied street were UAPA soldiers, attempting to hold their ground as large packs of voracious shreen continued to pour in through the main gate. Some of these shreen went straight to the dead soldiers, feasting on them. Some shreen branched out into alleyways and other streets. But most of the shreen focused on fighting against the UAPA forces on the main street.

Xander watched anxiously as a pack of thirteen shreen made its way towards a group of six UAPA soldiers on the side of the street. The soldiers managed to kill five of the approaching shreen quite quickly, blowing large holes in the beasts' bodies with their sonic rifles.

However, the UAPA soldiers simply didn't have the time to hit all of them before the pack closed the distance. After getting close enough, the remaining shreen pounced on the soldiers, tearing through armor and flesh with their corrosive saliva and countless rows of teeth.

UAPA armor was not weak, covering 80% of the soldiers' bodies in tough bullet-proof panels held between weaker, but still tough fabric. However, on top of weakening the armor with their corrosive saliva, it appeared as if the shreen were able to rapidly figure out where the weak points in the armor were located, targeting those points with their teeth and ripping off the tougher armor plating from the sides, so that they could get at the exposed flesh beneath.

Xander wondered if this technique could have come from their experience hunting *ghittles*. Ghittles are large creatures with dense exoskeletons that Kyara told him about earlier. Apparently, they were one of the shreen's main food sources before their populations were devastated by pollution in this region. Regardless of the explanation, though, it was horrific to watch.

"How could any animal act like this?" Xander asked in shock. "I mean, hunting for food is one thing, but they're practically throwing their lives away here."

Xander looked over at Kyara. While he was filled with a sense of dread, Kyara only appeared sorrowful as she looked out at the battlefield.

"This is what happens when you push an entire species to the brink," Kyara responded somberly. "I may not have known the shreen before now, but I know animals. I've lived among many of the most ferocious predators, and the *only* times any of them acted like this was when they were at their most desperate."

"Is that really enough to cause this kind of behaviour?" Xander asked with a hint of incredulity.

"You'd be surprised what desperation can do—to animals or people alike," Kyara responded as she wiped a stray tear from her cheek. "Albeit I wouldn't be surprised if there was a retribution component that may be going on here as well."

"Retribution?" Xander asked. "Really? You think they're able to even know that UAPA are to blame for their problems?"

"Well, it's probably not as blatant as that," Kyara explained. "However, many animals are smarter than you might think. I fully believe that part of the shreen understands the pain that this camp has caused their forest. It's only a hunch, but I suspect that has a role in their viciousness here."

"I never would have thought of that," Xander remarked. "Nature can truly be terrifying sometimes."

As they were talking, more UAPA reinforcements continued to join in, shooting down as many shreen as they could. Many of these soldiers looked tired, likely half awake, running on adrenaline after being woken up from their bunks to deal with this emergency in the middle of the night. However, more packs of shreen continued pouring in from the gate as well. It was clear that this conflict wasn't going to end anytime soon.

In that moment, they could hear gunfire from projection rifles—the kind that Oppori Qala uses—sounding out from a bit of distance behind them.

"It sounds like the main forces have made their move," Kyara noted.

"So, where are we going?" Xander asked. "Are we close yet?"

"Yes, we are very close," Kyara answered. "But you might not be as happy about that as you'd think."

Kyara pointed to a building across the battlefield. "The processing building is just over there, down the street, near the gate."

"Damn," Xander replied. "Well, are we going to take the long way around to it then? I suppose we're still trying not to be seen, right?"

"Actually, stealth is no longer necessary now that our main forces have made contact," Kyara stated. "Now, besides Matlex, our only other objective is taking out as many soldiers as we can along the way. We'll achieve that best and save lots of time if we take the direct route. However, if you don't feel up to that, we can maintain our stealth and go the long way. I will leave the choice to you."

Xander was not expecting to have to make a choice like this. The main street in front of them was a living hell.

However, he didn't want to wait any longer in his search for Matlex.

It also wasn't lost on him that they might be able to really help contribute to the success of the entire raid here. It was clear that the shreen were starting to lose ground to the continued influx of UAPA reinforcements. If the UAPA soldiers were to take out the shreen here, they could better prepare themselves for Oppori Qala's main forces, which could cause some real problems for the raid.

"Ok, let's do it," Xander affirmed. "We'll go straight for the processing building, but we'll take out as many UAPA soldiers as we can along the way. Hopefully that will give the advantage to the shreen here."

Kyara nodded to him. "Sounds good to me."

Kyara put her bow away, and then drew a pistol and pulled a dagger from her belt.

"Wait just a second, you use guns?" Xander asked, sounding a bit surprised.

"I mean, I've had it there on my hip the whole time," Kyara pointed out, scratching her head in mild confusion at the question. "What did you think it was there for?"

"I don't know," Xander shrugged. "Maybe as a back-up if you lost your bow? At this point, I just assumed that arrows were kind of more your thing."

"I use whatever tools are best for the job," Kyara asserted. "Bows are great for stealth, but guns have their own advantages too. This pistol here not only has better mobility than my bow, but it also packs quite a punch."

"I suppose that makes sense," Xander replied tepidly.

Xander took out his chiambra and bow. He took comfort in the fact that at least this time he wouldn't have to quiet himself as he cast his aurimancy.

"Do you think you can take out the soldiers up above?" Kyara asked.

She pointed up at two rooftops. One was on the eastern side of the street, nearer to them with four soldiers on top, and one was on the western side of the street farther from them with three soldiers on top. All of these soldiers were firing at the incoming shreen from their high vantage points.

"Absolutely," Xander answered. "I prefer to fight from up high, so that works well for me. I suppose I'll take them out and then provide you support from above afterwards. I mean, if that sounds alright to you?"

"Sounds good to me," Kyara nodded to him. "Now, let's go."

Chapter 19

Aren could feel the fatigue really setting in. He drained a ton of his energy in that last fight. Also, now that his adrenaline was dying down along with its painkilling effects, he started to feel a throbbing soreness in his chest. He no longer had any doubts at this point that he fractured his sternum when taking that blast from the sonic cannon.

However, he knew he had to continue moving. He grabbed the eight nutrient bars and the two caffeinated electrolyte drinks from his pouch and quickly downed them all.

After he finished eating and drinking, he took a deep breath and collected himself. This wasn't the worst condition that he had to complete a mission in. Not only that, but this operation was far more important than his usual. Continuing on here was an easy decision for him, mentally speaking, even if his body didn't quite agree.

"Ok, everyone injured, get ready to come with me," Ollit ordered to the group. "We're going to gather our fallen and head back to base. Lieutenant Chave and everyone who is still in the condition to continue, report to Aren. He's in charge of the operation now."

"Yes, sir!" the operatives responded in perfect unison.

Aren could see why the E7 Resistance Cell was considered one of the best in Oppori Qala. Throughout the ambush, Aren had noticed that they all kept their cool, keeping their movements fast and calculated, which was one of the biggest reasons they didn't have more casualties. Overall, their discipline, coordination, and skill were quite impressive for members of a rebellion, which generally consisted of inexperienced volunteers.

As the team was getting prepped to move, one of the operatives pulled a large metal device out of their pack. Aren recognized it immediately as a compact hovercart, used for many applications across the galaxy.

This operative unfolded the cart, revealing a thin metal frame that extended just over six feet long and three feet wide. In the center of the frame was a sturdy synthetic mesh for containing the load. The frame and mesh looked thin and frail, but Aren knew those things were designed with highly resilient materials that could carry a load weighing several hundred pounds without issue.

The operative placed this cart on the ground and then pulled out a long, retractable metal handle from the frame, which allowed the cart to be pushed or pulled manually. After pressing a button on the handle, the device began to emit a buzzing sound, and started hovering over the ground.

While the operative was doing this, the others gathered up the bodies of their three fallen comrades, and carefully piled them onto the cart.

Aren knew well that it was not always possible to bring the bodies back of fallen soldiers or operatives during an operation, but he was glad that Ollit and the E7 cell had the opportunity to do so here. This would undoubtedly be very meaningful for the friends and family of the deceased. Antallian funeral rites typically weren't religious, but they were ceremonial, and the tradition was that the deceased's body be present for it.

Elmenz approached Aren as he was watching the operatives and cleared his throat.

"I must say, that was some very impressive magic back there," Elmenz commended him, while stroking his beard. "From the council meeting, I knew you had some impressive skills, but I had no idea you had that kind of magical prowess."

Elmenz cleared his throat again before continuing. "Not meaning to brag or anything, but I'm considered to be amongst the best sorcerers here on Antal—an expert in Mivana—but I will openly admit, I certainly couldn't cast like that. The shielding spells and that lightning spell were both incredible. Even the fire spell you cancelled was unusual. To be honest, I'm very curious what magical arts those spells fall under, if you don't mind sharing? Although I could be wrong, I don't believe those were Mivana."

Aren looked at Elmenz thoughtfully. This sorcerer was old, with deep wrinkles, a large, gray beard, and frizzy hair, but despite his apparent age, he did not appear frail. He held himself with confidence and a strong posture that made him look taller than the 5'6" he stood at in reality.

It was little surprise that Elmenz brought up Mivana when asking about the magical arts that Aren was using. Not only because Mivana was Elmenz's specialty, but it was also the most commonly known and used magical art across the galaxy by most serious sorcerers.

This was because Mivana is an incredibly broad magical art with countless applications across many fields and connections to many other magical arts. Yet, despite its incredible utility, Mivana also is considered one of the easier magical arts to learn magic with. This makes it a great foundational magical art to start with, regardless of whatever branch of magic a sorcerer wanted to get into. However, Mivana also contained more than enough advanced and powerful spells that its users would never have to branch into other magical arts if they chose not to.

Consequently, it was quite common for most sorcerers to stick only to the art of Mivana from the beginning to end of their magical careers. In fact, Mivana had come to be so dominant in the scene that many sorcerers had stopped using the term "Mivana" altogether and had come to refer to it as simply default "magic". These sorcerers would only identify specific "magical arts" when they involved spells outside of Mivana, as if Mivana was not a magical art itself. However, Aren knew this was a flawed concept and was glad to hear Elmenz identifying Mivana as its own magical art.

"That's a good catch," Aren commended him. "None of those spells were Mivana. They were all Dracanis."

"Dracanis?" Elmenz said in wonder. "You can't mean the Dracosian magical art...? I've heard tales of it, but I didn't think that there was anyone alive in the galaxy who still knew it."

"Well, there's at least me," Aren grinned cheekily. "But truth be told, I actually don't know if there's anyone else."

"Interesting," Elmenz responded. "In any case, I'm glad that you're on our side."

As the operatives finished up their prep, Ollit walked over to Irven and helped him stand up using his uninjured arm. Irven put his arm over Ollit's shoulders and leaned on Ollit for support as he stood on his one good leg.

"Alright, let's move out," Ollit ordered, before turning to Aren and the others who were remaining. "Good luck to you all in your mission."

Ollit and the rest of the injured began walking back to base. Those who were left included Aren, Elmenz, Henrika, and seven of the E7 agents. Altogether, this was just over half of the people that they had started with.

One of the agents approached Aren.

"Hello sir," the man greeted. "My name is Lieutenant Chave. With Commander Irven gone, I am the ranking officer of E7. I know I speak for all of us when I say that we appreciate what you did back there. We are ready to take your orders whenever you're ready to give them sir."

"I'm glad to hear it," Aren nodded to him.

Looking over, Aren saw the remaining operatives of E7, lined up behind Chave, while Elmenz and Henrika were hanging back behind Aren. Aren could see that these operatives were diligently following their training, but despite their rigid posture and their attempt at keeping cold expressions, Aren could see the pain and worry in their eyes.

"Alright, now I know a lot of you are probably shaken up," Aren asserted. "What just happened was no small thing. Somehow, they must have found out we were coming. There will be time to figure that out and to grieve the fallen later on.

"But, for now, we have a very important mission ahead of us. It may be tough to move forward now, but I promise you, I will do everything in my power to ensure that no one else here will die on my watch.

"Nevertheless, if any of you feel that you need to take your leave, now is the time. I'm giving anyone full permission to head back if they aren't prepared to continue with this mission."

The operatives stood silently, without moving a muscle. Aren looked across their faces. They were clearly shaken, and yet he could still see an unmistakable, steadfast resolve in the eyes of every one of them.

"Alright," Aren announced. "Now, are you all ready to follow me and show the world the truth about UAPA?"

"Yes sir!" the group exclaimed in unison.

"Good," Aren asserted. "Let's get moving."

It didn't take Aren long to find the hidden hatch to the CNPF. It was concealed by a large maintenance panel, which was located exactly where the blueprints indicated it would be. This maintenance panel was easily removed, and behind it was a large, reinforced hatch and a keypad.

Aren could hear a humming sound and see visible vibrations in the air over the hatch, indicating that a sonic repulsor shield was actively protecting it. He pulled out the data card containing officer credentials from his pocket, inserted it into an open slot beneath the keypad, and then pressed a few buttons.

While UAPA used bioscanners for most of their automated identification systems across the globe, the CNPF worked differently because it already had state-of-the-art security systems when UAPA took over, and replacing these systems was deemed too expensive and unnecessary. Instead, they reprogrammed and continued using the old system, which used personalized credential codes for ID that were kept on data cards like the one Aren had just inserted here.

A prompt appeared on the display above the keypad, reading:

Welcome, Inspector Worist.

The humming sound suddenly stopped, the vibrations over the door disappeared, and the door opened. Aren removed his data card, putting it back into his pocket, before turning on his comms and speaking into his earpiece.

"Hello, Orita?" Aren addressed. "You said you wanted me to tell you when I accessed the facility, right?

"Oh, yes," Orita responded back into his earpiece. "So, I take it that your officer credentials worked then?"

"Yes," Aren responded. "I was a little worried when it looked like they were prepared for us, but it seems they still didn't know about the code I copied since they didn't update it."

"What do you mean 'it looked like they were prepared for you'?" Orita asked. "Did something happen?"

"Yes, unfortunately, we were ambushed," Aren responded. "And I'm guessing they knew I was going to be there, since they used gaucifin to cover their scent. We lost three people in the attack."

"Wow, seriously?" Orita asked in shock. "Do you have any idea how they could have known?"

"I don't," Aren answered. "However, we don't have time to worry about it right now."

"Right," Orita acknowledged. "Ok, well, since you opened the door, I was able to access their network through the remote router you're carrying. I can make sure the doors on the inside will open for you, but like I suspected, it's looking like I can't get to any of the really good stuff wirelessly."

"Wow, you work fast," Aren responded. "You did that while we were talking?"

"It's no big deal," Orita responded. "UAPA network security is crap. I could circumvent it in my sleep."

Aren laughed. "You know, you remind me a bit of someone I used to work with a lot. They were very good with computers as well."

"Is that so?" Orita responded. "Did you like this person?"

"They were a good friend," Aren replied with a hint of sadness. "Anyway, if wireless access isn't enough, I'll just have to hook you up when I get to the broadcast room like we originally planned, right?"

"You got it," Orita replied. "I'll be coordinating with you and Henrika from here on."

"Henrika?" Aren asked. "What do you mean? I thought she was just here to assist with the physical infiltration."

"Oh, right," Orita responded like she just remembered something. "Well, it doesn't really matter. The point is, I'll need you to connect me directly to the server when you get to the broadcast room."

Aren thought that her response was a tad strange. It was true that Orita was notorious in Oppori Qala for being a bit of an airhead at times, despite her high IQ and incredible skills with computers and hacking. It was very plausible that Orita simply mentioned Henrika by mistake.

Yet, Aren couldn't help but feel a tingling of suspicion that maybe there was something more going on. Either way, he decided not to pursue it. For now, he just had to move forward with his team.

He made a signal to the team to follow him, and then together they moved in.

Swiftly, they made their way through the halls. Along the way, they encountered a group of three guards. After seeing them, Aren lunged forward and cut them down in an instant, before they could begin firing on the group. While he did not kill them, he did make sure to destroy their rifles and left them with deep enough cuts across their torsos to put them out of commission for a while.

Two more guards came out from one of the side rooms, looking for the source of the commotion they just heard, but the operatives behind Aren instantly shot them down. Aren was impressed by the speed and accuracy of the E7 operatives, having aimed successfully for the weak points in the enemy's armor. Now that they were no longer at the disadvantage of an ambush, their skills were really shining through. However, he couldn't be impressed for long, as his thoughts were interrupted by a voice coming from the building's PA system.

"I had a feeling it was going to be you," The voice spoke. "The Devil of Hivich... It was no surprise to me when I found out that you've been working with Oppori Qala all this time. And here you are, with that vile thief and that second-rate sorcerer."

Aren's ears perked up, instantly recognizing the voice. The one speaking was unmistakably Commandant Reinault—the officer he had faced against back at the Silver Note Cabaret, and the one who was in charge of the CNPF.

"Reinault," Aren called out. " How's your neck doing?"

As Aren spoke, his voice was picked up by the security mics, which transmitted the audio to the Commandant.

"It's fine, thank you very much," Reinault sneered. "As an esteemed UAPA officer, I have access to the world's best medical care... Speaking of, I hope you don't think you'll get any mercy from me just because you were idiotic enough to make your cut too shallow to finish me off. Your death sentence was set in stone long ago."

"Oh, I wouldn't think anything of the sort," Aren countered, as their team took out several more soldiers rushing them in the hallway.

"Good," Reinault asserted. "I've been waiting for you, you know."

"Really?" Aren responded. "If that's the case, why don't you come out and face us directly."

"Ooh, yes," Henrika agreed. "I'd love to say hello. And maybe I could take a sneak peek at your vault code while we're at it. I hear you keep some rather valuable materials here."

"Oh, I think I know better than to show my face around you lot," Reinault laughed. "I'm not even in the building anyway. I happened to have business elsewhere today, but I just wanted to say hi. Don't worry about my absence there, though, you'll all be dealt with soon enough anyway."

"Is that so?" Aren questioned. "It's been quite the surprise party so far. I look forward to seeing whatever else you've got for me."

"Yes, well, it's unfortunate you survived the tunnel ambush," Reinault vociferated. "I warned that belik General that I would need more reinforcements, along with tanks and turrets to deal with you lot, but he just wouldn't listen."

Aren continued moving down the halls, leading the team as they spoke.

"Having said that, I'm glad to see you weren't unscathed," Reinault commented gleefully. "The first report from my people said there were eighteen of you to start. I only see ten now. Looks like that ambush wasn't totally worthless."

"You know, perhaps you could tell me how you knew we were coming," Aren requested. "Since we're having this lovely conversation and all, and you seem to have had such advanced notice."

"Oh, I think telling you would hardly do you any good," Reinault asserted. "Especially considering that you're not going to be getting out of here alive."

"You sound quite confident," Aren responded. "I almost feel bad that I'm going to be proving you wrong pretty quickly here."

"We shall see," Reinault declared. "In any case, I have business to attend to. I shall leave you to your fate. Have fun, rebellious scum."

Aren jumped and slashed the security camera, ending the conversation.

"Well, he was certainly cheerful," Henrika commented.

Aren laughed, but then turned to the agents more seriously. "Lieutenant Chave, you and your people are clear to destroy all security cameras and mics from here on. Consider them a second priority, behind guards and other immediate threats."

"Understood," Chave affirmed, turning to his operatives. "Did you all get that?"

"Yes, sir!" The E7 operatives chimed in unison.

The broadcast room wasn't far now. Their goal was feeling closer than ever. However, as they turned a corner, they were forced to stop. Blocking their way was an improvised steel blockade built into the hallway and covered by the appearance of vibrating air, marking that it was reinforced by a portable sonic repulsor shield.

"Damnit," Chave cursed. "How are we going to get past this?"

"Any remote chance that your magic could get us through?" Elmenz asked Aren.

"Maybe, but it would take too long," Aren responded. "We need to get to that broadcasting room as soon as possible. We're a bit behind schedule."

Aren turned to Henrika. "What about you, Henrika? Could you teleport us past that with your shadow magic?"

Henrika created a shadow and attempted to walk through but it appeared something was blocking her way.

"Sorry, love," Henrika responded. "It seems there's some kind of enchantment in the area stopping me."

"An enchantment to block teleportation magic is not an easy thing to accomplish," Elmenz noted. "Those kinds of enchantments are only temporary too, so they must have done it recently. They must really want to keep us out."

"Or perhaps, they want to make sure we go through the hangar instead," Aren theorized. "We need to be cautious. We have no idea what we'll see in there."

"That's a good point," Elmenz stated. "I agree, we should be very careful as we proceed."

"To be safe, I'm going to go ahead into the hangar on my own for now," Aren declared. "The rest of you, hold back for the moment. I want everyone to remain some distance away from the door until I can get a chance to see and assess whatever's waiting for us, assuming there is anything."

"Yes, sir," the operatives affirmed the order.

Aren opened the door to the hangar and walked through cautiously. It was a typical mid-sized industrial hangar. There were some random metal crates and barrels stacked in a few places, as well as a dock for a small craft, but the majority of the space was dedicated to the loading bay, likely for the delivery of equipment and supplies.

To Aren's surprise, nothing seemed wrong in this room, at first. There were no tanks, turrets, or soldiers that he could see waiting around for a second ambush.

However, not long after entering, he started to sense a powerful surge of raw magical energy gathering behind one of the stacks of metal barrels at the opposite end of the room. Whoever was preparing this spell was making no effort to "quiet" their magic.

Although Aren did not know what spell was being cast, he didn't take any chances, and quickly dove far out of the way. He was just in time to avoid a giant beam shooting out from behind the barrels. This beam cut through the metal barrels like a knife through butter, and then shot straight into the door that Aren came from.

Aren found himself panting more than he expected from the exertion. Normally, a little jump like that would be nothing to him — especially under Antal's weaker-than-average gravity. This just further demonstrated how seriously low his energy reserves were.

Aren looked back and saw a huge hole in the wall where the door had been. He was grateful he told the team to wait some distance away. This was exactly the kind of thing he had been worried about. It didn't appear that the beam made it much further after destroying the thick metal door and surrounding wall, but it still would have caused some significant injuries if the operatives were behind it at the time.

Henrika walked up to the giant hole in the wall.

"Damn," She commented. "Was that some kind of magic?"

"Yes, it was," Aren affirmed, impressed that she was able to tell based off of the little she saw from the other side.

Aren looked over at the source of the magic. Now that the barrels had been destroyed, Aren could clearly see the caster. It was a tall orren man, smirking over at him from across the room. He had medium-long, gelled-back hair, a well-groomed, braided beard, and he was wearing elaborate, expensive-looking, silk robes with ornate, golden accessories over the shoulders. Behind him stood a group of people in much simpler robes that featured the same colors. Aren counted twenty-two altogether, including the man at the front.

"Well, well, I see you managed to dodge my attack," the bearded man laughed. "Bravo. Although, I'm not surprised, really. Reinault warned me about you. It's part of why I took this job—so that I could face this so-called legendary Devil of Hivich, and further demonstrate my power to the world. But it's no matter. That was only a warm-up shot. The next one will be far more powerful, and will follow your body heat, so you won't be able to escape so easily. An easy feat for one as talented as I."

At this point, Lieutenant Chave and two other E7 operatives had gotten into position behind the hole in the wall and began firing at the man. However, the bullets stopped in mid-air as they hit an invisible barrier and fell to the ground. Aren could see four of the sorcerers near the back of the group muttering quietly, and he realized they were casting cyclical incantations to conjure this protective barrier. It was clear that this group of sorcerers were not unaccustomed to battle.

"Nice try, but you'll have to do better than that," The bearded man taunted. "I've been shot at many times, but never hit once."

Elmenz was curious at this familiar voice he was hearing from in the hangar. He carefully peaked around the edge of the opening in the wall to get a better look. As he peered into the room, he gasped as he saw who the caster was.

"Everyone, stay back," Aren ordered. "I'll deal with these mages."

"Aren, be careful!" Elmenz cried. "That man is Maximilius Olant. He's the most deadly sorcerer on Antal. I know your magic is strong, but the power he commands is even greater."

"Is that so?" Aren asked.

Elmenz nodded. "He made a name for himself during the Raider Wars, and with good reason. I've seen his spells level entire buildings before. Even that sonic cannon from earlier pales in comparison to the damage he can do."

"Interesting," Aren responded. "I take it those are his support casters behind him then?"

"Indeed," Elmenz confirmed. "He's the only one I've ever seen who is capable of coordinating and focusing the magic of so many support casters. You might have had the power advantage if it was one-on-one, but you won't come close when his full coven is with him."

"Is that Elmenz I hear over there?" Maximilius called out. "Why it's been such a long time? Why don't you come out into the open and greet me properly?"

"I think I'm good back here," Elmenz yelled back. "I have no interest in greeting a UAPA supporter."

"Come now," Maximilius responded. "You're just jealous of me, as always. You've been sore ever since I was voted Antal's greatest sorcerer in *The Antallian*... But you know, if you change sides now, and help me destroy that Devil of Hivich, I can promise you a lucrative job at UAPA. They treat turncoats quite well here."

"Thanks, but I'm not interested," Elmenz called back. "And to be clear, I have no issue with you beating me in that silly publication ranking. My only issue is your support of tyrants."

"Fine then," Maximilius shrugged. "You can die along with that devil."

Elmenz looked over to Aren and spoke quietly. "You can't win against him in a game of power. However, if you used that incredible speed of yours—the one you showed off at the council meeting—you should be able to go around that shield and get to him before he casts his next spell."

"Thank you for the warning, Elmenz," Aren said gratefully. "I think I know what to do."

"You know, I could teleport over there and knock him out if you want, Aren," Henrika offered. "It would be a piece of cake."

"Thank you for the offer, Henrika," Aren replied. "It's appreciated, but I've got this."

"Alright, love," Henrika nodded at him.

Aren began walking steadily forward towards Maximilius, straight out in the open.

"Aren, what are you doing?" Elmenz cried out. "You need to use your speed, or you'll be killed. You don't stand a chance against that level of magic. My gods, I mean, you can barely even stand."

"I understand your concerns, but it's fine Elmenz," Aren assured. "Trust me."

Aren knew that Elmenz was right about one thing though. He was very exhausted. His body's energy reserves had been drained along with all the life energy he had used. He was going to need a huge meal and long sleep when this was all over. But for now, he could only continue walking forward.

"Do you have a death wish?" Maximilius shouted to him, laughing heartily. "Or do you foolishly expect that you can dodge at the last second again? I wouldn't be so cocky if I were you, but if you insist, it certainly makes my job easier."

Maximilius gave the signal to his coven, and they all began muttering a new incantation, quickly producing a large ball of raw magical energy in front of Maximilius, that he held in place using his own power as he prepared himself.

Aren kept walking steadily, slowly making his way towards them without any change to his pace.

"I think it's time to say goodbye," Maximilius grinned maliciously. "This is the end for you, Devil of Hivich."

Maximilius muttered a quick incantation under his breath and began transforming the magical sphere into a giant beam, much larger and more powerful looking than the one before. This one was likely to do a lot more damage, especially considering it didn't have to go through a stack of full, steel barrels first.

"No!" Elmenz cried out desperately as the devastating beam, far larger and brighter than before, shot out towards Aren.

Chapter 20

More than a year before the raid on the CNPF, in an abandoned parking lot in eastern Marann, Anya was pacing back and forth impatiently along the pavement.

When she first arrived on this lot, she found that she enjoyed the beauty and peacefulness of the setting. Not only was it surrounded by gorgeous trees and chirping birds, but it was also pleasantly quiet. Being located on the outskirts of a ghost town meant that there were no sounds of the city nearby. It also meant that there were no people around to interrupt or snoop on the meeting. All-in-all, it was an ideal location for a rendezvous point.

Although, at this point, she was starting to wonder if the meeting was ever going to happen.

She looked down at her wristcomm. The time it displayed confirmed she had been waiting for him for more than an hour now.

She sighed frustratedly. It had been a bad enough day already without having to deal with tardiness on top of everything else.

I knew I shouldn't have trusted this to a bounty hunter, she thought to herself. *This was too important to leave to some flakey contractor.*

In truth, she had been rather impressed with this bounty hunter when they first met. Not only did he come from a renowned organization, but he had also successfully managed to capture a prolific serial arsonist from offworld who had been hiding out on Antal.

However, the fact that he was a bounty hunter at all, working purely for money, had put her a bit on edge. She was not used to collaborating with people from that line of work. Those she worked with were generally passionate people who fought because they believed in their cause, and not for the money.

Nevertheless, she decided to go out on a limb to hire this man because she needed the help and he had impressed her at the time. Although, at this point, the fact that he was now more than an hour late made her question whether that decision was a mistake.

She looked down at her wristcomm again.

I think it's time to call it, she decided. *I can't wait forever for someone who's probably not even going to show up.*

While she was upset about the failed meeting, there was a part of her that felt a wave of relief. It was unfortunate to not have this bounty hunter's support, but they could make do without him. Either way, she did not begrudge having some alone time right now. Today had been a dark day, and she was not holding up well. She was more than ready to just go home and pass out in her bed until the start of the operation tomorrow.

She began walking over to her auto-car when suddenly she heard a noise. She perked her ears up. It sounded like a vehicle was on its way.

She turned around and cautiously put one hand over the pistol on her hip as a large truck entered into the parking lot. The truck pulled up in front of her and then parked with the back of the trailer facing her.

She was tense as the truck's cabin door opened, but then relaxed as she saw Aren emerge from the vehicle.

"It's about time!" she called to him, taking her hand off of her holster. "I was about to leave, you know."

"I'm terribly sorry," Aren apologized. "I had to make an important stop along the way, and I ended up getting held up for a while."

"Well, I'm glad you're here now," Anya expressed with a light sigh. "But if it happens again, that'll be the end of us working together."

"Of course," Aren assented. "I can assure you that it won't."

"Anyway, are you ready to get down to business?" Anya asked.

"Yes," Aren asserted. "Let's get started."

"Well, before we begin, as a special agent of Calantia, I wanted to express thanks on behalf of my government for your assistance in this matter," Anya said gratefully. "Lateness aside, it is still most appreciated."

"It's my pleasure," Aren responded with a bow.

"Now, as for the plan," Anya began.

She paused for a moment, trying to push through her head fog.

Ok, Anya, she thought to herself. *You can get through this.*

She exhaled and then pressed a few buttons on her wristcomm, which began projecting a detailed hologram showing the layout of a large facility. There were several distinct, colored lines running through the halls and rooms, which seemed to indicate routes through the building.

"These are the digital blueprints to their headquarters," Anya explained. "The red line indicates the route you will take. After we finish our meeting here, I'll send you the file. It should help you with your side of the operation."

"Right," Aren stated. "So, you said they were called the Steel Riders gang, right?"

"That is correct," Anya affirmed. "As I said before, this gang has been causing some major problems in the area, and we need to put a stop to their operations. To tell you the truth, their gang used to be smaller and less significant until around a year ago, when they began secretly receiving money and weapons from UAPA, which led to them becoming one of the most prolific gangs in Marann.

"The Steel Riders have been clandestinely kidnapping and killing on UAPA's behalf ever since—doing the dirty work that Hamish and his administration want to pretend they're uninvolved in."

"Right, ok. And the contract was for me to take out their leader?" Aren asked.

"Yes, precisely," Anya affirmed. "Once we raid their headquarters, our people will take care of the rest of the gang."

Anya pressed a few buttons on her wristcomm, which began projecting a hologram of a large, burly man with a deep scar on his left cheek. "This is the one we need you to take down. He's a fearsome fighter and a giant of a man, known as 'Gron the Bear.' He's built up a pretty terrible reputation across Antal over the years. We've sent a squad of operatives after him before, but he ended up killing every single one of them. I don't wish to take any chances this time, which is why I hired you. I advise that you don't take him lightly tomorrow."

"Understood," Aren replied. "So, what happens after the gang is captured? I can't imagine UAPA will hold them accountable, considering the Steel Riders are secretly working for them, right? Is your own government going to hold them?"

"That's exactly right," Anya nodded. "There are empty prison cells waiting in Calantia with each and every gang members' names on them. All we have to do is capture them, and the rest will be taken care of."

"Sounds good," Aren nodded back.

Anya suddenly noticed that Aren had been staring her in the eyes with a worried look on his face.

"Is there something wrong?" She asked, feeling slightly annoyed. "Do you have any questions about the plan?"

"Not exactly," Aren replied. "However, if you don't mind, I was wondering if something was bothering you. You seem… off."

"Excuse me?" Anya interjected with a hint of indignation. "What do you mean by 'off'?"

"Sorry, I didn't mean to be rude or anything," Aren apologized. "I could be wrong, but you seem… upset, like something is troubling you."

Anya paused for a moment. She was taken aback by the question. People tended to always just assume she was doing well—largely thanks to her own efforts to always try to appear strong for the sake of those around her. But it seemed that her walls had fallen a bit in the midst of everything today.

"In truth, this past week has been difficult," She confessed. "We received some new intel recently, and it's... well, I'll just say it's not pretty."

"What kind of intel?" Aren asked curiously.

Anya looked up at him. Her first instinct was to immediately rebuke him. There was no reason he needed to know. However, her resolve quickly softened as she looked into his eyes. There was a deep sincerity in them that made her feel unexpectedly warm and safe.

She swallowed and hesitated for a moment in thought. She knew she absolutely couldn't tell him specifics. This information was too sensitive. If UAPA found out that they knew about the camps, it could be a major problem. However, she had felt really hopeless and alone today. Maybe sharing just a small nugget wouldn't hurt.

"Well, to be honest, today I learned that UAPA has been doing some pretty horrible stuff in secret," Anya shared sorrowfully. "We had our suspicions before, but it turns out that it was actually worse than we were expecting. I can't share too many details, except to say that people, including some of my own good friends are going through hell right now."

"That's awful," Aren empathized.

"I just—," Anya fought to hold back tears. "I just don't understand how some orrens—how some people—can treat each other that way."

"I don't either," Aren related somberly. "All I know is that some people need to be stopped. I mean, that's why you folks are fighting, right?"

"Well, to be honest with you, sometimes, I don't even know why we're fighting," Anya shared candidly. "I mean—don't get me wrong—I'd gladly give my own life if I thought it'd secure victory, but that's the thing... I'm not so sure that's a possibility any more. Part of me is starting to think this might just be a lost cause."

"A lost cause?" Aren questioned. "Come on, there must be part of you that still has hope."

"Hope?" Anya asked blankly, her frustration seeping out in her tone. "All I've ever had is hope and look where it's gotten me."

Anya paused for a moment before laughing out loud. "You know, after the Raider Wars ended, back before UAPA was a thing, I had been going for my degree in gods damned sociology? I wanted to help form social policies and programs that would help people, not fight an unwinnable war against... against monsters."

Anya leaned back against her auto-car, covering her face with her hand. Although her expression appeared superficially amused, there was a profound sadness that was emanating from beneath the surface.

Her instincts were screaming at her to stop. To close her mouth. To just be quiet. This was not her usual, private self who was used to pushing her emotions down. And yet, she couldn't stop herself as the words continued flooding out, like water bursting through the cracks in a dam.

"Despite everything this planet had gone through back then, I still had high hopes for the future of Antal," Anya remarked with a morbid chuckle as tears rolled down her cheeks. "Those hopes have been crumbling little-by-little with each and every nation that UAPA has conquered; with every victim that they have killed or enslaved; and with each person that they have roped into their cause with their lies and propaganda. Gods, 'hope' is starting to feel like nothing more than a distant dream at this point."

Anya suddenly looked startled at herself.

"I'm sorry," Anya apologized, shaking her head. "I don't know what came over me. I'm not usually so… morose. That wasn't professional of me. It won't happen again."

"No, no, please, I'm glad you shared your honest thoughts," Aren asserted. "I just am sad that you feel that way. I think that hope is the one thing that no one should ever lose."

Anya looked at him cynically.

"I appreciate the sentiment, but I'll be honest, it feels a bit empty," Anya replied. "Some hope is false, you know—keeps you hanging on—torturing yourself for no good reason. Not all troubles can be overcome. Not all fights are winnable, not all enemies beatable."

"I don't see it that way," Aren contended. "I think that hope is what makes the unwinnable winnable—what makes the unbeatable beatable. You just have to keep fighting—no matter how bad things look. That's what will lead to victory in the end!"

Anya looked over at him incredulously before laughing out loud. "I'm sorry, I suppose because of your skill and the clan you're with, I overlooked that you're still quite young. No offense, but it's clear that you have much to learn about the hard truths of life."

"I mean it," Aren asserted without wavering. "I know UAPA must seem daunting, but I fully believe you can win."

"Oh, really?" Anya rolled her eyes. "And what are you basing that confidence on? Your years of experience fighting against them?"

"No," Aren dismissed, looking at her with starlight in his eyes. "I'm basing it on *you*."

Anya was stunned at the assertion. "W—what do you mean by that exactly?"

Aren paused in thought for a moment before responding. "I mean, just, everything that I've seen in you—your intelligence, your resourcefulness, and more important than anything, the drive that I see in your eyes. While people like you exist on this planet—people who will stand and fight, evils like UAPA will never be able to endure."

Anya was taken aback. She didn't exactly consider his point to be particularly cogent, and yet, there was something about him, about his words, that stirred something deep inside of her. It was like standing in the summer sun after a long and miserable winter.

She shook her head. Whether or not he was refreshing to listen to, there was still no mistaking his message for anything more than naivete.

"Hmph, well then," Anya responded, coming back to reality. "No offense or anything, but maybe you can start by just capturing Gron first before talking to me about how supposedly beatable UAPA is. I mean, as is, you can't even seem to manage to show up to meetings on time."

"Hm, well, I suppose now is as good a time as any," Aren said, pressing a few buttons on his wristcomm.

"As good a time as any for what?" Anya asked curiously.

She was startled as she heard Aren's truck's trailer begin to automatically open from the back. As a reflex, she pulled her EK12 lightning rifle off of her back and aimed it at the truck, uncertain of what she was about to see.

What is he opening the trailer for? Anya wondered. *Don't tell me... is it even possible? He didn't capture Gron already, did he?!*

She looked on in anxious anticipation. She couldn't deny that capturing the Steel Riders' leader would be a highly impressive feat to pull off without the support of the team she was planning on sending with him.

However, as the trailer door finished opening, her eyes went wide. She took her left hand off of her rifle and used it to cover her mouth, not believing what she was currently seeing.

"I-is that—" Anya began. "How—"

"I didn't really feel like waiting until tomorrow," Aren shrugged.

Anya relaxed the aim on her rifle as she walked into the trailer, careful where she stepped.

As she suspected, an injured Gron the Bear was in here, chained to the back wall of the trailer, where he was fruitlessly grunting and squirming against his binds. However, what she hadn't expected to see was the trailer's floor filled from wall-to-wall with those she recognized to be the other members of the Steel Riders gang, all bound and gagged.

"My gods," Anya uttered in shock as she finished a headcount of the prisoners. "You got every single one of them. All forty-four of the gang's members."

"Well, it would have been unprofessional to leave any stragglers behind," Aren asserted, a tad cockily. "Besides, I knew how badly you wanted the entire gang. I figured I'd save your people the trouble."

Anya put her rifle away and then looked at Aren perplexed for a second, before laughing out loud. "I think I may have underestimated you, bounty hunter. It seems you're more than just words, after all. You've certainly earned your pay. I'm only sorry we can't afford to give you any extra for this."

"Oh, no," Aren replied. "This one's on the house. I saw what they were doing to some of the people they had kidnapped, and… well, let's just say that I'm happy to have helped get these people off the street. Besides, I'd rather see that money go towards your cause."

"Won't your clan be expecting payment though?" Anya asked, puzzled. "I can't imagine they'd have a policy on allowing jobs to go unpaid."

"To be honest, I never actually registered this job with the clan," Aren admitted. "As far as they're concerned, this job was never even requested and therefore never existed. So, really, it's fine."

"Wow, I can't thank you enough," Anya replied, bowing deeply to him. "On behalf of the Calantian government, I thank you for your service."

Aren looked at her quizzically for a moment.

"You can be honest with me—you don't really work for the Calantian government, do you?" Aren asked casually.

"Of course, I—" Anya began to protest, but paused as she realized it was in vain. "How did you know?"

"It never really made sense that Calantia would send agents all the way up here just to deal with some gang in Marann— especially when they're in the middle of dealing with war on their own territory at the moment," Aren asserted.

"Fair enough," Anya responded, looking at Aren thoughtfully. "You know, there's something about you, bounty hunter—something that makes me feel like I can trust you."

She hesitated thoughtfully for a moment. "I'm going to do something that I don't normally do here—I'm going to share the truth with you."

"Oh?" Aren voiced curiously. "And what is this truth?"

"Well, the fact is that you're right," Anya announced. "I mean, truthfully, I really do work *with* the Calantian government from time to time. However, I am not really a Calantian agent. My true name is Anya Allister. I am Vice Chair and Second-in-Command of the resistance organization, Oppori Qala, working within the conquered UAPA territories to bring them down."

Anya paused for a moment before continuing. "Of course, now that you know this, you could make a lot of money if you captured me and took me to UAPA for the reward money.

"However, if you're as good of a person as I suspect you to be, then I would instead ask if you would be willing to work more with me in the future. I may not be able to afford a continual contract, but I would certainly love to have your assistance from time to time whenever we are most in need of someone with skills such as yours."

Aren grinned, flashing his sharp teeth. "Well, it's nice to properly meet you, Vice-Chair Anya. My answer is yes, I'd love to work more with you in the future."

"Excellent," Anya took another satisfied look at the cargo full of tied-up gangsters as she spoke. "You know, I'm used to working with people who are rather predictable, dependable, easy to manage…That's my usual preference if I'm to be honest. But I think it might be nice, for once, to work with someone who seems to carry their share of surprises."

*/

Hanging back just outside the CNPF hangar, Elmenz was wracking his brain, trying to think if there was any magic that he could possibly cast to help Aren here. Things were looking dire, but he was struggling to think of any spell that would help at all.

Come on, Elmenz, he thought to himself. *How can I call myself Oppori Qala's top magic expert if I can't stop a single solitary spell?*

However, as much as he tried to come up with something, there was simply no time, and even if there was, there was just not much he could really do against the incredible, raw power that Maximilius brought forth with the help of so many support casters. He had advised Aren to dodge, but for some reason, Aren stubbornly insisted on just continuing to walk straight towards Maximilius.

Why is he doing this? Elmenz frustratedly thought to himself as he helplessly watched Aren walk towards his death. *Has he lost the will to live?*

Whatever the case was, all Elmenz could do was cry out and watch in horror as Maximilius' giant, devastating beam shot out towards Aren.

However, in the next moment, his horror was overtaken by a perplexed curiosity as he watched Aren suddenly stop walking forward and extend his hand outward towards the coming beam.

"*Ingeir sorbeo,*" Aren cried out.

Elmenz had braced himself for the worst. But, as the beam came into contact with Aren's palm, he was shocked to see Maximilius' *Mountain Leveler* spell stopped dead in its tracks, somehow dissipating as it hit Aren's hand.

Hardly believing his eyes, Elmenz looked closely at Aren to see if he had some shield or ward up that he was using to block the spell but neither appeared to be the case. It looked to Elmenz like the spell was somehow being sucked into Aren's palm, if such a thing were even possible.

After the spell was over and the last of the beam had disappeared, Aren calmly put his hand down. To Elmenz, it didn't look like Aren had taken any damage at all, nor that he was even struggling, like he was after taking the blast from the sonic cannon. If anything, Aren somehow looked better than he did when the spell started.

"What trickery is this?" Maximilius cried out angrily. "How are you still alive?"

"My gods, that feels much better," Aren rejoiced as he brought his arm back down. "I had drained a lot of life energy before this, so I appreciate the top-up."

"Are you implying you somehow absorbed my spell?!" Maximilius cried out incredulously. "That's impossible!"

Aren shook his head.

"That magic of yours is so raw, it makes it all too easy," He declared. "It would have been much harder if you bothered to translate or refine the energy whatsoever. Hell, dynamic warding could have done the trick too. But as it was, it took very little effort to absorb what you cast."

"Preposterous!" Maximilius refuted.

Aren took a deep breath, feeling invigorated.

"Honestly, I knew I could relax when I saw all of those support casters behind you," He explained. "A true master focuses on refining their own magic instead of relying on others for help."

"Nonsense!" Maximilius rebuked. "Support casters can give you way more energy than you could ever access on your own. It doesn't matter how strong you are, you'll always be stronger with support casters. And none are stronger than I, with the skill to use twenty-one at once."

Aren shrugged. "Quality over quantity. You can have all of the energy in the universe, but it doesn't matter if you don't know how to control it—as I just demonstrated."

While Aren's explanation rung true to Elmenz, he still found the claims a bit shocking. Such applications simply went beyond what he had ever been taught about magical energies.

Nevertheless, he could not deny what he saw with his own two eyes. As he looked at Aren, Elmenz could not help but think of the tales he had heard of rare sorcerers across the stars who were far more powerful and intricate in their magical abilities than the sorcerers of Antal. It would seem that he had finally come across one.

"Enough," Maximilius cried. "I don't know what trickery you used, but I'm not going to fall for it. My bet—this is all just some bit of illusion magic. But whatever the case, you won't get so lucky again. I'll end you even if I have to bring down this entire facility."

Maximilius gave the signal to his coven to begin the next spell.

"Put everything you've got into it this time!" Maximilius ordered his coven.

"I think not," Aren asserted. "As much as it might give me another nice little boost, I feel I've entertained you long enough here."

Maximilius and his support casters had already begun their incantation, but Aren wasn't going to let them continue for a second longer.

"*Kurami envelo,*" Aren called out.

Elmenz was startled as a wall of black suddenly appeared before him, blocking off the hole in the wall to the hangar.

He tentatively stuck his hand out towards this dark barrier. To his surprise, his hand went easily through it, revealing that the wall was intangible. Curious, Elmenz stuck his head through next.

All he could see was pure black, but when he pulled his head back into the hall, he could see normally again.

He realized that Aren must have cast a spell that devoured all light in the hangar, enveloping the room in darkness, but ending where the hangar met the hallway. This darkness spell must have been so potent that it even absorbed any light from the hall the instant it made it into the hangar, which is why this barrier appeared so solid.

In the next moment, a violent commotion could be heard from within the darkness, along with scattered cries. Shortly after, the light began to return. As it did, Elmenz could see Aren sheathing his sword as the twenty-one support casters and Maximilius were on the ground.

"You can all come out," Aren permitted. "It should be safe now."

Elmenz and the E7 operatives all came out and joined him. However, Henrika was already leaning on the wall next to Aren, clapping her hands.

"Not bad," Henrika praised with a grin.

As Elmenz got closer, he could see that most, if not all of the fallen coven were deeply wounded and unconscious but did not appear to be dead.

"Extraordinary," Elmenz gasped. "Although, to be completely honest, this was what I expected from you to begin with—something based on your speed and skill with a sword. I certainly wasn't expecting you to completely stop one of Maximilius' infamous spells."

Aren laughed. "I might not have been able to take them at all if not for that, to be honest. That energy was just what I needed."

"So, you truly made his spell's energy your own?" Elmenz remarked. "That's astonishing."

"Thank you, but it's really nothing," Aren asserted. "Given a month, I'm sure you could learn the same spell yourself. It comes from a meta-magical art called Orivanx. Absorbing raw magical energy is one of the easier applications, so it really isn't a big deal."

Although Elmenz was starting to realize how big the gaps in his magical knowledge really were, he still had confidence enough in his understanding of the foundations of magical energies. It was through this confidence that he knew that Aren was full of it—such a spell would be absolutely anything but "easy" to learn.

"Very interesting," Elmenz acknowledged to Aren, stroking his beard thoughtfully. "I appreciate the insight."

"No problem," Aren nodded to him, and then motioned to the group. "Let's get moving, everyone."

Aren opened the door, emerging into the hallway on the other side of the steel/sonic blockade. Their destination was just ahead after one more turn into another hallway. However, Aren could hear movement some distance away. It seemed that more of the enemy were on their way.

"Get ready everyone," Aren ordered. "We've got company."

"Yes sir," the E7 members replied in unison.

Lieutenant Chave put up a hand signal with four upright fingers to the rest of the team. The operatives immediately understood and along with the Lieutenant, got into a seven-pointed W-formation with four at the front and three in the back. The four operatives at the front took steel devices off of their back which folded out into large shields. These shields were then turned on, which activated minor sonic repulsor shielding helping protect their fronts.

Although sonic rifles were a technology that was exclusively controlled by UAPA, sonic repulsor shields were an older Antallian invention with no locking controls on most of them and availability of units across the planet, making it possible for Oppori Qala to attain some for themselves. They did not have many, and most of the ones they did have were smaller and weaker units, such as these, but the ones they did have proved useful from time to time.

The members in the front knelt a bit lower, behind the shields, while those in the back stood a bit higher, depending primarily on the front members for cover. Elmenz stood behind the team, pulling out a catalyst stone that he used to help focus his spells, which began to levitate over his left palm, while he held his right palm open, behind the stone. Henrika stood casually behind the group, yawning as she leaned against the wall.

Aren drew his sword. As the enemies from the righthand side drew nearer, Aren started to hear more of them coming from left as well. The first group, coming from the right, he estimated to include about twenty-five people. The second group, coming further away from the left, was harder to estimate, as they were a bit more scattered, but he guessed around twenty. Most likely, the last remaining soldiers in the compound had all been called to come down here in a last-ditch effort to stop them.

As he heard the first enemies starting to come around the corner, Aren didn't waste any time. He lunged at top speed just as the soldiers came into his vision, cutting down four of them in an instant. From there, he jumped into the middle of the soldiers and rapidly began cutting them down, one by one. The other agents got busy as well. The E7 operatives took down one after the other with a hail of bullets, as Elmenz supported with his magical projectiles. The entire wave of soldiers was taken down in no time.

Just as they were finishing, Aren could see the soldiers from the left hallway started to pour in from three adjoining hallways at once. These soldiers very quickly filled the hallway, in a haphazard formation. The ones at the front noticed him and began to take aim from a bit of a distance away. However, he already had his arm stretched out, with his palm pointed towards them.

Well, I might as well use all that energy I received, he mused silently.

"Scintilla ekrix!" Aren shouted out, sending a spark flying at them, dodging a few sonic blasts at the same time.

"Veit!" He cried out.

The spark exploded into a giant ball of flame, consuming all of the roughly twenty soldiers across the hall in an instant. This variation of Green Dragon's Spark had a massive radius and although Aren had activated it over a hundred feet away, the flames nearly reached all the way to him. Like with most of his flame magic, the heat was only enough to cause first and second-degree burns during the brief period that the soldiers were exposed to the fire. However, the magical flame incinerated straight through their life energy like it was nothing, instantly killing several of them, and knocking the rest out cold.

Aren looked back at the E7 soldiers. He relaxed as he scanned over everyone and could see that not a single person on their team was hurt.

Lieutenant Chave looked over furiously at Henrika, who was still leaning against the wall, and currently focused on a palmcomm she was messing around with in her hands.

"Excuse me, what was that back there?" Chave scolded. "Were you seriously on your palmcomm the entire time? We could have used your help, you know."

Henrika put her palmcomm away and yawned. "Nah, you seemed to have it well in hand."

"Just because things turned out fine in the end, that doesn't excuse sitting back and doing nothing," Chave retorted. "You're supposed to be this *legendary thief*. You could have done something. Anything at all."

"Chave, that's enough," Aren reproached. "She didn't come here to help with the fighting. That's not her specialty."

"All due respect sir, you've shown yourself to be a very proficient and reliable warrior," Chave sputtered. "But you can't really be ok with this, can you? I mean, it's one thing to take up a support role, but playing on a palmcomm during a firefight? Really? We lost some good people earlier, and we could lose more. The complacency is insulting."

"Insulting?" Aren asked incredulously. "You know she's the main reason you're all alive now, right? Back at the ambush, I wouldn't have been able to cast that lightning if she didn't move you all first, and she was the one to disable the cannon. Most of us here might be dead if not for her. So, 'with all due respect' you owe her your lives. You should show a little respect."

Aren hesitated for a moment before continuing more softly. "And come on, really? We have more than enough fighters without her, don't you think? I've been told that Henrika's been clear about her disinterest in fighting from the beginning. There's no reason we can't respect that."

"I- I'm sorry," Chave apologized. "I guess I didn't really think of all of that."

"I'm not the one you should be apologizing to," Aren asserted.

Chave nodded and turned to Henrika with a chagrin expression. "I'm sorry Henrika."

"It's fine," Henrika reassured, patting Chave gently on the shoulder. "I can assure you that I didn't care about your opinion anyway."

Chave looked to the ground with mixed emotions but remained silent.

"Alright everyone, let's go," Aren ordered. "We have a mission to carry out."

Chapter 21

With his chiambra and bow in hand, Xander began playing. With rapidly executed riffs, he boosted his jumping capabilities, giving him the ability to launch himself into the air, and onto a cloud he conjured mid-jump. He jumped again, landing on another cloud. He then did this again, and again, until he was around a hundred feet in the air, far above the buildings below.

That should be about far enough, he thought to himself.

Not only did coming up here give Xander a better vantage point against the soldiers on the rooftops, but it was his general preference to attack from up high regardless. Although Xander did have the ability to conjure shields for protection, he much preferred to avoid getting hit in the first place, which was much easier to achieve when attacking from up high in the air. He only had to make certain that he was close enough that he was still in range to use his spells.

Xander estimated that there were around two-hundred UAPA soldiers between where they were and their final destination. Not only that, but more groups of reinforcements kept joining in. However, there were also currently well over a hundred shreen in this same stretch of street. Both of these groups were incredibly dangerous on their own. However, with both focused on fighting the other, it gave Kyara and Xander a fighting chance in getting through them.

As Xander played his chiambra, making his way through the air, he looked down at the UAPA soldiers in the street. He could see a couple of them looking around with confused looks on their faces.

"What the hell?" voiced one of the soldiers. "Is that... music??"

But the soldiers had no time to investigate. Kyara had already begun to make her move. From the alleyway, she fired out a series of shots from her pistol, taking out six soldiers in a near instant. Before the remaining soldiers could even figure out where the firing was coming from, Kyara had already pounced over their heads, firing downward in mid-air and taking out another two of them. Once she landed in another alleyway across the street she continued firing again, taking out yet another four soldiers.

Xander was mesmerized. It had been only seconds since they had begun their attack and UAPA was already dropping like flies. He couldn't help but compare what he was seeing to Aren's fighting at the Silver Note Cabaret. Kyara and Aren's fighting styles seemed to be quite different, but their speed and their skill were undoubtedly comparable.

Xander knew he didn't have the time to keep watching her though. He had his own job to do.

He looked over to the four soldiers on the east rooftop first. These soldiers were so focused on firing at the shreen that none had noticed him yet.

Although Xander found it grizzly to consider, he realized that the sounds of all of the screaming, howling, and rifle blasts helped cover up the sound of his playing. And the soldiers who did seem to notice it, like the one who called out earlier, were either too busy trying to deal with the shreen or with Kyara to look for the source of his music.

This gave Xander the perfect opportunity. With a flourish of his bow across the chiambra, he cast a bolt of black lightning into the center of the group, taking two of them out.

"What the hell was that?" One of the two remaining soldiers on the rooftop screamed out.

The other looked around frantically, until they saw Xander standing on his cloud in the sky.

"Up there," They yelled. "I think it was him."

Both soldiers pointed their rifles at Xander, but it was already too late. He cast a black flame that swept across the rooftop, engulfing both remaining soldiers. Xander's flames worked similarly to Aren's Green Dragon's Spark spell, burning through the life energy of both of these soldiers caught within it, knocking them out cold.

When he looked over to the other rooftop, he saw one of the soldiers yelling and pointing in his direction, causing the other two to look his way. It appeared his casting was finally drawing some attention.

The rooftop soldiers began to take aim at him. Xander needed a quick moment before casting more energy-demanding offensive magic. So, he launched himself into the air as they began firing, jumping from cloud to cloud. From this distance, their accuracy was a lot worse and Xander found it rather easy to dodge their shots.

His biggest worry was about the possibility of one of the soldiers forming a bio-lock on him with their rifles.

This was something that he learned about from Anya. The first thing she had taught him was that, while it was possible to dodge a bio-lock shot, it was much more difficult. The easier alternative is to simply avoid allowing the bio-lock to be made to begin with, which is not an impossible task against UAPA soldiers.

With the older bio-lock tech used by UAPA, it takes about 10-15 seconds of pointing in the general direction a target unimpeded in order for the targeting AI to form the bio-lock. He knew this would be more than enough time for him to make his move.

Xander was about to cast a bolt at them when he saw something shocking. Two shreen were climbing up the side of the building he was targeting. With the soldiers focused on Xander, they were completely unaware as these creatures used a combination of their six sticky feet and claws to rapidly scale the wall.

Xander held back from casting for a moment. Instead, he just watched as the shreen made it to the top of the building. The rooftop soldiers' eyes widened as they saw the beasts jump up next to them. They stopped firing at Xander and aimed towards the shreen, but it was too late. The shreen quickly pounced on the soldiers, knocking their prey to the ground, as they descended on them with claws and teeth.

It was a brutal scene, but Xander knew he couldn't waste any more time here and had to continue moving forward. He looked away and jumped forward to new magic clouds several times in quick succession, hoping to catch up to Kyara.

When he got closer, he could see her in the middle of a group of UAPA soldiers, fighting in a frenzy. Looking more closely, he could see that she was relying primarily on her pistol, shooting down soldier after soldier, aiming for the weak points in their armor with every shot. However, she occasionally struck with her dagger, aiming for the neck or under the armpits. Her movements were so quick and sporadic that soldiers didn't know where to shoot.

He saw a short row of soldiers attempting to take aim at her. He quickly played a riff on his chiambra, summoning forth a burst of black flame that knocked out all four of them.

As Kyara took out the last one in the group, she surprised Xander by turning around and heading backwards.

He quickly realized why as he saw another group of ten soldiers that were coming in as reinforcements, a bit behind them. It was clear that Kyara was gunning for them. Xander speedily worked his chiambra sending out a bolt of black lightning to help support her. Kyara started with a pounce with her dagger out, slitting two of their throats in a single swoop. In no time the two of them took the full group out together. After finishing them off, Kyara looked up at Xander and nodded to him way up in the sky.

Kyara turned around again, continuing towards the processing building, and Xander followed from his conjured clouds in the sky.

Xander was happy to see that their destination wasn't too far ahead at this point, and all of the biggest UAPA threats had been removed. He began making his way down, jumping between clouds in a descending beeline towards the processing building's front door.

He noted that Kyara was now mostly leaving the remaining UAPA soldiers alone, likely because those who were left were actually helping to distract the shreen more than anything and were unlikely to pose a threat while they were struggling for their lives like this. Nevertheless, the few soldiers who so much as glanced in their direction she instantly shot down.

The two of them were more wary of the shreen than UAPA soldiers at this point and were trying their best to avoid confronting any of them, especially since these shreen could still provide useful support in this raid. Thankfully, so far, all of the shreen had been too busy attacking UAPA soldiers to even seem to notice Xander or Kyara. Xander was hoping that this would last.

The door was nearly within reach now. Xander landed several meters away and ran alongside Kyara. However, just as they were almost there, an unusually large shreen, nearly twice the size of the others, pounced in front of them, blocking their way as it growled deeply and gnashed its teeth at them.

Kyara held her pistol up and was about to pull the trigger when she noticed the growling quieting down. She made eye contact with the beast.

Despite its continued approach, she decided to listen to her instincts, relaxing her trigger finger and lowering her weapon.

"What are you doing?!" Xander asked in shock.

She stood perfectly still as the beast brought its face next to hers and began to move its tendril feelers from its upper lip across her face.

"Kyara!" Xander yelled out.

But to his surprise, the growling stopped, and the beast looked away.

"What in the world," Xander exclaimed.

Xander watched curiously as the creature scanned over the area. A moment later, its eyes caught a UAPA soldier nearby who was running away from his station. The creature's bloodlust immediately returned with a loud, guttural shriek as it started to run for the soldier.

"That was strange," Xander noted pensively.

"It was," Kyara confirmed. "But we don't have time to worry about it."

Kyara opened the door ahead of Xander and waited for him to go through before running in herself, closing the door behind them.

The building was eerily silent as they entered. The only sounds they could hear were coming from outside. Xander had prepared himself to face off against however many guards were in here, but there was no one in sight.

Nevertheless, they didn't waste any time. Briskly, they began walking through the halls looking for the records room. They peered into each room they crossed, but all of them were empty. It really appeared that everyone had either fled or gone outside to face the shreen.

After a bit of searching, they came across a room labeled: *Restitution Program Worker Records.*

"Ah, this has got to be it!" Xander declared triumphantly.

He put his chiambra away as he entered into the room. Looking around, he could see several filing cabinets, a computer on a desk, and a table. He went straight to the computer and clicked a couple of buttons to access the records.

Bio-scan required, a prompt on the screen read.

"Dammit," Xander cursed. "And of course, there are no soldiers here we can use like we did at the security station."

He sighed. "We'll just have to hope they have some kind of physical records of him, I suppose."

Kyara was already over at the filing cabinets, looking at the cabinet labels.

"Over here," She motioned to him. "I think this might have what we're looking for."

Xander walked over and looked at the filing cabinet. It was a fairly large one, labeled *Worker Intake Logs*.

Antal most typically used compartment-style filing cabinets, which were popular in a number of planets across the galaxy. These cabinets were divided into a series of labeled, cubby-style compartments housing series of documents in each one. In order to safeguard more sensitive documents, these compartments often were protected by locked, swinging cabinet doors. In some cases, these doors were small, with one door for each compartment, similar to mini lockers. However, often there would just be one large, locked door guarding all of the compartments at once, as was the case here.

Higher-end, modern filing cabinets used by military and corporations often were made of tough alloys and used advanced locking mechanisms. However, it appeared UAPA opted to save money by sticking to wooden filing cabinets with simple key-locks built into them.

"Yes, I think you're right—this seems to be exactly what I'm looking for," Xander stated excitedly. He turned to Kyara with an inquisitive look. "You wouldn't happen to be able to pick this, would you?"

Without a word, Kyara gently grabbed hold of the cabinet handle.

Oh, I suppose she's checking to see if it's unlocked first, Xander surmised. *Probably a smart idea.*

Xander blushed, feeling silly that he didn't think of that himself.

But his thoughts were interrupted by a thunderous cracking sound, startling him, as Kyara ripped the cabinet door open with her bare hand. The only piece of the door still left in place was a chunk of splintered wood surrounding where the lock was still holding tight.

The rest of the door swung all the way open, revealing a series of compartments inside.

"Gods!" Xander voiced in shock. "I suppose that works too."

Kyara stepped aside. After collecting himself a little, Xander got a bit closer and looked at the compartments. They were all labeled by month. The top row had all of the months of the current Antallian year, 610. In this row, months 1-10 were full of documents, while the compartments labeled 11-16 were empty.

Despite his time on this planet, Xander was still a bit less familiar with the Antal calendar, so he had to pull up his wristcomm and open a calendar conversion application to convert Galactic Standard dates to Antallian. Antallian days and years were both slightly longer than those in Galactic Standard. The years between both systems also were divided differently. Antallian years were divided into 16 months, with 21 days per month and 7 days per week. Galactic Standard, on the other hand, had 12-month years, with 32 days per month and 8 days per week.

However, while many people and planets utilized Galactic Standard as their primary clock and calendar, there were also many planets, like Antal, that relied on their own global systems instead, generally based on each planets' own rotations on their axes and orbits around their respective suns.

For many planets, this was simply more practical than relying on a universal time system. Nevertheless, there were many planets with unusual day and year cycles that were not practical to follow, in which case Galactic Standard would typically be used. For instance, some planets had days that could last an entire year. For such worlds, it would make little sense to create a calendar based on planetary rotations.

However, even on planets like Antal, with their own clock and calendar systems, most inhabitants were still typically acquainted with Galactic Standard. Those who regularly dealt with interstellar affairs, such as starship pilots, would even sometimes fully rely on Galactic Standard, despite the Antallian calendar being predominant on the planet.

As he looked at the numbers he was plugging in, Xander thanked the gods for his wristcomm's calendar conversion application. Math was not his forte.

The program on his wristcomm showed that the current date was 31/9/699 NE in Galactic Standard and 13/10/610 on the Antal calendar. Both of these were in the standard day/month/year format.

Matlex had left his message to Xander on 26/7/699 NE and went missing sometime shortly after that. After plugging the numbers in, Xander's wristcomm showed that the converted date of Matlex's message was on 16/7/610 on the Antal calendar. This meant that it was the 7th month of the current Antallian year that Matlex would have been taken.

Xander pulled all of the documents from the compartment labeled "7/610" and placed them on a table in the center of the room. Although there were fewer documents in this compartment than in many of the previous months, the pile was still quite thick, with likely somewhere between 250-300 forms.

He quickly scanned over the first document. He then flipped to the next one and then the next. He let out a frustrated sigh as he started to realize the problem with these papers.

"Gods dammit," Xander cursed. "There are no names on these forms. They're all labeled by the prisoners' RPW ID numbers."

He dropped the papers onto a desk and sighed frustratedly. "I did see reference numbers we could probably look up in the system if we could just get into that computer."

Kyara picked up the pile of papers and began to flip through them herself.

Xander looked over at the computer as he tried to think. "Is there possibly any way we could hack into that thing? I don't know much about computers."

Kyara continued scanning over the documents thoughtfully for a moment before responding.

"I don't think that will be necessary," Kyara asserted. "Look here."

She brought the papers down into Xander's view and pointed at a particular part of the top form. This part of the form read:

Assigned Residency Building: H

She then flipped to the next form, then the next, and then the next. They each referenced the same residency building.

"Huh, so everyone imprisoned on this month was assigned to the same residency building?" Xander inquired.

"It certainly appears that way," Kyara stated. "I know where this one is too. The letters for these things are displayed quite blatantly. This one is near the center of the camp. We should be able to get there relatively quickly. Are you certain he was taken this month though?"

"I'm pretty sure," Xander asserted. "He left me the message in the middle of the month, so he was free then, but he went missing the next day. I don't think there's much doubt he would have been brought here in the seventh month if he was brought here at all."

"In that case, if he is here, he must be in Residency Building H," Kyara concluded. "I'll lead you there. Are you ready?"

"Yes, let's go," Xander nodded.

The two of them quickly made their way back to the building's exit.

"Wait," Kyara ordered just as they were getting to the door.

Xander stopped dead in his tracks. Kyara brought out a tiny spray bottle. She sprayed Xander with a few spurts of misted liquid from the bottle and then did the same to herself.

"What is that?" Xander asked.

"It's a chemical called gaucifin, commonly used by hunters," Kyara explained. "I probably should have used it sooner, but I have a very limited supply, so I wanted to wait a bit. It's very effective at masking your scent. Unfortunately, this is not perfect against shreen who hunt just as much with their ears as they do their noses, but it should help some."

"Understood," Xander replied. "Thank you."

Xander got his chiambra back out and braced himself. No matter how many soldiers or shreen lay ahead, he felt he was ready.

However, as he opened the door and looked out into the street, he realized that, for all of his bracing, he was completely unprepared for what was awaiting them.

I don't know if this is better or worse, he thought to himself with a shudder.

"Wow," Kyara murmured under her breath.

Instead of a massive battle between shreen and UAPA, like they had just seen out here minutes ago—there was absolutely nothing on the street. No fighting, no soldiers, no shreen, and not even any dead bodies. The only evidence left of the battle was damage to the buildings, some abandoned rifles, and a large amount of blood covering the street, thick and pooled in some areas, and thin and spattered in others.

Xander could hear the scattered sounds of some howling and gunfire in the distance, but in comparison to the raucous battle here earlier, it was eerily quiet in this street.

"What happened?" Xander uttered shakily. "Where did the shreen go? Where are the soldiers? Where are all the dead bodies?"

"I can't say that I'm certain," Kyara answered contemplatively. "I might just have a theory, but we don't really have time to investigate."

"I suppose not," Xander responded with a shudder. "I guess we should probably just get going."

Kyara nodded in agreement.

Still feeling unsettled, Xander collected himself and began following Kyara as she made her way through the streets. Through their first few blocks, they continued to see no shreen or soldiers, living or dead. It was almost peaceful if not for the blood everywhere, and the distant sounds of battle. And yet, this somehow felt more disturbing to Xander than the brutal and chaotic scene from before.

After making it some distance from the southern gate, they eventually started seeing some more small conflicts between soldiers and shreen again. Although things were starting to seem more normal again, it still did not answer the question as to what happened to everyone back at the main gate.

Kyara suddenly stopped and kneeled down. Xander looked over her shoulder curiously as she carefully scanned over the ground in front of them. After a few moments, she ran her finger along a trail of blood and then looked closely at the crimson liquid on her finger.

"What is it?" Xander asked.

Kyara stood back up and began cleaning her finger with a handkerchief she had in her pocket. "I know what happened."

"What?" Xander asked skeptically. "How could you possibly know that from looking at some blood on your finger?"

"That isn't the main thing," Kyara responded. "This was just to confirm how old the blood is."

"Ok," Xander said uncertainly. "Then how?"

"Take a look around," Kyara responded. "Things were too messy back at the main gate for me to be sure of anything, but the patterns are clearer here."

Xander couldn't really see what she was talking about. Their surroundings looked like pure chaos to him. There were signs of battle everywhere, from sonic blast holes to acid corrosion from shreen saliva. There was also a large amount of blood, along with bloody footprints going in every direction, from both shreen and soldiers.

"I'll be honest here, I don't really see what you mean," Xander stated, scratching his head. "It looks like a mess to me here too."

"Look more closely," Kyara instructed. "Pay attention to the blood spatter and footprints."

Xander wasn't sure what he would see, but he knelt down and looked more closely, nevertheless. It took him a few moments, and he was just about to tell her that it was pointless when suddenly, he saw it.

While all of the spattering of blood appeared random at first, there were some signs of trailing in a few places. It was subtle, but definitely there, and appeared to all be going in the same direction. Once he noticed it, he also began to realize that a fair amount of shreen footprints also seemed to be heading in the same direction as well.

"Ok, I think I see it now," Xander asserted. "There's some trailing in parts the blood, and some of the shreen footprints appear to be headed in the same direction."

"In fact," He continued nervously. "It kind of looks like the direction we're going. But what does it mean?"

"You are correct," Kyara confirmed. "As for what it means—well, you'll see for yourself pretty quickly. We're probably not too far at this point."

Kyara started walking again, signaling for him to follow.

"I mean, sure, I guess," Xander replied nervously.

He was apprehensive about moving forward without knowing what was ahead, but he trusted Kyara, so after taking a moment to collect himself, he anxiously followed behind

After making it into an alleyway, they stopped dead in their tracks as they heard the sound of sonic rifle blasts up ahead. Both of them stealthily peered into the next street. Ahead of them was a group of roughly fifteen UAPA soldiers facing off against a pack of growling shreen who had them surrounded on all sides.

These soldiers were shaking and firing sporadically with unusually poor aim, as they backed up closer into each other. One by one, these soldiers were taken out by the shreen, who openly devoured the guards in front of their allies.

While the soldiers managed to take out a few shreen, most seemed to be falling to panic and desperation, clouding their ability to fight back. One broke formation and tried running for it. They were immediately pounced on and killed. Another dropped his rifle and fell to his knees, holding his head in his hands in despair, awaiting his fate. Half of them were screaming for help, begging for anyone who would listen.

"Please!" One cried out. "Anyone! I have a family. I'm begging you!"

Xander was taken aback. This was nothing like the confident aggression that he was used to seeing from UAPA soldiers. To him, they had always seemed like unfeeling machines at best, or monsters preying on the weak at worst. But these ones, they didn't just seem pathetic, they seemed like real people. He began to feel empathy—sorrow. It was one thing to die in the heat of battle. It was another to suffer as these ones were.

"Let's move," Kyara urged him.

Xander hated this, but what could he do? He couldn't, in good conscience, let armed UAPA soldiers go, who could harm others, but he didn't feel that he could just let this happen either.

"I need one second," Xander asserted.

Without another moment's hesitation, he grabbed hold of his chiambra and bow and began playing. The level of precision he needed here required very delicate and technical playing, but he knew he could manage it. It took some extra work to focus with the harrowing scene before him, but he put everything he had into it.

As the notes flowed from his string instrument, black flame rapidly engulfed the weapons of the UAPA soldiers, one by one, causing them to be dropped to the ground. After all of the soldiers had been disarmed, Xander quickly switched to louder, more bombastic playing. The shreen were eager to descend on their now-helpless prey, but Xander was not going to allow it. Bolts of lightning came down from the sky, taking out four shreen on one side of the UAPA soldiers, creating an opening for them to escape.

The rest of the shreen growled and a few pounced, but straining himself to his limits, Xander quickly conjured a wall of black flame in a U-shape around the soldiers, protecting them from the shreen while maintaining an opening towards their escape route. The shreen hissed and shrieked at the wall of flames but did not attempt to cross them.

"Go!" Xander yelled. "And if this means anything to you, you'll retire immediately and never work for UAPA again!"

Most of the UAPA soldiers, while clearly shocked, did not even take a second to question what was happening and went straight for the opening, running for their lives. Only one of them ended up turning back. This was the one who yelled about his family. He nodded to Xander gratefully with tears in his eyes before running off.

The black flame wall dissipated after the last UAPA soldier made their escape. Xander was completely exhausted. He took a moment to recuperate. That was a lot of very difficult casting in a short period.

Dammit, he thought to himself while he panted and sweat dripped down his brow. *What was I thinking? I need my energy to save the prisoners, not these goddamn slaving fascists. Why did I save them?*

As the wall of flame died down, the remaining shreen turned their attention towards Kyara and Xander, growling furiously. It did not appear they would be let off as easily as they were the last time they came face-to-face with one of them.

Kyara calmly drew her pistol in one hand, and pulled out her dagger in the other. She walked forward intently, with a cutting focus on the beasts as they turned their attention towards her.

There was a moment of tense calm as she walked smoothly towards them, and they growled at her. This calm was broken as three shreen ran at her at once. With a single sweep of her gun arm and a rain of bullets from her pistol, she took that first wave down in an instant.

Another pounced forward, gnashing its rows of teeth at her, but she ducked down and launched her knife arm upwards at the same time, dodging the attack, while landing her dagger into the beast's heart from beneath. As she pulled the dagger out, the beast kept going from its momentum until it hit the pavement on the other side of her, where it died within the next second.

As the next shreen launched itself at her, she shot it directly in the head. The beast's body went limp, falling into her. She grabbed it with her gun arm, wincing as some of the beast's corrosive saliva dripped onto her shoulder, penetrating through her thin fiber armor and burning into her skin. However, she didn't let it slow her down and immediately threw the body at a high velocity at another shreen who was running at her, knocking the shreen back before she shot that one twice.

While she was firing, two more shreen jumped at her simultaneously. In a 360-degree spin, she sliced both of their throats before they could get to her and then ducked, allowing their bodies to fly overhead past her. Both of them fell to the ground, where they convulsed and bled out for a few moments before passing away.

The final shreen growled at her and reared back onto its hind legs, ready to pounce, but Kyara relaxed her pose and shot the beast directly in the head before it had the chance to move a muscle.

Xander, although very low on energy, had held himself, prepared to cast spells and help her at any point, but she seemed to have it well in hand from beginning to end.

Nevertheless, she didn't come out completely unscathed. She grabbed her water canteen and poured it on her injured shoulder, washing the vestiges of the shreen's caustic saliva away. The shoulder's armor had some uneven patches burned through, exposing some of her damaged, lightly bleeding skin in a few areas.

"Are you ok?" Xander inquired worriedly. "I'm really sorry you got hurt."

"Yes, I'll be fine," Kyara responded. "We should get moving."

"Ar—aren't you going to berate me for what I did?" Xander asked anxiously. "Aren't you going to tell me it was risky? Unnecessary? Helping the enemy?"

"No," Kyara answered. "I mean, I might have taken on that attitude in the past. But to be honest, I get it. Frankly, it's pretty clear that UAPA has lost here. Any survivors are likely only trying to flee at this point. I might not have done the same myself, but I can see why you'd want to save them from senseless anguish."

She looked at him with a hint of pride. "And besides, you showed good foresight to disarm them first. With weapons, they could have still posed a threat to our plans."

Xander looked at the ground quietly. Her words made sense, but he still couldn't help but feel guilty.

"I—" Xander sputtered, trying to find the words to express his remorse. "Well, still, I am sorry. You got hurt as the result of my actions."

Kyara nodded to him supportively.

"I appreciate the apology," She reassured him. "Maybe next time, you can communicate before doing something like that."

"I—I will," Xander assured. "But do you think it was the right thing to do if I had communicated?"

"To be honest, I have no idea," Kyara scratched her head. "I'm not sure if I'm the right person to ask. I find morality confusing.

What I will say is that I know it can be hard to make these kinds of calls in the heat of the moment, but you did what you felt was best, which I think counts for something."

Kyara looked at Xander, seeing his expression was still grim and decided to add. "Really, if I had to say, it was probably the right thing, for whatever that's worth. Oh, and my shoulder is fine, so don't worry about that."

Xander looked up at her.

"Thank you, Kyara," he said appreciatively.

"Now, come on," Kyara urged. "Let's go."

Xander looked her in the eyes and nodded.

The next part of their trip went without incident as they made their way through the streets. However, as they began to near their destination, Xander heard a strange sound emanating from somewhere nearby.

Kyara motioned for them to slow down and move quietly. Xander walked forward cautiously behind her. The sound got louder and louder as they got closer. It was a strange, repetitive sloppy sound, almost like wet suctioning along with soft tearing.

As they came to an intersection, Kyara carefully peeked both ways, using a building on the corner for cover. As she turned to the right, her eyes focused on something. She motioned to Xander to come over and take a look. Xander walked up to her, slowly turned the corner and peered over at what she was looking at.

Xander covered his mouth in horror at what he saw. Up the street, around two-hundred or so feet away, was a mountainous pile of dead bodies, both of UAPA soldiers and of shreen. Although it was hard to tell, it looked like there might have even been at least one or two Oppori Qala operatives in there.

The pile was horrifyingly massive, with likely well over a thousand collective bodies in it. It was clear that this was where all of the bodies from the area around the main gate had gone, alongside plenty of others.

Xander realized that the sound he had been hearing was coming from the dozens of shreen standing all over and around the pile, who were feeding on these bodies. While this was happening, more shreen were coming from various directions, carrying even more bodies over with their teeth. The bodies carried by the shreen were mostly half thrown over the shreen's back, likely making it easier for them to be carried. However, blood still continued dripping from some of the bodies, which would have been the reason behind some of the more subtle blood trails that they had seen earlier.

"Why are they doing that?" Xander asked, feeling sick to his stomach as he looked at the scene.

"Food-hoarding," Kyara explained. "There are many animals that do it, often to store food for the winter. This is the right time of year for the shreen to be doing it. It's often called their 'Winter Feast.'"

"This is normal for animals?!" Xander asked in horror.

Kyara shook her head. "It's not normally like this. For one, carnivores are a bit less likely to do it in larger quantities, due to how quickly meat usually spoils, but Antal's colder autumn and the shreen's strong immune system make them an exception."

"Ok, but like, is this normal for shreen then?" Xander asked.

"Well, I have limited experience with them, but from what I've read, it doesn't seem to be," Kyara noted. "It's not usually this big, and they wouldn't normally engage in cannibalism either."

"Damn," Xander shuddered. "UAPA has really fucked them up, haven't they?"

"Indeed," Kyara nodded sadly. "Their mutations, their starvation, their pain… It's no wonder the shreen are going overboard here; this is likely their first shot at some real prey in a long time, and it's a feast."

"As sad as it is, it's hard for me to feel much of anything besides the need to vomit right now," Xander heaved a little as he spoke. He looked worriedly over to Kyara. "Please don't tell me we have to pass near that thing to get to our destination."

"No, we don't turn in that direction at all," Kyara mentioned. "We cross and continue straight down this street, and our destination is just up ahead on the left-hand side."

"Good, I'm glad," Xander replied with a sigh of relief. "Let's get moving then."

The two of them waited until the coast was clear of any nearby shreen and then quickly ran across the street. He noticed that Kyara's footsteps were weirdly quiet. However, his own were as noisy as anyone else's. With the shreen's good hearing, he worried that some might come after them. However, the beasts at the pile thankfully all seemed too focused to bother with them.

To be safe though, he didn't slow down as he booked it down the dirt road, continuing at full speed all the way through the next block until finally, they came a residency building with a large letter _H_ on its side.

As Xander caught his breath, Kyara walked straight up to the front door. She grabbed a round device from her belt and attached it to the door, next to the handle. She pressed a couple of buttons.

There was a mild buzzing sound, and then a small but powerful boom came from within the device. Kyara grabbed the device and pulled it off of the wall. There was a clean round hole underneath where the device had been attached, positioned half over the door and half over the wall next to it.

Kyara grabbed hold of the handle. Now that the locking mechanism had been destroyed, there was nothing stopping her from opening it. Yet, she hesitated and looked at Xander first, while holding the door in place.

"Before we go in, I should mention," Kyara noted. "There are more than five-hundred enslaved people in each of these residency buildings. Even if Matlex is here, it may take a bit of time to find him. Also, well, in my reconnaissance…"

"In your reconnaissance, what?" Xander inquired.

"To put it bluntly, I noticed that some of the prisoners here seem to have some difficulties with speaking or responding," Kyara expressed. "Some of them seem practically non-verbal. If Matlex is like them, well, there's the possibility that he might not respond, even if you call out to him. It's something that could make finding him more difficult."

Xander stood stunned for a moment. He had never even considered something like that.

"Thanks for letting me know," Xander replied as steadily as he could muster. "I'm prepared to deal with whatever I have to."

"Alright," Kyara acknowledged. "Are you ready?"

"Yes," Xander asserted.

Kyara swung open the door.

Xander took a deep breath before entering. It didn't matter how long it would take. If there was even a remote chance that Matlex was in this camp, he would check every face in every building, starting with this one. And if he wasn't in this camp, then Xander would keep looking until he was found, wherever he was.

Xander exhaled and then slowly entered the room, preparing himself for the search ahead of him. As he took his first step in the building and brought his eyes up from the floor, his jaw dropped. He stood in place, stunned, as the man across from him looked equally surprised.

"Xander?" Matlex asked in shock.

Chapter 22

Matlex tossed around restlessly in his top bunk. He was trying hard to relax and go to sleep. He knew he would regret it the next day if he didn't get a good night's rest. UAPA had them working fourteen-hour shifts, seven days a week. On normal days, he went to his bunk so exhausted that he would collapse into a deep sleep almost immediately.

However, tonight, for some reason, he was feeling rather unsettled. Although insomnia was not an entirely uncommon problem for him, it had been weeks since it last plagued him, so it still caught him off-guard. His insomnia often was paired with anxiety and tonight was no exception.

The last time it happened was around the beginning of his time in this work camp. In his first few days here, it had been particularly bad, likely related to his anxiety adjusting to life in the camp. Although, this did not last long, as eventually the brutal exhaustion from the daily work won out, allowing sleep to come more easily for a while.

But now, for whatever reason, over fifty days after his last insomniac night, it had come back with a vengeance. It had been over three hours since lights out, and he still felt no closer to sleep. He pondered whether it might be that his body was finally adjusting to the work, so the exhaustion was no longer able to beat out his insomniac tendencies any more.

How can I be so tired and yet so awake at the same time? Matlex thought to himself frustratedly. *I swear my body just hates me sometimes.*

He sat up in his bunk, and then paused suddenly. There seemed to be a faint sound coming from outside. It was hard to make out, but it sounded like distant shouting.

He perked his ears up but couldn't hear anything anymore.

Did I imagine it? He wondered to himself.

"Hey, Matlex, you awake?" He heard a whisper coming from one of the bunks next to his.

He recognized the voice as coming from the closest friend he had made while he was here, Ruland.

Ruland was a Nolinthian chaemid who had been transferred into the Restitution Program from the Penal Servitude program when the changeover between them happened around three years ago. Altogether, he had been working in indentured servitude for a collective twenty-eight years between his time working for UAPA and Nolinth.

"Yes, what's up Ruland?" Matlex whispered back. "I'm surprised to hear you're still awake."

"I often like to spend part of my bunk time just sitting and thinking before sleep," Ruland responded. "We don't get much time for solitary thought while we're working."

"Really?" Matlex asked. "Don't you get tired? We're working long days; I feel like we get barely enough time for sleep as it is."

"Oh, well chaemids don't sleep as long as orrens do typically," Ruland explained. "Still, it is true, I do get tired sometimes, but it's worth it. I enjoy getting to escape in my thoughts for a little while each night."

"Interesting," Matlex replied. "So, what do you think about?"

"Oh, all kinds of things," Ruland responded. "I like to think about the outside world and wonder what's going on out there. I like to think about Ovanicx, the planet of my ancestors. And sometimes, I think about my father—the songs he used to sing and the stories he'd tell me. He was a wonderful singer and storyteller."

"Is he the one who taught you how to sing?" Matlex asked. "If so, he did a great job. You have a beautiful singing voice."

"This coming from the great Matlex?" Ruland beamed. "Thank you, but yours is the voice we truly all look forward to hearing. I regret that I wasn't out during your rise to fame to see you in concert. You have the voice of a siren, mesana."

"You're too kind, Ruland," Matlex smiled. "Anyway, once we get out, I can promise you free tickets to all of my concerts for life."

"Once we get out, is it?" Ruland smirked. "I admire your spirit, mesana. I hope it never fades."

"Well, it's been tough, but I mean, I've only been here for a few months," Matlex responded. "To be honest, I'm more curious about how you've kept your spirit up after 28 years in hellholes like this. How have you kept going all this time?"

"My, my, what a question," Ruland responded. "I think the better question is how could I not? I sing the songs that I do because I could never stand to see the spirit die within my comrades here. Too many lose their hope too quickly in these camps, but it is hope we all need, mesana. It is hope that allows us to carry on, even as we struggle under the bootheels of our captors."

Matlex took a moment to ponder what he said. "You know, I never asked, Ruland, but what did you do to receive this sentence?"

"Nothing so noble as you, mesana," Ruland answered.

"What?" Matlex asked. "Oh, no, that was nothing."

"So humble, mesana," Ruland responded. "The other prisoners told me all about how you were convicted for speaking up against the UAPA fascists. They said you broadcast some scathing interviews on fringe radio networks, I believe?"

"That's correct," Matlex confirmed. "They're the only ones left outside of UAPA control. Still, we hit a lot of ears though. But anyway, we've gotten off-topic. I still want to know what you were arrested for?"

"Well, if you must know," Ruland began. "I was arrested, quite simply, for love."

"Love?" Matlex asked. "What do you mean?"

Ruland took a moment to respond, as if he was lost in the memory.

"Well, back when I had just graduated from foundations school, me and a young woman fell in love with each other," Ruland told him. "It feels like a lifetime ago now. The problem was that she was the daughter of one of the top officials in the Nolinthian government.

"When her father found out about us, he was beyond furious. The idea of his daughter dating a chaemid—rather, the idea of his daughter dating anyone non-orren—sickened him to his stomach. He banned us from ever seeing each other again."

"Wow," Matlex responded. "I'm so sorry... Some orrens are just so backwards in their thinking."

"It is ok," Ruland responded. "Some people are just like this, I know."

Matlex nodded. "So, what happened next? Did you listen to him and break up?"

Ruland chuckled. "Of course not. We were young and in love, and so we ignored his orders and continued seeing each other in secret.

"But the problem came one day, when he caught us in our secret meeting place—a hidden part of their garden. He immediately had me arrested and charged with trespassing."

"You got sentenced to Penal Servitude for trespassing?" Matlex asked in shock. "Was that kind of sentence normal back in pre-UAPA Nolinth?"

"Generally, no," Ruland answered. "But alas, at the time, I happened to have my ceremonial *calva* stake with me. In my culture, it is standard to keep with you at all times. It is dull and fairly harmless, but her father nevertheless used that to increase the charges from trespassing to burglary with a deadly weapon.

"The maximum sentence for such a charge in Nolinth is a lifetime in Penal Servitude, and as everyone in Nolinth knows, if you're an offworlder like me, the maximum sentence is basically a given. I've been imprisoned in work camps ever since, first in Nolinth, until eventually UAPA transferred me out here."

"That's awful," Matlex commiserated. "Honestly, that doesn't sound too different from how UAPA operates. I remember them talking so big about how Restitution Program was so much more compassionate and fair than the Penal Servitude program. As far as I can tell, it really doesn't seem like very much has changed to me."

Ruland shook his head.

"Absolutely nothing has changed, mesana," Ruland asserted. "If anything, it is only more secrecy and that this program seems to be working on a much bigger scale than Nolinth ever tried for. It's certainly not any more merciful though."

"Damn, well, I can't say I'm surprised," Matlex responded. "Things seem to be as bad as they get here."

Matlex rubbed his wrists near where they were cuffed. In the mornings, the prisoners' chains were remotely released, and they were expected to hang them up on hooks along the walls of the building. This was to maximize their efficiency as workers. However, at night, after a dinner in one of the dining halls, they were expected to cuff themselves first thing upon their entry back into the residency building. After cuffing themselves, they would be allowed a very brief reprieve for hygiene and conversation before it was lights out for the night.

Sometimes, some of the new inmates would try to get away with not cuffing themselves in the evening, trying to take advantage of the fact that they often went unchecked through the night. However, on occasion, UAPA soldiers would perform random checks at lights out. If any of them were ever caught without their cuffs on at night, they were punished so severely they would never think of doing so again.

Regardless, the chains seemed like a pointless precaution as the enslaved prisoners were always locked up tightly in the residency building at night anyway. Not only that, but even if they did somehow get out of the building, they still were in the middle of a large compound full of armed guards, surrounded at the perimeter by high walls with sensors and locked gates. On top of all of that, they also were all implanted with tracking chips in their necks that made them easy to find even if they did somehow get off the property.

Matlex believed that, as much as it was unnecessary, these chains were forced on them each night only to remind them of their place as slaves. The only minor comfort was that these chains were made from a softer, less noisy industrial-grade plastic, rather than metal. These were favored by UAPA because they were cheaper than steel and surprisingly tough.

"Matlex, I—" Ruland began.

"Wait, hold that thought," Matlex interrupted him.

He could hear the distant shouting from outside again, this time paired with a bizarre shrieking sound.

"Did you hear that?" Matlex asked.

"No, I don't believe so," Ruland replied. "But I don't have the same hearing you orrens do. If it was a scent though—now, that would be a different story."

The shouting and shrieking both got louder. In the next instant, he could hear sonic rifle blasts from outside.

"Ok, now that I did hear," Ruland stated.

Suddenly, the front door opened. Ruland and Matlex instantly fell silent.

Although this was later than usual, it was not uncommon for UAPA officers to come into the residency buildings late at night. There were generally two reasons this might happen. The first was for random inspections, and the second, more heinous reason, was when the officers came looking for an inmate to take back to their quarters with them to warm their beds. On occasion, they even allowed lower ranked guards to do so as a reward for good work.

The only positive side for the inmate in this is that they generally were allowed the following day off of work if they went along with it. However, if they resisted, they were beaten and then made to work the next day no matter how injured they were, as an example to the other inmates. Even just speaking up against this practice led to similar corporal punishment. Matlex got brutally beaten a few times for speaking out before realizing it wasn't making a difference anyway and quieting down.

However, tonight, Matlex realized the guards were not here for that purpose, as the lights in the residency building were suddenly all turned on at once. Whenever officers came for a "comfort slave," they always left the lights off and just used a flashlight to navigate around—as if that somehow made it less noticeable to the inmates.

Matlex looked over and saw a UAPA officer standing near the entrance, facing them, with two armed guards at his side.

"Attention all inmates," the officer's voice came out loud, projected from a cybernetic amplifier implant that he had attached in his mouth. "The camp is currently on red alert. You are all to prepare for possible evacuation. More orders will be coming soon."

The officer and the two guards then promptly walked out, locking the door behind them.

People all over the residency building were grumbling and cursing as they began waking up.

"What do you think is going on?" Matlex asked Ruland. "I've never seen this in the time that I've been here."

"Honestly, it's really hard to say," Ruland responded. "An evacuation like this would normally happen if there were major safety concerns."

He sniffed curiously. "There is a strange smell in the air... Perhaps some of the toxic chemicals we have warehoused have begun leaking into the ground around here. That would certainly be a problem."

"But then, why was there shooting?" Matlex asked. "They wouldn't shoot toxic chemicals, would they?"

Ruland shrugged. "Perhaps another inmate got out of their building and sabotaged one of the warehouses. A thousand blessings to whoever it is, should that be the case. Anything to give those beliks trouble."

But Matlex was not so certain. Nevertheless, he got up and started getting himself and his bunk ready, preparing for evacuation, as he had been ordered. But just as he was finishing, he heard more shots being fired from outside.

It was disturbing to hear, but there wasn't anything he could do, so he just continued on his routine. He would have liked to change his clothes, but the evacuation policy was to keep the ankle and wrist cuffs of prisoners on, so that wasn't an option. Nevertheless, he grabbed his toiletries and headed over to the large, shared bathroom. Showering wasn't permitted before an evacuation, as it took too long, but since most people were still just waking up in their bunks, this was the perfect opportunity for him to claim a sink to clean up a bit and brush his teeth.

Surprisingly, most sinks were already taken by the time he got in there. But there was one still open. He walked speedily over to it, claiming it before anyone else could, and began his cleaning routine. It started with washing his face, then shaving, then brushing his teeth. Unfortunately, UAPA did not supply hair products or moisturizer, so both his hair and his skin were suffering as a result— not that this was even near the top of his problems here, but it certainly didn't make things any easier.

As Matlex went through the routine, yet more shouting and gunfire could be heard from outside. It sounded like there was a full-blown battle happening outside.

He finished up and went back to his bunk. Ruland joined him a minute later, rolling back over in his wheelchair. Ruland had severe muscle damage in one of his legs from an accident several years ago due to the unsafe working conditions in the camps. While this level of injury could be fixed in most modern hospitals across Auros, the medical care in these camps was nowhere near the level required for such an operation, making the injury effectively permanent.

However, this did not get him out of working. As soon as he was well enough, he was re-assigned to train other slaves, helping them learn the technology and procedures for working in the factories.

Emotionally speaking, while the damage to his leg had been devastating, Ruland insisted on maintaining his bright and positive spirit, still singing his songs and speaking of his hope that one day they would all get out of this barbaric program.

"Still set on your theory?" Matlex asked him. "It sounds like there's a lot more going on than one lone saboteur to me."

Ruland nodded.

"Aye, it sounds that way to me too," Ruland agreed. "And I don't have your ears, mesana, but even I can hear enough to be sure you're right about that."

"Not to mention," Ruland added, again sniffing the air. "That is most certainly the scent of blood that has just wafted in. Must be more than a little to make it through the tiny cracks in that door."

Matlex shuddered at the observation.

Ulus, the inmate on Ruland's bottom bunk, joined their conversation. "You don't suppose someone's attacking the camp, do you Ruland? Maybe someone coming to save us?"

Ruland laughed. "One can always dream, but I would advise against getting hopes too high. Hope is a beautiful thing, but letting it inflate too much at once can lead to terrible, bitter disappointment. The truth is that any number of things could be happening."

Matlex fidgeted anxiously. "I think I'm going to go wait next to the door."

Ruland looked at him quizzically. "Are you sure that's a wise idea, mesana? You know that the evacuation procedure is to wait next to your bunk with your belongings after you are ready. You could get in trouble for breaking procedure."

"I don't care," Matlex said firmly. "I want to be there to get a firsthand peek outside the next time that door is opened. If there's even a chance I can get a glimpse of what's going on, I want to take it."

"Very well," Ruland relented. "In that case, I shall accompany you."

"Are you sure, Ruland?" Matlex asked hesitantly. "You yourself just mentioned the risk of breaking the evacuation orders. I can always tell you what I see."

"It is fine, mesana," Ruland assured. "There is nothing they can do to me that they have not already done a million times before. Besides, I would like to see for myself whatever is causing the UAPA beliks so much trouble. Who knows? Maybe I will get lucky and could even give thanks to whoever or whatever is the cause."

"Perhaps a tad optimistic," Matlex chuckled. "But very well then. Let's go."

"Good luck you two," Ulus wished them as they headed towards the door.

After they made it to the door, they stopped and began waiting. Matlex felt a weird emotion, somewhere between excitement and anxiety. He was certain he would be in trouble the next time an officer opened the door, but he was extremely curious to get even a glimpse of what was going on outside to the point where he was willing to endure any possible punishment. The increasing sounds of shouting, shrieking and gunfire continued to make it clear that whatever was happening out there was no small crisis.

After a brief while, there was quiet. This sudden quiet was, in a way, more disturbing than all of the sounds that came before it. The silence lasted for several minutes while Ruland and Matlex continued waiting stiffly next to the door.

Finally, Ruland broke the silence. "Is it perhaps over? Do you still hear anything?"

"Shh," Matlex shushed him, raising his curled index finger, and putting its first knuckle next to his mouth, signaling for Ruland to be quiet.

He could hear someone fiddling with the door outside. Matlex worried that they may have missed their chance. With no audible commotion outside, there might be nothing worth looking at, and with an officer opening the door, they may be about to receive beatings for nothing.

Nevertheless, he maintained his resolve and stood still, holding on to the off-chance he could catch even the smallest glimpse of what had been going on out there when that door opened.

Then, out of nowhere, a loud blasting sound came from the door, causing Matlex to jump back as a circular chunk of the door and wall next to it was blown out in what appeared to be a small-but-powerful, controlled explosion.

"Get yourself ready Matlex," Ruland calmly instructed. "Whoever is behind that door is clearly not an officer."

Matlex looked over to Ruland, his green scales glistening in the residency building's lights. He had never seen his friend look so serious, let alone so stoic, before. Ruland had gotten up out of his wheelchair, with all of his weight balanced on his good leg, and was holding himself in a sturdy, defensive position a bit in front of Matlex with fierce, steeled determination in his eyes. All four of Ruland's arms were braced for combat, likely in case whoever was coming happened to be hostile.

Matlex had never been in a fight before, but he gulped nervously and tried to brace himself as well, balling his hands into fists and shakily holding them up. Even with only one working leg, Ruland was a more capable fighter than Matlex could ever hope to be, but if there was someone hostile coming, Matlex wanted to at least try and help his friend out.

In the next moment, the door swung open. Walking through it was a strong-looking, beautiful human woman with light brown skin and dark hair. Coming in shortly after her was a skinny, young human man with pale skin and blonde hair who Matlex instantly recognized.

His fists released and his arms fell to his sides as his jaw dropped in surprise.

"Xander?" He asked in disbelief.

*/

The half-dozen UAPA soldiers still in the CNPF's broadcasting room immediately surrendered after Aren and the rest of the Oppori Qala team stormed in.

The E7 operatives quickly went to work tying up the soldiers. In addition to tying and gagging the soldiers, the E7 operatives also put blindfolds over their eyes and locked silencing headphones over their ears. This was not an abnormal procedure during sensitive missions such as this one. The reason for it was to reduce the chance of the enemy seeing or overhearing anything they shouldn't. Experienced operatives, however, still tended to avoid talking about anything too highly confidential in front of these guards, just in the off-chance something went wrong with their headphones.

"Huh," Elmenz remarked. "You know, I have to admit, I would have expected to see at least a few civilians in the building. I mean, I know that UAPA re-classified the CNPF as a military facility, but I wasn't expecting to see nothing but soldiers everywhere. I don't think we've seen a single civilian since arriving here."

"UAPA doesn't trust civilians to work in a building like this," Henrika explained. "Which is deliciously ironic, considering even the UAPA Capitol Palace is full of them."

"Wow," Aren smirked. "I suppose Hamish's precious radio networks are more important."

"Yes. Gods forbid something goes wrong and some cooking show has to go uncensored for ten seconds," Henrika cackled.

"Oh my gods," Aren laughed heartily. "Careful now, we don't want to give him a heart attack."

"But don't we though?" Henrika retorted with a devilish grin.

Both of them were surprised by raucous laughter coming from Elmenz behind them.

"That's brilliant," Elmenz remarked. "Too true, too true."

Aren smiled at him before turning to the group.

"Alright everyone, I need to contact Orita," Aren stated. "Give me a second here."

He clicked a few buttons on his wristcomm. A moment later, he heard Orita's voice in his earpiece.

"Well, hello there, Mr. Mercenary," Orita greeted him playfully. "I take it you're calling because you've accessed the broadcasting room."

"You got it, Ms. Computer Expert," Aren responded back in the same playful tone. "Am I all good to plug you and the officer codes in now, or is there anything you need first?"

"Nope, it's all good," Orita assured. "Just stick me in there, baby."

Aren first inserted the data card with the officer codes. After the monitor said the codes were accepted, he then took the small device given to him by Orita and plugged it straight into the computer.

"Oh, that's the stuff," Orita moaned teasingly and then giggled. "God, UAPA firewalls are such a joke. I'm not even sure we really needed those officer codes for this part. They shouldn't have messed with the old CNPF software. That stuff was much harder to crack… erm, not that I would know."

"I'm sure you wouldn't," Aren chuckled. "Anyway, is that it? Are we good to broadcast now?"

"Yup, that's it," Orita confirmed. "That's all I really needed. I have remote control over more than 90% of the CNPF's systems. If you could stick around though, I could use your support a bit during the broadcast. It would be helpful if you could flip the live switch over there to actually start and stop the broadcast. Otherwise, yeah, we're good."

"Glad to hear it," Aren stated.

Aren turned around and looked at the rest of his team.

"Fantastic job everyone," Aren praised. "We now officially have control over the CNPF broadcasting systems."

The operatives cheered.

"I'm glad to hear it, sir," Lieutenant Chave rejoiced. "With your permission, I'd like to take those of us from E7 to secure the halls and surrounding area while you take care of things in here. I'm pretty certain that we've cleared out most of the soldiers at this point, but it would be better operation security if we set up a perimeter nonetheless."

"Permission granted," Aren stated. "That's a good call, Chave."

"Thank you, sir," Lieutenant Chave replied, before turning to the other operatives. "Alright, let's move people."

"Yes, sir," The operatives responded in unison.

Lieutenant Chave and his people exited the room.

"If you don't mind, I'd like to head out for a bit myself," Henrika stated. "I'd like to stretch my legs."

Aren eyed her suspiciously.

"Really?" Aren asked doubtfully. "I don't suppose you'd be after that CNPF vault with the rare and expensive hardware, would you?"

"Come now," Henrika smirked at him. "You should know better than to expect a girl to reveal all of her secrets."

"Very well," Aren relented. "I suppose we don't actually need you here at the moment. Permission granted. Go 'stretch your legs' all you want."

"Thanks, love," Henrika leaned down and planted a kiss on his cheek. "Not only hot but a good leader too."

Aren smiled and was about to respond, but Henrika had already left the room.

"She's quite the devilish one, isn't she?" Elmenz chuckled.

"She's certainly something," Aren replied, rubbing his cheek where she had kissed him. He felt a warmth in his chest, thinking about the feeling of her lips.

He still felt uncertain about Henrika's intentions. Between Orita's earlier slip and Henrika's current "walk," it felt like something more was going on here. However, he decided not to worry about it. While he may not have known Henrika well, his intuition told him that whatever she was up to was not likely malicious or harmful in nature.

"I don't think I've ever seen her take this much of a liking to someone before," Elmenz noted casually. "There are a lot of Oppori Qala operatives and officers I'm sure would be quite jealous to be in your shoes."

"Is that so?" Aren said, blushing lightly.

"Indeed, her beauty is so great that many are willing to risk being robbed blind for a chance at courting her," Elmenz remarked with a light chortle. "Having said that, she doesn't seem interested in most herself, to be honest. The only others I've seen capable of holding her attention even in the slightest were Anya, Morgas, and maybe Orita at times."

"Interesting," Aren blushed, uncertain of what else he could say to that.

"But anyway," Elmenz pivoted. "Now that we have a moment, I actually have a question for you, if you don't mind."

"Ask away," Aren permitted.

"Well, earlier, against Maximilius, you said that true masters didn't use support casters," Elmenz recounted. "I have to ask; do you really believe that? I mean, I understand your quality over quantity argument, but can't you still get more energy with the help of support casters? Assuming the quality is there, would more energy not be a good thing?"

Aren looked thoughtful for a moment. "I suppose that's technically true. You are accessing a larger life energy pool, so of course you'll have a higher raw output."

"Exactly," Elmenz concurred. "So, why would you say that masters would never use them?"

"I see where you're coming from," Aren expressed. "However, the part you're missing is that the goal should be to stop relying so much on life energy, not to simply access more of it."

"Could you elaborate on that?" Elmenz requested curiously.

"Well, the fact is, the universe is full of all kinds of massive pools of energy, both cosmic and beyond," Aren expounded. "A mage's end-goal should be to try to learn to tap into some of these energies. Of course, there are limits to this, but a true master could, in many cases, gain even more energy and power output than all of Maximilius' coven combined. That's why support casters are only a crutch."

Aren's explanation was very intriguing to Elmenz. Using some environmental energy to support your spells was not an unknown technique, but what Aren spoke of seemed to go far beyond what Elmenz had ever heard of.

"That's very intriguing," Elmenz commented, stroking his beard thoughtfully. "May I ask, have you attained a mastery of this skill, yourself?"

Aren laughed "Not remotely. And if I relied on support casters, I don't think I ever would."

"Fair enough," Elmenz responded. "I have just one more question though."

"Go ahead," Aren assented.

"I understand your full argument now," Elmenz began. "However, the only thing I don't understand is, well, I was under the impression that some legendary sorcerers have used group casting to accomplish some incredible feats. Are you telling me that they were relying on a 'crutch' as you so put it?"

"Well, no, but there's a difference between group casting and support casting," Aren explained. "It's a bit complicated, but basically, group casting involves performing different spells that are weaved together into the same complex, multi-layered ritual. Support casting, on the other hand, has a group all lending their power towards the same spell. It's a completely different thing.

"Masters do use group casting to produce some incredible magic sometimes. It's really a specialized skill in and of itself. On the other hand, you most likely wouldn't find a real master ever relying on support casting."

"Hmmm," Elmenz murmured. "Listening to you speak on magic makes it abundantly clear that I have been a bit complacent in my time on Antal."

"Oh?" voiced Aren.

"Yes," Elmenz responded. "You know, I am recognized as one of the best sorcerers on the planet, and yet, I've always known there's more across the stars—concepts that are all-but-unknown in this world's magical circles."

"Your magic is still impressive," Aren responded. "I've seen your projectile spells—those are a work of art. You have a lot to be proud of."

"Thank you, but no, please don't get me wrong here," Elmenz responded. "I'm not meaning to get down on myself or anything. On the contrary, I think it's inspiring. Listening to you—it makes me feel like I want to go out there, explore, and learn all of the magic I can across the galaxy. How incredible it would be to go out there and develop my own skills in the way that you described."

"Well, why don't you?" Aren asked.

Elmenz laughed. "I mean, I know I look good for my age, but… You must have noticed I'm not exactly a young *jonta* anymore. I'm much too old for such things at this point."

"Why do you say that?" Aren inquired, sounding confused.

"It's just—it's how it is," Elmenz explained. "At a certain point you get to be too old for going out on adventures, for learning new things, for all of that kind of stuff. It's just how things work."

Aren took a moment to consider his words.

"But does it really have to be?" He asked.

"I—well, I mean," Elmenz stammered.

"Look, I know I'm young, so maybe I have no right to talk," Aren began. "But I don't know, if it's something you truly want to do, I just don't see why age should get in your way. If it's about physical or medical difficulties, there are treatments and supports in this day and age that can help.

"Besides that, I just don't see the issue, personally. I've met people older than you who are still dedicated to learning and following their passions, you know, and they seem quite happy… Maybe you could be too."

"I… well, I suppose maybe you have a point," Elmenz responded. "I'll think about it, in any case."

"I'm glad," Aren smiled warmly at him.

"On a related topic, I've been wondering," Elmenz said. "How old are you, if you don't mind me asking? You don't need to answer if you don't want to, but I'm just curious. You seem incredibly young for a man of your skills."

"Well, thank you for the compliment," Aren replied gratefully. "I don't mind at all. In both Galactic Standard and Antallian years, I am 19 years old."

"Really?" Elmenz asked in shock. "Incredible. That's even younger than I expected, to be honest. Where did you learn—"

They were interrupted by an incoming call on Aren's wristcomm.

Elmenz immediately quieted down, recognizing that any call during this mission took precedence.

Aren answered. "Hello."

"Hey Aren," Xander greeted cheerfully. "We're ready."

Chapter 23

Xander ran up to Matlex and wrapped his arms around him in a deep and tight hug. Xander couldn't help but feel that the situation was surreal, and yet amazing at the same time.

After a moment of dissociating, Matlex fell back to reality, and he grabbed Xander back, taking him in a big bear hug and lifting him up off the ground. It was a moment of pure joy to see his old friend like this and hold him in his arms. If this was some kind of hallucination, Matlex did not want it to end, but the longer he held Xander, the more he could feel that this was reality.

"Hey there, Little Songbird," Matlex greeted him sweetly. "It's been quite a while."

"Too long," Xander said, burying his face into Matlex's soft chest.

After a few moments, they pulled away from each other.

Xander looked with concern at Matlex. "You've lost so much weight in such a short time. And those bruises on your arm."

"Don't worry about me, I'm fine," Matlex assured him. "More importantly, why are you here? Don't take this the wrong way—I'm very excited to see you, but you're honestly the last person I would have expected to see coming through that door."

"I came because of your message," Xander responded. "As soon as I found out you never made your flight, I couldn't let that go."

"Wait…" Matlex paused for a moment, processing his shock. "Are you really telling me that you came all this way, traveled through a locked down forest, and infiltrated a secret, military camp, all because of a holo-message sent by your ex-boyfriend that you hadn't seen and barely talked to in nearly three years?"

"Of course, I did," Xander replied assertively.

Matlex laughed openly. "You really haven't changed, Little Songbird, have you?"

Matlex looked at him more seriously.

"I do have to ask though: what's going on in this camp right now?" Matlex questioned in a concerned tone. "And also, how did you find me? I'll admit, I'm a bit perplexed all around. I'm still not convinced I'm not dreaming."

Matlex looked over to the woman that Xander came with. Although her expression appeared to be calm and kind, Matlex still somehow got the sense that this was not a woman to be trifled with.

"And also, who is this you came with, if you don't mind me asking?" Matlex inquired.

"Ok, well, first, you're not dreaming," Xander chuckled. "Second, this is Kyara."

Kyara bowed to Matlex. "Nice to meet you, Matlex."

"Likewise," Matlex bowed back.

"Kyara and I both joined Oppori Qala recently, which should give you some idea what's going on in this camp right now and how I found you," Xander continued.

"Wait, Oppori Qala is here??" Matlex asked in shock. "And you joined them?"

"Yes," Xander answered. "We're taking this camp and freeing all of you."

While they were talking, Kyara pressed a few buttons on her wristcomm and stepped aside to make her report to Morgas.

"Seriously?" Ruland wheeled up to Xander and asked. "You think you really have a chance to help us here? You're not just fanning fog in our eyes, are you?"

"Ah, please forgive my manners," Matlex apologized. "Xander, this is Ruland, the closest friend that I've made here. He's one of the veterans of this camp. Between Nolinth's Penal Servitude program and UAPA's Restitution Program, Ruland has been enslaved for 28 years altogether."

"Wow, 28 years," Xander was shocked. "I thought this residency building was just for the inmates who arrived in in the seventh month of this year."

"Those from that month do make up about two-thirds of the inmates in this building, but the rest have been in the system much longer," Ruland explained. "UAPA adapted Nolinth's system of pairing up new and old inmates so that the new ones can learn how to behave from the so-called 'veterans'."

"I suppose that makes sense," Xander acknowledged. "At least from their viewpoint."

"Indeed," Ruland responded. "Now, I ask that you please give answer to my question. Do you truly believe you have a chance at freeing us?"

"More than a chance," Xander asserted. "I'll admit, things may have gotten a bit messy, but UAPA has already been all-but-defeated in this camp."

Ruland put his head in his hands, quaking in a way that looked like sobbing. However, as Ruland began to pull his head back up, it became clear that, although there were tears in his eyes, he actually was not sobbing but laughing. Or, on second glance, it may have been something between the two.

"Gods," Ruland cried out. "I knew this day would come. I knew it. I always said it would, didn't I, mesana?"

"That you did Ruland," Matlex smiled at him and patted him on the back. "And you were always right."

As the two were speaking, Kyara finished making her report to Morgas.

She looked around herself. The facility appeared more like it was designed to be a warehouse than a residence. The majority of the building was a wide-open space, most of it dominated by bunks—252 bunks in total, in rows of 18 by 14 with two beds per bunk. The only closed off room appeared to be a large communal bathroom at the back.

The area she was currently standing in was an open entry area, which stood between the front door and where the bunks began. This area was quickly filling up with curious inmates, while others stood next to their bunks, watching the events from some distance away.

Many of the inmates looked confused or curious, while some appeared somewhat hopeful. However, more notable was the condition most of them were in. Over half of the inmates were bruised and battered, and most of them had signs of malnourishment, from mild to severe.

It was a sad sight to see, but Kyara knew she had a job to do. She pulled out two devices that were attached to her hip and stepped forward. She handed one to Xander, and then motioned with her hand to the crowd to get their attention.

She took a deep breath. Public speaking tended to make her feel uncomfortable, but she pushed that discomfort to the back of her mind.

"Everyone," She announced in a loud booming voice that echoed across the building. "We have come to free you from this place. I ask that you please be patient as, over the next while, we will be working on getting you out of here and to somewhere safe, out of UAPA's reach."

She held up the device in her hands so most could see it. "To start with, this is a device that will disable your trackers. Please come up one at a time, and Xander and I will use these on each and every one of you."

"What about our chains?" One of the inmates asked, rattling the hard plastic chains still attached to his wrists and ankles.

"There are operatives currently working on those," Kyara explained. "Your chains will all be remotely deactivated as soon as they have successfully hacked into the inmate management system."

"Is that device of yours going to remove the trackers?" Another inmate asked. "I don't want this thing in my body a second longer."

There were some murmurs of agreement among the crowd.

"I apologize, but this device will not remove the trackers," Kyara expounded. "Those trackers were deliberately placed near vital blood vessels, making it risky for any non-medical professional to remove them. The devices we have brought are only meant to disable them. However, there are doctors on standby at your final destination who have volunteered to give all of you check-ups and to surgically remove your trackers. But for now, please line up so that we can begin the disabling process."

The inmates eagerly formed two lines down half of the rows of bunks, which funneled towards Xander and Kyara. Both lines were of identical length and in perfect symmetry with one another.

Xander was impressed at how fast and orderly they were in following Kyara's instructions. Most crowds would be considerably slower and need much more guidance to form lines this well with this many people.

However, while the incredible discipline of these inmates sped the process up considerably, it saddened Xander to think about the implications of it. They likely had this discipline instilled in them at the edge of a whip or similar implements, as they were made to follow orders like these regularly.

Looking over the prisoners, their terrible physical conditions only reinforced this theory. These people were clearly beaten, battered and starved, and Xander was sure the mental injuries were likely worse than anything physical he was seeing.

Tears welled up in Xander's eyes, as he thought about what the prisoners went through. As much as he tried to hold back, he began to cry, even as he continued working.

"It's not pretty, is it?" Matlex said sadly.

"No, it really isn't," Xander sniffled.

"Hey, try to keep your chin up, ok?" Matlex replied, wiping a tear off of Xander's face. "You know me, I have nothing against crying, but this is a merry moment—one to celebrate. We're going to be free and out of here soon, thanks to you and Oppori Qala. You should try to focus on that, Little Songbird, ok?"

"I suppose so," Xander responded softly.

"Come on," Matlex scolded. "I think you can do better than that."

"Alright," Xander relented with a sigh, wiping his remaining tears as his crying stopped. "I'll try my best to stay positive, ok?"

"There we go," Matlex smiled at him and ruffled his hair. "That's much better, Little Songbird."

Xander couldn't help but give a small smile in response to his old friend's shining, positive attitude. Matlex had always been like this, and Xander was glad to see that a few months here had not changed the man's attitude.

"Hey, you wouldn't happen to have anything to eat, would you?" Matlex asked hungrily.

"Oh, of course," Xander replied. He reached into his pack and brought out a protein bar, handing it over to him. "Here you go. There'll be a lot more coming after we get out of here too."

"Thank you!" Matlex eagerly removed the wrapping. "Rations are not good here… They're also inconsistent. Apparently, before I arrived, there were some *weeks* people had to survive on half-rations—some kind of shortage according to the officers. I'm glad I came after; their regular rations already feel like half-rations."

Matlex was about to mow down on the bar, when he looked up and saw another prisoner looking hungrily at it. He sighed and broke the bar in half.

He paused for a moment, and then broke both halves into quarters, doing so with all of the reluctance and care of someone destroying a beloved heirloom or a priceless work of art. He handed one of the pieces to the prisoner who had been staring. This prisoner bowed rapidly in gratitude before devouring it ravenously.

Matlex then walked over and handed another piece to Ruland and the third, biggest piece, to Trymis, a woman who appeared particularly skinny and frail due to being withheld rations a few times this past month as punishment for her refusal to work. They both thanked him before similarly devouring their pieces.

Matlex quickly downed his own quarter before anyone else could get a chance to see and ask. The bar was delicious, much better than the reconstituted gruel and dry bread served here. As he gulped it down, he felt quite unsatisfied—a natural consequence to divvying the bar up into such small portions. Nevertheless, he was grateful to have another bite to eat in his stomach, however small.

As this was happening, Xander continued disabling the tracking devices. The process was fairly simple. Just as Anya had taught him, Xander started with each inmate by positioning the tracking disabler over the tracker location. This was easy to find, as it was always somewhere close to the RPW ID tattoo on the inmate's neck. He would then press the activation button for a few moments, until a beeping sound from the device indicated that the tracker was disabled. The inmate would then leave the area, so that the next person in line could have their turn.

After Matlex finished his bite to eat, he returned and began chatting with Xander as he worked. Xander was delighted to be here with him, his old friend who he had worried he might not ever see again. It also just felt good to catch up, considering how long it had been since they last saw each other. Despite how close they had been at the academy, after Xander left Antal, for various reasons, they didn't talk to each other very often. It had been two-and-a-half years, and there was a lot to tell each other about.

As Xander was working, he was suddenly startled by a loud series of beeping sounds coming from the prisoners' ankle and wrist chains. The cuffs suddenly all opened up and fell straight to the floor. True to Kyara's word, they had all been remotely disabled.

After a moment of silence, the inmates began to cheer. Up to this point, most of them seemed to be just going through the motions. However, as soon as those chains hit the ground, the atmosphere suddenly became more bright and upbeat. It was as if, with the chains gone, the idea of actually getting free was starting to feel a little more real.

Xander could feel the difference in that moment himself, letting out a sigh of relief. Up until that point, there had still been a part of him that felt like maybe he spoke too soon, and worried that maybe they weren't actually going to succeed. After all, things weren't exactly under control while he was out there. But seeing these chains fall to the ground like this was proof that things were going according to plan.

This renewed hope had put a spring in Xander's movements as he continued disabling tracker after tracker. It felt like he was really getting into the groove of things.

However, as Xander was working, he was startled by the sudden sound of the door to the outside opening behind him. He quickly dropped his tracking disabler and grabbed his chiambra, fearing the worst. He twirled around, ready to fight, just as a hand connected with his shoulder.

"Glad to see you on your toes," Morgas chimed pleasantly, patting his shoulder lightly. "It's good to stay alert—especially in enemy territory."

Xander watched as seven Oppori Qala operatives entered the building behind Morgas.

"You two can stop now," Morgas instructed to Kyara and Xander. "A6 and B15, you take over for them. Don't stop until you are certain every tracker has been disabled. A8, B7 and A4, I want you checking the inmates for major injuries and providing whatever minimal treatment is required. I want everyone ready for transportation in the next hour. D30 and D31, start getting things ready here for the broadcast."

"Yes, ma'am," the operatives all replied in unison.

Xander was impressed by the way Morgas spoke. Her words were confident, assertive and professional, and yet, he could also feel a kindness and a respect for her subordinates in her tone.

Xander and Kyara both stopped what they were doing, allowing the operatives to take over, continuing the work of disabling each of the prisoners' trackers. Three of the other operatives went and quickly began work setting up a temporary medical station, while the last two started setting up recording equipment.

While they worked, Morgas stepped forward and lifted a miniature amplification device she was holding up to her mouth.

"Everyone, listen," Morgas ordered. "I have an announcement."

Anyone who was chatting stopped, and all eyes went over to Morgas.

"It is my pleasure to announce that this camp is now officially free," Morgas proclaimed. "We still have to get everyone prepped and transported, but as of this moment, you are no longer under UAPA control."

The crowd cheered loudly. Many of the inmates hugged each other. Some were laughing, some were crying, while others simply looked stunned in disbelief.

Morgas turned to Kyara and Xander.

"Excellent job all around, you two," Morgas praised. "We couldn't have done this without your help. Not only did you disable their security for us, but to then find Matlex as well? Simply outstanding work."

"Thanks," Kyara responded.

"Oh, thank you," Xander also replied to Morgas. "I'm just glad that he's ok."

Xander looked over to Matlex. It appeared he had just finished up a conversation with some of the other former prisoners and was now headed in Xander's direction.

As Matlex approached, Xander motioned to him. "Speaking of, here he is."

"Indeed, I am. Matlex Winslow, at your service," Matlex greeted in his deep, smooth voice, bowing his head to Morgas. "You must be the infamous Morgas Yen. I'm a big fan of your work."

"And I of yours," Morgas smiled. "Come, I'd love to talk to you a bit, if you don't mind."

"Oh, I don't mind at all," Matlex responded. "I'll see you in a bit, Little Songbird."

Xander nodded at him "I'll see you in a bit."

"Xander!" He heard his name called out.

Xander looked over to see Anya coming in with three more operatives behind her. She put her rifle on her back, and then ran up to him, throwing her arms around him.

The embrace was unexpected. To Xander, Anya had always seemed very professional and maybe even a bit distant at times. But here she was, hugging him deeply and warmly. He put his arms around her, returning the embrace.

"I'm so glad you're ok," Anya rejoiced. "I'm sorry we sent you into this. I never thought things would get this bad. That must have been terrifying to go through with just you and Kyara alone."

"Why are you just singling me out?" Xander asked, going red in the face. "You know, Kyara was there too."

Anya released her hug.

"Of course, and I'm very happy you're ok too , Kyara," Anya said to her, before turning back to Xander. "But out of the two of you, you are technically the civilian, Xander. I'm also sure Kyara's been through situations like this many times. But if I knew it would get this bad, I never would have accepted you going ahead of the rest of us like that."

Xander rubbed the back of his head sheepishly.

"I guess you have a point," Xander admitted. "But it all turned out well, didn't it? Largely thanks to Kyara, but still. Honestly, I don't know if I'd have accepted it if you told me I couldn't go anyway."

"I didn't do all that much," Kyara responded. "Xander is being humble. But yes, I would say that it went well."

"I'm glad to hear that," Anya replied. "Still though, I'd like to avoid putting you through something like that again, Xander."

"Gosh, you keep talking like I'm so breakable," Xander chuckled. "I guess I'll admit things did get a little crazy. Those shreen are seriously something else. Speaking of, Morgas said we have control of the camp. Does that mean the shreen were dealt with, then?"

"Yes," Anya replied. "Honestly, it wasn't easy. Our short-range deterrents weren't doing much, unfortunately. Thankfully though, they seemed much more interested in UAPA soldiers than us through this whole thing."

"Really?" Xander asked. "Well, if the deterrents weren't doing much, then how did you get them out of the camp?"

"Honestly, it's a little gruesome," Anya warned. "Are you sure that you want to hear it?"

"After everything I've seen today, I don't think it will bother me," Xander assured. "Go ahead."

"Alright, well, we realized that the main thing keeping the shreen here was their food," Anya explained. "It appeared that they finished up hunting not long ago. I suppose they finally decided they had enough to last the winter. The shreen who remained were all gathered around their 'Winter Feast,' if you know what that is?"

"Yes, that enormous pile of bodies," Xander replied while grimacing. "We saw it before we came here. I won't lie, that was pretty disturbing to see."

"You're not wrong," Anya commented in an unsettled tone. "I have no doubt that thing will be appearing in my nightmares for some days to come."

Anya shuddered for a moment before continuing. "Anyway, we found a bulldozer and an excavator at a construction site in the camp, and we decided to use those to move that Winter Feast out of the compound. It wasn't pretty, to say the least, but we managed to get the pile moved to the forest, and the shreen were quick to follow. Surprisingly, the few bodies that we missed were actually picked up by the shreen, who carried them over to the pile's new location on their own."

"That was a smart move," Kyara praised. "Food is going to be a stronger motivator for the shreen than pretty much anything else right now."

Anya nodded. "That was my thought as well."

"Anyway, from there, we followed the original plan, disabling our virus on UAPA's system, and turning the camp's sonic deterrents back on to keep the shreen from coming back."

"Wow," Xander replied. "That's… that's quite the method. I'm just glad that it's over."

"I am too," Anya agreed.

As they were talking, Morgas returned next to them.

"Hey Xander," Morgas greeted as she approached. "I hope I'm not interrupting anything. I have a question for you."

"What is it?" Xander inquired curiously.

"How would you like to make the opening statement for the broadcast?" Morgas asked him. "I know it's last second, but I think you'd be the perfect person for the job."

"Wait, do you mean the broadcast that's going to be sent around the entire planet and beyond?" Xander inquired incredulously. "I thought you were going to open for the broadcast yourself. Or if not you, how about Matlex?"

"Originally, it was going to just be me," Morgas explained. "But since you're here, I actually think it would be better if you were the one to start it off. As for Matlex, he has graciously agreed to be a part of it as well, but him and I will both be coming later."

"But why me though?" Xander asked. "What is it that makes you convinced I'd be the right person to open?"

"Well, in truth, I've seen you speak in interviews in the past," Morgas explained. "You may be young, but you have impressive oratorical skills. You're more than just charming when you speak. You have a compelling intellectual side beneath that cavalier exterior, especially when it comes to matters of justice. That one speech you gave on marriage equality in Gazef was very touching and well thought-out."

"Beyond that, the work you've done with us has only further convinced me of your passion for the cause. And if all of that wasn't enough, you're also pretty popular on Antal at this moment thanks to your music. From all angles, it's pretty clear that you're the right person for the job."

"Wow, well thank you. I'm honoured," Xander stated proudly. "Of course, I'll do it."

"Excellent," Morgas beamed.

Morgas pressed a few buttons on her wristcomm. "I've just sent you the notes. We don't have long here, but you can take a little time to get prepared. Just tell us when you're ready. If you'd like, you can also be the one to call Aren and inform him when we're ready to start the broadcast."

"Well then," Xander nodded to her. "I suppose I should start getting ready right away."

He sat down on a nearby chair, pulled up his wristcomm and began reading the notes Morgas had sent him.

Within moments, his eyes had widened in surprise. "So, they're here too, huh?"

Chapter 24

Around the world, countless people were tuned in to global internet radio networks before the start of the broadcast. These networks comprised a core part of Antallian culture and were the most popular global sources for both entertainment and information media on the planet.

However, Antallian radio broadcasts were not just limited to Antal. Thanks to the upgrades that the CNPF received over two centuries ago, most of Antal's broadcasts were now on the ISB (Interstellar Broadcasting), which extended across the Auros galaxy through faster-than-light, dark radio waves.

In their prime, Antal had been one of the most popular interstellar broadcasters, with billions of active listeners across Auros. However, since UAPA took over more than two years ago and began focusing their broadcasts on propaganda, the popularity of Antallian ISB stations decreased dramatically, from billions of active listeners down to only tens of millions.

The Supreme Executive of UAPA, Hamish Drulth, had originally considered cutting off all ISB stations when their ratings plummeted, keeping Antallian radio isolated to Antal. He would rather just stop broadcasting outside the planet altogether than admit they were doing poorly. This move would have been easy to rationalize to the people since his political platform was already built on promoting Antallian independence from the rest of Auros.

However, his advisors pointed out to him how much money he would lose in advertising revenue if he did this, and in the end, the financial incentive won out and the broadcasts continued. Instead, Drulth decided to go the opposite direction and publicly claim that Antallian radio was now greater than ever, dismissing the idea that their ratings were down, and asserting that any interglobal viewers they did lose were either uncultured or simply could not handle the truth.

One thing that was true was that their Antallian audience numbers had not decreased very much within the bounds of the planet. While there were many Antallians who were vehemently against all of the UAPA propaganda, most of them did not care enough to stop listening to their favorite programs. In fact, some detractors even went out of their way to listen to the propaganda out of morbid curiosity and wanting to stay informed on what "new nonsense" that UAPA was preaching to the public from day-to-day.

Thanks to Antal's persistent strong audience numbers within the planet, there was always at least a million people viewing and/or listening to Antallian radio at any one time, even during the hours with the lowest audience numbers.

Therefore, even though it was somewhere between late night to mid-morning for most of Antal's population when Aren flipped the switch to start the broadcast, there were still over two million Antallians tuned in to the 148 networks controlled by the CNPF. Every single one of them who were paying attention were on the edge of their seats throughout the entire program, as the reality hit them that this broadcast was going to change everything.

*/

"Hello everyone," Xander began. "I am sorry to interrupt your programs.

"My name is Xander Ardentes. Many of you likely know me from my music. However, today I am addressing you all as a fellow person; as someone who lived for years on Antal; as someone who loves this planet deeply; and as someone who can no longer abide by the evil that has been taking place here right under everyone's noses.

"As you all are aware, UAPA is in the midst of a conquest across Antal, invading and conquering nation after nation, leaving a trail of death and destruction in their wake. They have attempted to justify their brutality by claiming it is all for the sake of unity and for a better future for Antal. This is a lie. The real truth of the terrible organization that is UAPA is much uglier and more sinister. This broadcast is intended to reveal that truth to you all.

"The accusations we are about to make do not come without evidence, mind you. We ask that you all download the three information packets we have attached to this broadcast, which will provide evidence of our claims. The first of these packets includes every study and statistic suppressed by the UAPA government, showing how much worse things have actually gotten under UAPA control, from increasing wealth disparity, to worsening health outcomes, to increasing hate crimes, and beyond.

"However, those studies are not the main reason I came to talk to you today. The main reason is to talk about UAPA's Restitution Program.

"When UAPA dissolved Nolinth's unpopular Penal Servitude program nearly three years ago and shut down Nolinth's work camps, they promised that their new Restitution Program, despite still clearly being a system of slavery, would be much more compassionate.

"They claimed that they would greatly reduce sentencing into the program. They also claimed that it would only be reserved for the worst of the worst criminals.

"Both of these were lies. The approximately 18,000 Restitution Program 'workers' that the public knows about make up only about 12% of the actual total of people currently held in the program. The true number of Restitution Program slaves is nearly 150,000, which is a number has been growing more and more every day. In fact, this number would have already been thousands higher if it weren't for the obscene mortality rate that these enslaved individuals have gone through.

"The reason you do not know this is because the vast majority of the people in the Restitution Program were convicted in secret trials and were sentenced into hidden work camps in places that the public does not have access to. The public face is a mere façade to help hide the true program.

"Most of those convicted in these secret trials were not hardened or violent criminals. You can see for yourself. The second information packet includes the confidential court records for every person taken into the Restitution Program, secretly or otherwise. These records show that most were only given convicted for small offenses or even just for politically opposing UAPA in gods damned summary trials where the judge often didn't even see the defendant in person before making each judgment.

"This evidence also shows that non-orrens are far more likely to be convicted, making up approximately half of Restitution Program convictions, despite non-orrens making up less than 11% of UAPA's total population. In many cases, judges specifically cited the convict being an 'offworlder' as part of the reasons behind their conviction."

Xander looked down for a moment, with a pained expression. He turned off his wristcomm that he had been glancing to for notes.

"But I think that's enough numbers. I didn't come on here simply to cite basic facts and statistics to you all. I came to speak to you from the heart. And my heart knows that UAPA's actions are, well, there's no better word for it than *evil*. Hamish Drulth and his administration are cruel, selfish cowards who do not care who they harm, as long as it increases their wealth and power.

"Recently, I joined the resistance organization Oppori Qala. Tonight, we raided all fourteen of UAPA's hidden slave camps and freed all of the people they had enslaved. What we had witnessed in these slave camps would shock and horrify you all. The most sickening part, however, was that this was not merely a small conspiracy by a handful of individuals. These camps took the collaboration of thousands of UAPA soldiers and workers on every level of that corrupt government to run and to keep a secret. The fact that so many could be so devoid of morality is… beyond disheartening.

"If you don't believe it, the third information packet has pictures, videos and audio recordings taken both before and during the raid, showing many of the horrifying things going on at these camps.

"And if you still have doubts, we will be releasing more documents and testimonials from the formerly enslaved people themselves in the days to come. Among those who plan to testify include the ecologists who infamously went missing in Grimveil Forest. I was shocked when I recently learned myself the truth of their fates, which was that they were captured and forced to join the work camps by UAPA soldiers.

"More than just them though, all of the former Restitution Program slaves who consent to it will have their names and information released to the public and many will be available, giving their own testimony on underground radio stations.

"If you do not know how to access underground radio, the third information packet also includes a tutorial on how to tune in to such programs through most media devices, including most common wristcomms and palmcomms.

"However, before all of that, I am going to hand off this broadcast so you can hear from one of the survivors of this program firsthand. He is someone quite special—a personal friend of mine and someone you all know, Matlex Winslow."

"Thank you, Xander," Matlex said as the audio and video of the broadcast switched their focus to him. "Now, like Xander alluded, for the past few months, I have been trapped here in this camp, living and working, most frankly, as a gods damned slave to UAPA."

As Matlex spoke, he grabbed the camera and moved it around to show them the room, with all of the rows of cramped bunks, the countless chains across the floor, and the hundreds of former slaves who were currently getting ready to leave.

"This is the residency building where all of us prisoners had to sleep at night. This camp alone has fifty-two buildings like this, most of which are just as full as this one.

"I can tell you that my time here has been a living hell. I don't know how much longer I could have taken this, and I've only had to endure it for a few months. Many of the people here have been in this program for years. Hell, some of them transferred from the Penal Servitude program and have actually been enslaved for decades— well, at least out of those who have survived.

"But I tell you, this Restitution Program is nothing like that happy, positive 'work to pay off your debt to society' program that

UAPA's been fakin'. Like many here, I was arrested and convicted for nothin' more than 'dissidence.' In other words, I openly criticized UAPA's war-mongering and fascist policies to my fans.

"It's funny—UAPA shills have always claimed to be passionate advocates for free speech, when all they really wanted was to make sure their voice was always heard by everyone. Now that they are in control of things, they are more than happy to censor other people, to lie, and to enslave their critics to prevent the free speech they claim to care about."

He stopped for a moment and sighed. "But my friends, that's enough talk. Y'all know me—I can sometimes prattle on here and there, but music is how I truly communicate. And so, me and some of the other former prisoners here, we've got a song for you. While this song plays, we'll be showing you some clips of what we had to endure under this program. I warn you, it will be quite graphic.

"The song we'll be singing along with those clips was written by Ruland Oh'ah, a good friend of mine, a strong leader and an excellent singer. I will now pass the broadcast on to him to introduce the piece."

"Thank you," Ruland said appreciatively in his thick Ovanicx accent. "This piece is called 'Chains of Sand.' I wrote it back in a Nolinth work camp, with a friend of mine who is no longer with us. Truth told, he was executed for trying to escape."

Ruland paused for a moment as tears fell from his eyes. He cleared his throat before continuing "I tell you all, things are no better under UAPA now than they had been under Nolinth. Maybe worse. But of course, even Nolinth was hardly the first time such terrible mistakes were made on Antal.

"This piece is loosely based on the freedom songs that were sung by the Antallian slaves over a thousand years ago during a dark period in our history.

"In the factories, we would sing this song in my mother tongue to avoid the guards from understanding, but we originally wrote it in the common tongue. I am now happy we will get to sing it together for you in the language it was meant to be sung.

"Without further adieu, here it is."

Switching from the camera feed, the following message came onto the screen over a black background:

The following video contains brutal scenes of victimization taken from UAPA Restitution Program slave camps. We received permission from the victims featured in this video to broadcast. The few victims we could not receive permission from, we blurred the faces of. This is only true of the victims. None of the slavers nor soldiers were contacted, and none of their faces have been blurred.

The video feed began showing footage of the slave camps. As it did, the singing began, with Matlex and Ruland at the lead, and the rest of the former slaves in the residency building singing together as back-up.

"Chains of sand weighing us down,
Chains of sand, chains of sand.
Chains of sand weighing us down,
Under these chains of sand, we firmly stand."

The footage showed guards tasing and beating slaves on the factory floors. Meanwhile, the audio was overlayed with Ruland's song being stoutly sung by a full chorus of the former slaves in the residency building.

"Our captors may want us broken,
They may beat, torment, degrade.
But spirits will never falter,
No matter how our bodies are flayed.

These chains of sand can't hold us,
These brittle bars mean naught.
While our captors sneer, we will draw ever closer
To the freedom we have sought.

Chains of sand weighing us down,
Chains of sand, chains of sand.
Chains of sand weighing us down,
Under these chains of sand, we firmly stand."

The clips continued moving through shocking and haunting imagery. One of the videos showed Oppori Qala operatives storming in on what appeared to be a slave brothel, where prisoners with RPW tattoos appeared to be forced into lecherous acts with all kinds of people. At least one of the slaves, with their face blurred, appeared to be tied down whilst enduring an apparent assault before the Oppori Qala operatives jumped in and saved them.

"So, we'll keep working their factory floors,
Knowing everything is alright.
One day we'll leave with heads held high,
And we'll walk into the light.

Until that day comes, we'll hold our freedom
In our hearts deep within.
We'll be patient until the day our bodies can join
Where our souls have always been."

All of the clips shown throughout the song were dark and hard to watch, featuring all kinds of different injustices against the enslaved people. The final of the clips showed an execution of Restitution Program slaves conducted on camp grounds. Seven victims were simultaneously shot against a wall in broad daylight by UAPA soldiers.

"Chains of sand weighing us down,
Chains of sand, chains of sand.

Chains of sand weighing us down,
Under these chains of sand, we proudly stand."

There were a few moments of silence and darkness on the broadcast. Audiences around the world and galaxy were on the edge of their seats, wondering if that was the end of the shocking program. But then, Morgas appeared.

"Hello all," Morgas greeted. "I am Morgas Yen, the Chair of Oppori Qala and former veteran of the Raider Wars.

"You know, here on Antal, we often speak about our history quite proudly, fondly even. And it is true, Antal has overcome many obstacles and accomplished many incredible feats since our founding. However, many seem to forget that not all of our history is so glowing.

"In fact, there was a time, long ago, when our Antallian ancestors had gotten complacent. Things had been good for a long time, and we became arrogant in thinking it would always be this way. In this time, our leaders became corrupt, and our people became apathetic.

"Things remained this way for many years until, about 1700 years ago, a terrible natural disaster devastated our planet, killing many, and destroying the majority of our farmland and infrastructure. The warning signs had been there and our planet's forebears had no one to blame but themselves for how unprepared they were. What's worse, even after the disaster was over, mismanagement and greed only continued to make things worse until we were in the nadir of a terrible famine and the worst economic depression in all of Antallian history.

"What followed from this was a brutal war across our globe for resources, during which, countless people were captured and sold by rogue soldiers for money. This new slaving practice grew rapidly in popularity across the globe. Even after the war itself had ended, it only became more rampant. Eventually, the leaders of all of our nations caved to pressure, one-by-one, until slavery was legalized across the planet, thus beginning the darkest chapter in Antal's history.

"Our historians generally agree that this did not save the economy. All it did was transfer and magnify some of the suffering from the captors to the captured.

"It would be 600 years before slavery was finally outlawed in all nations across the planet when we finally learned our lesson that people are not possessions.

"Yet, it seems, over a millennium later, many of us have somehow forgotten that lesson. We all stood by and did nothing as Nolinth introduced the Penal Servitude Program, which turned convicts into slaves. We turned a blind eye because most of us figured it didn't affect us. That was wrong of us. We should have done something back then.

"But we will not stand idly by any longer. This Restitution Program of UAPA's is nothing more than a re-emergence of this planet's darkest and most shameful history, and it will not be tolerated for a second more.

"And so, I say this to Hamish Drulth and to the so-called United Antallian People's Army: your days are numbered. We *will* be coming for you.

"By now, most of you will have heard of the Devil of Hivich. He is one of ours. But truly, UAPA may consider *all* of us as devils. For we will assume whatever form it takes to see your horrific organization come to an end, be it soldiers, angels, or even devils.

"As to everyone else, a brighter time will be coming soon for Antal. This, I promise.

"We shall be seeing you all again very soon, but for now this is all we had to share. As we say in Oppori Qala: For love and freedom!"

Morgas brought a fist to her chest proudly just before the broadcast ended.

*/

With a click, Aren ended the broadcast, suddenly switching all networks back to their usual programming. Thanks to Orita's hacks, the supplemental information packets would likely still be available to the public for download for 15-20 more hours until UAPA would work out how to take them down, but the broadcast itself was now over.

"Alright," Aren spoke into his team's radio channel. "Everyone, the mission has been a complete success. Now, let's get out of here."

"Sounds good," Elmenz replied.

"Roger that," Lieutenant Chave responded through the same channel.

Aren quickly exited the room, greeted by Henrika on the other side of the door. On her back, she was carrying a sheer cloth bag containing what appeared to be several complicated looking computer parts, and a few glowing stones, encased in glass.

"Well, hello there," Henrika greeted him in a seductive tone.

"Hey," Aren greeted back, looking over at the haul on her back. "I see you had a nice 'walk' then, did you?"

As they were talking, the rest of the team joined them, and together, they began moving back towards the underground tunnels that they came from.

"Indeed, I did," Henrika smirked. "It's good to stretch your legs sometimes, you know."

She flashed him a sly smile. "Perhaps I can show you how far they can stretch sometime, if you'd like."

Aren laughed and blushed, looking away. "Do you make offers like that to all the boys?"

"Hm," Henrika voiced coquettishly. "What makes you think only boys?"

Aren blushed more deeply as he chuckled lightheartedly.

As they made their way down the halls, Aren saw a window into a large room full of computers. As he got to the door, he could see that the label read: *Censorship Processing*.

"One second everyone," Aren stated.

He stopped suddenly in front of the door to the censorship room, opened it and pointed his palm towards the equipment inside.

"*Lasaer ferven!*" Aren cried out.

Unlike Green Dragon's Spark, the flame that came from the Red Dragon's Breath spell did not burn life energy hardly at all. However, it made up for that by having a flame that was far hotter than Green Dragon's Spark, burning at over 2000 degrees Celsius.

As the red flames rolled across the entire censorship room, the fire rapidly began to burn and melt through all of the computers, monitors and various other equipment, rendering all of it useless over a period of several seconds.

"Damn," Henrika laughed as she looked into the room, seeing the molten chunks and seared husks that were left after the spell. "I don't remember this being part of the mission."

"I made a judgment call," Aren asserted.

"I knew there was a reason I liked you," Henrika winked at him. "Now come on. You're falling behind."

As Aren headed back to the hatch leading into the tunnels, he felt a powerful sense of relief, pride and accomplishment over their victory. And yet, with each step forward, he couldn't help but feel a pit forming in his stomach. Victory or not, he knew in his heart they were far from the finish line, and that the real battle had yet to begin.

Acknowledgments

I would like to give my deepest gratitude to every person who helped me along my journey to writing this book. The first to thank are my parents, who provided invaluable support through the writing process, as well as my grandparents who provided their own support.

The next to thank are my friends who both helped and supported me through my writing. Out of those friends, I must give special acknowledgment to my best friend—the one I affectionately often refer to as my soul mate—who has been there for me every step of the way and has always assisted me in my creative processes, brainstorming sessions, and more. I also must acknowledge my other best friend, who graciously allowed me to use them as a sounding board, both allowing me to read/talk out loud to them as I worked through my process, and who gave me feedback and opinions when requested.

More people I must thank include my cover artist, who did a superb job on the cover art, as well as those besides my best friends who helped with test reading and providing feedback as I was writing this novel. Even those who only read isolated sections were helpful. These test readers allowed me to see my writing through other perspectives, which helped me to not only improve the writing itself, but also to grow as a writer.

Furthermore, I would like to thank all of the fantasy, sci-fi and other fiction writers and creators out there who helped me realize my love and passion for fantasy, sci-fi, and other stories throughout the years. I was enthralled and inspired by countless sources on my path to writing this book, from J.R.R. Tolkien to Gene Roddenberry to Yoshihiro Togashi to George Lucas, and many, many more. I learned so much about stories through the works of so many great writers and creators, and I would not remotely be the same writer without them.

Finally, I must thank you, the reader. You are the one that I wrote this book for. It is thanks to you that I have people I can share my journey and my passion with. I hope that it has been a positive experience for you, and that you continue reading future installments in this series as well as others that I have a hand in.

Every person who contributed gave something a little different, and all brought their own unique value into the mix, which I greatly appreciate. From the bottom of my heart, I am deeply grateful to each and every person who was involved in helping me with the creation of this book. Thank you, one and all.

Appendix

Table 1, Calendar Comparison Table

	Earth	Galactic Standard (GS)	Antallian (Antal)
A Week	7 Earth Days	8 GS Days	7 Antal Days
A Month	28-31 Earth Days	32 GS Days (4 GS Weeks)	21 Antal Days (3 Antal Weeks)
A Year	12 Earth Months (365.25 Earth Days)	12 GS Months (384 GS Days)	16 Antal Months (336 Antal Days)

Table 2, Time Unit Conversion Table

Earth	Galactic Standard (GS)	Antallian (Antal)
1 Earth Day	1.077 GS Days	0.938 Antal Days
1 Earth Week	0.943 GS Weeks	0.938 Antal Weeks
1 Earth Month	1.025 GS Months	1.360 Antal Months
1 Earth Year	1.025 GS Years	1.020 Antal Years

Follow us

 facebook.com/ajenfictura

 @ajenfictura

 @enfictura

 www.enfictura.com

Milton Keynes UK
Ingram Content Group UK Ltd.
UKHW020637230124
436534UK00016B/561